# THEIR SHIP SLAMMED INTO THE ALIEN CRUISER . . .

The soldiers could hear Master Sergeant Pepe Stuart bellow, "In!" Then Pepe himself was hurtling forward, his shoulder slamming into a Hothri's midriff and its roar echoed around him in the pea soup the aliens called atmosphere.

Pepe saw a sword-tipped barrel slashing toward his eyes, and he rolled aside, pulling the trigger of his own rifle. The Hothri's head vanished in a splatter that Pepe didn't stay to see, but another Hothri blasted him with a scatter gun. There was a sharp sting in his shoulder, a reek of methane in his nose, and he knew his helmet had been holed. He knocked the Hothri's shotgun up with his rifle barrel, slammed the butt into the cricket's helmet, reversed the weapon and pulled the trigger. The white-hot fury seared through his back and everything went black. . . .

# THE WAR YEARS
## 2
# ★ THE ★
# SIEGE
# ★ OF ★ ★
# ARISTA

## FEATURING
## CHRISTOPHER STASHEFF
## EDITED BY
## BILL FAWCETT

A ROC BOOK

ROC
Published by the Penguin Group
Penguin Books USA Inc., 375 Hudson Street,
New York, New York 10014, U.S.A.
Penguin Books Ltd, 27 Wrights Lane,
London W8 5TZ, England
Penguin Books Australia Ltd, Ringwood,
Victoria, Australia
Penguin Books Canada Ltd, 2801 John Street,
Markham, Ontario, Canada L3R 1B4
Penguin Books (N.Z.) Ltd, 182-190 Wairau Road,
Auckland 10, New Zealand

Penguin Books Ltd, Registered Offices:
Harmondsworth, Middlesex, England

First published by Roc, an imprint of New American Library,
a division of Penguin Books USA Inc.

First Printing, January, 1991
10  9  8  7  6  5  4  3  2  1
Prologue and Interludes copyright © Bill Fawcett and Associates, 1990
"The Bottom Line" copyright © Janet Morris, 1990
"Papa Don't 'Low" copyright © Christopher Stasheff, 1990
"The Last Katana" copyright © Steve Perry, 1990
"Brig Rats" copyright © William Dietz, 1990
"Suspect Terrain" copyright © Elizabeth Moon, 1990
"Rage of an Angel" copyright © S.N. Lewitt, 1990
"Unreality" copyright © Jody Lynn Nye, 1990
"Breakout" copyright © Robert Sheckley, 1990

For Anne McCaffrey, David Drake,
Kirby McCauley, Darwin Bromley,
Bob Asprin, and all those
from whom I am still learning

—B.F.

# Contents

# Prologue:
# The Great Lurch Forward
## by Bill Fawcett

Man did not expand into the galaxy. He exploded into it with an optimism and level of energy that hadn't been seen in several millennium. There was no plan to this explosion, no form or purpose. Individuals, governments, traders, and criminals generally followed the paths of least resistance across the hundreds of worlds capable of supporting Terran life.

One of the more unusual results of this erratic expansion was that man settled a long string of stars stretching outward along the upper edge of the spiral arm in which Earth was situated. Several hundred light-years out they discovered the Far Stars Cluster, containing six thousand stars and over a hundred eminently habitable planets in a relatively small volume of space. Man encountered often fierce resistance from the races already living in the cluster, but within three centuries was entrenched in the cluster. Even a major war against the powerful and militaristic Gerin only served to strengthen and unite all the worlds under the banner of the xenophobic League of Man.

Fifty years after the Gerin War, the Far Stars were crowded, civilized, and safe. They were too powerful to attack and too prosperous to allow change. Those with too much ambition, or too little sense, once again began traveling beyond the known worlds. As always, those who led this lurch outward were the desperate and those who had to be the first on new worlds. With no FTL radio, each of the newly settled planets was still basically on its own. The men who first explored—and often were the first to die on—the new planets often gave their names to worlds they found. Worlds such as Shelling, Silvercase, and Douglas. Arista itself was named after the wife of its discoverer, Christopher Blancmont. After the loners, came the exploiters, those who were attracted by the easy wealth the first men found. Fi-

nally, there came those who were to stay, to settle, and
those who came to live off of them, the bureaucrats and the
merchants.

Arista was settled early in this new wave of human expansion. It was a rich world, full of fertile soils and easily
mined minerals. It was ideally located to serve as a con-
nection to the distant League and dozens of developing new
planets. The population grew quickly as did the world's
wealth. The Aristans parlayed this advantage into a growing
mercantile empire. The total population of Arista when the
war started was five million.

Soon the small but aggressive Aristan navy directly controlled a massive volume of space and a half-dozen worlds.
Many other planet's settlers and non-human races now found
they now had no choice but to deal through Arista. On
Arista, a generation grew to assume prosperity was their
right, no matter what the cost to others. Others, equally
rapacious, became wealthy almost overnight. Arista had the
feel of a boom town, and its leaders soon became interested
only in keeping the boom going with little regard for the
consequences.

# THE BOTTOM LINE
## by Janet Morris

"DID SOMEBODY FART?" Michaels said, too loudly, hitching up his weapons belt as he stood over the aliens' table. The nonregulation buckle on the Aristan SOG major's belt said, "I'm the Guy Your Mother Warned You About," in raised titanium letters; the belt was cutting into the major's gut because the flamethrower slung on it was so heavy.

The giant ants seated at the table bent their noseless heads together and made whistling noises at each other. Then one of them twitched in Michaels' direction, as if to rise to its full seven-foot height.

Michaels' flamethrower came out of its quick-release scabbard already flaring, leaving a track of smoldering, scorched wood that actually ignited in places as the major brought his weapon to bear on the enemy.

The giant ant was breathing a methane-based atmosphere which he'd brought with him in a feeder tank. Which was too bad for the ant. The tank, the hoses to it, whatever the ant used for a nose, and every breathing passage inside of the ant exploded as soon as the flamethrower whooshed up his tall, slender black body.

McMurtry could see the whole thing in the mirror behind the bar where he waited for his drink. At the table, the other two giant ants, called Hothri, started unfolding themselves into erect positions—maybe to go for weapons, or perhaps just instinctively to help their fellow.

The first Hothri was already down on the wood floor, looking a whole lot worse than the family cat had, the night McMurtry's brother had lit it back on Arista.

The other two, who either had hive-minds and couldn't help themselves, or just had an inordinate amount of respect for the about-to-be-dead, were down on the floor trying to extinguish their flaming fellow when Michaels depressed his trigger a second time and fried the other two ants, stepping back as he did so because they popped some when their tanks and lungs went.

In the mirror, it looked like a fireworks display gone to shit, rather than alien beings gone to glory in the first salvo of a trade war.

All around the bar, the rest of Michaels' Special Forces team were keeping order. All but McMurtry. McMurtry didn't think this was any kind of good idea, and Michaels knew it. So McMurtry's job was to keep an eye on the bartender and everything else, using the bar's mirror to make a covert record of the encounter through a minicam he wore pinned to his collar.

Since McMurtry was the COA (Cover Our Asses) officer on this little foray, he picked up his black beer and sipped it calmly, keeping one eye on the bartender, and the other on the mirror in case something went wrong.

Nothing was going to go wrong that the bartender had anything to do with. McMurtry had put his Aristan Military Industries machine pistol on the bar when Michaels approached the ants, just to make sure.

The bartender was watching the pistol, and McMurtry was watching the bartender—when he wasn't watching the spitting multilegged bonfire and the frightened locals who were trying to get out the door any way they could.

Of course, you couldn't get out the door—Sonny and Raven had the door covered. Sonny might have figured that the civilian Portu women, at least, ought to be let outside where the smell wasn't so bad, but Raven was a hard case. Michaels had told Raven, their S-3, that nobody left.

Therefore, nobody left.

You couldn't do Special Operations Group missions any way but by following orders. Even when the orders were dumber than Portu locals. McMurtry knew that. So he'd kept quiet when Michaels told everybody what the objective was: "Take out the local ant trading mission—all of 'em. Arista doesn't want Portu aiding and abetting these Hothri scum. We're harrying and destroying Hothri wherever we find them, until the Portu humans get the message that harboring aliens isn't a good idea."

So it was economics at the heart of this: Arista didn't like Hothri competition. To McMurtry's way of thinking, that wasn't a reason to field SOG personnel. But nobody was asking McMurtry what he thought.

Except, before they'd deployed here, Michaels had pulled him aside: "Something you don't like about this mission, Sergeant?"

"No, sir," McMurtry had said, looking straight into Michaels' blue eyes. "You've got real survivability here, sir. However . . ."

"However?" Michaels had said.

"If we're goin' out purposely to get Hothri shit all over our shoes, shouldn't we be sure we've got some way to wipe it off later—sir?"

"That's a command decision, McMurtry. Not Mine. You know that."

"Yes, sir," said McMurtry, and was willing to leave it at that. Fry the aliens the way Michaels had originally ordered, let the brass worry about repercussions.

But Michaels knew McMurtry better than to leave it at that. A Special Forces sergeant can usually run a good team without the team leader or the operations officer, and McMurtry had outlived two previous holders of Michaels' slot, and Raven's slot.

Michaels said, "Tell you what, McMurtry. You go in wired and I'll do the shooting, this time."

It wasn't a consultation. It was an order. It was also close to a goddam slap across the face.

But it was Michaels' team while he was ambulatory.

So McMurtry played eye-games with the bartender and watched the mirror to make sure his lapel-pin videocam was recording the proceedings.

Damn, if it hadn't smelled real bad in here before, it sure did now. McMurtry had an almost unbearable urge to go to the bathroom: he wasn't really a part of this action, and yet the "pucker factor"—the adrenalin rush that pulled his guts in tight—was real high in here.

McMurtry couldn't sit out any more of this. He picked up the machine pistol, ported it, and turned—slowly, for the camera's sake.

What patrons weren't cued up trying to make Raven let them out, were trying to get away from the stinking, black smoke.

Lucky the whole place hadn't blown. Nobody knew what would happen when you set fire to an ant that big, wearing methane-atmosphere augmentation.

But you couldn't tell anybody back on Arista anything.

Back on Arista, it was Arista forever; Arista, right or wrong; everything for the greater glory of the newest trading power in this sector of the universe.

Aristan trade usually meant exclusivity, high prices, and "protection." Most of the time, the army was engaged in "protection."

Right now, McMurtry would have given anything to be protecting a caravan, a trading mission to Hui Whey, a boat or a hypersonic. There was something about this mission that felt purely wrong.

He wasn't in the pest extermination business.

And neither was his team. They didn't know enough about what they were dealing with to come in this heavy-handed.

But here they were.

And so far, so good.

The ants hadn't gotten back up out of the flames. There was an occasional crackle from the pile that used to be the Hothri traders. As McMurtry watched, a leg or an arm bone broke in a cascade of sparks, falling on the pile, making the burning heap shift a bit.

But that wasn't serious.

The serious stuff was all happening over at the doorway where Michaels was putting the appropriate face on the mission, telling the locals what they'd just seen—winning hearts and minds, as the saying went, before he let them out to spread the word.

From over McMurtry's shoulder, the bartender said, "Want another beer, soldier? On the house? This one's got black scum on the top."

"Yeah, okay," McMurtry said, still watching Michaels and Raven.

Raven, their S-3, was this amazing female with a tiny waist and a real knack for logistics, strategy and tactics. If she'd been a woman of the sort McMurtry understood, he'd have been crazy in love with her. But she scared him, even after half a tour, so he kept his distance. When she was up and running, Raven was something to see. All grace and speed and lethality, with none of the split-second hesitations even the best of men displayed.

Raven, comforting a blond woman a full head shorter than she, was doing a passable imitation of a feeling being.

Only McMurtry knew better. The single one who might

give him an argument about Raven's purely murderous nature was Sonny, who (rumor had it) was sleeping with her.

But you didn't ask if rumors were true. And you didn't think about stuff like that. Raven was as good an S-3 as you could have for the low-intensity-conflict sort of mission that McMurtry's Team 12 specialized in: she'd lasted twice as long as her direct predecessor.

If she weren't so damned beautiful, with that wavy mane of dark hair and those big velvet eyes that looked at you over a pair of upward-tilting breasts, then maybe having her directly above him in the command chain wouldn't make McMurtry so uncomfortable. But there she was. And he had to look at those breasts when they weren't safe inside hardsuit armor, like—

Raven's breasts blew apart. Her trunk spewed blue-purple-white-brown organs and pureed flesh mixed with spine.

The concussion of the blast that took out the door came slightly afterwards.

The bartender was just saying, "Here's your beer—"

But all McMurtry could see was Raven with no chest and the surprised look in her big velvet eyes as her body was thrust forward by the force of whatever had holed her.

Then she fell, slowly—much slower, seemingly, than McMurtry as he dived for the wood floor boards, his machine pistol looking for a target.

There wasn't a target.

There was almost nothing to shoot at, according to the feed he was getting from his sight control electronics. The rest of the twelve-man team had hit the deck, and taken the civilians with them. Everybody was down and covered.

The little shocks the pistol was feeding to his right wrist told him that it was still set for an ant target.

He reached out to set it to nondifferential, so that he could shoot at anything he wanted to, when the whole wall before him, front facade included, disappeared, taking with it what was left of Raven's corpse in a bellow of physics and a pulverizing explosion.

Part of McMurtry's job was to know where all his people were, every minute.

He knew where everybody else had been, and one blink into the billow of explosion in front of him told McMurtry that there was no use waiting around to see if he had wounded or dead he could carry back.

Anyhow, there was only one priority at a time like this:
get the intelligence back.

He scrambled backward, trying to get behind the bar,
kicking over something as he did. He blinked repeatedly,
trying to see something more than the mass of black/red/
gold smoke and the silhouetted casualties in its midst.

He couldn't. And he couldn't hear anything either except
the buzzing tones and electrical whine that was the blood
in his ears.

When he made it behind the bar, he was panting and
didn't realize he was climbing over the bartender, until the
man shoved at him.

The bartender's face was bloody from a heavy scalp
wound, so that his eye-whites looked yellow and his teeth
were pink.

McMurtry yelled: "Another way out?"

The bartender gestured.

McMurtry ran without a backward look.

He could still see Raven's chest exploding. Damn, why
couldn't it be the vision of silhouettes flung before the explosion that he was left with?

But it wasn't. It never was, he thought as he stumbled
through a back room full of kegs and dove through a door
into loamy dirt. It never was the easy stuff you remembered.

He'd had a bad feeling about this mission all along, he
told himself as, against his better judgment, he crawled
around the side of the building to get a peek at what had
totaled its facade.

And then he saw ants. They'd never really seen ants before, he realized. They'd seen . . . a couple ants. Nothing
like this.

Must be the hive mind thing. Lots of ants . . . kill one,
the rest react.

The whole goddam main street of Portu Prince was covered with ants. The sky above was dark with ant aircraft—
big stuff, not just little flyers—that must have been deployed
from low orbit.

Shit. Now, McMurtry *had* to get out of here. The ants
were methodically hosing down everything standing in Portu
Prince.

The sound of the whistling ant language, coming through
amplification devices, mixed with the rumble of ground ve-

hicles and the whine of air cover, nearly masked the steady stream of curses coming from McMurtry's own throat.

Damn Michaels. Damn SOG Command. Damn the whole Aristan Senate, and its Aristan Military Industries constituency, who hadn't bothered to research the ants.

*Hadn't anybody wondered how they'd react?* he asked himself as he sprinted along the alley, throat raw, machine pistol slippery in his grip?

Didn't anybody remember the difference between trade war and real war? Business enemy and mortal enemy?

These ants were on the town of Portu Prince too fast, too hard, and too heavy for McMurtry to mistake what he was seeing back there.

And intel had to know. He had to get back with his record of the proceedings. Otherwise, Arista wasn't going to know what kind of war it had just started, until the Hothri fell on the next unsuspecting human settlement—or the next. Because no Portu humans were going to be doing any talking about what had happened here—or what was happening here.

The gouts of flame, from area denial munitions pounding the main street behind him, attested to that.

McMurtry tried to leap over a barrel that had overturned and was rolling into his path. He miscalculated, and fell on it—with it, rolling.

Damn, too much noise.

The next thing he knew, he was crawling inside the barrel. He could hear that whistling, coming closer. Something overhead was screeching in a language he didn't understand.

He huddled in the barrel, his machine pistol cradled against his chest as if he were some frightened little boy with a teddy bear, until the whistling receded and the thud of chopped air lessened as the air cover went on its way.

If he ever found out whose idea this was, he was going to kill the son of a bitch. He kept seeing Raven's chest, exploding, all that pureed lung and heart, sprinkled with shards of bone.

Well, he thought, if it was any consolation, he'd been right about there being something wrong about this mission.

The damned ants were telepathic, or empathic, or group-minded, or somesuch. You'd think somebody would have thought of that.

But you'd think the brass would think, just once in a while, about something besides the bottom line.

Of course, people never set out to screw up. They just set out to win in their terms. The problem came when those terms weren't terms on which everyone involved could win.

Right now, winning in McMurtry's terms meant calling for pickup somewhere that didn't get himself and his automated dust-off craft hosed down along with the rest of Portu Prince.

"Ants," said Ace Baldridge with a shudder, pulling his big arms in to encircle his chest. His dog tags jittered on their chain as he shook his head. "Uh-uh. I hate bugs. I got this thing about bugs. Come on, Sally, don't put me into this. You can find somebody else."

The ONI officer shook her head at Baldridge pityingly. "I'm sorry, Ace, I really am. I need you. And I've got you." She tapped a disk against the bulkhead. "You and I are the only two people on this ship who are cleared for McMurtry's verbal debrief. I had enough trouble getting any regular army officer cleared for this."

Ace Baldridge sat up and flexed his arms over his head, gripping both wrists with his hands. The gesture was one which betrayed a long, unconscious familiarity with the confined spaces of aerospace fighter-bombers.

"You're telling me that the fucking regional commander of fucking Special Operations Command had to be specially cleared to hear one of his own people's reports?"

"That's what I'm telling you, Colonel. Now, you want in on this bug thing, or not?"

Baldridge shifted uncomfortably, hands still over his head. His triceps jumped. "You said 'direct contact with the ants.' I'm really not up for a pow-wow with bugs."

"Direct contact may not be the talking kind," said the woman from the Office of Naval Intelligence. "We're having an interagency meeting, with your single sergeant as our briefing officer. At the end of that meeting, everybody involved does whatever's necessary—personally, to surgically solve this problem before it spreads. Now, are you up for it?"

"Why didn't you say that in the first place?"

She'd scared him, wanting to have this 'private talk' in

the cramped cockpit of one of the fighter-bombers in the big carrier's hold. Security, she'd said.

Sally Holden was a significant power on the carrier *ASS Hollywood,* not simply because she held Commander's rank. Everybody knew how much money there was in the Holden family, how many Holdens had been senators, how much stock in Aristan Military Industries the Holdens had.

She was in line to head ONI. And that made her really significant. So when Sally wanted to hunker down in a fighter-bomber's C4I cockpit to have a chat where she could control security, you wondered if the world was ending.

Bugs. Ace Baldridge was forty-four years old and he'd hated bugs for at least forty of those years with a pathological hatred that sprung from an uncontrollable fear. His mother had been bitten by some kind of bug and died when he was very young, on a colony world that later was abandoned for reasons that were still classified.

Ace had been making worlds safe for human colonization for his entire adult life, and he always started with defoliants. And followed that with bug spray. And had managed to get a special bug-repellant for his Special Forces troops that nobody in the regular army had. All because he hated bugs. He sure hoped that whatever McMurtry had to say about these ants was something that didn't involve dancing cheek to cheek with one.

Sally looked at him critically. "Are we finished with the calisthenics?"

He was still flexing and relaxing his arm muscles. "It relaxes me."

"So would a ten-year old Scotch, I'll wager. Let's go up to my office and have one."

"You brought me all the way down here for just a yea or nay?"

Sally Holden looked at him out of the corner of one green eye. "Ace, I want to be sure you understand what's about to happen. Once you're in, there's no going back."

"I don't need a mother, Sally. I had one. Did everybody else get this private pep talk?"

She was beautiful and she was powerful, and he'd slept with her before he'd realized how powerful, beautiful women could mess with your life. Then he'd stopped sleeping with her, because all of a sudden he stopped getting ground missions.

He'd never wanted to be too valuable to lose.

Now she was doing it again. And he'd nearly let her get away with it—seduce him into it—because he hated bugs, and because he knew she could get him out of whatever this was. He could use Sally's clout as a shield between him and anything he didn't want to do.

Now he understood why they were down here, in the little fighter-bomber. ''You're doing it again,'' he said warningly, letting his arms fall. His hands twisted in his lap. ''You want to get laid, I can handle that—it's been a long time. But not the rest.''

''Before you say that, look at this.''

She leaned forward and put a disk in a slot. The fighter-bomber had five screens between the copilot and pilot's stations.

The data came up as video on the screen at the bottom of the console's T-shaped configuration. Ace Baldridge involuntarily sucked in his breath.

Damn. Ants. Lots of ants. The hair on his arms rose. His skin turned to gooseflesh. He watched the massacre in silence. Then he said, ''That's Portu Prince, right? Or was?''

Had to be, if McMurtry was the briefer for the upcoming meeting.

''That's right. Russell's people got their butts chewed out there, good. Only one came back, Mc—''

''—Murtry.'' McMurtry would always come back. If you had a team with twelve McMurtrys in it, you could pack up and go home and wait for the mares to foal.

''So that's how come I hadn't heard anything.'' Russell, from the intelligence side, had borrowed an SOG team for something in Portu Prince. Since it came up through Sally, Ace had signed off on it, no questions asked.

Now he was getting back one guy, McMurtry, a sick stomach, a spine full of chills, and a very incendiary situation with the Hothri.

''That's how come. The Hothri hosed down a whole town, and then kept going. They haven't stopped yet, on Portu, as far as we can determine.''

''So we stop them.''

''Any idea how, without starting an interstellar war?''

''Sally, it's too late for that. When the senate sees this footage—''

''Nobody sees this but us. And the rest in the briefing.

We started this, Ace—Michaels' team had a mission definition which touched off this result.''

"Terrific. Still, we stop it.''

"How?''

"Blow the Hothri ships, here and now—all of them.
Nothing gets out of Portu orbit.'' Ace shrugged. Women
never wanted to get right to the nitty-gritty. In war, there
were occasions when it was counterproductive to engage in
foreplay, no matter how clear it was to you that justifications
were going to be important when committees convened, after the fact, to study what you'd done.

"I can't just authorize—''

"We can, together. Don't brief the others.'' Out here,
Ace Baldridge was the equivalent of a Joint Chief. Sally
represented all of ONI's muscle. If they didn't let the alert
status get contemplative, didn't even think about looking for
a quorum, they could react. "If we wait, we'll be impo-
tent.''

"It's Russell's team,'' she reminded him.

"It's my team,'' he reminded her.

"Let's go listen to McMurtry. Maybe we're both overre-
acting.''

"You can't overreact to that many dead noncombatants,''
Ace said, but either she didn't hear him, or she didn't care
to hear him. She pulled her disk, shut down the flight deck
electronics, and palmed open the fighter-bomber's hatch.

Once that was done, there was nothing to say: words
bounced around the huge bay of the carrier like photons;
you never knew where any single one might end up.

Sally Holden wanted to retch, once she'd seen McMurtry
face to face and watched the record he'd made on Portu
while listening to his verbal briefing.

When all that was left to watch was the rescue and dust-off,
McMurtry said, "That's really it, sirs.''

The lights came up. Everybody blinked. Russell, bone-
less in civilian clothes, was picking his teeth with a toothpick from his survival knife.

Ace was sitting backwards in one of the briefing room
chairs, performing some arcane isometric ritual.

The ship's captain was sipping tea and tapping his stylus
on the keyboard in front of him.

"So, given the foregoing," Sally said dully, "how do we respond?"

Russell raised his fine, graying head and stared at her for an instant before he said, "McMurtry, you did a fine job, getting back here with this record. We're sorry about your loss. You want to sit in on this, it's fine with us: you're our situation expert."

*She* should have said those things. She blushed. Russell never dropped a stitch, on duty. Sometimes she thought she wasn't in his league. He thought so all the time. ONI wasn't professional enough for the civilian intelligence component's liking. And Russell was the representative of that component: he was everything Arista wanted its best and brightest to be, only he was a little bit more.

"Thanks, sir," said McMurtry. "I just wanta go down the next time, if we're going to even the score."

"You can and we are," said Russell positively, shifting the toothpick with his tongue. He was one of those big, fair men that aged beautifully, all size and sinew and testosterone—a born leader, Sally's father would have said. "How about your personal take on these ants?"

Russell took things personally. And she could tell from the way his face was planed with tension that this was no exception.

"My take is, we just started somethin' that ain't gonna finish unless there's none of us or none of them," said McMurtry, shifting from foot to foot. "They were too quick. They've got some kind of herd instinct. They're not going to cool out and walk away."

"Neither are we," Sally said, regaining control of the briefing as best she could. "Captain, what can you give us for odds of success if we try to take out every Hothri vessel in orbit, within twelve hours?"

"With or without communications jamming?" the captain wanted to know.

"Jamming should have started when McMurtry's data reached this vessel," Russell critiqued softly, looking at his toothpick. "Too late now to be effective."

Sally shot a look at Ace. Baldridge's hands were white on the chair. "Ace? You haven't said anything yet."

"I keep thinking that I want to know who's bright idea it was to record an Aristan picking a fight with a Hothri trading party. Was that supposed to make it okay that we killed three of their people? How the fuck did you expect them to react, Russell?''

''I didn't cut these orders, Baldridge. Homeworld thought up this stunt. Ask Holden which of her father's friends thought that, if the Hothri were to lose face and a few bodies, they'd cut and run, leaving Portu Prince for Arista to loot.''

''Sally?''

''I can't tell you anything like that, Ace. You should know better than to ask.''

McMurtry shifted again, then slid onto a bulkhead.

''McMurtry, something to add?'' Sally said.

''I . . . don't think I belong here. Maybe I should go see that this data gets shunted back to Arista. . . .''

Sally was about to say he needn't worry, but Russell stood up. ''I'll go with you. If the Hothri don't confine their hostilities to the planet's surface, we'll want this data in the hands of the senate. . . .''

''In the hands of your shop, you mean,'' Sally said.

Ace said, ''If you send that back, now, we won't be able to do anything about this until we get orders on how to proceed. And you know it, Russell.''

''I don't know any such thing. Maybe you people have to wait for permission to wet your pants, but I can piss myself just fine on my own out here.'' The big civilian turned. ''Come on, McMurtry, let's go do it.''

''Russell!''

Russell turned, his face bland-looking if you didn't know what those planes meant, so carefully arranged to show no emotion.

''You're not going anywhere yet,'' Sally said.

''That's right. I'd like your copy of that data. I want to class it so high, and compartment it so deep, that only three wizards at supergrade level'll be able to look at it, and that only after they've entered a clean room.''

''I—''

It was Russell's operation. His neck. He was telling her that he knew that, was accepting it, and could keep the blame from affecting the rest of them.

''Yes, all right.'' She gave McMurtry's data to him. He took it and, with an arm over McMurtry's shoulders, left the briefing room.

Nobody said anything until the doors snapped shut again and the dogs shot home.

"Okay, where does that leave us?" the captain wanted to know.

"Ace?"

"Mounting a sterilizing operation, starting from orbit." Ace shrugged. "Can we shoot down anything that comes up off Portu? Blanket jam their coms? Keep 'em bottled up?"

"For a time. If I deploy all my assets, including kinetic kill smart mines and telerobotic orbital sweepers."

"Do that," Sally said. "If you will, Captain."

"That won't help on the ground."

"On the ground," Ace said, "we've got to get some kind of bug spray working. It's our only chance. Something that bonds with methane and kills the bugs, while leaving the humans alone."

"Chemical/biological weapons are in violation of every—" Sally began, and stopped.

"I know, sweetie. I just want us to live long enough to face court martials."

Ace grinned at her.

She smiled back.

The captain said, "I wish the colonel wasn't right, but he is."

"You bet I'm right. And, unless I'm mistaken, we're going to be one vehicle short: if I know Russell, now that he's got that sergeant of mine and the record of what happened in Portu Prince, the two of them are down in the jump bay picking out a two-man scout that will get them home to Arista as soon as they can get cleared for separation."

"We've got to stop them," Sally said, getting to her feet.

"Why?" Ace wanted to know. "Don't you think that somebody ought to be personally carrying word home about what happened here, in case these ants are better at thinking like us than we are at thinking like them?"

The captain said, "So, bottom line, you think you're going to take your people back onto the surface, with whatever chemical agent we can come up with, Ace?"

"Bottom line, I don't see any other way."

"Well," Sally said, trying to talk without her voice thickening, to look at the two men without tears overwhelming her desperate attempt not to shed them. "Let's get to it, gentlemen. I'll take the coms. My intel contingent will give you at least a few hours of fratricide-free communications while the Hothri systems are—I promise—useless."

"Right," said the carrier's captain. "We'll count on that. And we'll coordinate the freqs for all the telerobotic hunter-killers, so that we can give you a clear orbital path and good drop zones, Ace. Don't figure on deploying for at least six hours: it'll take that long for me to get your spacelane's drop-windows cleared."

"Great. I'll go see if anybody in Special Weapons can make me a bug killer we can spray. Save me some tactical fighters: I'll need at least ten first-stage-to-orbit vehicles with nozzles where their cannon used to be."

"No problem," said the captain. "Just be sure you find something to spray through those nozzles that'll kill ants, but not children, or we might as well self-destruct right now and save ourselves some grief."

"Must be something," Ace said.

"Let me see if my people can help you find it," Sally said, knowing, as everyone else here knew, that they were just going through the motions.

Barring a miracle, every one of them was walking dead. To make things worse, they'd just witnessed the start of a war that would kill millions, on both sides, before it ended.

"God, I wish we hadn't done that now," Sally said, getting up from beside Ace, beautiful and naked in the subdued lighting of her cabin.

"I'm glad we did. Maybe you'all up here'll make it through. Maybe you'll have pity on a poor dead soldier and give me a posthumous son—"

A pillow hit him in the face.

"You're a morose, manipulative bastard, you know that? Go sell it to the sperm bank."

He might have, if he really believed that the carrier had any more chance of getting out of here alive than he did of getting down onto the planet, and off, alive.

When the real shooting started, there was no way in creation that a few paltry humans were going to fend off the fury of those ants, once aroused.

He kept trying to tell himself that he shouldn't go groundside, but he wanted to go. You had to confront your fears. You couldn't send men on a suicide mission, while you sat safe in orbit above their heads. You couldn't say, "Yep, that was a suicide mission, all right." Not when you knew you were going to get just as dead waiting around to count the bodies.

She came into his arms. "Maybe we could jump out of here, the way Russell and McMurtry did. . . ."

There'd been one free throw—one surprise exit, one shot at getting home. "Russell's quick. He's good. He'll probably make it. But the ants'll be waiting for us to try it, now. They're alerted."

"So why didn't you say something?" She was girlishly lovely in her cabin's low lighting. All Daddy's money wasn't going to help her now. She knew it. He knew it. And she knew he was impressed with how she was holding up.

"It's been nice knowing you," he said.

"You'll come back from there."

"Yeah, probably. But will you still be here when I do?"

They'd done a count of the Hothri ships. Unless the carrier's captain could mount a surprise attack to beat all surprise attacks, there was no way that Aristan battle management could muster any force or counterforce up to handling the ants' group-mind response capability.

This ship, everybody on it, and everybody who went groundside, were equally doomed. Barring a miracle.

"Do you believe in miracles?" he asked her.

"Only today," she said.

"How's that?" he asked.

"That McMurtry got back at all—that was a miracle."

He thought about it, running his hands up her round, white arms, and then over and across one of her round, white breasts. "Yeah, you're right. Okay, do you believe in two miracles?"

"On one day?" She grinned wickedly. "Well, I got you back into bed, so I guess I'll have to say yes to that."

"You what—?"

Then he was sorry he'd asked, embarrassed. Women always confounded him. "Damn," he mumbled at last, "if I'd known you were that hard up—"

"We're both hard up, Ace." She settled into his lap. "I still think it might be worth it to get a Portuan who speaks good Hothri and try to talk our way out of this—even pay reparations."

"Is that what you want me to do?"

He really wanted to use his bug spray. He had his heart set on it.

"Yes. That's what I want. Even knowing that, if I'm wrong, then we've lost whatever element of surprise we have left," she said dreamily.

"Yeah, but I'm not so sure—"

*Bang.*

The first salvo of the Hothri attack on the carrier blew their compartment to smithereens, and settled that argument for eternity.

Human vermin, like any other vermin, had one saving grace: once they were dead, you could eat them. Or so the Hothri command structure consoled itself as it continued firing upon its self-appointed enemy.

The Hothri's second salvo, from a closing globular formation of dreadnoughts, staggered so that no friendly fire would hit a Hothri vessel, ripped the Aristan carrier apart at midships.

The cleanup, ordered by the Hothri command structure in order to make sure that the enemy did not have time to warn its bases, took less time than expected.

When all of the human aggressors were dead, on the planet and around it, the Hothri turned up the shipboard infrared and let the crew bask for a while, as was the right of the victorious.

In the command echelons, some considered the possibility that one of the enemy spacecraft had escaped early on. But the command males and females were already twisting in the hot red light of celebration, and these could not be convinced that their victory was anything but complete.

Victory complete, peace assured. War was, after all, a thing to be avoided. War ravaged economies, destroyed trading cultures. Witness what had happened on the planet below.

All that was left of their human trading partners was fit only for food. Hothri cryoengineers were readied for debarkation to the planet's surface. There they would attack the task of preparing to transport all that food shipboard.

A way must be found to store all the human meat. The Hothri did not waste food. It was a sin against nature to waste food. It was also a sin against the species that had attacked the Hothri. A dead enemy was no longer an enemy.

A dead species, even one that breathed only barely-palatable atmosphere, was still protein.

Some way must be found to take the rusty taste out of so much valuable protein. Otherwise, nature would be offended. Nature was always offended when its bounty was misused. A way would be found to make this dead flesh of human enemies palatable—if not to the Hothri themselves, then to some other trading partner.

Of course, no thing capable of life and death was ever truly useless. Fertilizer was in demand on some planets. Calcium was highly sought in other places. One of the Hothri recollected a race which liked to carve bone and had carved all its big mammals to extinction.

Some use would be found for the bodies of the enemy. This was certain. That way, the slain Hothri's souls would not be offended when they returned through new eggs to life.

Not that the conquered planet itself couldn't be useful. Breeding stock to repopulate it was now the most pressing priority to the Hothri—Hothri breeding stock. It was a lucky thing that, wherever these human monsters must be eradicated, Hothri could thrive. Once planets were sterilized of this now-hereditary enemy, Hothri colonizers could be brought in to settle. Thus, eventually, trading would resume.

In the meantime, there was much to be gained by collecting what was left of the enemy artifacts and studying them. Even though peace was at hand here and now, wherever and whenever Hothri met the hideous human enemy, war would begin again. Whenever Hothri met human, if that human was living, that human would be considered a hideous enemy.

It was important to learn as much about the enemy, and his capabilities, as possible before man and Hothri met again.

The Hothri sent out salvage parties to bring back every shard of human equipment that had escaped total destruction. Soon the Hothri flotilla was as busy as a hive, with workers coming and going, storing bits of enemy and bits of enemy equipment.

The command elements watched, lazy in the bright glow of infrared luxury—the prerogative of command—as order was restored above the world they had just taken as their own.

It was not important, they told themselves, whistling softly, touching heads and scratching eyes, if one of the enemy had escaped. The advantage, they told themselves, was still theirs.

They had met this enemy once and defeated it easily. The scoured planet below was proof that, if confrontation came again, nature was on the side of the Hothri.

They were still in the Portu light cone when McMurtry saw the flare on his topo monitor.

He yelled, "Russell!"

Russell, who was readying for the jump out of Portu spacetime, yelled back, "What, damn you? Can't you see I'm busy?"

McMurtry was out of his web harness by then, over at the bulkhead.

They were approaching half–C, where spacetime was breachable. Anybody but a crazy man would be sitting in his goddamn acceleration couch, not bucking all that G-force in order to roam around a flight deck where everything, including people, ought to have been battened down tight.

Russell turned from the waist, very carefully. You didn't try to turn your neck at these speeds. Spacetime affects and G-forces could combine with human stubbornness to snap your neck and kill you, if you were very unlucky. Most of the time, you just bought yourself one hell of a headache and some extremely sore muscles.

But there was McMurtry, on his feet. Leaning against the bulkhead.

Russell carefully reached up and pushed back his helmet enough to really hear what the sluggish sound waves were carrying toward him in real-time: *thump; thump; thump.*

Russell had probably heard it through his com link; he'd just ignored it.

Now he couldn't: McMurtry was slowly, methodically, pounding his head against the bulkhead wall next to the expert-system rackmounts.

"McMurtry, sit the hell down. You're going to kill yourself."

Of course, that didn't work. Russell had seen men do lots

of crazy things during after-action stress-outs, but he'd never seen a man with quite as much hysterical strength as McMurtry was displaying.

At least it was aimed at McMurtry himself, and not at Russell. Russell had been leading men into and out of tight spots for most of his professional life. He ought to be able to talk McMurtry down—at least talk him back into his seat so that Russell could execute the jump.

But you never knew.

So Russell slipped a stunner out of his couch's map pocket and chambered a wire-guided round before he said, "Come on, McMurtry. Sit down. We'll talk this through together."

*Thump.* "They're dead." *Thump.* "They're all dead."

"On the carrier, you mean? Probably. I know what you saw. I saw it—the topo flash—too. They're dead and we're not. I save your ass, and this is the thanks I get." Russell knew he was taking a terrible risk. Special Forces people grew unhealthily close to their teammates on long hauls. And McMurtry had been out a long time. "Maybe I should have left you to die with your buddies," he continued when he got no response, "but I didn't want to. Know why?"

*Thump.*

Oh, great. "Because we need you, alive and well, to back up what's on that disk for any number of senators and industrialists who flat aren't going to *want* to believe what's on that disk unless there's a man there to look them straight in the eye and say, 'I was there. I did it. I saw it. We're in deep shit, gentlemen. You have my word on it.' "

*Thump.*

Rusell actually considered trying to get out of his acceleration couch at this speed—or slowing down enough that doing so made sense. But that was crazy. As far as Russell was concerned, he was still fleeing possible Hothri pursuit.

"Now, look, McMurtry, if you're not going to help me with my problem on Arista, you might just as well have stayed back there and died. But I can't let you stop me from making the jump. Somebody's got to get word home. Don't you think the human race deserves some decent intelligence—just this once, when it really counts?"

Russell held his breath.

For a long time, McMurtry didn't say anything. But the thumping had stopped.

Then, when Russell, looking to his AI for guidance, saw

that he had sixty seconds to either prepare his dual-flow engines to jump or throttle back into normal mode and try another run up to speed, McMurtry said, "Yeah, okay."

And the brawny special forces sergeant made his way carefully back to the copilot's couch, sat in it and strapped his webbing on, all as if he wasn't bucking some serious g-force to do it, even with grav-adjust.

Russell let out a deep breath. He was no hot dog pilot. If not for the expert system, he'd probably have blown them both to hell by now, trying to hover at the jumpspeed threshold.

"You know, McMurtry, you had me worried." Carefully turning his whole torso from the waist, Russell looked over at the SF sergeant.

McMurtry had a bunch of hematomas on his forehead that made him look like he had a case of volcanic acne, but otherwise, he looked better than Russell had hoped.

Tears were streaming openly down the sergeant's face—tears of grief for lost comrades.

Men who cried didn't run amok and kill everybody in their general vicinity. Russell took a deep breath and said, "It's okay, man. They did great. You did great. We'll find a way to make it worth it. This was bound to happen, sooner or later, the way those ants behaved: they were ready for you guys. Waiting for a pretext. Trust me. This is my area of expertise."

"Yeah," McMurtry was nodding through unashamed tears. "We'll warn everybody. We'll get prepared. It'll be . . ."

Russell pushed the button and even McMurtry couldn't talk under the onslaught of Dirac-transforms that popped them out of relativistic spacetime into an expert-calibrated n-space.

". . . worth it, if we save everybody," McMurtry continued when he could, as if the breaths in one dimension and the breaths in another were connected.

Russell said, "Look, intelligence is the only edge we've got: the kind between our ears, and the kind we can give them back home. You've got to hold on with me, McMurtry. We can, and will, win this eventually."

"How can you say that?" McMurtry wanted to know.

"Because we're men, damn it. We think for ourselves.

We reason. We don't just react like those ants do—some huge knee-jerk response to stimuli.''

"You saw what they did to us back there. . . ."

"We walked right into it. You step on a snake, it's going to bite you. You tromp a hill full of red ants, they get pissed. Little ants didn't overwhelm mankind. Big ants won't either."

McMurtry was palming his face dry. "I should have died with my—''

There it was. Russell wasn't going to let that one get started. "Hey, soldier. You got a job to do. You aren't responsible for your orders, or command screwups that gave you mission parameters that were bound to get people killed. You were responsible to do the mission and survive if possible, right?''

"Right," said McMurtry with a sniffle. Rough-hewn SF sergeants didn't cry enough that they knew what to do when their noses started to run. McMurtry wiped his hand under his nose. "But you know you can die in performance of—''

"Some sensible damn duty, which this wasn't. Nobody asked for suicide commandos on this. Nobody with brains does that, ever. There's nothing that isn't survivable if its planned by the right people and executed by the right people—nothing that should be planned and executed. Got me?''

"You civilian intel—''

"Yeah, we're nasty. We play dirty. We know we're good and we're proud that we stay alive by breaking the rules. You bet. And if you'll let me, I'm going to teach you lots of things you didn't learn in jump school, mister. Enough things that you can fight this war to the finish and end up, alive, with your foot on a Hothri nest, if that's what you want.''

"That's what I want, all right," said McMurtry with a bleak grin.

Predictable, Russell thought. But he said, "Okay, we've got a deal: you brief 'em till they cry for mercy, and I'll get you over on my side of the playing field, where one guy can do the damage of a hundred grunts, no matter how special, and live to bitch about the assholes who sit around wringing their hands over the nasty way we go about winning. You have me on your scope, sergeant?''

"Yep," said McMurtry. "I'd join up with the devil himself, long as I get to kill ants."

"I promise you, you'll have all the ants you can stomp, and then some."

Russell flipped his earpiece back over his right ear and faced front. He still had to get this piece-of-crap ship docked, and get McMurtry, safe and sound, into the right briefing rooms. But he'd do everything he'd promised the marine he would.

In Russell's line of work, where everything was off the record and nonattributable, your word was your bond.

And McMurtry was the only weapon that Russell had at hand to make sure that the human race didn't get caught with its pants down.

Again.

But he'd been living by his wits long enough to get a good gut take on the situation. And his gut was telling him that McMurtry's eyewitness account of what had happened back there in Portu Prince was going to be enough.

And that was all you ever asked of the universe: a fighting chance, a second of warning—just enough.

Once more he looked at the marine, hoping McMurtry understood that, even if he did feel like he'd started this whole war all by his lonesome, he was still the only man who could whip Arista into readiness.

And readiness was what counted. More, even, than intelligence itself.

The AI beeped and Russell flipped through his heads-up displays until he found the topo map it wanted to show him.

*This way to Arista, Mr. Russell,* he could almost hear the AI whisper. *Time to save the world.*

If you can. If they'll let you. If you can convince them. The shaken marine sergeant would go a long way toward convincing anyone who saw him.

The rest was a matter of putting things in terms that the Aristan senate could understand: wounded global pride, financial risk, possible profit.

And, of course, personal survival.

Russell hadn't gotten this far—alive—by under-estimating the lure of personal survival. To anyone.

On his side of the house, the civilian side, the professionals knew who and what they were, and what good they were to Arista.

Other people thought about manifest destiny and history and the Aristan ethic.

Russell's kind thought about survival. So that was what they called themselves, among themselves—the survivors.

They survived administrations. They survived general staffs. They survived wars and famines. They survived purges and peaces.

If he could just show McMurtry that one man, well placed, with good intelligence and experience, could make a difference, then McMurtry's life was going to make one hell of a difference to Arista.

And to McMurtry himself.

Sometime during the flight home, while Russell was getting in line for a parking orbit, McMurtry leaned over and grabbed his arm.

Since it was Russell's throttle arm, he took the touch very seriously.

He froze and said, slowly pulling his headset back off his ear, "Yeah, McMurtry. What can I do for you now?"

"I just want to thank you, sir—Mr. Russell—not only for saving me in the first place, but for talking me down."

"Don't sweat it, McMurtry. I have every intention of taking that little favor out of your hide for the next two or three months."

McMurtry grinned and let him go.

It occurred to Russell, as he resumed throttling down, that McMurtry might not know that Russell never lied unless it was absolutely necessary.

After all, safeguarding the truth was part of Russell's job.

And the truth was about to come home to Arista in a big way, in the person of a Special Forces sergeant named McMurtry, just in time to keep the human race from blundering into Armageddon one more time.

# Weapons of War
## by Bill Fawcett

Both the Hothri and humans had star drives that were fairly efficient. Maximum speed was in theory unlimited, but navigationally, few ships could surpass ten light-years per day. Due to fuel costs and strain, most merchants and transports could actually travel at little more than a fifth of this speed. The entire FTL drive for the smallest ships was the size of a Ford van.

The most dramatic weapon system was actually totally defensive. This was the ship's shields. The shield is actually a projection of the same system used for FTL flight. It acts by shunting the effects of opposing letters into the same otherspace that allows ships to travel at multiples of light. Most ships were shielded. Ships as small as corvettes could now generate screens powerful enough to protect against anything but multiple hits. Unfortunately if a shield receives more power than it could shunt aside, it would simply fail in a burst of sparks, often taking the ships engines with it as well.

The design of most Hothri ships often lacked the elegance of human space vessels. Only those which were designed to penetrate a planet's atmosphere had any streamlining at all. These tended to natural forms emphasizing arcs and ovoids. The Hothri also preferred larger ships, on which they could be accompanied by a large number of their fellows. The insectoid aliens also preferred to fight in large formations and tended to advance cautiously. This was speculated to be a side effect of their group awareness. There had to be some reluctance to take losses when you feel a little bit of your fellow soldier's pain. Only later was it found that the Hothri were much more capable of suspending this group sense than was suspected and rarely employed it unless aware of definite danger.

The Hothri were also reluctant to attack at any odds until

they had achieved a definite advantage. This led to long pauses between battles and longer delays after any defeat. These periods of relative calm lulled many of Arista's leaders into a false sense of security, but also provided extra time at crucial points during the war. Time that proved vital to Arista.

Another racial imperative meant the Hothri were unable to tolerate even the smallest pocket of resistance. Combined with their natural tendency toward caution, the need to react massively to every threat was reflected in nearly all of the Hothri's tactics; both in space and during actual landings.

The ships of the Aristan Navy were initially comprised of fifty of the most recently designed human vessels. One-on-one, they repeatedly proved themselves superior to their insectoid opponents. Unfortunately the Hothri fleet outnumbered the Aristan by at least ten-to-one. The regular Aristan navy was supplemented by several hundred hastily-armed merchant ships. These were limited in combat effectiveness because few of them could be shielded effectively. Nearly half of the Aristan Navy was lost trying to defend trading outposts in other systems before the Aristan siege actually began. Mercenary ships filled only part of the gap.

The offensive weapons of both ships were comprised of both beam weapons and torpedoes. Most beam weapons were easily stopped by a ships' screens. The beams often served more to soften a screen, thus enabling a torpedo to penetrate. It took a lot to cripple or destroy a ship, but when hit, most ships simply vaporized. Aerial mines using balloons or anti-grav units and smart bombs that seek out specific targets are used extensively to defend Arista. Neither side had bombs powerful enough to blow apart a world.

On a personal level, the intention was still to deliver enough energy into your opponent to disrupt his cell structure. Whether done by a sharp stone, a titanium and steel pellet, a plasma round, or a laser beam, the effect was the same. As always, armor in the Siege provided more of psychological than real protection.

There has never been an era when there was not a direct relationship between those who fight the wars and those who labor at home. In the middle ages it took several hundred peasants to support an armored knight and his retinue. In the twentieth century no real distinction was made between soldier and those who supplied them with the means to make war. Carpet bombing, and atomic weapons didn't bother to determine who was carrying a gun, who made the gun, and who was cowering in a shelter. While less appreciated, and certainly less flamboyant, those who make the weapons have been just as important to a war effort as those who fire them. They can't by themselves win the war, but they certainly can help lose it.

# PAPA DON'T 'LOW

## by Christopher Stasheff

THE DREADNOUGHT WAS BIG, but it was still out-gunned by the six Hothri cruisers, especially since they were coming at it from all sides—and above and below, too.

"Out!" the lieutenant bawled. "Those ants need something else to think about!"

But he was talking to their backsides; Papa had kicked his platoon into motion before the lieutenant finished his exclamation point.

They shot into the scout, catching grab-handles and swinging down into their chairs, stretching their shock webbing over themselves, then sitting, hunched over and tense, eyes glittering, watching Papa.

"Any second," Papa growled, still upright, hanging onto a grab in the ceiling. "They'll shove off any . . ."

Then a huge boot kicked them all in the seats of their pants and, for a moment, they had weight again—too much weight, as the little vessel shot out of its berth in the dreadnought, spearing straight toward a Hothri cruiser.

"Okay, web off," Papa said. "We'll be boarding in a minute." He didn't bother with the "if"—if the Hothri didn't shoot them down before they grappled; if they were still alive when they hit the bigger ship. They all knew that, or thought they did.

But Papa knew it for real. He'd been in a landing ship that got blown. He was the only one who'd had the presence of mind to crack his emergency oxygen, the only one who'd lived—and would keep living, because Papa was a survivor.

Master Sergeant Pepe Stuart, alias Papa, had been a marine for ten years, and had climbed the ladder of noncom rank by the simple process of staying alive when all the other Aristan marines were dying. Of course, he was good, too—a good fighter and a good boss. More importantly, though, he had an instinct for staying alive, and he took his platoon along with him. He knew when to hide and when to hit . . . and where, and how hard. He fought and bled, but he came away—and went back to fight again.

Their ship slammed into the cruiser with a jolt likely to jar his implants loose. Papa turned to yank the hatch open—then stepped back out of the way, because Mulcahy was kneeling right behind him with the cutting torch. He triggered it as Papa stepped clear, and the beam sprang to life, connecting his hands with the side of the Hothri ship. The coherent light heated the armor plate cherry-red, nothing more—but the liquid explosive that sprayed on just behind it began to roar with its continual, directional detonation, blasting the armor plate ahead but nothing behind. Then Mulcahy closed the circle, and the torch winked out. He tossed it aside, leaping to his feet and leveling his rifle—just as the explosion stopped, and the circle of armor fell out with a clang they could feel in their feet, though they couldn't hear it through their helmets, or the vacuum around them.

But they could hear Papa bellow "In!" through their earphones.

In he went, jumping through the glowing circle with balletic grace, incongruous on a body hurtling like a bullet, which was why the Hothri's first shot went over his head and his shoulder slammed into the giant cricket's midriff. It was a big target, a little taller than himself but half again as long, its abdomen sticking out four feet in back, its thorax leaning forward with a grin beneath its black-plate eyes and long arms reaching for him with three-fingered hands—armored hands, natural bug-case armor with razor-sharp serrated fringes along their backs. Its roar echoed around him in the pea soup that the aliens called atmosphere, the murky red they used for light—but the monsters were snapping their helmets closed now as their fog drained into Papa's ship.

That delay was just what the platoon needed. They were through the hole and all around now, the air staccato with bursts of fire, ripping through Hothri suits and Hothri flesh. Then the monsters rallied with whistling screeches that must have meant fury, and tore into the men. Papa saw a sword-tipped barrel slashing toward his eyes, and he rolled aside, leveling his own rifle and pulling the trigger. The Hothri's head vanished in a splatter that Papa didn't stay to see—he had rolled to the side and ducked, just in time, as another Hothri blasted at him with a scatter gun. There was a sharp sting in his shoulder, a reek of methane in his nose, and Papa knew his helmet had been holed. He knew their smog had enough oxygen to keep him going for a little while, though—certainly long enough. He knocked the Hothri's shotgun up with his rifle barrel, slammed the butt into the cricket's helmet, then reversed the weapon and pulled the trigger.

Then, the white-hot fury seared through his back, and everything went black.

He woke up seeing white. For a moment, he panicked, thinking he was blind, and swung his head to yell for help. But he saw a door, and a pale-yellow wall. That steadied him; wherever he was, it wasn't a ship and it wasn't Hothri. After all, he was breathing sweet air with no methane or chlorine, though he didn't have a helmet.

Who did?

Who had taken his suit off him?

Or had they? He looked down and saw a sheet, a blanket—and something in him relaxed. He was in a hospital; he was safe. More importantly, there were the right number of lumps under the blanket—he had both legs. He held up his hands, relieved to see they were both there, then ran them over the rest of his body. Everything was there, everything seemed to be in good order. His back was a long, flaming ache, which must have been why they had him propped on his side, but all his pieces seemed to be right.

The door opened, and a nurse came in. Not worth fighting for, but still awfully good to see. Anyway, she smiled when she saw his eyes open. "Just a second, Sergeant. I'll get the doctor." The door closed.

And Papa was tense. If she'd gone for the doctor, there was something she wasn't supposed to tell him. But what? He was all here!

The door opened again, and the man of medicine came in, wearing long, white coveralls and a nice set of exhaustion lines. Nonetheless, he managed a smile. "Good morning, Sergeant."

"Good morning, Doc," Papa answered. "Which one?"

That brought the doctor up short. "Which what?"

"Which morning?"

"Oh." The doctor sat down in the bedside chair. "Wednesday, Sergeant."

Papa stared. "Two whole days? Was I out *that* long?"

The doctor nodded. "It took us a little while to rebuild your back, Sergeant. New tissue takes time to grow, even when it's forced."

"I *knew* there was something wrong back there. What'd the crickets do to me, Doc?"

"Basically burned your whole upper back. We thought there might have been some damage to your hindbrain, but all your reflexes checked out. How do you feel?"

Papa frowned. "Logy, slow in the head."

"That's the hangover from the sedatives. If you find anything unusual in the way you think, any strange surges of emotion, let us know—but we think you're okay."

"Think?" All Papa's defenses went up. "That means you're not sure."

"Not yet—but we have every reason to think you'll recover completely."

"When?"

The doctor blinked. "Excuse me?"

"How long before you send me back to combat?"

"Oh." The doctor relaxed. "Can't say, really. Could be a month, could be six. But figure you've got at least thirty days R & R, Sergeant. You've earned it."

"But now, wait a minute, no!" Then, for a second, Papa forgot what he'd wanted to say. But only for a second; he knew that what the doctor had said was wrong somehow, that it wasn't what Papa should do. "No, now . . . You see . . ." His brain seemed to be working in low gear, as though he were pushing his thoughts through molasses. "See, it's . . . it's . . ."

"What is it?" The doctor's gaze sharpened, weariness falling away. "What, Sergeant?"

What *was* it? Then Papa remembered. "My pluh . . . platoon. My mmmenn, they nnneeed meee . . . You've . . . got to . . ."

There was a black space, then, and he found himself opening his eyes again. The doctor was standing up, his face only a couple of feet away and directly overhead, the ceiling behind him—and there were two nurses, too. How had the second one gotten there? But his brain was still fuzzy, very, and it was a major chore to collect his wits enough to ask what he needed to. But what was that? Oh, yes. "Why . . . nurses?"

"Just in case we need her. And this is Dr. Lakin, Sergeant. She only has to finish her test, now."

"Test?" Then Papa realized there were gossamer tendrils running from someplace above him to the younger nurse—but no, she was a doctor. Why? He lifted his hands to touch his head, find out where those threads went . . .

The doctor stopped him with a gentle touch. "Please, Sergeant. The test's almost over; then she'll remove the threads. But you do need to wait a little longer."

Papa decided that was okay, if the doctor said so. Obviously, what was being done was what needed to be done, and everything was okay. That meant he could sleep for a while, so he cheerfully slipped back into oblivion.

When he woke, the door was stained orange. He realized that had to be the rays of the setting sun reflecting off the wall—must be a window behind him. He was amazed at how clearly and quickly he was thinking. That made him realize that he shouldn't be amazed, which made him remember how slowly his mind had been working when last he woke.

Then he remembered the hat check.

He sat bolt upright and hit the call-bell.

The door opened in two minutes, and a new nurse looked in. "Oh! You're awake, Sergeant!"

"Yeah." Papa frowned. "What happened, Nurse?"

She stared, at a total loss. "Happened?"

"They gave me some kind of test."

She shook her head. "Not on my time. Hold on, I'll get your doctor."

Papa wanted to protest that she could look it up in the records, but the door closed, and he had to choose between being a grouchy patient and hitting the call bell, or being grouchy but patient. He chose the latter—after all, he knew what it was like to be just taking orders.

Finally, the door opened and the doctor came in. He still looked exhausted, but now he looked fresh-wakened, too. Papa felt remorse. "Shouldn't you go home, Doc?"

"Not when I'm needed. They gave me an apartment on the top floor." The doctor stepped over, pulling out a tiny light, lifted Papa's eyelid, and blinded him with a pocket-sized beacon. Through the glare, Papa asked, "What happened?"

The doctor snapped off the light, letting go of the eyelid and straightening up, giving Papa a look that weighed how much he could take.

Papa braced himself. "I've seen men die, Doc, and I've seen the color of my own blood, by the bucket. I can take it."

The doctor nodded once, satisfied, but he was still braced as he said, "You had a seizure."

Not the last one, as it turned out. Papa had another that night, and a third the next day. Then they hit the right pill, and he didn't have another one for a week. They couldn't take a chance on fixing the brain damage, because they might have caused more while they were trying—but after that first week, they had him charted well enough to install a little gadget inside his skull, and he never had another one.

"But it might break down, Sergeant. You might run out of power supplies. It might be damaged if you fell."

Papa braced himself again. "I can take it, Colonel. Hit me straight."

The colonel's face was stone, no matter how he felt—probably pretty badly, if he had to glower that way. "You can't be a Marine any more, Sergeant."

"*What?*"

"You can't." The colonel braced himself against the man's anguish. "The gadget might fail in the middle of combat, and you might shake up your whole unit."

"Shake up *Marines?*"

"You saw your own sergeant shot when you were a corporal," the colonel reminded "How did it hit *you?*"

"I was shaken, but I picked up the pieces and commanded my squad! We finished out the mission!"

"But you might not be lucky enough to have a corporal who is that good." The colonel shook his head. "Or you might have a seizure during a night attack—and you would do some yelling when it happened, Sergeant. You could give away your platoon's position."

That brought Papa up short. Taking a chance on death in battle was one thing—he'd done it every time he went out. But risking his men's lives was another matter.

"It's not the end, Sergeant." The colonel's voice softened. "There are defense industries. You can still serve."

"But not in uniform! The Corp has been my life, sir!" Then Papa sat up straighter, a glint in his eye as the idea hit. "If I can serve out of the Corps, I can serve in it! Give me a desk job, sir! Give me a way to back up the poor rankers who have to go out there!"

The colonel sat frozen, his face still set in concrete while he weighed the chances. There was a time when keeping a disabled man in uniform could have resulted in his accidentally being assigned back to combat. But that couldn't happen now; once he was coded as a non-combatant, the computers would keep him at a desk. And if he stayed in, he'd have all the fanatic dedication of a convert whereas, if he were cashiered, he'd grow bitter, and might even just sit on the sidelines—or worse.

"All right, Sergeant. You're back in. But you might not like it."

"That doesn't matter." Papa felt a huge surge of relief, even gratitude. "As long as I can serve."

"Oh, you'll serve, all right," the Colonel said. "You'll serve."

Papa ripped the cover off the crate.

"Look," the deliveryman said, "it doesn't matter whether you like 'em or not. That's what the Quartermaster sent, so that's what you get."

"Might be." Papa lifted a rifle out, sighted along the barrel, checked the action, then took out the clip and swapped it for one from his pocket.

The deliveryman frowned. "What do you think you're doing? That's not part of the shipment!"

"No, but it's for the same make and model. What's the matter, friend? Afraid it won't work?"

"Me?" The deliveryman stared. "Hell, no! What difference does it make to me? I just deliver 'em! Come on, now, sign, okay?"

"If it works." Papa sighted at the target on the other side of his depot and squeezed. The huge cavern filled with the drumming of magnum rounds, then went silent.

The deliveryman stared at Papa's hand, the trigger finger still tight. "What the hell did you do?"

"Nothing," said Papa, "but the rifle did. It jammed."

The deliveryman swallowed. "Look, this ain't no business of mine! I just haul'em, Sergeant, I don't make 'em!"

"You can just haul this crate back, then," Papa said. "I don't accept delivery."

The deliveryman began to sweat. "Look, if you don't sign, they'll think I'm goldbricking!"

"Not if you give me a different case."

"I can't do that," the deliveryman objected. "The rest of the load is for Company D."

"So?" Papa waved at the back of the truck. "They get this crate, I get one of theirs. Same guns, right?"

"Well, sure, but . . ."

"So you're giving them what they ordered. What's the problem?"

"But we're giving them guns that won't fire!"

"And it's okay to give them to us?" Papa hurried on while the deliveryman was hung up on common sense. "Let *their* quartermaster find that out. It's his worry, not mine—or yours."

"That makes just enough sense to sound wrong." The deliveryman frowned, eyes straying to his load. "So what do I do if *he* turns 'em down?"

"You take 'em back to Stores, with his note saying why he won't take delivery."

"And let his tail get in the sling, not yours?" The deliveryman turned back. "I think I understand how you're thinking now, Sergeant."

Papa shrugged. "Maybe nobody's in a sling. Maybe the quartermaster will send 'em back to the factory."

"Come on, Sarge! You know factories don't take things back!"

"Maybe. Or maybe nobody ever *sends* 'em back." Papa grinned. "Come on, Corporal—take a chance. Start a revolution."

"*Start* it? *You* did that. All I can do is get caught in it! Give me one reason why I should, Sarge—just one!"

"For the guys on the line."

The deliveryman just stared at him for a moment. Then he said, "I did say just one, didn't I?"

"Want another one?"

"That'll do." The deliveryman turned away and swung another crate of rifles out of the truck, slamming it down at Papa's feet. "Have another, Sarge. One for the road." He

picked up the crate of duds and swung them back aboard
the truck, then turned to find Papa calmly stripping the
packing off one of the rifles from the new crate. "Aw, come
on! Don't tell me you're not going to accept delivery on that
one, too!"

"Oh, sure I will." The Sergeant slapped a new clip into
the rifle and raised it to his shoulder. "Just as soon as I
make sure it works."

He had to salute; it was a lieutenant. He even had to try
to stand up behind his desk, though there wasn't really room
enough.

"At ease." But the lieutenant's frown didn't seem to in-
spire a relaxed attitude. "What kind of racket are you running, Sergeant?"

"Sir?" Papa kept his eyes on the lieutenant's, but noticed
the quartermaster's patch on his pocket. Not that he needed
it—he knew the clerks from his own brigade.

"All the rejections, Sarge! You keep refusing deliveries!"

"Beg pardon, sir. I've never sent anything back."

"No, but you've sent 'em on to other companies! What's
the matter, Sergeant—didn't you ever stop to think that every
crate of good material you get, is one less for another com-
apny?"

"Not my problem," Papa said, straight-faced.

"No, but you sure as hell make it mine!" The lieutenant's face reddened.

"It's simple." The captain spread his hands. "You keep
rejecting the duds, and instead of each company having a
crate or two to scrap, you don't have any, and all the others
have more. Let it go long enough, and the Tenth will be the
only company in the battalion whose rifles work."

Papa dug his heels in while his stomach sank. "Just doing
my job right, sir."

"Yes, you are." The colonel picked up a stylus and
bounced its tip on the desk. "And you know there's only
one thing to do about it, don't you?"

The sunken stomach turned into a hollow pit, but Papa
still didn't back down, even though visions of civilian
clothes flitted through his head. "Yes, sir. I know."

"Good." The captain nodded. "Then go back and clean

out your desk, Sarge, and move your gear over to company HQ. You just became battalion quartermaster.''

Papa stared, unable to believe his ears. "Sir?"

"What's the matter?" The captain looked up with a frown. "Don't understand orders?"

"But, sir. There's a lieutenant in that job!"

"Good point—you just got promoted. Congratulations, Lieutenant Stuart."

The room seemed to become a litle unstable. "Uh—Sir! Thank you! I'm . . . I'm . . . But!"

The captain leaned back with a sigh. " 'But,' Lieutenant?''

"We already *have* a battalion quartermaster!"

"We developed a sudden and urgent need for him in one of the orbital stations. You'll just have to manage somehow, Lieutenant. Dis—miss!"

Alice had been in combat, but she'd only seen one mission—and she'd been terrified every minute, as much by the appearance of the Hothri as by the danger. Then her right arm had been burned off at the elbow; she remembered screaming and blacking out—she remembered, but she tried not to. She remembered waking up, too, seeing what was left of her arm, and screaming again. That time it was the sedative jet that had put her to sleep—and after that, she remembered the counseling, the exercizes to get her used to her prosthetic arm, and her amazement at how much it looked and felt like her real one. That was why she hadn't opted for a graft, of course—she would have felt very strange with arms that didn't match. The prosthetic felt like the real thing; the only time she knew it wasn't was when she had to pick up something heavy. The mechanical arm was much stronger than the real one. That had taken some getting used to, and a good many broken drinking glasses.

Now, a year later, she could do everything with it that she'd been able to do before. But it was her right arm, and the Navy didn't feel like taking chances on a malfunction, so she'd been rotated back to the Reserves, and given a civilian job. All in all, she guessed she was happy about it, but there was always that sneaking guilt.

Well, if she couldn't be firing a rifle in Arista's defense, she could at least be making them. She tried to relax into the boredom and let it pass while she let her gaze rove over the tell-tales, watching for red lights. There was scarcely ever any trouble—the robot factory was so completely efficient! Metal roared as the truck dumped into the giant hopper, but the tell-tales said it was all feeding down to the assembly line without trouble.

Something rang like a gong, then clattered, and Alice turned back, alerted. Sure enough, a bar of pig iron had slipped between the truck's funnel and the hopper. She jumped back, judging its trajectory and stepping aside just in time to avoid its hitting her toes. Then she scooped it up with the prosthetic arm—so much stronger than her real one!—and started to toss it back into the hopper.

But she stopped with a frown, hefting the bar. It felt lighter than it should have. Flesh and blood couldn't have told the difference, but the circuits in the prosthetic were sensitive to very slight differences in weight and texture. And the pig iron felt wrong. She frowned, looking at it closely, and saw the multitude of tiny, almost microscopic, bubbles, as though the iron were foamed. It didn't really matter, she supposed—the machines on the assembly line would melt it down or forge the air out of it, wouldn't they? But it did bother her, that the Company was paying for solid pig iron, but getting foam.

Or maybe they weren't. Maybe they were paying for foam, and getting what they paid for. She summoned resolve and tossed the pig back into the hopper—it was none of her business. That was what the company had managers for, and she wasn't about to make a fool out of herself by reporting something they already knew.

But it nagged, and nagged—maybe they *didn't* know. She just had to tell someone—but who? Nobody from the company, of course. But who?

Lunch break came, and with it, Clothilde. Alice had to reconcile pleasure in human conversation with a friend, with her irritation—Clothilde was sure to try to set her up with another man. She always did. Clothilde had finally married, and was now evangelizing with all the fervor of a convert, trying to make sure all her friends were as happy as she.

The trouble was, Alice wasn't at all sure a man could make her happy. Not judging by the ones she had met, and the few she had dated. She supposed she was just too plain to attract the really good men—and she wasn't about to settle for anything less.

Sure enough, they'd scarcely sat down before Clothilde started in. "Jerry introduced me to this wonderful friend of his last night, Alice! His old sergeant, who was injured and pushed out before Jerry was."

Clothilde's husband was out with an honorable discharge, of course—too badly wounded to be patched up and sent back. Those were the only men around—except for soldiers on leave. Inwardly, Alice sighed and braced herself. She managed a tired smile. "Really? I thought men didn't like their sergeants."

"They do after the sergeant's saved their lives a few times. He thought Lieutenant Stuart was an angel, or maybe a devil."

"Or both." Alice smiled. "But I thought you said he was a sergeant."

"Well, he's a lieutenant, now. They kept him in, at a desk job—he made too much of a fuss when they tried to discharge him."

Alice stared. "He was that badly wounded, and he wanted to stay *in?*"

Clothilde nodded. "Crazy, huh? That's why I figured you wouldn't want to date him."

"No," Alice said slowly, thrown off balance as much by the denial as by the strangeness of the man Clothilde described. "No, I think I might like to meet him." Then, quickly, "But nót a date, of course."

Clothilde's eyes lit with the joy of the huntress who had bagged her prey. "Not a date," she agreed.

Papa frowned. The tank looked right, drove right, and fired right—but felt wrong. Somehow, he just knew there was something bad about it. "Let me keep it around for a couple of days."

"Heaven's seven's, Lieutenant!" the salesman snapped, exasperated. "If your corps accepted it, you have to accept it."

Papa's hackles went up, and his head went down. "Not if I don't think it will do everything I need, Mr. Snell. No."

"Oh, come off your high horse! What difference could it make? Who the hell is gonna use a tank in a space war, for crying out loud?"

Papa turned a very unfriendly gaze on the salesman. "Then why is your company making them?"

"Why . . ." the salesman floundered. "Because the Force is buying them!"

"Does that give you the right to make junk?"

"Look, Lieutenant." Snell drew a deep breath and fought for calm. "I don't make them. I just sell them."

"Not to me, you don't." Papa turned back and scowled at the tank.

"Quit stalling, Lieutenant!" Snell decided to let the whip show. "There's a contract! If we deliver them, you have to take what we give you!"

Papa shook his head slowly. "If I had to, they wouldn't have sent you down here to talk to me into it."

"Just because you won't accept perfectly good materiel . . ."

"The first one shattered its barrel on the third shot," Papa reminded him, "and the second one lost its left tread in two hours."

"But they'll never be *used!*"

"They might," Papa said. "We might have to use them. We hope we won't, because we'll only need them if the Hothri smash through our defenses and land an invason force. But if we do need them, they have to kill Hothri, not us."

"They couldn't possibly kill . . ."

"That one over in Company D, that blew up its breech, killed its whole crew."

Snell reddened. But he bit his tongue and swallowed, then smiled and said, "We can't let you keep it if you don't accept it, Lieutenant."

"Fine!" Papa waved a hand. "Take it back."

Snell stared. "What?"

"I said, take it back."

"But if you don't accept any of our tanks, we'll lose the contract!"

Papa shrugged. "Not my job."

Snell clamped his jaw shut and waited till the wave of anger passed, then said, "Two days, Lieutenant. I'll see you in two days."

Alice had never been in Clothilde's apartment before—but then, Clothilde hadn't been in it that long, herself. She'd only moved in when she had married Jerry, a few months earlier. Until then, she'd only qualified for a cubicle in the unmarried women's dorm. Now they qualified for two rooms and a kitchenette, and Clothilde was working toward three.

For the time being, though, the single front room was arranged as both a parlor and a dining room. Jerry was sitting in one armchair, laughing and talking with a man in uniform. They broke off and looked up as Alice came in—and the eyes of the man in uniform widened. Then he was out of the chair and helping her off with her coat, all smiles. "Hi. I'm Pepe Stuart."

"Lieutenant, this is Alice Biedermann." Clothilde seemed irritated.

"Oh, I'm sorry, Clothilde! I should have waited to be introduced." The lieutenant turned toward the closet, but Jerry had caught up with him, chuckling. He took the coat, saying, "No way, Papa. You let the host do his own job, huh? Watch out for him, Miss—he eats pretty girls for breakfast."

"Lunch," Papa corrected. "It's *privates* I eat for breakfast. Only I'm on a diet, since they kicked me upstairs." But his eyes were on Alice the whole time. "Pay attention to him, Little Red Riding Hood. I'm the wolf."

Alice couldn't help it; she laughed, and her shyness evaporated. For the first time in her life, she felt pretty.

They had a wonderful evening, talking and laughing well past midnight, and Papa even managed to make his war stories seem funny. When he offered to take her home at the end of the evening, and Jerry started to object, Clothilde caught her husband under the short ribs with an elbow. He said, "Wuff!" and forced a smile as Clothilde said, "Yes, that would be very nice, Lieutenant. Do make sure she gets home safely, now."

He might not have—but on the way, Alice suddenly realized she was right next to a man who could tell her she was being silly. "All those stories about your job, Lieutenant—I owe you a few about mine."

"Oh?" No amusement, no belittling—he was instantly interested.

She suspected most of that was politeness, but she tried anyway. "I'm a cyborg, see, and . . ."

"Uh, problem with definitions." Papa took her hand. "You're delightfully organic."

She glanced at him, almost gratefully, and blushed. "That's the one that was shot off, Lieutenant."

Papa stared at it, then squeezed the fingers gently. "Doesn't feel any different."

"But it does to me—it's much more sensitive."

Papa dropped her hand like a hot rock. "Oh. Sorry."

"Not at all; I liked it. So what kind of job do you give a girl with a super right arm, Lieutenant?"

He frowned up at her, not understanding. "I give. What kind?"

"Super in a weapons factory. I get to make sure the incoming steel bars feed into the production line properly."

Suddenly, she knew she had his complete and total attention, but not as a woman. "Do you really!"

"Yes." She forced a smile. "Every now and then, I have to pick up a pig that drops out, and throw it back in."

"Noisy but absorbing work."

"Yes." She fought to keep the smile. "But since this arm is so much more sensitive, I get a surprise now and then."

His gaze bored into hers. "Nice surprise?"

Alice shivered. "I don't know. Just odd, I guess. But every third bar seems to be . . . foam, if that makes sense. Steel foam."

"Full of bubbles," Papa grated. "Perfect sense—for the company."

"But it doesn't matter, does it? The air gets beaten out in the forges."

"Sure." Papa gave her a hard smile. "But the company only gets maybe half the steel it paid for."

"So the company *does* lose!"

"No. They just buy more steel, and charge the government a higher price for the finished weapons."

"But . . . the government doesn't care, does it?"

Papa shrugged. "You tell me. They could buy three rifles with the money they're paying for two. Who wins?"

"Well, the Company, I suppose . . ."

"No. The Hothri."

Alice stared, appalled, the more so because he had finally put into words what she'd been worrying about, herself. "It's not *that* important!"

"Oh, yes it is," Papa said softly. "But what worries me is, what *other* short cuts is the Company taking?"

"Maybe none," Alice said, but her stomach was shrinking into a knot.

"I hope not," Papa said. "If they do, though, I'd like to know about it."

She stared at him, and his eyes seemed to be drawing her in, enveloping her, compelling her . . .

She tore her gaze away, looking at the buildings they were passing, recognized the doorway with relief. "This is my dorm, Lieutenant."

"So I see," Papa said, with regret.

She turned back to him, forcing a smile and holding out a hand. "Well . . . good night, Lieutenant."

"Good night." He ignored the hand, reaching out, almost touching her chin, but not quite. "And if you see anything else funny, let me know, will you?"

"Yes, Lieutenant," she said, feeling chilled inside.

But his sudden smile thawed her as he said, "And *that* has got to be the world's worst excuse for getting another date with a pretty lady. So find something wrong fast for me, huh?"

She managed to smile again. "Of course, Lieutenant, if you put it that way. If I can't find one, I'll make one."

"Thanks, Little Red," he said softly, "but you really should be more careful about wolves."

She would, Alice decided firmly as she closed the door behind her. She would be very careful about this particular wolf—but maybe not the way he'd meant.

Papa found the flaw on the morning of the second day, when he tried to start the tank and the gauge read empty. It took him another half-hour to find out that the power plant was still functioning just fine, but with no outlet for the energy it had built up. The linkage had burned out.

"A bomb." The general seemed very happy about it. "It was a rolling, shooting bomb. It would have killed its whole crew, and half the ratings near it."

"Sir." Papa stood at parade rest, eyes carefully focused an inch above the general's left shoulder.

"Oh, sit down, Lieutenant! You're not an NCO any more." The general leaned back, studying Papa as he sat warily in the straight chair before the acre of desk. "You realize you're creating difficulties, don't you?"

"No, sir."

"Oh, really?" The general raised one eyebrow. "And

may I ask why you think we can't get enough tanks to man every post?''

"Because General Munitions isn't producing enough good ones, sir.''

"Not producing.'' The general held his gaze steady. "It wouldn't be because you're not accepting delivery of the ones they *do* make, would it?''

"Absolutely not.'' Papa shook his head. "A tank that doesn't work, is the same as no tank at all—maybe worse, if it explodes and kills its crew.''

"Valid.'' But the general still held his gaze on Papa. "How do you think we can boost production, Lieutenant?'' Papa opened his mouth, but the general added. "Don't try to say it's not your problem.''

"Begging the General's pardon . . .''

The General didn't move, but his gaze sharpened to a diamond. "Yes, Lieutenant?''

"I'm only responsible for receiving and distributing deliveries of sound equipment, sir. I don't have anything to do with procurement.''

"I *told* you not to say it wasn't your problem!'' The general leaned forward, eye narrowing, hands clasped. "But since you insist, we'll *make* it your problem.''

"Begging the General's pardon, but a battalion quartermaster can't have that kind of responsibility, sir.''

"Very true—so we're making you quartermaster for the whole Corps.'' The General's hand opened, revealing a new, glittering set of insignia. "Congratulations, Major.''

That night, Papa came home, touched his doorman, and heard Alice's voice say, "Grandma, what big ears you have.''

Grandma's was crowded for so early on a Wednesday night. Of course, there were always soldiers on leave, but it seemed a little odd that there were so many factory supers in here, too. Alice wondered if it was just her imagination.

But there was no mistaking the one empty table, empty except for a stocky man in uniform. The mere sight of him sent a flood of relief through Alice, and she wended her way over to him with a smile. He stood, aware of her before she'd even seen him, and lit up the room with his grin. He held her chair, and she slipped in, grateful for the anachronistic gallantry. The glow in those eyes warmed him, and he sat down beside her, almost sorry they had business to discuss.

She lowered her eyes, maybe blushing—he couldn't tell; the lighting was dim—then looked up with a roguish smile. "How did you manage to keep the table clear, Lieutenant?"

Pepe shrugged and pointed to his insignia. "Rank. Keeps 'em at bay."

Alice looked, and looked again. "You were promoted."

"Thanks for noticing." He grinned. "Things happen fast in wartime."

Then the jarring note registered, and Alice looked around in surprize, really noticing her surroundings for the first time. "This is an enlisted man's place!"

"Not officially, no. And as you can see, there are a lot of civilians."

"Yes, but they're all rankers, too. Isn't it wrong for you to be here?"

"Not really." Papa grinned. "The place is civilian, not under military jurisdiction—and I'm a ranker who made good."

"Oh." Alice felt something relax inside, something she hadn't known was tensed. "You were an enlisted man?"

"Yeah, but they had to promote me to make me a quartermaster. Don't think they really wanted to, either."

He made it sound like a joke, but Alice caught the undertone and frowned. "Why not?"

She suddenly had his total attention again, and his eyes devoured hers. "Because I'd been on the line. I knew what faulty weapons meant."

Alice shifted nervously, and broke the gaze. "Well—that's what I came to tell you about. You see, Major, I . . ."

"Yeah, it is a little crowded in here, isn't it?" he said, too loudly. "Sure, let's try a restaurant. I'm hungry, too."

She looked up, startled, then followed his lead, standing up. "Major, I . . ."

"After all, I did ask you out for dinner," he said, still too loudly. "We can get cocktails while we're waiting on the chef."

She shut up, letting him help her into her coat again, then moving with him toward the door—and wondered, as the crowd seemed to part around him. Then they were outside, and she said, "Is it really that bad?"

"Dunno," Papa said cheerfully. "Depends on what you were gonna tell me. But it's a lot harder for the walls to have ears when we're outdoors. In there, no telling who might have been listening—or with what. So, spill it, Super. Let's get it out of the way, so we can pay attention to the important things."

Her heart skipped a beat, and she decided not to ask what the important things were. She'd rather have her illusions. "Okay, Major. One of the bars broke open today, when it fell—and it wasn't just foam, it was hollow."

Papa stared at her for a long minute. Then he said, "That's more than somebody pulling a sharp one on somebody else. That's collaboration."

He turned away, frowning as he strode along, and she suddenly felt hurt, locked out. But he turned back to her and said, "Think you could get a promotion?"

"Why—I don't know," she said, startled. "I never wanted one, really. I make enough to live on, and . . ." She didn't finish; she would have had to say, *"and I'm safe."*

"Try," Papa urged. "I'd like to know what happens to that flawed steel. Nothing, I hope. But if the Company's willing to pay so much for so little, they might have other arrangements going, too."

"You mean . . ."

"Nothing." Papa shook his head. "I don't mean anything—yet. Too many possibilities. Hopefully, I'm wrong, and all we're looking at is a little bit of mutual back-scratching. But try, okay? You deserve a better job, anyway."

*But I don't,* she thought helplessly.

Papa noticed. He frowned. "Why not? You're a wonderful woman."

She turned away. "You don't know me—yet."

"Yet," he agreed, and her heart thawed. "But what could you have done, that would make you think you're not great?"

Her voice turned flat. "I deserted my unit."

Papa frowned. "I thought you were invalided out."

She tossed her head, irritated. "Invalided, deserted— what's the difference?"

"A lot," he snapped. "I know."

She looked up at him, startled. "I'm sorry . . . I didn't mean . . ."

"Of course not." His smile shone again. "But if it's not true for me, Alice, it's not true for you, either."

He had used her name! She turned away, rattled. "You don't understand. I was *glad* I couldn't go back."

"Ahhhh." But there was no judgement in that, only warmth, only sympathy. "Glad they didn't order you to, huh?"

She nodded, feeling herself sink inside.

"Because you would have had to go, if they had?"

"Yes," she hissed. Why was he tormenting her like this?

"Then you didn't desert."

Alice stopped still for a second, then looked up at him. "What?"

"You didn't desert," Papa explained. "If you'd have gone back if they'd ordered you to, then you didn't desert."

Alice turned away and started walking again, numb. "I guess I didn't, did I?"

"Not a bit," Papa assured her. "A scared soldier is still a soldier, and I've met a lot of 'em—me included."

"Thank you, Major," she murmured. "Thank you *very* much."

"My pleasure. So will you apply for a promotion?"

Alice gave a short nod. "Yes."

"See?" Papa's voice was full of warmth. "I told you you're not a deserter."

She beamed up at him, and her face was filled with sunlight. He let himself drift downward into her eyes, then opened his lips against hers.

After a while, he straightened up, taking a deep breath. "Yes. Well, now. It seems I said something about dinner some while ago, didn't I?"

"I don't need it," she said, beaming up at him.

"Maybe not, but *I* do." He took her arm, hooking her hand over his elbow. "Someplace with bright lights, okay?"

"Anything you say, Major." She floated along on his arm, feeling very sultry.

"Well, we're both reasonable men." The sales manager leaned back, caressing his snifter. "Surely we can come to some kind of accommodation."

'Reasonable' and 'accommodation' were both words that

rang alarm bells in Papa's head. With a two-alarm wariness, he said, "I doubt it, Mr. Gleed."

The sales manager looked pained. "Please, Major Stuart! Certainly we can deal with first names, can't we?"

"That's only for personal situations, Mr. Gleed, and this is official. After all, if your STOs won't detonate, they won't detonate. And that's all there is to it."

"One." The sales manager held up a finger. "One out of five you tested—at considerable cost to Arista, I might add."

"That's one out of five Hothri battleships coming through to blast our cities, Mr. Gleed."

"A fluke." The sales manager waved it away. "You happened to get one of the very few duds, Major."

"All right. Give me five more to test. Only this time, don't charge the government for them."

The sales manager reddened. "Major, that would be prohibitively expensive for us."

"It would be even more expensive for you if those missiles fail when the Hothri blast through."

The sales manager took a long breath as he sat back, eyeing Papa with a new and different gleam in his eye. He started to say something, caught himself, and said instead, "Our missiles won't fail when the time comes, Major."

"Then," Papa said, "make sure they don't fail *now.*"

The sales manager leaned forward again. "Major Stuart, my company has put aside all other projects to develop this surface-to-orbit missile, and the government has an ironclad contract to buy them."

"True," Papa agreed, "when the Navy accepts delivery."

"There is no reason not to!"

"Twenty percent don't work, Mr. Gleed."

"Major . . ." Gleed drew a long, shaky breath. "Any delay in processing this sale could be ruinous for General Munitions. We have invested sixty percent of our capital in the development and production of this weapon!"

"Then invest a little more, Mr. Gleed. Fix the detonators."

The next week, they had a new detonator in production, and a mugger jumped Papa on his way home.

He liked to walk the mile to his apartment—it was the

only exercize he ever got any more. And okay, sure, it was late—it always was when he came home—but not *that* late.

Still, the kid who jumped him wasn't worrying about the rules. Papa was walking past the corner park when something hard and rough closed about his throat, yanking him back, and steel flashed in the dark.

Old reflexes took over. Papa kicked back, heard something crack, and the steel went wide as the mugger groaned and loosened his hold—just a little, but enough for Papa to drop down, straightening his legs as he bowed and pulled—sending the mugger flying over his head. Papa hung on to the arm, and the man slammed down on the ground with a howl—then howled again as Papa bent his arm back and yelled for the police.

By the time they got there, the man was very ready to talk. Why not? He'd already told everything, and had been outraged to find out that Papa couldn't really do anything about the dislocated shoulder.

But he didn't really have anything worth saying. Someone had paid him five K to beat up Papa—"Want me to kill him, too?" "We're not fussy."—and promised him more afterward. Other than that, Papa couldn't really hold a grudge—the poor guy had been maimed in battle by the Hothri, and couldn't remember directions for more than a few hours any more. Too proud to go for Vets' Aid, too, so he eked out a living any way he could. Papa struck a deal. He didn't press charges, and the mugger went to live in the Vets' Home.

He didn't stop walking home. But he did start carrying his sidearm again.

The foreman called her over as she came in the door, before her clock-chime had even faded. With heart pounding, she came over. What had the boss-lady found out?

"Bertha's sick, over in Quality. We can put that trainee on your job; you go fill in for Bertha, okay?"

Alice stared, appalled. "But I don't know anything about quality control!"

The fore shrugged. "What's to know? You look at the gadget as it comes along, look at the diagnostics, and let it go by."

"But how'll I know if there's anything wrong with it?"

"Wrong?" The fore's tone somehow managed to convey both the extreme improbability of the event, coupled with the imbecility of Alice. "The diagnostics will tell you, of course! Now, get going."

Alice tried for a little bit more information when she arrived at her station, but the other checkpointers only shrugged and said pretty much the same.

"Nothing to tell," Alberta assured her. "If there's anything wrong, the screen will light up with red danger calls."

"But how about if it's something the machines can't see?"

Alberta gave her a look that implied there was something wrong with her. "Well, if you see anything wrong that the machines don't catch, tell me, will ya? It'll be a first."

Alice's face flamed, and she felt as though she were dwindling right there and then, but she plucked up her courage and asked, "Don't the screens tell you anything else?"

Alberta shrugged. "Well, they'll light up in yellow if there's something questionable, and they'll light up in blue for something that's wrong but doesn't matter. So what it comes down to is, you only scrap the item if the screen shows red."

Alice stared, not believing her ears.

Alberta finally noticed. "Well, it's not as though we had much choice, lamebrain. After all, each of us has to pass four hundred items each day—and there's one coming down the line every thirty seconds! How long do you think you'll keep your job if you stop the line every time there's a yellow flash?"

"I don't know," Alice answered. "I really don't know."

But she found out very quickly. The yellow letters flashed for every fifth gadget, it seemed, usually in the words "CASTING FLAW," and the blue showed once an hour. If she had pulled each one, she could never have sent four hundred to packing. Three hundred, maybe, but not four. She almost pulled the first one off the conveyor, but at the last moment, she remembered Pepe telling her to just find out as much as she could for him, so she glanced at the other checkers, to take her cue from them.

Two others had yellow words on their screens, but they stood by, arms folded, looking bored, and reached out at the last second to punch the button that routed the item off to packing. Alice swallowed heavily, and punched her button, too.

Fifteen minutes later, every checker's screen had flashed yellow at least once, and not a single item had been pulled off the line. Alberta had been right—they didn't stop for anything but red.

So Alice held back, and let the item go by.

Papa didn't like talking to strange admirals.

He sat down at the little table, trying to hide his wariness. A full admiral didn't usually meet with a colonel, even a quartermaster, in a restaurant—a small, very expensive restaurant. And certainly not with a civilian in a very expensive suit beside him, a civilian who had iron-gray hair and iron-gray eyes, and whose finger gleamed with a watch worth two months of Papa's pay.

"Good of you to invite me, sir."

"Not at all, not at all, Colonel! The top brass should stay in contact with their juniors, don't you think? Outside the office as well as in."

Not that Papa had needed any remainder that the admiral could give him orders—he'd just been making sure. "Still an honor, sir." He turned to the civilian. "Don't believe I've had the pleasure?"

The man gave him a tight-lipped smile. "Names don't matter here."

They certainly didn't—not when the man's face was as well-known as his company's name—L. C. Lamprey, Chairman of the Board of Industrial Munitions.

"Let's just say I represent the private sector, Colonel."

The alarm bell in Papa's head started clanging, and irritation surged. He decided to go on the offensive. "The people we rely on, yes. The good people in industry who make the armor that protects our boys, the weapons that keep the Hothri from gobbling them up."

Anger flashed in the civilian's eyes, and the admiral said, "No, we can't do without them, Colonel. We'd go naked into battle, if it weren't for the manufacturers."

"True, sir." Inspiration nudged him, and Papa decided to stab. "Of course, it would be much more efficient if the Navy just built its own factories. Fewer middlemen, greater quality control."

The admiral stared, appalled, and the civilian's gaze turned to a glare. "Don't try to threaten me, Colonel!"

"Me, sir? I don't have anything to do with policy."

"Of course not," the admiral said quickly, but the civilian's gaze was still carving and slicing. "And the notion is ridiculous. Why, the expense to the Navy would be intolerable.''

''Not really, sir.'' Papa began to realize that the idea might be worth exploring. ''We're already paying the same amount to private enterprise—and without their profit margin, we'd actually save money. An amazing amount, in fact.''

''That will be enough!'' the civilian snapped.

Papa rounded on him. ''I think that's for the Admiral to say, don't you, *mister*? If you want to give orders, find a clerk!''

''That will do, Colonel!'' the admiral snapped. ''You will treat this man with all due courtesy!''

''That's what I was doing . . . sir.''

The civilian only narrowed his eyes, but the admiral turned red. ''That will be enough impertinence, Colonel! Or I'll break you out of your job!''

Papa stared at him, then smiled, just a little. ''Fine.''

The admiral stared back, then snapped, ''I'll transfer you to the front lines!''

Papa's eyes glowed. ''Thank you—sir!'' He rose and saluted. ''Have I the Admiral's dismissal?''

''Don't be an ass!'' the civilian snapped. ''Sit down, you fool!''

Papa spun, caught up the man's snifter, and threw the brandy on his suit.

''Colonel!'' the admiral cried, appalled.

But Papa was saying, in cold fury, ''Armed Forces personnel do not take orders from any civilians, *Mr.* Lamprey—especially from men of acceptable physical condition who decline to serve!''

Lamprey's eyes were as void of emotion as outer space. Slowly, he stood, eye to eye with Papa. ''You will regret that insult sorely, Colonel Stuart—sorely, and at great length.''

He turned away and stalked out.

''Do you realize what you've done?'' the Admiral said, in a shocked whisper.

Slowly, Papa turned back to his superior officer. ''Oh, yes, sir. But what, may I ask, were the two of *you* doing?''

''I don't think that matters, now,'' the admiral said, rising slowly. ''Report to the stockade, Colonel, and turn yourself in for arrest!''

"Oh, yes, sir, I will," Papa said softly, "and, of course, I'll have to make out a full report as to why."

"I don't think that will be necessary. My word . . ."

". . . will be evidence at my court-martial," Papa interrupted. "I'll have to request one, of course."

The admiral stared. "Do, and you'll be cashiered!"

"Only if the verdict goes against me," Papa assured him.

By the time he got to the stockade, orders from the admiral were waiting, commanding him to return to his duties. The guard could only stare as Papa smiled at the paper, then folded it and turned away. "Uh . . . Colonel?"

"Yes, Sergeant?"

"May I ask, sir—what you needed here?"

"No, Sergeant. Seems it's not my business to answer."

"And that's 'checked by hand!' " Alice told Pepe, still seething.

"Yeah, well, at least a human being made the decision."

"The machine should have made it! They've got the sensors, they know what's wrong! We don't!"

Papa shrugged. "Then they'd just set the machines to only kick out the code red's, anyway. They can set the warning levels wherever they want, you know. That much *is* done by hand."

"And the hand isn't a checker's! What good did I do, Pepe? What good?"

"A lot of good." His voice was soothing—no, admiring. "You did wonderfully, Alice. You found out about it, and you didn't blow your cover."

"Oh, yes, I found out!" she exploded. "And I can't stand it! You'd think they were manufacturing wallets or something!"

"Wallets made of bad leather, with pockets that would let the cash fall out," Papa reminded her.

"Any company that did that would go out of business! And I helped them! What good did I do, Pepe?"

"Let me worry about that," he reassured.

She looked at his face, and saw the grin of a hunting cat. Even as her heart quailed at the sight, she felt buoyed up. Still, she had to demand, "Can you stop those yellow letters from coming on my screen?"

"Sure." His eyeteeth showed. "All they have to do is

code those flaws for red. By the way, what were these 'items'
you were checking?''

She took a deep breath and said, ''Reflectors. For laser
cannon. And they know those reflectors are flawed, but they
don't give a damn!''

''Sure.'' Papa shrugged. ''What difference does it make
to them, if the beam doesn't come out of the muzzle?
They're not the ones who're going to be standing in front
of a raging Hothri.''

''Not even that,'' Alice snapped. ''I swear they don't even
think that far! All they can see is, sure, this is wrong, but
it's not my job to fix it, and if I say anything, I'll just get
fired. They don't even think!''

''Not paid to,'' Papa murmured.

''But they're paid to produce *weapons!* Ones that *work!*''
Alice scowled. ''It makes me wonder, now, about that
Hothri who got past my shots to take my arm.'' Her breath
caught. ''I could have sworn I had him dead in my sights—
at point-blank range!''

''The rifle spat out a slug, didn't it?''

''I wonder. I was looking at the Hothri, not my rifle.''
Alice drew a long, shuddering breath. ''I tell you, Peppy,
it makes me so mad I wish I'd never been promoted!''

Oddly, he found his mispronunciation of his name en-
dearing, not irritating. ''Sorry to make you go for it,'' he
murmured.

''Oh, it's not your fault. Besides,'' she grumbled, ''I suppose I wouldn't have forgiven myself if I'd missed a chance
to catch this.''

''How did you?'' He judged that she had calmed down
enough so that it might be safe to ask.

''I saw it myself,'' she snapped, ''in the test readout from
the quality control unit. But the standards are set so low
that the program didn't flag it—and the controller told me
if the bosses didn't care enough to set the specs higher, we
shouldn't, either. Oh!'' She jammed her fists into her coat
pockets, glaring again. ''Just thinking about it makes my
blood boil! I tell you, Peppy, if you hadn't wanted me to
take that job, I would have quit right there and then!''

''And they would have just gone right on making more
cannons that would quit working in the middle of combat.''
Papa shook his head. ''No, it's much better this way. You
let me take care of it, angel.''

"Angel!" She stared up at him, the job forgotten.

"Why not? You're guarding all our kids on the line, out there."

"But I'm not . . . I can't . . ."

"Do anything?" Pepe grinned like a wolf. "You already did. But I can't follow it up until tomorrow, and we both need to eat if we're going to be able to keep fighting the baddies. What restaurant tonight, Fury?"

She smiled, oddly flattered by the nickname. "How about my place?"

"Oh, no!" Papa grinned. "Don't trust me in your cottage, Little Red, if I won't trust myself! Come on, we'll try Pomona's!"

And he whirled her away to the high life, or at least as much of it as he could afford. It was a wonderful evening, but she was still disappointed.

The admiral tried again, of course. Papa had figured that he would—after all, he had his orders, too. The fact that they didn't come from anybody military was only incidental.

And of course Papa met with him—after all, orders were orders, even if they did come in a plain unmarked envelope. Besides, the embankment was beautiful that time of year. Since it was chilly, though, Papa wore his heavy overcoat, with no valuables, and a wet suit.

"Industry's good is Arista's good, Colonel," the admiral said, "and without the profit incentive, industry is never very productive."

"True." Papa had read his history, too. "But if the profit motive gets out of hand, sir, industry lowers costs by cutting quality."

"Competition will take care of that."

"Only if there really is free competition, sir. And when all the industry is controlled by three companies, it's very easy for them to watch what the others are doing, and all produce substantially the same goods at the same price. Not that they would, of course."

"Of course." The admiral gave him a whetted glance. "If they start showing losses, though, they'll stop making weapons."

"But that's a purely hypothetical case, isn't it, sir?"

"Not necessarily." The admiral turned to face him. "We

have to make sure they have a decent profit margin, Colonel. After all, even if only five out of ten rifles fire, that's still five rifles.''

"Would you want to be holding one of the other five, sir?''

"Of course not,'' the admiral said impatiently. "The other five, we throw away. It's worth it, to keep industry producing.''

"Why not just subsidize them, sir?''

"You know the Senate would never stand for that.'' Finally, anger began to show. "They couldn't see any reason to subsidize a profit-making company!''

Neither could Papa. "Doesn't that depend on their profit margin, sir? I mean, if they have to cut corners to maintain a healthy percentage, they *need* a subsidy.''

The admiral was reddening. He couldn't come right out and say Industrial Munitions was raking in a 50 percent profit margin, but he knew that Papa knew it, too. "What the Senate won't do, we'll have to do, Colonel—or the factories will close down, and we won't have *any* weapons.''

"I wouldn't mind paying more, sir, for reliable equipment. If they boost quality control, they won't have any problem.''

"I don't think that's for you to say, Colonel. From now on you will accept at least twenty percent of all weapons and equipment that you consider to be defective! Is that understood?''

Papa wondered if the admiral was on Industrial Munitions' payroll, or just a stockholder. "No, sir. Not clear at all. I can't believe an admiral of the Navy would order me to accept defectives.''

"You will do as you are commanded, Colonel—for the good of Arista!''

Papa stared straight into the admiral's reddened eyes and realized he was going to have to play it by the book—for the good of Arista. "Yes, sir.'' He pulled a brace. "I will implement the order the moment I receive it, sir.''

"You *have* just received it, you impertinent imbecile!''

"Begging the Admiral's pardon, but orders to the Quartermaster must be cut in triplicate on Form A–394–C, sir, and signed by the senior officer.''

The admiral just stared at him, turning light purple. "Why, you insubordinate, goldbricking, malingering, cowardly lackey! You do as I command you, or there'll be hell to pay!''

Papa felt the rage churning inside him and kept his face carefully wooden. He decided that there *would* be hell to pay—and that he would send the admiral the bill.

The order never arrived, of course, and Papa made sure his staff kept on sending back the defectives. And there was no summons to a court martial—Papa had known there wouldn't be. But it did shake him, knowing that a full admiral, one of the high command, had sold out to the profiteers. So he did send the admiral the bill.

He stayed late one night, checking out the admiral's requisitions personally—everything for his own porkbarrel use, down to the aftershave and razorblades. Then he locked himself in the computer room alone, and cut routing slips guaranteeing that every single item that went to that admiral was defective.

It was almost satisfying—but not quite, because he never did hear the admiral squawk. He couldn't, after all. He'd made sure there was no trail to show who had cut the routing orders.

But he didn't doubt for a minute that the admiral knew. Especially after the next attack.

"Biedermann!"

Alice turned away from the time clock and toward the Fore with a thudding heart. "Yeah?"

"Boss wants to see you." The fore jerked her thumb toward the office.

"What for?"

"Not my problem." The fore shrugged. "I did see all those rejects you've been piling up."

Alice couldn't pull every code yellow off the line, or she would have been fired for sure—but she had pulled all the blues as well as the reds. "So I'm up for termination."

"Hope not." The fore met her gaze. "You have the lowest absenteeism rate of anyone on the shift. Besides, you never come drunk, and you don't make trouble. No, I hope not. But you're probably in for a dressing-down."

"Thanks." Alice smiled, with warm surprise at the woman's support. Then she turned toward the office and went in, breathing slowly and deeply.

The under-manager was at her desk, flanked by a clerk who looked up and said, "What's it about?"

"You tell me," Alice said.

The under looked up. "Biedermann?"

"Yeah."

The under looked down at her screen. "You have a lot of rejects, Biedermann."

"Not much in point in letting the blues go by," Alice answered. "They'll just come back to us."

"But the yellows won't?"

"I send the yellows for hand-checking."

"That loses a lot of time, Biedermann—and twenty per cent of your yellows have to be scrapped. You know what you're costing the company?"

Alice kept her face rigid. "A thousand a day?"

"More like five. Why are you so finnicky, Biedermann?"

"Isn't that what I'm there for?"

"Guess so." The under looked up. "The Company wants better quality control. They want a fore just for that—and you're it."

Alice could only stare.

"But why?" she said to Pepe that night. "You can't tell me they weren't trying to foist off duds on the Navy before!"

"Wouldn't dream of it," Papa assured her.

She gave him a narrow look. "No, they'd only plan on it! So why all of a sudden this push for high quality?"

"Well," Papa mused, "it might be because I just rejected a whole shipment of cannons."

Alice spun to face him, wide-eyed.

Papa shrugged. "After all, I found flawed castings in the breeches of one out of every five—and the three I tested exploded at the breech after a dozen shells. Well, one lasted long enough to make a hundred."

"How long did that take, ten minutes?"

"About. So I told them to re-check the whole load." Papa grinned. "You should have seen the salesman's face!"

"I'll bet! No wonder they want to boost quality control!"

"Yeah. Saves time and money to do it right the first time. I'll bet you're going to be getting that load of cannon back, though one piece at a time."

But Alice wasn't really listening any more. She turned

haunted eyes toward him "Peppy, I don't like this. They weren't supposed to notice me."

He saw the fear and reached out to squeeze her shoulder. "They won't. They have no reason to link us up, or even to think about it. So you're going out with a cashiered soldier. So what? Don't most of your fellow workers? And even if they did, they wouldn't dare try anything. Don't worry, beautiful."

She looked up at him, startled. "What did you say?"

"I said they wouldn't try anything. Well, they might fire you, but that's all. Come on, let's think of happier things— like shellfish and steak."

She let him whisk her away to a nice restaurant and a bottle of champagne to celebrate her promotion. She floated through the rest of the evening in a happy daze. He called her "beautiful" twice more that night, the second when he kissed her at her doorway.

She closed the door behind her, hit the lights, and turned to look at herself in the mirror—nose blue with cold, eyes teary, wisps of hair straying from under her hood. Beautiful? No—he had to have been lying.

But she felt very warm inside, anyway.

Winter had turned the corner, and was heading toward spring—not that Papa would have known it from the weather. It was still dark when he arrived at his office, dark again by the time he started home. But he took quick glances at the stars as he strode along toward home and saw that the spring constellations were peeking over the horizon.

Not that he could do much more than peek. He still walked home, and meant to keep doing it—only fresh air he got anymore—but he had to be alert. That meant no rubbernecking.

His glance roved over the street ahead, the shop door-ways, the windows above. Nothing out of the ordinary; nothing suspicious ahead.

Behind was another matter. Two tall, dark figures in Burleigh coats had been following him ever since he had come out of HQ. He slowed down, they slowed down—he sped up, they sped up. Not much chance of mistaking—they were shadowing him.

Of course, they weren't being *that* obvious about it. They mingled with the crowd, one on one side of the street, the

other on the other, always several people between them and
a block behind. If he stopped to look in a shop display, the
one visible out of the corner of his eye would already have
stopped to read a news screen or pick his way around an
icy patch. And every so often, one of them would disappear,
but almost instantly, Papa would see a new man way ahead
of him.

It sent the thrill of danger coursing through his nerves—
good, good! It had been too long since he'd been in combat,
too long. He opened his coat, the better to be able to reach
the pistol under his arm. The knowledge that he might die,
hollowed his stomach—the Colonels of Industry might not
be homicidal, but their lieutenants would love to see him
dead.

Well, if it happened, it happened. But there was no point
in letting the assassins name the time and place when Papa
could force the issue. He strolled onward, scanning the street
ahead, picking out a good alleyway.

When he came up to it, he lurched aside as though he'd
stumbled, into the alley, out of sight—where he sprinted for
cover: a worn-out sofa waiting for trash pick-up.

Papa would be the trash man.

He waited about three minutes, long enough for his shadows to realize he might get away, long enough for them to
race up behind him.

One of them swung into the alleyway, flashlight stabbing
out from his silhouette. Papa squinted against the glare and
leveled his pistol, just as the second shadow came up behind
the first. "Hold it right there!"

The shadows froze.

"Lower the light," Papa commanded. "You know who
I am, so you know I'm armed. And you know I can see you
against the street lights behind you. Lower the light and put
your hands up."

There was a quick, whispered conference, while Papa
waited, strung tight as a lyre, ready to duck and dodge to
the old armchair in front of the couch. But the flashlight
beam dipped, and the two shadows lifted their hands slowly.

"Just so you're okay, Colonel," one of the voices said.

"Sure." Papa smiled without mirth as he slowly stood
up, still ready to dodge—but the two silhouettes stood frozen. "All right, now." He stepped closer, his pistol glinting
in the dark. "Put your hands on the wall. Who sent you?"

"Naval Intelligence, Colonel."

Papa stopped. Then he said, "ID?"

"Inside my coat, on my left."

"Take it out," Papa said. "Lay it on the ground and back off."

Slowly, the shadow did as Papa said.

"Farther back. All right, that's good enough." Papa stepped forward and bent down, still keeping his eyes on the two men. He picked up the flat, slick case, flipped it open without looking, and finally took a quick glance down, then back up. That told enough; he looked down, studied the ID, then slowly stood up, lowering his pistol. "All right, boys, you can put 'em down. I never like to hang up a friend."

The shadows relaxed visibly. "No problem, sir. We shouldn't have alarmed you."

Papa shrugged, stepping into the light to get a good look at the agents' faces. "You'd have to be almost supernatural to keep me from noticing."

The taller agent nodded. "An assassination attempt tends to do that."

"So that's why you boys were detailed to me?"

"Yes, sir," said the shorter one. "HQ figured you wouldn't like the idea of bodyguards, sir."

"Well, they were damn right!" Papa let some of the irritation show. "I can take care of anything I come up against, myself!"

"Yes, sir. With all respect, sir, there's a real chance the enemy might send half a dozen men after you, sir."

No need to say who the enemy was—and Papa had to admit he didn't like the sound of the odds. But he glowered and said, "I've had worse than that in combat."

"So have I, sir—but I had a spray-rifle and grenades, not just a pistol."

Papa looked at the man more closely. "You were in combat?"

"Both of us, sir," said the shorter man.

"Rank?"

"Sergeant, then. They booted me up to lieutenant when they put me in Intelligence."

"They need you a hell of a lot more on the line than down here protecting a broken-down ex-sergeant from bogeymen!"

"We're hoping to be rotated back, sir. But we realize what we're doing here is more important."

"*More* important?" Papa shouted. "Don't even think it, Lieutenant! I'm just as expendable as any man on the line! Every soldier has to take his chances."

"Uh, by your leave, sir." The shorter agent looked down at the pavement, then up again. "We can't afford to take chances with your life, sir."

"Every soldier's as important as any other, Lieutenant!"

"Yes, sir. That's why your life is vital," the taller man said. "I wound up with a rifle that jammed in combat. I used it as a club and got a Hothri rifle, and it worked well enough to save my life—but it was close."

"They don't have so many rifles that jam up these days," the shorter man said, and the taller agreed. "Not since you took over as quartermaster."

The shorter man nodded. "We figure you've saved ten thousand lives, give or take a thousand, Colonel."

Papa stared, dumbstruck.

"As you said, sir," the taller one said softly, "no soldier's life is any less important than any other. That's why we have to keep you alive."

"All right, all right!" Papa turned away. "You can stick around. Just don't get in my way, damn it!"

"Yes, sir. If you can cuss, we're doing our job."

Papa snarled and turned away, stomping down the street, feeling sheepish and somewhat ashamed—but underneath it all, secretly elated. His mind churned, reeling over what the Intelligence men had said, reviewing the impossible notion of saving ten thousand lives, feeling humbled and exalted at the same time—and absolutely certain that they had to be wrong, that he couldn't be that important.

Which is why he didn't notice the movement in the shadows as he passed the alley . . . didn't notice until hard hands grabbed him, slamming him against the wall. He shouted and lashed out, but iron fingers seized his arms and yanked them up and back while a gag jammed into his mouth. Another hand darted into his coat, yanked the pistol out, and a voice snapped, "He's wearing armor."

"Under the hood, too," another voice said, and yanked Papa's cowl back to show the helmet.

"We'll go for the spine." A shadow hulked before him, slamming a fist into his belly, another into his jaw. He tried not to fold, but hard hands forced him down, and steel glinted in the night, flourishing high. . . .

Guns barked, and the hulking shadow spun away, slamming into the wall. The man who held Papa's gun fired back, a split second before he whirled and folded. The third one just gave off a tired sigh as he wilted.

Struggling for breath, Papa looked up at the two Intelligence agents, amazed. One of them turned away, checking the assassins, but the other was right there by Papa, holding his arm. "Are you hurt, sir?"

Papa shook his head, trying to wave the man away, trying to unkink his diaphragm long enough to take a breath.

The Intelligence man seemed to understand. "Try to relax, sir."

Finally, air came in—only a trickle, but enough to start his belly pulling in more.

The taller man came up. "Two dead, but the last one will live. Maybe he can tell us something."

Papa caught enough breath to say, "Don't count on it. He probably only knows an electronic voice and a public phone number."

"Probably," the taller man agreed, with some regret. "They look to have been professionals."

"Not as much as you two." Papa finally straightened up and forced out, "Thanks, Lieutenants. Seems it was something I *couldn't* handle."

"Glad to help, sir." The taller one's voice was neutral, but his eyes glowed.

"Just doing our job." The shorter one actually smiled.

"Glad you were." But that wasn't enough. "About my . . . snarling at you, before. Sorry."

"Perfectly all right, sir," the shorter one assured him, and the taller one answered, "This is a fine assignment."

Alice noticed the discrepancy her first day on the job. The weights on the receipts didn't match the weights ordered. Not surprising—they were for pig iron.

"If I tell my department head, they'll suspect me," she told Papa.

Papa shook his head. "Not with your record. After all, they promoted you because you managed to boost quality control, didn't they?"

She turned away, frowning. "I've been thinking, Peppy."

"You can get in trouble that way."

"Oh, be quiet! And listen. It occurred to me as I was going over those purchase orders and receipts that by promoting me to paper-pusher, they got rid of me in quality control."

Papa nodded. "We do that in the Marines, too. It's called 'kicking someone upstairs.' "

"And with me gone, they can start turning out shoddy equipment again."

"Right. Which means I have to double my scrutiny. As soon as you told me about the promotion offer, I put in for a dozen new privates and some very elaborate diagnostic machinery."

She looked up at him, astonished.

"Why so surprised?" He smiled, amused. "Just because it takes a dozen soldiers to make up for you."

"I—I'm flattered."

"That's right. Now, about that discrepancy?"

Alice frowned, jolted back to her worry. "You think they're expecting me to catch it?"

Papa shrugged. "If it's so obvious that you caught it your first day on the job, and without looking for it, they meant for you to find it."

Alice lifted her head slowly. "So they'll be suspicious if I *don't* find it."

"That would be my guess. And, of course, if you tell them and they fire you, then that gets you out of the whole sticky situation."

"Yes . . ." Then she looked up, startled. "You'd like it that way, wouldn't you?"

"I don't want you to do anything dangerous, Alice," Papa said. He stopped and turned to her, slowly. "Not *anything* dangerous."

Her heart skipped a beat, but she said, "I won't, Peppy. Not if I can help it."

The under-manager frowned. "Let me see."

Alice showed her the hard copies. "That's just the one, ma'am. There are three more current. And I haven't even checked the histories."

The department head shoved back her seat and swung around the desk. "I want to see this for myself."

Alice led the way, the under marching stiffly after her.

Alice wasn't worried about her immediate superior—the woman had lost both real legs in the first Hothri attack, and was rabid at the thought of defective weapons going out to the soldiers. It was the big bosses who worried Alice.

They came down to the loading dock, where a dull-eyed super watched the pig iron roar into the hopper. Alice stepped up, waved to the worker to show it was all right, and punched the button that stopped the dumping. She disengaged the hopper, reached into the truck, and started pulling out pigs, weighing them in her artificial hand. On the fourth one, she nodded, set it aside, and engaged the hopper again. She gave the swab-O sign to the worker, who pressed the green patch, and the roar started up again.

Alice picked up two bars as the under swung up to her. She held the bars up, then dropped them both.

One of them bounced. The other broke.

Alice held up the broken halves. The under took them, staring. Then, outraged, she turned one broken end for Alice to see, and pointed to the myriad of bubbles in the metal, around a hollow core.

The three Hothri dreadnoughts floated in the void, each surrounded by its six daughter cruisers and thirty-six destroyers—except that they weren't really floating, but hurtling toward Arista at tremendous velocity.

Well, they had that much advantage, at least. Human ships came in groups of ten—five fingers on each hand. But Hothri squadrons came in sixes. Six fingers total; ships in multiples of six.

Not that Papa could see them, of course. All his eyes saw were yellow blips on a vast wall-screen marked with concentric circles, at whose center was Arista—but memory and imagination provided what the battle monitor couldn't; in his mind's eye, he could see the Hothri battlewagons, gleaming in the distant light of Arista's sun, as they hurtled toward the double cluster of Aristan ships that drifted, waiting for them, grouped around the moon's two orbital stations.

He sat at the back of the Operations Room, watching over the heads of the dim, low-voiced forms before him. Pools of yellow light on desk-tops showed hard copies; small data screens glowed amber here and there about the room. On a raised dais in its center sat the rear admiral, watching the progress of the battle, ready to respond to any calls from the fleet commander at the site.

But the whole room was dominated by the huge situation screen at its far side, flanked by smaller screens that showed the view from each of the battle stations around the moon. All those showed were the silvery forms of Aristan cruisers and the glints of destroyers; the approaching Hothri fleet wasn't even a glimmer.

On the screen, the triple yellow cluster approached the two smaller, green clusters steadily, remorselessly—but Papa could envision the Hothri dreadnoughts, oblong and many-hatched, like huge mechanical hives, each with its cruisers and destroyers going before it like so many warrior ants. But those hatches would open to reveal the barrels of cannons, not tunnels.

This was his greatest single privilege of remaining in uniform, his greatest reward for rank—the ability to watch the progress of the battles, to ache with the anxiety of his fellow soldiers, to share the joy of their victory, or the horror of their defeat. Under it all ran the guilt of being safe here on Arista, while they staked their lives on the strategies of their commanders—and the quality of their weapons.

The weapons Papa had allocated to them.

There! On the side screen, a circle of points of light became visible, points that swelled to discernible disks. And on the big screen, the Hothri swarmed down on the battle stations like the pincers of a giant mantis.

Then the screen filled with red streaks as the battle computers strained to track each torpedo, each laser strike. The side screens showed distant flares of light as Hothri ships blew up.

But there were closer flares that filled the screen, then died with supernatural quickness as the computers subtracted them.

"One hit on the eastern Hothri fleet." A yeoman called out the information; the computer needed all its capacity to track the battle.

"*Jones* is hit," a closer yeoman responded. "Screens down . . . *Jones* is dead." His voice tightened at the end of the sentence, but showed no more emotion than that.

Papa felt all the agony the man had repressed. Had it been his screen generator that was at fault? His laser cannon that had failed to bring down the torpedo?

On the big screen, the western battle platform was suddenly denuded as half its destroyers, and two cruisers, shot off toward the Hothri line. The side screen boosted magnification, showing them as a circle, tightening around the Hothri dreadnought.

Hothri cruisers scurried to intercept them, and the dreadnought hurled its stings.

"Center and eastern Hothri dividing laterally," chanted a distant yeoman. "Center and eastern accelerating toward eastern platform."

Papa's heart sang—the Hothri had missed a bet! They should have pounced on the western station!

"Western sally force engaged," the nearby yeoman recited. "Screens down on *Wallace*. . . . Screens down on *Boru*. . . . Hothri destroyer exploded. . . . Second Hothri destroyer exploded. . . . Hothri destroyer in to *Wallace*. . . ." His voice caught. "*Wallace* dead. . . ."

"Eastern fleet responding," called the distant yeoman. "Torpedoes off and away. . . . Hothri cruisers' screens down. . . . *Nobunaga* in toward Hothri cruiser. . . ."

Light flared on the side screen.

"Hothri cruiser dead," the near yeoman said, his voice carefully neutral. "*Nobunaga* drifting, screens down, controls dark. . . ."

And *Nobunaga* was probably dead, too, Papa realized, with a wrench of anguish. There was little or no chance that some Hothri destroyer would not pick off the wounded ship, almost no chance it would survive the battle.

"Hothri center veering," called a lieutenant, "top and bottom. Hothri center pinching western fleet. . . ."

And the western fleet was down to half its normal strength! They had no choice; they fell back on the orbital platform.

In the screens, columns of light jabbed out from the platform, spearing the Hothri cruisers.

"Hothri cruisers dead one . . . two . . . three . . ." the lieutenant sang. "Hothri dreadnought accelerating. . . . *Potemkin* accelerating above its plane. . . ."

A maze of red lines filled the big screen between the orbital platform and the *Potemkin* on the one side, and the center Hothri dreadnought on the other—but the dreadnought kept coming, kept coming. . . .

"Dreadnought's screens down!" the lieutenant shouted.

"Dreadnought's screens overloaded! *Potemkin* accelerating. . . ."

Papa's fists clenched the arms of his chair, sweat broke out on his brow. *Potemkin* was going to ram the dreadnought, and die with its enemy.

But there was no alternative. It was the only way to save the platform and, with it, the moon.

"Eastern Hothri closing moon-side of platform," chanted a yeoman. *"Porlock* and *Birmingham* accelerating toward upper Hothri cruisers. . . . *Adelaide* accelerating toward southern Hothri. . . ."

The orbital platform spat ruby streams toward the Hothri. It was dangerous; if they missed the cricket ships, their beams could scar the moon with new craters—where domes had stood.

"Western Hothri dreadnought dead," the lieutenant called out. "Hothri dreadnought's a new star—and *Potemkin* is dead within it."

That lieutenant would get a reaming tomorrow, Papa knew, for losing his composure enough to use such colorful language. But he couldn't blame the man; he, too, mourned and celebrated *Potemkin's* glorious death.

"Eastern Hothri cruisers dead from platform beams . . . one . . . two . . ." the yeoman recited. *"Porlock* and *Birmingham* closing on third cruiser. . . . *Porlock* sustaining damage from enemy destroyers. . . . Third cruiser dead. . . . Enemy destroyers dead. . . ."

"Center Hothri dreadnought withdrawing!" another yeoman cried in triumph.

And so it was; on the big screen, the center pulled back, sucking its cruiser-dots and destroyer-sparks with it.

*"Adelaide* engaging Hothri cruiser," another yeoman announced. *"Adelaide* sustaining damage. . . . Hothri sustaining damage. . . . Hothri's screens down. . . . *Adelaide's* screens down. . . . Hothri cruiser dead. . . . Route clear to eastern dreadnought. . . ."

The right-hand screen filled with ruby light. The big screen showed the eastern platform bonded to the dreadnought by a scarlet column.

"Dreadnought's screens loaded full," the yeoman sang. "Dreadnought withdrawing. . . ."

Finally, the rear admiral spoke. "Recommend do not

chase," he said. "Fleet commanders, base recommends, do not chase."

As they might have, in the flush of victory—and been cut to pieces by the retreating Hothri cruisers.

"Admiral," a commander said, with full formality, "the battle is ours."

And the moon was still theirs, too, Papa knew—but the price had been heavy. Cruisers dead, one battleship annihilated, and he'd lost count of the destroyers. Thousands of men and women gone to glory in a moment of light. . . .

How many his fault? How many of his weapons had failed in battle, how many screens?

He'd know tomorrow. Maybe some, maybe none. So he put the thought aside, and let the elation of victory fill him, as he slowly stood, feeling the aches of a body overstressed with tension, and turned to leave the room.

The weights of iron started almost matching the weights ordered, and Alice relaxed, her faith in Gerta, the Head, validated.

"It'd be asking too much for the weights to match completely, wouldn't it?" she asked Gerta on the way out of work one day.

"Too much," Gerta agreed. "But keep track of the shortages, okay? We'll hit them with a bill at the end of the month, and they can make it up."

Alice decided that she liked Gerta very much. Liked her enough to bring her news of the shortages she spotted in silicon shipments, and ceramic clay, and a dozen other materials. Then, one lunchtime, Alice overheard some workers talking about a fire in the plastics-casting section, and told Gerta about that, too. Gerta tested the plastics and found some that burned very quickly and brightly. And all the shortages eased, and the incoming plastics started being tested. They developed a great resistance to heat.

So it wasn't really a surprise when Alice stepped into Gerta's office one morning and found her packing her personal items.

"So." Alice's mouth went dry. "They finally fired you, huh?"

"You could call it that." But it was a grin Gerta turned on her. "They let me go."

" 'Let you go!' Those sanctimonious, hypocritical . . ."

"Whoa, whoa!" Gerta held up a hand. "Letting me go to Amalgamated Defense! They heard about me, and asked Industrial Munitions to send me over to clean up *their* procurement division."

"Oh." The anger abated, making Alice aware of a hollowness in her stomach. "I'll miss you, Gerta."

"Oh, we'll still get together now and then." Gerta grinned. "Because, you see—they're giving you my job."

Alice could only stare.

"They asked me who I could recommend," Gerta explained. "I figured it was the least I could do."

"But I don't *want* to be a department head!" Alice wailed to Papa. "I don't *like* to give orders!"

"You'll get used to it," Papa assured her.

"But I hate administration!"

"What do you think you've been doing these last two months?"

"Well . . . yes," Alice admitted, "but that's different. That's a detective game, trying to catch all the shortages and profiteers."

"Then keep playing. It's your duty to Arista."

Alice tossed her head impatiently. "Arista's just a giant ball of dirt. It doesn't care."

"All right—it's your duty to your brothers and sisters on the line."

Alice was quiet. Papa paced alongside, hearing her footsteps crunch in the snow, waiting.

"You would have to bring that up, wouldn't you?" She made it an accusation.

Papa nodded, with a cheery grin.

"All right," she grumped. "I'll keep playing."

"Good woman!" He squeezed her shoulder. "Just one thing. . . ."

"What's that?"

He stopped, turning her to face him. "Don't get caught, huh?"

She let herself drift into his eyes and said, "I'll play by the rules, Peppy."

"I have to *what?*"

"Attend a board meeting," her secretary told her patiently. "That's one of the disadvantages of being a department head—if the directors need information for a meeting, you have to be there to give it.''

''But they could punch it up on a screen.''

''Maybe they figure you'll see some point they've missed.'' The secretary shrugged. ''Or maybe they just like to have their juniors waiting on them. Either way, you've got to go.''

Alice went with her heart in her throat, overwhelmed and feeling very much out of place. What was she, an ordinary line worker, doing in a meeting with the high and mighty? But she sat down, squared her keypad in front of her, and reminded herself that she was wearing a new suit and new hairdo.

It helped.

Of course, the presidents, the dozen vice presidents, and the chairman all outshone her in their quiet, elegant way—outshone her to the point of making her feel insignificant. Their suits must have cost six months of her pay, their styli and jewelry were gold and platinum, and their grooming must have been done by a professional just that morning—and every morning. Nonetheless, she plucked up her courage and waited.

And waited. And waited.

The meeting droned on and on around her, the chairman asking for information that he could have had on his screen in an instant, but getting it from each of the presidents who in turn demanded it from each of their vice presidents. Every now and then, the chairman would state an idea and ask the presidents what they thought of it. As one, they turned to their vice presidents and asked for information, then reported it back to the chairman, who nodded wisely and stated that he was glad to see his opinion supported.

Finally, Alice began to grow impatient. She realized that the chairman was setting not only the tone of the meeting, but also the opinions that were going to come out of it. There was no real opportunity to say ''no'' or to disagree in the slightest way. She finally began to realize that she was embedded in a ritual, in which the only purpose was to make sure everybody else in the company was doing what the chairman wanted, in the way he wanted it done. It was disguised as discussion, but it was as much an issuing of decrees as any emperor or dictator had ever exercized.

Then, suddenly, it all became ominous.

It started easily enough, with the chairman, Mr. Lamprey, turning to the president of sales and asking, "How's the competition doing, Mr. Dunbright?"

"Sales down five percent for Amalgamated, sir, and . . . Mr. Wron, what was the figure for Interstellar?"

"Four percent, sir."

"Yes, four percent." Dunbright turned back to the Chairman. "Down nine percent total, sir. That boosts our share of the market to just a little over a third."

"Not good, but better than last quarter." Lamprey frowned. "How are their prices?"

"That's the good part," Dunbright said, with a gloating smile. "They've had to boost prices an average of eight percent."

"So." Lamprey nodded, with the ghost of a smile. "We can boost ours five, then." He turned to the president of production. "You disagree, Mr. Kriegspiel?"

"Oh, not really, sir," Kriegspiel said quickly. "But wasn't our market gain due to our underselling the competition?"

"Of course—and we'll still undersell them. While we're on the subject, any idea why they had to boost prices?"

"Yes, sir. Cost increase, of course." Kriegspiel turned to his vice president for cost control. "What did you say was the prime factor in that increase, Immer?"

"Quality control, sir," Immer answered. "They had to add on personnel, and recycle much more than we did."

Alice stiffened.

"Nice to know we're ahead." But Lamprey frowned. "How were we able to spend less on quality?"

"We already had the systems in place, sir," Kriegspiel said proudly, "and at a fraction of the personnel." He turned to Immer. "What's our total number in quality control?"

"We don't have a separate department, sir," Immer explained. "It's part of procurement."

"Procurement?" The chairman frowned. "How did *that* happen?" He didn't sound happy about it.

Immer turned an expressionless face to Alice. "Ms.

Biedermann, you're the under-manager for that department. How did quality control come under procurement?''

"Our people caught the discrepancies between weight ordered and weight received, sir,'' Alice managed. "We investigated and found that the shortage was due to defects in the materials we were receiving.'' She didn't mention that she was the one who had found out. "And since we were investigating, production routed quality control to us, to do our testing.''

"And you hired more people.'' Suddenly, she had the chairman's full attention—and felt as though she were a butterfly pinned to a board. But she spoke up bravely.

"Yes, sir—we added four checkers. Then, when raw materials improved, we put two of them onto output quality control.''

"I should have thought you would have let those two go.'' The chairman's gaze was a needle through her.

And, meeting his gaze, she suddenly knew that this man didn't want high quality control, didn't want to produce sound weapons for soldiers, didn't want anything that would reduce his profits or slacken the flow of money into his coffers.

She stammered out a reply as best as she was able, and that awful gaze swung off her and back to Immer, who assured President Kriegspiel that they'd rectify the situation, and the president assured the chairman that, really, there was no cause to expend monies needlessly—and, finally, the long meeting dragged to a close. Alice pushed herself out of her chair and managed to find her way out into the corridor, numb with the certainty that the chairman, and therefore all the presidents, and the vice-presidents, and the managers, and the under-managers, and almost all of the workers wanted as many defective weapons as possible going into the hands of Aristan soldiers.

"I couldn't believe it,'' she told Papa that night. "I still can't. There he was, the chairman of Industrial Munitions, making it very clear to everybody in that room that his company should deliberately produce as many duds as he can get away with!''

Papa scowled. "That makes a lot of sense, Alice. Too much sense.''

Alice hugged herself and shivered. "I could stand it

when I thought it was just an accident, Pepe—just a side-effect of their wanting to cut costs and not caring about whether or not the weapons were any good. But to do it deliberately!''

"Of course, he couldn't come right out and say it," Pepe mused.

"Of course not! But everybody in that room knew it, oh yes! And knew that their careers depended on doing what he said, too!"

"Sure. The only real purpose of a meeting like that is to make sure everybody knows what he wants, Alice—to make sure they all think the say way."

"But what about *ethics!*" she cried.

"Ethics are whatever the chairman says they are."

Something nudged Alice from inside her head. She looked up, frowning. "You know, this could all just be the way I saw it. I couldn't prove a word of it. It could all be in me—I could be imagining things."

"You could," Pepe said, without emotion.

"I notice you aren't exactly straining to prove I'm wrong."

"Not a bit." Papa agreed. "Mostly because I don't doubt you for a second. It makes an awful lot of sense, Alice. Too much."

"Too much?" She peered up at him. "Why 'too much?' "

"Because Amalgamated and Interstellar are running the same way. Their track records could be copies of Industrial's. They even cleaned up their quality control almost as soon as Industrial did—and let it go just as quickly, too. When you think of it as their producing as many duds as possible, until I made it clear they couldn't get away with it, it makes sense. I put the heat on them, and they cleaned up—until I quit snarling so much. Then their dud rate went up again."

But she caught the hint of something else in his tone. "What else, Peppy? Tell me what else!"

He sighed. "No fooling you, is there?"

"Not a bit." She swung around in front, blocking him. "What else is there?"

Pepe sighed and said, "There've been a couple of tries . . .''

"Not at killing you!"

"Only a couple, I said." He held up a palm. "I hated to believe that they'd try to assassinate me just to save money on quality control—but if they're really on the Hothri's side, it's easier to believe."

"On the Hothri's side!"

"Why else would they *want* to produce duds? Once the system's there, they wouldn't lose money by keeping quality up."

"But . . . *traitors?!*"

"Different people believe different things, Alice," he said softly. "I've heard of people who hate the human race, don't think it should exist."

She stared at him, then shook her head, faster and faster, trying to deny it.

Papa shook his head, too, but sadly. "They're there, Alice. Anyway, I've read about 'em." After all, he couldn't be sure he'd met any.

Alice turned away, walking down the street, numb and silent.

"That's why we have to stick together," Papa said. "All the rest of us."

Alice nodded. "Because we're not the only ones who are sticking together."

"Oh?" he asked. "Who else?"

"Amalgamated and Interstellar—or their chairmen, at least. How else could they all be turning out duds, and all have the same prices?"

"By watching each other," he answered. "Believe me, informal price-fixing is nothing new. They don't have to get together and agree on a price. They just watch each other and make sure they don't charge too much more than the other guy."

"So." She frowned. "And cost-cutting could work the same way?"

"Sure." Papa shrugged. " 'If General can get away with twenty percent defectives, why can't we?' So they set the quality-control monitors lower, and they're all producing the same."

"So." Alice turned away, walking through the swirling snow again. "One man is enough. Just one—if he's chairman of the board of one of the Big Three."

"Yes, one would be enough." Papa matched her pace.

"And he could just be pushing for maximum profit, and the hell with everybody else."

"Could be," she said, "but he's not."

Papa walked along beside her, matching her pace for a while.

Then he said, "How would you explain it?"

"By somebody telling them to produce as many duds as they can get away with," she answered.

Slowly, Papa nodded. "That makes sense. So you think the chairman is taking orders?"

She swallowed heavily and nodded.

"From whom?" he asked. "One of the admirals?"

"No," she said. "The Hothri."

Papa stopped, stunned. Then his mind cleared and he nodded slowly. He didn't have to ask why.

"There's got to be evidence," she said. "I'll search the computers and find it."

"Don't you dare do any such thing! Any file you find would have such a loud alarm on it that you'd be strung up within minutes. No, you let me take it from here, Alice."

"But I can't just stand by and . . ."

"Alice." Papa rounded on her, looking deeply into her eyes, his shoulders hunched, face solemn. "Since you started getting upset about flawed steel, the dud rate from all Arista's industries has gone down from twenty percent to about five. You have probably saved the lives of almost as many young soldiers as the entire Medical Corps. They haven't just been standing by—and you're too valuable to risk."

She stared up at him.

"Don't worry," he said gently. "The other companies cleaned up their quality control almost as quickly as Industrial did. No one suspects you yet."

She paled. "Yet?"

Pepe nodded, his gaze locked with hers. "I've been worried about that. Wouldn't take the risk. If there was the slightest sign, Alice, I'd ask you to quit."

"But . . . if they're really suspicious . . ." She stared at him. "Have they been following us?"

Pepe shook his head. "Believe me—I'd know if they were."

"That's right, you're always so careful. But . . . Pepe!"

Her stare turned to a glare. "You've been seeing other women, haven't you!"

He nodded, slowly and easily, eyes still on hers. "Of course, Alice. Of course. Wouldn't want them to think I only had one girl friend—they might start wondering where I get my ideas. As it is, it's bad enough that I only date the other ones for maybe a month at a time, while I've been seeing you for more than a year now. Bad enough—but not too bad. There are always three or four I'm seeing." He forced a smile. "Of course, I don't *do* anything with them, beyond talking—but a shadow wouldn't know that, would he? He'd never come inside a dorm to a room door."

"And you always see your ladies home," she breathed. "So *that's* why you never stay."

"Not even for a drink," he assured her. "Believe me, Alice, that's the only reason."

"Well, I wondered. . . ."

"Uh, sorry." Papa actually looked abashed. "Didn't mean to hurt your feelings."

She decided not to ask him about kisses. After all, he had to make it look good.

"But it could have turned dangerous for you, see," Papa said, "if anybody got the idea we were more than friends. As it is, Industrial might have some suspicions about you, but nothing dangerous—and if they *do* get nasty ideas, we can always pretend to break up."

"You wouldn't!"

"To make you safer? Of course I would." He turned to face her, a pleading look, almost lost. "I know I'd risk losing you—but I'd rather you found another man than an early grave."

She managed to keep looking sharp while she melted inside. "I won't find either one! And we won't need to break up."

She turned away and marched down the street to keep her knees solid. Papa hurried to catch up.

"Besides," she reminded him, "we never said we were going together, or anything. Nothing formal."

"Can we go together?" he asked, very meekly.

She turned a radiant smile on him. "I thought you'd never ask! But we can't be obvious about it."

"No," he confirmed. "That would be too dangerous for you. Nothing formal."

He turned solemnly, and she waited, scared but thrilled—and he said, "That's why I can't propose, either."

Peppy had told her not to, but the knowledge of his love inspired her. Besides, Alice was tired of being such a passive link, and perhaps a little guilty, too—she didn't think she'd really been taking any risks.

Of course, she couldn't ask Pepe to help her do what he didn't want her to do—so she went to the technician who serviced her arm.

"You want a *what?*" He stared, incredulous.

"A video camera," she repeated, "hooked to a memory chip, inside my arm. I do a lot of paperwork now, Jules. It'd make things a lot easier if I could just point my finger and make a copy."

Jules sighed and shook his head in wonder. "Well, I must admit it's a new one. Give me a week, Ms. Biedermann, okay?"

A week was time enough to make friends with her president's secretary, who was friends with the chairman's secretary. Then, over a month of lunches, she managed to work in a few questions about the chairman's business trips. She relayed the information to Pepe and was very surprised when he became upset with her.

"You're sticking your head into the lion's mouth!" he stormed. "This isn't the small time, Alice—these boys play dirty! Please keep out of it!"

Pepe knew that Alice was hurt. He apologized for being so nasty, and he made it up to her—but that only strengthened her resolve. Especially since she was sure he was putting her information to good use.

So she did a little investigating with her data screen—nothing definitely outside her bailiwick, though it was certainly on the border. Records of expense accounts; records of travel accounts—and she copied down the chairman's expense records while she was busy being numb at the amount any one trip cost the company. Rank had its privileges—and the private shuttle that was, for all intent, for the chairman's use only, cost an almighty lot for any one trip.

But there were two dates he had traveled, that weren't on

the accounts—one three years ago, and another only one year ago.

She remembered Pepe's reaction, and didn't tell him this time. She decided to wait until she had all the information she could get. That way, Pepe would only get angry with her once. It was quite reassuring to know how upset he could become at the thought of her being in danger. But it was also scary while it lasted.

The anger proved that, if nothing else, he loved her. So she shrugged it off.

Then, one morning, her secretary looked up as she came in, and said, "The chairman wants to see you."

Alice stood stock-still, every nerve stinging at the thought of danger. "What about?"

The secretary shook her head. "Didn't say. Just wants you to get in there as soon as you come in."

It was wrong, Alice knew—he was bypassing channels. And if it was all that urgent, his secretary should have called her at home. Prudence dictated that she turn around, go out, and get to Pepe as quickly as possible—but curiosity said she might gain some more information with which to hang the chairman.

She went.

Maude, his secretary, looked up and smiled when Alice came in.

"Good morning, Alice. What were *you* up to last night?"

Instantly, Alice relaxed a bit, and smiled back. "Nothing but a good book."

"Well, you *are* looking a little pale. Don't choose such exhausting books, okay, dearie? You can go right in; His Nibs is waiting." She leaned forward, lowering her voice. "What's it about?"

Alice stared. "I was hoping you could tell me."

"Hm." Maude frowned. "Well, I don't know *everything* that man has on his mind—but it's rare, when it involves the help." She shrugged. "Go on in."

Alice flashed her a grateful smile and went into the chairman's office.

The door closed behind her; the office was empty.

Alice frowned, puzzled, and started to turn . . .

A huge pain flared in her head, then was gone—and so was everything else.

An acrid reek seared through her head, and she snapped awake, coughing. When the racking subsided, she became aware of an enormous pain filling her whole head, but pulsing outward from a spot on the back.

"So sorry to jolt you from your slumbers with so bitter a smell."

She looked up, startled, and the pain pulsed harder. She blinked away tears and saw, through a film of moisture, the chairman standing before her, immaculate in a gray pin-striped suit, fingers caressing a fob on the end of his vest chain. She sat in a pool of light, just barely able to see beyond the chairman's form. She could make out plain stone blocks and nothing more.

"However, the matter is rather urgent," the chairman went on. "I really could not wait for you to awaken naturally."

Alice mustered her courage and tried to stand but jolted against bindings. Looking down, she was astonished to see that she was tied into a chair.

"Quite necessary, I'm afraid," he said. "because you're apt to try to move about rather violently when we commence."

She stared up at him, the first feelings of terror blooming inside.

The chairman stepped up, caught her hand, twisted it over, and slammed it down on the metal arm. Alice cried out.

"Go ahead," he urged her. "We're quite alone—and quite far underground, beneath my office. Private elevator, don't you see."

He pressed the fob against her wrist and she felt a coolness. It wasn't a fob—it was a hypodermic jet.

She stared at her wrist, numb, then began to feel very light-headed.

"There's no point in trying to hold anything back," he told her. "The drug is very effective. All I have to do is mention a topic and you'll tell me everything you know about it. More than I want to know, probably. Now—Colonel Pepe Stuart."

"I met Pepe at a friend's house. He walked me home, and I told him how I was worried about the bubbles in the pig iron . . ."

On she went, and on and on—but inside, she was horrified to hear herself telling every detail about herself and Pepe, every detail. For once, she was grateful to him for not giving her anything terribly carnal to talk about.

But she babbled everything she'd told him.

"Me," the chairman suggested, and she was off again, gibbering, babbling. She talked and talked, until it was all told.

Then, as she sat panting, the chairman's eyes narrowed, and his face paled. He drew a short metallic stick out of a pocket and swung it at her temple.

Consciousness nudged her, and she thrust it away. But pain bored in, and she had to face the fact that she was once more aware. She was about to force her eyes open when she realized the chairman was talking.

"Those were not the terms of our agreement. You contracted to provide transportation away from Arista whenever I chose!"

A warbling falsetto answered him—Hothri speech. Over the trill came the vocodered words of a translator. "It is no longer expedient to arrange your escape."

Carefully, Alice opened her eyes the tiniest bit, peeking through her lashes, and could just barely make out his shadow in front of a glowing screen—a screen that showed the image of a Hothri.

"Such an attempt would be detected," the alien explained, "and it is quite possible that the ship would be eliminated. It could result in the deaths of several Hothri."

"Then you must risk it!" The chairman's face was red with anger. "You made a binding commitment!"

Even through the throbbing pain in her head, she felt panic at the thought that she was missing this. Summoning the tiny remnants of her will, she pulled with all her strength. The artificial arm tensed, strained—and the rope that bound it snapped apart.

The chairman didn't notice. "You contracted for sabotage and information! In return for information regarding weapons research, your agent would deposit bullion in an anonymous account on Aries!"

"Such has been done," the translator answered over Hothri piping.

Trembling, Alice brought her artificial wrist near her real fingers, and pressed the patch that started the camera. Then she pointed her index finger at the chairman and lowered the arm, resting it on her real one. She hoped he was in the field of view.

"What good are millions on Aries, if I cannot go there to draw them?" the chairman snapped. "In return for my assuring the production of defective weapons, you contracted to provide for my escape!"

"For your escape, when the Hothri conquered Arista" the alien reminded him. "That event has not yet transpired. When it does, we will happily provide you transportation to Aries."

"Yes, so that I can provide further services for you there! But do you not realize that I will not be able to do so if you do not remove me from Arista at once? The Navy is alerted to my activities; they will find some manner of proof! No trail can be covered completely! My transmissions to you must have been noted and logged, scrambled or not!"

"Come now, dear Chairman." The Hothri was enjoying itself. "If you have been discreet, nothing can be proved."

"Proof is not needed—only grounds for suspicion! They will remove me from office, at the least! I will no longer be able to aid you, in retirement!"

"That is regretable," the Hothri admitted. "But if so, it is not in our interest to aid you in any way."

"I have adhered to our agreement!" The chairman began to sound frantic. "I have produced as many defective weapons as I could manage! I have sent you word of every bit of weapons research undertaken!"

"You have indeed," the Hothri confirmed, "but by your own admission, your usefulness is ended. You can no longer assure defective weapons, or provide information, on Arista; and surely, your disappearance here would confirm suspicion and negate your usefulness on Aries."

"I will assume another identify on Aries! I will invest heavily in their defense industries; I will rise in their ranks till I am once more privy to secret information!"

"You will not," the Hothri contradicted. "Your record will not bear scrutiny. No, dear Chairman, I am afraid you can be of no further use to us. Farewell."

The screen filled with multi-colored snow. The chairman spun away from the screen with a curse.

And saw Alice's arm pointing at him.

The gun was in his hand before she knew it; the flat, sharp crack filled the room before she could cry out. the tearing pain seared through her chest; but, as consciousness dimmed for good, she saw a rectangle of fire behind the chairman, saw him whirl as the door fell to ashes, and saw a familiar form filling the doorway with flame jolting from his hand.

The chairman recognized Pepe, and his teeth writhed back in a snarl. The pistol in his hand cracked again, and Papa rocked as the bullet slapped into his armor—but he fired a moment later, and the chairman slammed back against the wall.

Men began firing behind Pepe, and bullet after bullet slapped into the chairman, jolting the body—but Papa was no longer there to see. He had spun aside to kneel by Alice's chair, knife slitting her bonds. His heart turned over at the sight of the bruise next to her ear, then turned to ice as he saw the red stain around the hole in her chest. He grappled her out of the chair and touched her neck, feeling for the jugular for a pulse. . . .

"He's very dead." The Intelligence man came up behind Papa. "Must have known we were onto him. But he didn't guess how quickly we'd picked up his transmission, or recognized it as Hothri encoding."

Papa didn't answer.

"Sorry we doubted." The other Intelligence man came up behind the first. "You were right to make us keep a radio watch on this . . ."

Then he saw Alice, and stopped.

The first Intelligence man reached down to touch Alice's arm. "She has a camera in there, you know. It's still on."

"You can turn it off now," Papa said.

The Intelligence man reached down to press the switchpoint. "He wasn't ready for us. He couldn't guess that we could trace his transmission and find him so fast."

"Not fast enough," Papa said.

The Intelligence man frowned at something in Papa's voice, and looked more closely. When he saw the tears in Papa's eyes, he shut up. Finally.

\* \* \*

"Ms. Biedermann was buried with full military honors."

The screen showed Alice's coffin, draped with a flag, framed by the honor guard firing their salute.

The midday patrons shut up, staring at the screen in mute respect.

"Her heroism in recording the final proof of the chairman's guilt, cannot be overstated." The picture dissolved into the chairman's profile, seen from the back, lit by the screen in front of him with its image of the Hothri operator. "Here, again, is the evidence for which she gave her life, evidence of the treachery that cost so many lives."

The sound came up, and once again Papa heard the damning words, already burned into his brain, but all of which told him, again and again, that he had come too late.

The bartender took one look at his face and lowered the volume. A patron or two looked up to protest, caught the bartender's tight shake of the head, and turned back to watch the screen, sobered.

The door wheezed open, clicked shut, and the general stepped up to Papa's table. He stood, staring down at the bulky man hunched over his glass with a half-full bottle by his elbow. Finally, the general said, "Can I sit?"

Papa lifted his head slowly, frowning, then waved toward a chair. "Sure. Why not? It's a public place."

The general sat slowly, laying his hat on the table. He waited until Papa looked up at him again, then said, "The Senate met right after the broadcast last night. They talked nonstop till dawn."

Papa's mouth quirked into a bitter line. "Talk!"

"They decided not to nationalize the defense industries," the general said. "It was close, though."

"I don't really care," Papa told him.

"They did decide that all industry would have to be run by very tight government controls," the general said. "Very tight. They voted to establish a Board of Industry to oversee everything about them, Colonel Stuart. Everything."

"A little late, don't you think?"

"They want you to resign your commission," the general said.

Papa looked up, his mouth a hard, bitter line.

"They want you to head the Industry Board," the general explained.

For a long, long minute, Papa just sat there, staring.
Then, slowly, he relaxed, hunching over the glass again.
"That's great," he muttered. "Just great."
And he took another drink.

# The Hothri
## by Bill Fawcett

Like humans, the Hothri breathe oxygen, sort of. Their home planet has massive traces of methane left in its atmosphere and slightly less oxygen. This is probably the result of being early in its planetary evolution. The similarity of atmospheres enables both races to survive for short times in the other's air. Humans need filters and get winded a bit easier. The Hothri need to supplement the "tasteless" Aristan air with Methane. Humans breathing unfiltered Hothri air begin to cough after minutes and have lung damage after hours; a bit like breathing the air in a chlorine cleanser bottle. Any Hothri breathing Aristan air quickly finds itself unable to metabolize the oxygen.

The Hothri are insect-like—though not in the face or head. They are bipedal, average between six-and-one-half and seven-feet tall, and are slightly thinner than the typical human. Their bodies are lighter in density, with a standard gravity equaling .81 of Earths or .83 of Arista's. The Hothri have a projecting rear thorax which, while not scraping the ground, does act to counterbalance their slight forward-leaning posture. A Hothri is almost entirely covered by a chitin-like exoskeleton. They are slightly stronger and slower than a typical human. Their exoskeleton also means they have no waist, bending only at the legs.

All Hothri have two arms, shoulders mounted in ball joints, and three long fingers. Even the fingers are chitin-covered, except at the joints. There is also a jagged fringe to the chitin on the top of the hands, which is their chief natural combat weapon. The Hothri are tough, able to withstand as much or more damage than a human before submitting to death.

A typical Hothri's life span is about forty years. They have a greater sense of community than humans. There are four sexes. The males (sperm producers), females (egg producers), lovers (mate with males and females, mix the sperm and eggs which fertilize within them, finally screening and rejecting malformed or mutated fetuses), and the mothers (which receive fertilized eggs from the lovers, carry them to birth, and then nurse the newborn). The males and females are the active members of the race, doing all the fighting, trading, etc. The lovers are smaller and stouter. They are also weaker in the arms, though their bodies are tough. Lovers are normally kept in purdah. The mothers are much larger. They receive twenty to thirty eggs from a lover and incubate up to a dozen at a time.

The Hothri homeworld is a planet orbiting a red giant star. This results in high background radiation levels and low levels of visible light. The Hothri therefore see better in the dark than in daylight. To see, Hothri don't use eyes. They have sensors that detect heat and reflect infrared and a type of passive radar/sonar which detects movement.

The Hothri breathe through spiracles on their thorax, but they ingest through a mouth containing both grinding and tearing teeth, (as they are omnivores). Hothri teeth are made of the same material as their exoskeleton. They have no nostrils, instead detecting odors through certain of their spiracles. With forward-set sonar and side-set infrared patches, they possess about 270° of "vision."

In their dim light, the Hothri appear to be a glistening black. In bright light as on Arista they appear to be blue-black with patches of very dark brown, and their chiton has a slight prismatic quality. They communicate by a whistling language produced by air rushing through certain spiracles in their thorax. This is augmented by gestures and postures, as is the human language. Their alphabet is written using lighter areas on cool surfaces and read by their infrared senses.

# THE LAST KATANA

## by Steve Perry

SILK was prepared to die.

He had been prepared to die for a long time. That was the Way. That was the bushi's creed—death was not important. Only technique was important, and Silk was as good as they got. He was ready. He was like the ancient terran sword that hung in his quarters, the katana. His art had forged and tempered and sharpened him until nothing was left but the mirror shine of razored steel, so keen that you could cut yourself and not know it until the blood welled. Death meant nothing to the katana, for that was its existence, what it had been created for. In a one-on-one, hand-to-hand encounter, Silk was fairly certain he could defeat any human in the galaxy. He might die doing so, but he would win, that was the important part.

He had never had a family, save for his instructors. No mother, no father, no siblings. He was alone in the galaxy, never finding love. But he had found the Way.

The problem was, this time, Silk couldn't die, because this time, death would mean failure. They should have picked somebody else, but they hadn't. They'd picked Silk and the choice was final.

Damn, it was dark inside the Hothri ship. Dark, murky, and hot. The place smelled like a tropical barnyard on a summer day despite the plugs they'd injected into his sinuses. Bad enough that the air was full of methane. But better than if they breathed fluorine or chlorine. Not that he smelled much better himself, he thought.

The bean-like stuff the Hothri ate stank even worse. Silk had been buried in the food container for three hours, breathing from a bottle, before they'd finally lifted and delivered it to the ship. You'd think the whitesuits could come up with a sinus filter that could stop the stench. They were

in clean noncom berths back in the medfly and didn't have
to smell anything but recycled air. Life was hard.

He slid the spookeyes into place and clicked them on.
They were 10/gen bothsiders that could be shifted to work
the ultra or the red. The theory was that he'd be able to see
what the bugs couldn't, since their eyes played mostly on
the low end of the spectrum. If he had to hide, it had better
be someplace warm, they told him. He had to be able to see
as much as he could. The bugs had all the advantages. They
were stronger, didn't have to be quiet, there were a lot more
of them, and it was their fucking ship.

And an ugly ship it was, too. The Hothri were hosers—
they liked to throw a lot of firepower at something rather
than pinpoint shooting. As a result, the inside of the ship
was bulged by huge, clunky capacitor compartments and
battery bioplates. It was like walking through a maze to get
anywhere. And this wasn't even a battleship, it was the
broodwagon.

Ah, the man remembered why he came. *Come on, Silk,
get with the flow. You keep dreaming and you will be the
disappointment of the day here.*

Silk was passing a heat sink when the Hothri warrior appeared from the murk in front of him. Dumb luck was what
it was, but he'd take luck over money any day.

He couldn't tell if the warrior was male or female—there
were two other sexes, four altogether, the brains in MI knew
that much—but it didn't much matter. Either one would kill
you just as dead.

Silk had a Smith 10mm pistol crowed to his belt but he
didn't want to use it except as a last resort. The weapon
itself was silenced and it was loaded with subsonic ammo,
so there was no boom when it went off, and it didn't break
the sound barrier and boom then, either. But the bugs' black
chiton exoskeleton was tough, and you had to use armor
piercing or explosive rounds to get through it. AP rounds
just didn't work at subsonic, the stuff he was lugging
wouldn't punch 300 meters a second, so it had to be explosive. No way to silence that when it hit—it made a *big* boom.
It was too early to be making that kind of noise.

With the heat sink fuzzing the bug's sight, Silk had the
advantage. The Hothri were strong but not very flexible,
and not any faster than humans. Silk had been using the
makawara to toughen his hands. In addition, he wore hard-

skin fingerless gloves. His dotic boots were reinforced with stacked-carb at the soles. He could crack the plate—at least he had done so in practice on bug corpses.

The man froze against the background of hot metal. The Hothri warrior moved past in that stiff-jointed shuffle they used. If you moved they could see you a klick away through fog as thick as a shipwhore's wallet. But if you stayed still you were as good as invisible.

When the Hothri had its back to him, Silk set himself low in a wide horse stance and did a crossover sidekick.

The crossover sidekick was as slow as radio. Anybody who knew anything and was paying any attention could get out of the way and have time left over for lunch. What it lost in speed, however, it made up for in power.

Silk's heel slammed the thing over where the hips would be on a man, in the thin plate over the low back, and knocked it forward onto its face. The counterbalancing thorax didn't do it much good. The bug was a quarter-meter taller than Silk but probably weighed a third less than he did.

It chittered in surprise, but before it could get up, Silk leaped up into the air and came down on its back with both feet. Silk massed ninety kilos in one gee, and that was a little more than what the Hothri set their ships at, so the impact was considerable.

The bug's shell crunched and splintered, and the viscous yellow fluid that circulated in a membrane under the chiton splattered in all directions. The heavier air near the ground was disturbed, and it blew up to fight Silk's filters.

The thing chittered again. The Hothri were strong, but once you cracked their shells they went out like a light. It was like a human losing all its blood at once.

Silk hopped off the bug. It shivered a little, then lay still.

*Sorry, friend. We come in alone and we leave alone. Nothing personal, it's my job.*

Silk found he was breathing hard and he made an effort to slow his respiration. It was the atmosphere; they'd told him that might happen. He wasn't afraid.

There was a gap next to the heat sink. A live Hothri or human couldn't have squeezed into it, but with its shell ruptured, it was easy enough for Silk to stuff the dead bug into the space.

Maybe nobody would find it until he was offship.

Yeah, and maybe the local sun would go nova and fry everybody, too. The goddamned dickholes in MI had told him this was a downcycle for the bugs—that most of them would be doing what passed for sleep. Periodization, they called it. So within three minutes of stepping out into the ship, what happens? A bug nearly steps on him.

*That was yesterday, Silk. Get moving and get the job done. You can bitch when you get home.*

The MI clowns had drawn him a map of how they thought the ship would be laid out based on part of a hulk they'd recovered on the far side of Arista's moon. They were partially right. They had the food pods in the right place, and the escape ships were where they were supposed to be, at least some of them were.

Silk moved down the hall, freezing at imagined or real sounds, blinking dryly under the spookeyes at the chemlenses they'd stuck into his eyes to keep them from constantly tearing in the methaned air.

He could fly the four-passenger Hothri escape ship, and if the control panel was the same on the thirty-passenger lighters, he could make do in one of them. Once he'd accomplished his mission, he could probably get home. MI would not be displeased, they'd said, if he could manage one of the lighters; they had plenty of the little bug ships.

Dickholes.

But first he had to find the nursery. That was the easy part.

Score another point for MI, Silk thought. A sign in Hothri, visible with the spooks on infrared, spelled out the word he'd learned meant "Nursery." It had taken him twenty careful minutes to get there, and while he'd seen two bugs moving down a side corridor, they hadn't noticed him. So far, this was going better than he'd expected.

*You shouldn't have thought that, Silk.*

There were four guards outside the nursery door, all of them armed with those damned rakeguns they used.

Shit.

Silk pulled back as slowly as he'd stuck his head around the corridor turning. He was good, but nobody was going to dance with four armed Hothri in this sludge and expect to keep it quiet. Those rakeguns sounded like the wrath of God when they went off.

Why the fuck were there guards? There weren't supposed to be any. It didn't make much sense, unless they were expecting trouble, and there was no reason they should be expecting trouble, unless maybe somebody had found the dead bug next to the heat sink.

*Don't waste your time worrying about what motivates 'em, Silk. They are there. Deal with the reality of it.*

*Okay. Think.*

He had the paralytic, but that was for the mother. Given MI's record so far, it might or might not even work on the mother and probably wouldn't do shit to the guards. So that was out. He had the nest globe, but somehow he didn't think that was going to do much good. He had the Smith 10mm. He could slap off a round down the hall and hope the guards would run to see what it was, but somehow that didn't seem likely. A human guard who went tooling off down the hall to see what went *boom* would be looking at locktime when he got back.

Not good to depend on that.

Okay, what was left? He could turn around and find an escape ship and make vapor. Tell the MI clowns that it wasn't possible. There was no way they'd know differently, even if they did a brainstrain on him, because four armed guards were four armed guards.

Silk sighed. A mistake. That got him a mouthful of noxious vapor, as close to the floor as he was, sitting there like that. Shit.

Okay. The nearest escape ship was supposed to be about two hundred meters past the nursery in the other direction. He could make that in well under thirty seconds, even carrying the package. Figure that long to do the mother and pry her open, plus another ten seconds to welch the guards. Add thirty seconds for the shit. Under two minutes. Would he have that long?

Probably not. Probably not.

But—that was the choice. Try it or go home empty-handed.

It was all he had, but it was better to break the katana than give it up. Nobody cared whether he lived or died, and neither did he, so he might as well just do it.

The decision was made, Silk moved. He drew the Smith.

He edged his arm and shoulder slowly around the corner and just as carefully pointed the Smith down the hall. He was good unarmed, but he had blackpins in projectile weapons and throwing steels, too. He didn't aim, instead casting his mind into point mode. He took a deep breath, let half of it out, and snapped off four rounds as fast as he could pull the trigger. As the fourth round rechambered the fifth, Silk was up and running.

The sound of the four explosions echoed through the corridor almost as a single report. It hurt Silk's ears. He should have put the mutes in. Damn.

He reached the door as the last bug fell. In so doing, the guard triggered his rakegun, and the body of his nearest comrade shook and practically dissolved under the sleet of boilrocks. Intelligent beings always make weapons that serve best at destroying their own kind.

The panel was heavy plastic on an electric hinge. Silk snap kicked the door and knocked it open. He leaped inside, the Smith held ready.

The mother, three meters long, two meters wide, and a meter-and-a-half tall, tried to scuttle away from the intruder. Anywhere else and Silk might have smiled at how the thing moved. It looked like a Hothri, vaguely, but a grossly fat one lying on its belly. The legs it had were thin and weak, and its arms didn't help much. Something like a grasshopper with terminal obesity trying to run.

Silk pulled the paralytic from his belt, triggered it, and threw it at the mother. The cannister bounced from the thing's black back and fell onto the floor, then blew up into a dark cloud that looked particularly green through the spookeyes. Silk held his breath. MI said the paralytic wouldn't hurt him, but he trusted MI about as far as he could fly on a two gee world by flapping his arms.

The gas dissipated almost instantly, and Silk was at the mother's side before she stopped moving.

There was supposed to be a hatch-like opening at the rear, big enough for him to reach inside. It wasn't there.

Motherfucker! If he got back home he was going to kick those MI dickholes all over the base!

*Come on, Silk, come on! Get your nose out of your ass and do something!*

No opening. Fine. Make one.

He backed up until he was five meters back, pointed the Smith, and fired.

The tail end of the mother blew off, and pieces of the

chiton showered Silk. He felt it stick him on the face and forehead, tiny cuts, but that didn't matter.

The man ran forward and reached into the smoking mother.

*Sorry,* Silk thought. *It's my job.*

He felt a flash of sympathy for the Hothri mother, for what he was doing to her offspring. He'd never gotten around to fathering any children himself, never had the inclination when he was younger, and once the arts had claimed him, didn't think it wise later. His own raising in a creche without a father or a mother was painful. He didn't want to inflict that on somebody if maybe he wasn't going to be around. Too bad. He thought about it sometimes. He liked the idea of a little version of Silk being out there somewhere, but the whores he'd been with probably hadn't, so it was doubtful there were any copies of him roaming the galaxy, or given where he was and what he was doing, ever likely to be, either. Dying and leaving your chromosomes behind made it easier for some guys. Silk could understand that. But it wasn't fair to the child. Children need parents.

The first egg was pulped jelly. It had been an oblong about the size of a big man's head, but the clear outer gel was mashed, and the pinkish gray embryo inside was a shattered mess. The second, third and forth eggs were also mostly destroyed in the explosion. Dammit—

The fifth egg was whole. The gel wasn't scratched, and inside, the bug-to-be was curled into a tiny replica of the larger Hothri Silk had killed outside the nursery. The gel felt warm and slimy to his touch, and it gave under his fingers. Careful. These things looked to be very fragile. No protective outer shell.

Silk scooped out the rest of the eggs. There were half a dozen more. All were warriors, at least as far as he could tell. He didn't really have time for a fucking leisurely examination here.

MI wanted a mother, or failing that, a lover, but it would take whatever it could get. He only had room for one.

Silk pulled the plastic container from his back pocket and triggered the flatpack. The container expanded into a bucket-sized half globe. Moving quickly, Silk sprayed biofoam from the aerosol attached to the globe, half filling it. He put the egg into the nest of spongy white stuff and foamed over it, then pressed the self-sealing top half of the lid shut. In theory, you could drop the globe off a mountain and it would bounce but the egg wouldn't be harmed. In theory.

He hitched the container to his back, low, and stood.

*Time to leave, Silk. The party is over.*

He reached the door. There were at least twenty bugs in the hall, swarming toward the broken door.

*Oops. Wrong, pal. The party is just beginning.*

"Shit. We aren't going out that way, Junior," he told the egg. "And there doesn't seem to be a back door, either."

*No way out, Silk.*

He shoved the Smith in front of himself and full-autoed the last of the explo slugs into the hall. It made a hell of a noise. That ought to slow them down a little.

*Make your death-poem, get a couple of fresh magazines out, and see how many you can take with you.*

But as Silk pulled the spare ammo mags for his Smith from their pouches, he had an idea. He moved to the rear of the nursery. Maybe it would work. He didn't have anything to lose.

Inside ship walls were thin. There was no reason for them to be thick—they didn't have to fight vacuum or weather. And the door had been plastic and not metal.

He had four fifteen-round magazines of explo for the Smith. He pointed the gun at the wall and opened up.

By the second magazine he was stone deaf.

But by the third magazine he had a wall in front of him that looked to be made of torn paper.

Silk jumped at the shattered wall and went through. He stumbled, nearly fell, but kept to his feet. He was in a room full of cargo containers, that butt-ugly hex stuff the bugs liked to use. It was a big room with a door on the far side.

Silk ran for it. A slap plate on the wall opened the door, swinging it inward, and he went through the exit with his gun held ready—

Into an empty hall.

*Some god has taken an interest in you, Silk. What say you build him a temple when you get home?*

*You got it.*

Silk oriented himself. If MI had ever been right, they had better be right this time. He turned to his left and ran.

\* \* \*

Two bugs lurched toward him in the murk but Silk never even slowed as he blew them apart. *Come on, MI, don't let me down!*

There, just ahead, was the circular lock that indicated the entrance to the first of three four-place emergency ships.

Son-of-a-bitch.

As Silk cycled the lock closed behind him he heard the roar of a rakegun battering against the metal at his back. He hoped that the Hothri fire control was as bad as he'd heard, otherwise this little ship he was about to steal would be crisped before it got a hundred klicks away. Supposedly, the gunners were used to much bigger targets, and the auto-guncomps were set to avoid anything close for fear of setting off a suicide bomb or possibly hitting somebody else in the formation. Silk guessed he would find out soon enough.

He peeled the egg carton from his back and strapped it into the co-pilot's chair, then slid into the awkward and uncomfortable pilot's seat. It had a big hole in the back and he was practically standing up, but he could live with that.

"Come on, Junior, let's go for a ride, hey?" Silk said, as he reached for the controls.

The little ship fell away, kicked out of the broodship by what was basically a big spring. The destroyers and battle-wagons that flew formation around the broodship wouldn't shoot at him for fear of nailing one of their own—at least that was the theory.

He lit the engines and punched the little bird for all it was worth. G-force slapped him with its big paw, but Silk didn't care. He was pointed away from the fleet's line of travel and into the sun, and a hard parabola would take him behind Arista—if he made it that long.

He had time to get the ship back where MI could send somebody for him. He locked the coordinates into the comp. Even if he didn't make it, the package would. A pro until the end.

At that thought, his head seemed to explode. What was happening here? This wasn't like any radiation he'd ever heard of.

He stood and moved away from the pilot's chair. Something about the egg . . . something was—was there something wrong with it? Did it get a dose of what he'd gotten?

Silk was drawn to the egg.

Something was *moving* inside there.

He triggered the release for the globe's lid and peeled it off. The biofoam, engineered for the Hothri to the best of MI's knowledge, felt warm when he dipped his hands into it and touched the egg. The gel vibrated under his fingertips.

Silk lifted the egg from the foam. He set the egg onto the floor and squatted next to it, wiping the foam away.

As he watched, a tiny hand dug its way through the gel and punched free of the clear and soft mass into the air of the cabin. The jagged fringe on the back of the little hand was already turning dark in the ship's air. After a moment, the rest of the three fingers began to darken as well.

It was *hatching!*

Nobody had prepared him for this. He was just to pick up and deliver. Now what was he supposed to do?

The other hand unfolded from the body and began to worm its way through the clear gel.

The itch began in Silk's brain again.

He reached down and began to peel away the gel, helping the baby Hothri to free itself. "So, Junior, you couldn't wait, hey?"

"Ah, Bandit, Bandit, this is Hole in the Wall. Do you xerox?"

Silk stared at the TBR unit. MI was casting on the agreed tightfreaq.

"Hole in the Wall. Bandit here."

"Silk! You made it!"

There was some commotion on the other end of the circuit.

"Hey, fuck off, dickhole. You think it matters if the bugs know his fucking *name?*"

"Ah, Hole in the Wall, we are negative results here."

"What? Repeat that."

"I got off but without the package."

"Shit."

"Yeah, well, it doesn't look as if I'm going to be bringing you a new ship to play with, either, MI."

"What's the scat, Silk?"

"I took a few hits leaving the mama ship. I'll be visiting Arista in a little while but not—ah—under power."

"Ah, shit, Silk."

"Yeah, look for a bright light in the sky, boys. I'll aim for the darkside, maybe give the boys on the ground a shooting star to wish on."

"Buddha. I'm sorry. Any messages you want me to convey?"

"That's a negative. See you next incarnation, maybe."

Silk discommed and tried to lean back in the ship's chair. The tiny Hothri on his lap clutched at his shirt.

"Hey, take it easy, Junior. I got you."

He cupped the little alien with both hands and felt it relax against his bare skin. The Hothri felt warm to the touch.

It had been quite a shock when the last of the gel had been brushed away to reveal the baby Hothri. The thing had chittered up at him, and the itch had finally resolved itself, revealing itself for what it was: The Hothri baby was an empath.

The contact had only lasted a few moments, but it was enough for Silk to know more about the Hothri than he could have learned in a lifetime of intellectual study. And at the same time, the baby knew *his* thoughts and feelings, too. It wasn't permanent, the Hothri empathy. It was only a kind of imprinting available to the babies at birth. As they were hatched, they reached out with their minds to the mother who incubated them, and she in turn touched them. Silk knew all this to his core, as well as he knew anything. He communicated with an alien in a way he had never communicated with another human. For a brief time, they lived in each other's soul. MI didn't have a clue about this.

"Well, Junior," he said, "we won't have it easy. I guess I can come up with enough methane for you to breath down there, and I can swipe enough of that bean paste to keep you fed, but if either side catches us, we're in trouble."

The baby alien chittered softly. He didn't know what it meant, but Silk figured he could teach it to talk his language, there were supposed to be some who could.

He couldn't very well turn it over to MI. Not after what it had said when it was in his mind. There hadn't been any real language to it, but the meaning was clear, as clear and sharp as the katana that Silk had once been, no mistake about it. There was no way Silk could not feel it, connected as they had been. And no way he could leave it, not after what it said, what it felt, what he had felt:

"Daddy," the Hothri had said, full of love and innocence. *Daddy.*

And with that, the last katana had shattered . . . and become whole.

# Orbital Defense
## by Bill Fawcett

Once it became apparent that the final battle of the Hothri War would be a siege of Arista itself, the Hothri's cautious approach gave the Aristans several months to prepare. These preparations included the manufacture of hundreds of "floaters," mines hanging from balloons. These mines, in their very concept, acknowledged the inability of the Aristans to militarily control even their own atmosphere. More sophisticated homing mines were strewn in space above the most sensitive targets. Simplified weapons of all kinds were distributed to a population which was steadily being diminished by Hothri bombing raids.

After ten years of growing conflict, the Aristan high command was well aware of the Hothri's inability to bypass strong defenses. When it became apparent that the battle would soon be for the planet itself, the high command sought to take advantage of this Hothri weakness. But with no place left to retreat, the question was a serious one.

One of the solutions was the construction of defensive platforms in high orbits. Assembled in space from prefabricated components, the rapid construction of the platforms could have been considered triumphs in themselves. Built in less than three months, all the planned platforms were within ninety percent of completion when the final battles of the siege began. Sadly, it was a realistic commentary on the situation that only a few admirals maintained that the resources expended on the platforms should instead be spent on ships capable of offensive action and ftl flight. There was no place left to go. Arista had been driven from space.

The highly armored and heavily shielded platforms mounted firepower equivalent to three heavy cruisers. Each was also capable of supporting two full battalions of infantry. Armed with dozens of laser and missile tubes, the platform's greatest weakness was their inability to maneuver.

Another concern was that they were not completely supplied when the final battles began. Sitting alone, beyond any hope of support from the remnants of the Aristan fleet, the platforms were intended to attract the attentions of a large segment of the Hothri assault fleet. This would hopefully buy a few extra hours, or days, of survival for the Aristan world.

# BRIG RATS

## *by William C. Dietz*

ON MOST DAYS the military hall was an empty place, home to beams of dusty sunlight, and the occasional maintenance bot. But this day was different. Today it was overflowing with officers, all shuffling toward a large pair of double doors, filling the hall with the rumble of their conversation.

The officers nodded at ramrod straight marine guards as they passed through the doors, and did their best to avoid eye contact with Colonel Ras Kilgor. It was as if Kilgor had some sort of infectious disease. In military terms, he did.

Kilgor was seated just down from the double doors in a straight-backed, wooden chair. It was hard, overly ornate, and a size too small for his large frame.

Kilgor was a big man at six-foot-four and 220 pounds. He had even features, green eyes, and a nose which nature and a long succession of opponents had beaten flat.

He watched the officers with a crooked smile. Some hated him, but most were simply confused. What was he anyway? A cold blooded monster? Or someone who'd done the best he could with an impossible situation. In a few minutes the court martial would resume and they'd learn the answer.

The floating spy eye was swept sideways by an errant breeze and buzzed back into position. The device was supposed to eliminate the need for guards and protect Kilgor's dignity. It didn't. His butt was planted at the center of ground zero and everyone knew it.

The buzz of conversation was cut off as the double doors hissed closed and the marine guards went to parade rest. Kilgor was sure that any two of *his* troopers would have executed the drill with more snap.

His thoughts were interrupted by the click of boots on polished stone. The major was short and stocky. His uniform was perfect, so crisp that it crackled as he moved, causing Kilgor to take him for a pencil pusher.

Then Kilgor saw the golden star burst on the man's chest and revised his estimate upwards. *Way* upwards. A Medal of Valor! They didn't give those to pencil pushers or hardly anyone else for that matter. Kilgor knew. He had one himself.

"Colonel Kilgor?"

Kilgor stood. It felt good. "Yes?"

"The court stands ready, sir."

What was that in the major's eyes? Compassion? Pity?

Kilgor forced a smile. "Thank you Major. Let's move out. We wouldn't want to keep 'em waiting."

The major smiled. The colonel was okay. Too bad about the court martial.

The major gestured towards the massive doors. "Sir?"

Kilgor nodded and headed for the doors. The major was two steps behind him with the spy eye bringing up the rear.

The marines crashed to attention. They wore light duty ceramic body armor and carried Zitter IV blast rifles. Years in the Corps had scrubbed all expression from their faces.

Kilgor nodded to each of them as the doors hissed open. Now for the verdict. Guilty or innocent? The odds said "guilty," but Kilgor had allowed himself to hope. After all, General Kelly, better known to her troops as "Killer Kelly," sat on the tribunal and was sympathetic to line officers.

In fact, Kelly was widely known for stomping through rear echelon areas, grabbing staff officers, demanding to know how many bugs they'd killed during that particular campaign. God help the poor slobs who said "none."

On the other hand there was Admiral Wanto, more politician than officer, and a swabby to boot. Kilgor could expect damned little sympathy from him.

And at last, but not least, there was General Hurd. A "do it by the book" martinet, presently in command of Arista's military academy, and widely known as "Hard-Ass Hurd."

Still, there was hope, and Kilgor tried to believe in it.

A pair of boxy news cams swooped down to capture the moment. The public wanted to know: was Kilgor a man or a monster?

Not only that, but the trial was a political event as well, with implications for Arista's non-human allies. Would the

"Monster of Maldura" pay for his crimes? Or will he be released after a show of concern?

All eyes were on Kilgor as he began the long walk down the center aisle. The auditorium was so large that the members of the tribunal were tiny figures in the distance, and Kilgor couldn't tell them apart.

High windows admitted shafts of yellow-orange sunlight which splashed the audience below. The walls were paneled with richly polished wood and covered with hundreds of war banners. Many were torn and stained with blood.

Kilgor had entered the auditorium only twice before: Once when graduating from Arista's Military Academy; and once when receiving the Medal of Valor. Now, on his third visit, both honors were in doubt.

Kilgor remembered throwing his cap in the air with all the rest and wondered who got it. Were they in the audience today? Dead on some alien battlefield? Or just drifting through another day?

Kilgor's eyesight was extremely good, but the tribunal and the table before them was still a long way off. Kilgor could see the glitter of metal but nothing more.

Which way was the dagger pointed? Towards him or away? He couldn't tell, but by long standing tradition, the hilt signaled innocence, and the point guilt.

The audience already knew his fate. Those seated toward the front of the auditorium could see the dagger and were passing the word. It sounded like the long drawn out hiss of a snake. Then the process was over, and they waited for Kilgor's reaction.

Outside of the clacking sound made by Kilgor's boots, and the major behind him, there was almost total silence inside the auditorium. Time seemed to slow and almost stop as the distant blur resolved itself into three people and a table. And there it was, polished steel on dark wood, the harbinger of his future.

Kilgor felt something heavy fall in his stomach, and the blood rush into his face. The point was toward him. The verdict was "guilty."

The news cams whirred in close, the audience rustled, and Kilgor stopped before the tribunal. General Kelly looked grim, but Kilgor saw sympathy in her eyes. He knew without asking that she'd supported him and lost.

As for Wanto and Hurd, they wore satisfied expressions, and seemed almost smug about the verdict.

As the most senior officer present, it was Wanto's duty to read the verdict. The naval officer had a long thin face and hooded eyes. He checked to make sure the news cams had a good shot, cleared his throat, and picked up the fax.

"Having heard testimony, and having examined relevant evidence, we have reached a verdict. We find Colonel Ras Kilgor guilty of wrongfully destroying the village of Maldura on the planet Ulona II, guilty of murdering all two thousand four hundred and two of its sentient inhabitants, and guilty of disobeying lawful orders."

There was more, much more, detailing his lesser offenses and citing relevant portions of military regulation, but Kilgor didn't listen. He was light years away on Ulona II.

He remembered the reinforcements which never came, the supplies that never arrived, the air support which never materialized.

He remembered the stench of Ulona's swamps, the smell of his own unwashed body, and the stink of death.

He remembered endless days and nights of combat, of stumbling out of the command bunker just as tired as he'd gone in, of popping stims to stay awake.

He remembered bugs dropping out of the sky, tunneling up from below, and charging the perimeter.

He remembered the thump of mortars, the chatter of automatic slug throwers, and the whine of energy weapons.

And above all, he remembered the chittering sound the bugs made as they broke through the wire and swarmed into the bunkers.

Yes, he was accountable for his actions, and yes the league had the right to judge.

But only those who'd been there. Only those who'd seen men and women overrun by charging bugs, who'd heard their screams, and felt the waves of hate.

*Then* they could judge. *Then* they could place blame. *Then* they could assess guilt.

Wanto's voice came flooding back.

"And so it is the finding of this tribunal that Colonel Ras Kilgor, formerly commanding officer of the Fourth Battalion, League Guards, shall be stripped of all rank and honors, to serve the rest of his natural life at hard labor. This sentence to be formally imposed at evening parade."

The audience remained seated as Kilgor was escorted from the auditorium by a squad of armed marines and marched to his quarters. Now that he was officially "guilty," his dignity, or lack of it, no longer mattered.

It took him a full half hour to work up the courage to call his father. Chances were that he'd never get another opportunity. Military prisons aren't known for their amenities.

The call went through but was refused at the other end. Lt. General Alex Kilgor Ret. wasn't taking calls. Especially from his dishonored son.

It hurt, but less than expected. It seemed there was some sort of limit to the amount of pain he could feel. Good. More was on the way.

The afternoon passed slowly with nothing to do but stare at the walls of his small apartment and think how things might have been.

Finally, at sixteen-hundred hours, there was a knock at his door.

"Enter!"

The door opened and a Gunnery Sergeant stepped inside. He was a small man with lean, no-nonsense features and a garment bag draped over his left arm.

"Good afternoon Colonel. My name's Whippet. It's time to get dressed. Parade's about an hour away. Sorry things turned out as they did sir, but that's the crotch for you."

As a member of the Guards, Kilgor was army, whereas Whippet was a marine, and therefore in the "crotch," as jar-heads had referred to their organization for more than a thousand years. By tradition Kilgor could not be served by someone in the same uniform he had dishonored.

"Thanks gunny. I'm sorry you caught the duty. You on the outs with your C.O. or something?"

Whippet grinned. "Something like that sir. Now, if you'll just shuck that uniform, I brought you a brand new one."

Half an hour later Kilgor examined himself in the mirror. The gray uniform fit like a glove, as it should, since it had been tailor made for him that very afternoon.

Kilgor knew without checking that his comets and medals were only tacked on. That way Wanto could rip them off without spraining his wrist. Another exercise for the cameras. Kilgor sighed.

"Okay, gunny. Let's get on with it."

Whippet nodded, called for Kilgor's marine escort, and held out his hand. Kilgor took it.

"Good luck sir. For whatever it's worth, there's plenty who think you did the right thing."

Kilgor nodded soberly. "Thanks, gunny. Kill some bugs for me."

Whippet stepped back and snapped to attention. His arm came across his chest in a formal salute. "Sir!"

Kilgor returned the salute and stepped out the door. He would never see the apartment or Whippet again.

The escort's boots crashed down in perfect cadence as they marched Kilgor down a series of gleaming halls, out through a permeable force field, and onto the grinder.

The grinder was a vast expanse of gray duracrete also referred to by a number of more derogatory names. During his days in the academy, Kilgor had performed push-ups on just about every square foot of that hated surface.

The staff sergeant shouted some orders, and they marched towards the headquarters building. Although the spy eye had disappeared, two news cams were very much in attendance. They darted here and there gathering shots while a bored newswoman provided a running commentary from a studio hundreds of miles away.

The sun was low in the sky and warmed the right side of Kilgor's face. The air was soft and sweet, a reminder of Arista's beauty, and the many who'd died to protect her.

The signs of war were everywhere. A flight of delta-shaped aero-space fighters roamed overhead, and higher up, running along the very edge of space itself, a squadron of destroyer escorts streaked across the sky.

But they were only signs—unblooded portents of the horror yet to come. Out there, on planets like Ulona II, Arista was losing the war. In months, a year at the most, Arista would fight for its life.

Just ahead, a company of recruits wheeled and turned, marching across the gray surface of the grinder towards a line of distant barracks.

A single glance told Kilgor they were green, farm kids mostly, learning to obey orders. Orders that would cause many of them to die.

How many boys and girls would it take to stop the alien Hothri? How many were left in the peaceful farms and villages of Arista? Enough to save the planet?

Kilgor didn't know. Nobody knew.

Fluffy white clouds scudded across an otherwise blue sky and songbirds chirped the arrival of evening. It was the worst day of Kilgor's life, yet beautiful at the same time.

How could that be? Was there someone beyond the perimeter of the base for whom this was the best day of their life? For reasons unknown, had the weather sided with them?

"Battalion! Attenhut!"

On those words the two-hundred and sixty-seven surviving members of Kilgor's battalion came to attention.

Kilgor's escort wheeled him into place and took two steps backward. He was at right angles to the troops and senior officers.

Even now Kilgor took pride in the way the battalion looked, in their strength, in what they'd accomplished . . . In what *he'd* accomplished. The fact that these men and women were still alive proved that he'd made the right decision, done the right thing.

"Yes," a small voice said, "you saved them . . . and paid with more than two-thousand innocent lives. Blood for blood. Are you proud of that?"

"Yes!" Kilgor countered. "I can only do so much, be responsible for so many, and these lives were mine to protect."

Orders were shouted. Kilgor did a left face and stood alone.

Wanto, Kelly, and Hurd faced him, backs ramrod straight, medals gleaming in the afternoon sun. Once again Kilgor saw sympathy in Kelly's eyes and wondered what she was thinking.

Major Dieter stepped up on Kilgor's right. Once his X.O., now she commanded the battalion. She addressed Wanto.

"All members of the Fourth Battalion, League Guards, present or accounted for, sir."

Kilgor smiled inside. He'd always enjoyed that phrase. ". . . accounted for." It mean so many things: At various times it meant "drunk," "in sick bay," "wounded," or "killed in action."

Yes, more than a thousand members of the Fourth Battalion had been "accounted for" on Ulona II. And now, within the next few minutes, one more. Still unhurt . . . but a casualty nonetheless.

Wanto's eyes were like stones. "Colonel Ras Kilgor, about face!"

Kilgor obeyed. Now, by tradition, Kilgor faced the men and women of his command. They were professionals, lifers in a crack outfit, a truly dying breed. Their faces were impassive.

Admiral Wanto stepped forward to read the charges one last time. His words became a drone.

A drum roll began.

The sun came in hard and low.

A bird soared upwards.

Shame rolled over Kilgor in crushing waves. He wanted to cry, to run away and hide, to disappear and never be seen again. No matter what he told himself, no matter what he *knew* to be true, this was the ultimate dishonor and the lowest point of his entire life.

The words finally came to an end, but the drum roll went on. All three of the senior officers approached and stood two paces in front of him. Wanto was at the center, and it was he who took the final step. The news cams swooped in for close-ups.

There was satisfaction on the naval officer's face as he ripped the tabs from Kilgor's shoulders, jerked the bar of medals from his chest, and plucked each one of the gold embossed buttons from the front of his uniform. All went into a bag which would be ceremonially fed into a mass converter later that day.

Then, on some invisible cue, a staff sergeant came forward with a cushion on her arms. The cushion was covered with red velvet and bore Kilgor's dagger. The dagger given him the day he graduated from the academy. Handed to him by the same proud father who no longer acknowledged his existence.

Light twinkled off polished metal as Wanto held the dagger aloft. The blade was more than a ceremonial toy, it had saved Kilgor's life, and it hurt to see what they'd done.

The durasteel blade had been cut nearly in two leaving only a small bridge of metal to hold both halves together. The cut had been filled with a silvery paste to make it seem undamaged.

Wanto's voice was amplified and carried over the speakers which ringed the parade ground.

"Members of the Fourth Battalion, League Guards! This

blade has been dishonored! But *only* this blade, and *only* the officer who abused it. All Arista knows of your loyalty, of your courage, of your battles against the alien Hothri. By age old tradition I call upon you to judge one of your own.'' Wanto snapped the dagger in two.

It was an age old tradition but rarely used in modern times. By allowing the troops to endorse the tribunal's finding, Wanto hoped to maintain morale and score some more points with Arista's non-human allies. The news cams pulled back for a wide shot.

Kilgor waited for Dieter to give the traditional command. The battalion would perform an about face, and on her orders, march away. In doing so they would turn their backs on him and his dishonor as well.

Major Dieter did a neat about-face. "Fourth battalion! Attenhut! Preseennt h'arms!''

There was a double crash as 267 blast rifles came off the ground, hit hands, and snapped vertical.

It was unheard of! The battalion was saluting him! Refusing to turn their backs on him, and in so doing, voluntarily accepting his dishonor as their own. To erase the stain from the unit's record they would have to perform some act of future heroism.

"Battalion! Right face! Right shoulder, h'arms! Forward, h'arch.''

Stripped as he was of all rank Kilgor could not salute. So he stood there in silence, the tears rolling down his cheeks, and watched his battalion march away.

All prisons are brutal, but military prisons are the worst of all. Kilgor was well aware of this fact and understood the reasons behind it.

First was the fact that civilian style prisons look pretty inviting when compared to the average battlefield. That means conditions inside military prisons are intentionally worse than a night drop onto a bug-held planet.

Add to this the fact that unlike the population at large, some members of the military *like* to hurt others, and you've got the makings of an unmitigated hell.

And that, Kilgor reflected, was a pretty good working definition of Receiving Station Four.

RS-4 was located in the middle of a small desert. It consisted of eight large tents and an inflatable admin building.

Like the rest of the prisoners, Kilgor hadn't seen the inside of the air conditioned admin building and never would.

He was however extremely familiar with the tents. Tent one was the mess hall, tent two was the medical facility, and the rest housed prisoners . . . 241 of them to be exact. One-hundred and sixty men, and eighty-one women. The sexes were segregated everywhere but in the mess tent.

There was no wall, no razor wire, and no security system to keep them in. Only miles and miles of desert. They were, as Sergeant Major Giller liked to point out, "free to leave at any time."

However as long as the prisoners chose to stay, they would obey *his* rules, do things *his* way, and remember that it was *his* camp.

Kilgor had arrived at RS-4 sixteen hours before. Shortly after his arrival he had been stripped, shaved, and professionally beaten. It was a light beating, scientifically administered, and delivered to each one of the prisoners on one pretext or another. It was a time tested process similar to army boot camp.

First the prisoners were stripped of their previous identities. In Kilgor's case, the officer-authority figure. This was accomplished by confiscating all of their personal possessions, shaving their heads, and forcing them to wear identical fatigues.

Then the prisoners were introduced to a new set of rules, the consequences for breaking them, and a power structure in which they occupied the lowest rung.

Only after this process was complete would the prisoners be allowed to enter the navy brig at High Bluff.

RS-4 was similar to boot camp. In boot camp the goal is to break you down and build you up. But the purpose of RS-4 was to break you down and *keep* you down.

Due to his status as an ex-army officer, Kilgor had been placed with navy and marine prisoners, and would eventually end up in a navy brig. This was for his own protection since an army prison might include men and women who'd served under him and bore some sort of grudge.

It was a dubious protection however, since the marine guards had announced his previous rank immediately after arrival, thereby ensuring that most of the prisoners would dislike him. He was, after all, the only ex-officer in the entire group.

Divide and conquer. It's good military strategy regardless of circumstance.

Interestingly enough, few if any prisoners knew about Kilgor's offense, or if they did, didn't choose to mention it. Maybe they'd been off-planet, were preoccupied by their own troubles, or just didn't care.

At the moment, Sergeant Major Giller had them standing at attention in the hot afternoon sun. The prisoners wore heavy winter fatigues, body armor, and assault packs filled with forty pounds of metal for the men, thirty for the women. Every moment was pure torture.

Giller was a short man, with a heavily muscled torso, and bowed legs. As usual his puffy face was beet red, and he looked like he'd have a coronary at any moment. In spite of their fervent prayers, it never arrived. Making things worse was the fact that Giller enjoyed the sound of his own voice. Kilgor blinked sweat from his eyes and waited for this particular speech to end.

". . . And so," Giller went on, "you will enter the med tent in single file, strip off your clothes, and step in front of the scanner. Depending on what the scanner finds, you will either leave through the other end of the tent, or remain behind for further examination. Do any of you worthless, low-life scum have questions?"

Giller prided himself on the fact that he never swore. This didn't keep him from heaping lots of abuse on everyone.

Since any verbalization was worth forty push-ups, even when invited, no one asked any questions. Giller nodded approvingly. "Good. Take 'em away."

Giller's cadre of interchangeable corporals divided them into groups of twenty or so and double-timed them around tent city until it was their turn in the med tent.

Though careful to keep a straight face, Kilgor found the whole thing a bit amusing. Giller would abuse them, the medics would fix them up, and Giller would abuse them some more. It didn't make sense. Why bother? Wouldn't it be easier to let them die?

The answer was of course that death would be inhumane, and compared to life with Giller, relatively pleasant. Theirs was truly "a fate worse than death."

Kilgor laughed, caught a nasty look from the hulk known as Corporal Kostaza, and turned it into a cough. The trick didn't work. Kostaza's swagger stick hurt like hell.

By the time Kilgor fell into his rack at the end of the second day, the prisoners had divided themselves into subgroups, and a power structure was starting to emerge.

Kilgor watched this process rather carefully. Like anyone who'd managed to survive five years in the military academy, he knew a lot about life in a structured environment. There were two choices. Join a group, or go it alone.

Membership in a group had advantages and disadvantages. Members had people to watch their backs, but unless they fought for leadership, were forced to follow group rules. The first rule was to "hate all the other groups." Otherwise, why have groups?

In the case of RS-4 the groups were forming along service lines. The "grunts" and the "swabbies" had already divided Kilgor's tent into two halves and were exhibiting various kinds of territorial behavior.

Meanwhile, there were two kinds of loners. Voluntary loners and involuntary loners. The voluntary loners chose to stay apart. One was a black man named Struck.

Struck was big slab of a man, and that, plus a sort of glacial cool, allowed him some independence. No one knew much about him, except that he was a marine and an expert in unarmed combat.

Kilgor suspected Struck of leaking that piece of information on purpose. If so, Struck would be someone to watch. Tough and smart. Officer material.

Thanks to his status as an ex-officer, Kilgor fell into the other category of loners. The kind which had no choice. These were the geeks, the screw-ups, and the crazies. Men and women who didn't or wouldn't fit in. And, given the kind of people who end up in military prisons, there were plenty of them.

The loners didn't have to follow group rules, but due to their isolation, made perfect victims. Kilgor studied them carefully because he had a plan, and it hinged on them.

Some were in his tent, and some weren't, but he had a mental profile: First there was Red, a jittery young man with wild eyes and a talent for blowing things up. According to the scuttlebut, Red had taken a real dislike to his C.O. and wired an A-6 demo pack into her command car.

For weeks she'd driven it around while Red watched, played with the remote detonator in his pocket, and enjoyed his invisible power. Then one day she made the mistake of chewing Red out, and whammo! No more C.O.

Next was a skinny little woman called "Wires." Once a com tech on a battleship, she'd used her considerable technical expertise to set up a fleet-wide gambling network, and had been court martialed when a senior officer lost ten-thousand credits.

Then there was "Freese," a sometimes raving lunatic with three now-suspended decorations for bravery. He had slightly bulging eyes, a nose somewhat too small for his face, and a nervous tic in his left cheek. No one knew exactly what Freese had done and he wouldn't say.

And there was "Bugs," a monosyllabic maniac with cold wet hands and dead eyes. Word had it that Bugs had a pathological hatred for the Hothri, and while fighting them on a world called Isamba II, had assembled a huge collection of right index fingers . . . some belonging to prisoners-of-war. This explained his presence at RS-4. Bugs loved guns and was one of the few marines to score "expert" with every hand-weapon currently in use.

Finally, there was the woman called "Doc." She was pretty in a haunted sort of way and seemed to float through her days, as if only partially there. The rumor was that she'd machine-gunned a squad of marines trapped in a burning assault vehicle and been convicted of murder. Though always willing to treat members from either group, Doc had refused to align herself with either the grunts or the swabbies.

There were more, but these would do for a start. With time and work Kilgor would mold them into a third group. A group which would eventually dominate the other two.

"Sure," Kilgor thought to himself, "it'll work. But why bother?"

"Because I haven't got anything else to do," the answer came back. "And because it's the only way to hit back."

Kilgor smiled and fell into an exhausted sleep. Sometime during the night he stirred briefly as something went pop, pop, pop, but he went right back to sleep.

The next day got off to a brutal start. The prisoners arrived in the mess tent to find three bullet ridden bodies sprawled across the tables.

During the night two men and a woman had tried to cut their way into the admin building. No one knew what the plan was. Maybe they hoped to steal a vehicle, find some booze, or who knows. It really didn't matter.

The prisoners grumbled as they fell in. No one liked to miss breakfast, not when meals were their sole source of entertainment, and portions were so small. That's when they noticed that piles of sand that had sprung up overnight courtesy of Corporal Kostaza and the dozer he stood on.

Giller arrived a few minutes later. He had just stepped out of the air conditioned administration building. His uniform was freshly starched and had just enough wear to show he was a pro. Kilgor could practically smell the cool air still trapped in its weave.

Ignoring the women Giller headed for the men. Once in front of them, he wrinkled his nose as if confronting a garbage dump, and started his speech.

"Good morning, scum. I hope each and every one you low-life scuz-buckets had the worst night of your life. But, just in case some of you worthless hunks of putrescent meat had pleasant dreams, I will make your day a living hell." Giller paused to point his swagger stick at the mountains of sand.

"Men can move mountains, or so I've been told. You of course are not men, but pus-sucking vermin, sent here to try my patience. You shall have a chance nonetheless. Before you, stand two proud mountains. The mountain on the left is Mount Giller. It is *my* mountain, and I want *you* to move it."

Now Giller strutted over in front of the women. "Good morning maggots. You are, as always, some of the most repulsive slime balls I've ever seen." He pointed at their mountain.

"That's Mount Kostaza. It belongs to Corporal Kostaza. He looks up to me, and when the scuz balls move my mountain, he'll want you to move his mountain as well. And Kostaza will be very disappointed if his mountain arrives after mine does. Do you maggots understand?"

It was a no-win trap, and the women knew it, but they yelled "yes, sir!" anyway, sensing it was the less of two evils. They were right. The push-ups were hard, but easier than the laps Giller would've given out had they refused to speak.

The moment the push-ups were over, the real torture began. Line up in front of the mountains, wait while another prisoner loaded your pack with sand, then double-time to the other end of the camp where you dumped it out, double-time back, then start all over.

Hour after hour they ran, glugging the canteens of water the medics pushed their way, and swallowing an endless procession of salt tablets.

As time passed it became obvious that the men would finish first. This was not due to any weakness on the women's part, but because of the fact that Corporal Kostaza had intentionally over estimated the amount of sand in their pile, making it impossible for them to move their mountain in the same amount of time as the men.

Had there been some sort of central leadership among the prisoners, it would've instructed the men to slow down so that the women could tie.

But that wasn't the case, and seeing an opportunity to come out on top, the men sped up. Kilgor saw, and understood, but couldn't intervene. He had no power, and thanks to the circumstances, no opportunity to communicate his observations to those who did.

As the men hurried to move the last loads of sand Giller stood next to his mountain and grinned. And Kilgor knew why. This was the point where the analogy between boot camp and a military prison came to an end.

In boot camp almost all the activities forced recruits to work as a team. Here it was just the opposite. A single team would be harder to control, so Giller was busy sub-dividing them into smaller groups. Not only for his benefit, but for the benefit of subsequent guards as well—guards who depended on RS-4 to break prisoners in.

The men won a few minutes later, just as Giller had intended, and Corporal Kostaza flew into a calculated rage. The women were ordered to move their mountain back to its original position while the men went to dinner.

The women labored long after the sun had set, and by the time they ate their cold field rations and racked out, they hated the men with a living passion.

In the meantime Kilgor planned his next move. He was angry, and without knowing it, had substituted Giller for the "enemy." All his life Kilgor had been trained to defeat the enemy, and this was no different. Tomorrow, or the next day at the latest, he would implement the first step of his plan.

Actually, three days passed before Kilgor could take action. He needed an opportunity, a specific kind of opportunity, and it took awhile to develop.

It came just after chow, during the hour of so-called "free time," when the prisoners were allowed to clean their tents, wash their uniforms, and prepare for evening inspection.

Freese had both good and bad days, and as chance would have it, this one was bad. His eyes seemed to bulge even more than usual, his right check was twitching like mad, and he was muttering under his breath.

As a loner and resident of the grunt side of the tent, Freese got all the shit details. This gave the grunt leader, a one-time recon corporal named Hubashi, points with the men. Why should they clean the head when Freese the freak could do it for them?

Under normal circumstances Freese accepted his tasks without comment. But this was a bad day, a day when terrible memories were bubbling up through the surface of his mind, and Freese had less control.

So when Hubashi handed Freese a bucket, and told him to clean the head, something snapped. Freese crotch-kicked the unsuspecting grunt, chopped the back of his neck, and stomped him.

Hubashi's men yelled incoherently as they jumped Freese and tried to put him down. It wasn't easy. Freese was a hardass, a crazy hardass, and knew his stuff. Grunts began to fly in every direction. Seeing this as a marine struggle, the swabbies stood to one side and placed meaningless bets.

Kilgor watched and waited for the perfect moment. By going in too early he'd take more of a beating than he absolutely had to, and by being too late he'd miss a golden opportunity.

Freese fell under the combined weight of three men and Kilgor entered the fight. His goal was make it look good then lose before he was maimed.

Kilgor peeled two marines off Freese's back, helped the other man to his feet, and fought beside him until a concerted charge brought both of them down.

Then it was pay-back time as the grunts worked them over with fists and combat boots until the guards came to break it up.

The whole tent did extra PT that afternoon, but one thing had changed. Where two groups had existed before . . .

now there were three. Kilgor and Freese did their push-ups side by side.

The days passed, and one by one, Kilgor used similar tactics to recruit Wires, Red, Bugs, and finally Doc.

Doc turned out to be hardest, first, because everyone seemed to like her, and second, because she operated on some other plane. As far as Kilgor could tell Doc didn't care if she lived or died.

Strangely enough it was an attack on Kilgor that brought Doc into his group, and not because he'd planned it, but because she chose to come.

The incident seemed to come out of the blue, but Kilgor had his doubts, and suspected Giller of planning the whole thing. Perhaps the Sergeant Major had noticed Kilgor's recruiting activities and felt he was too big for his britches.

Whatever his reasons, the Sergeant Major made his move after evening chow. The prisoners had just finished eating their tasteless slop when Giller stepped into the mess tent, stood with hands clasped behind his back, and waited for their reaction.

This was the first time the Sergeant Major had interrupted their chow, but someone had the good sense to yell "Atten-hut!" and benches crashed over backwards as everyone hurried to obey.

Giller smiled. "At ease, scum. Take your seats."

There was an uneasy stirring as the prisoners righted benches and took their seats. What was Giller up to this time? Whatever it was boded ill for someone.

Giller mounted the nearest table and looked them over. His expression left no doubt as to what he saw. They were garbage. He cleared his throat.

"In a few days you leave Receiving Station Four and move on to a real prison where you belong. In the meantime however, I want your stay to be as pleasant as possible, so I've agreed to tell you a bed time story.

Like most good bed time stories this one's about a monster, the "Monster of Maldura" they called him, and that may be something of an understatement."

At this point Giller looked Kilgor directly in the eye and grinned. Some who'd long ago figured out who Kilgor was understood the reference. The rest waited to see what this was all about.

Kilgor felt an emptiness grow in the pit of his stomach and steeled himself against the pain.

"You see," Giller continued, "the monster commanded a battalion, the Fourth Battalion, League Guards if I remember correctly, and was fighting on some dirt ball called Ulona II.

"We didn't have much on Ulona II, so the bugs landed like flies on fecal matter, and the monster found himself over-extended. With that in mind he pulled back to a well fortified fire base and waited for the navy to bail him out." Giller looked around, eyes gleaming, enjoying the attention.

"As the monster pulled back, the bugs moved in to replace him, and occupied a village called Maldura. It wasn't much as villages go, just a collection of white-washed mud huts, but the indigs liked the place and called it home. There were two-thousand-four-hundred-and-two of the little one-eyed devils . . . all helpless as new born babies.

"Well the monster liked the indigs, or so it seemed, and the bugs heard about it. They heard how the monster used his troops to dig new wells, hold sick call, and repair storm damage.

"So they picked out two-hundred of the indigs, killed 'em, and sent their bodies to the monster along with a message.

"The message said 'surrender with all your troops or we will kill two-hundred indigs per day until you do.'

"Well, the monster gave it some thought. He couldn't surrender, there was no question of that, but he *could* try to retake the village and save the indigs."

Giller's eyes swept the tent like twin lasers. "Worthless though you are, I suspect most of *you* would try. But not the monster. Oh, no, the monster took a far different approach, an approach safer for him. Care to guess what it was?"

There was no reason to think that the forty push-up rule was suspended, so everyone was surprised when Struck stood up and took a guess.

"I'll take a crack at that one Sergeant Major. It's my guess that the monster's outfit was worn down to nothing. He knew they couldn't take the village, and went to option two."

Struck looked around as if challenging someone to say otherwise. "It's my guess that he knew the enemy would kill the indigs just as they said they would, realized there were about fifteen-hundred bugs occupying the village, and dropped a couple of missiles right on top of them. Boom. No more indigs, and no more bugs.'' With that Struck sat down.

Giller was so mesmerized by Struck's narrative that he forgot to hand out the usual push-ups. The opportunity to isolate Kilgor was gone, but Giller did his best to salvage it. He nodded sagely.

''Essentially correct. The monster played *God,* and took more than two-thousand innocent lives. And guess what? He's right here among us. Don't be bashful prisoner Kilgor . . . stand up and take a bow.''

Kilgor had little choice but to do as he was told. And as he stood something wonderful happened. Somehow, out of the hundreds of eyes which surrounded him, Doc's found and held his. They were filled with compassion and something more as well. Suddenly Kilgor remembered the story about the burning vehicle and understood. Doc knew what he'd been through.

Kilgor took strength from her support. Giller was wasting his time. Kilgor's followers had already taken pride in their status as outcasts. They wore rejection like a badge of honor. In fact, the news that their leader was the ''Monster of Maldura,'' would probably strengthen their respect for Kilgor.

Still, Giller's comments were like salt in an open wound, and hurt like hell.

They had no opportunity to speak, but later, when Kilgor went to sleep, he dreamt of a woman with luminous eyes and the ability to see his soul.

The rest of Kilgor's time at RS-4 passed in a weary succession of long days and short nights.

Bit by bit he strengthened his group of outcasts until they saw themselves as a cohesive whole. It was a delicate process since people like Red, Freese, and Bugs were inherently unstable. Just by the nature of things, Kilgor was forced to spend a lot of time stroking them and resolving minor feuds.

Still, the process was worth the effort because over time the ''Brig Rats,'' as Wires had christened them, were slowly gaining influence. The fact that half of the Rats were certifiably insane prevented others from harassing them, and Kilgor's leadership kept things from getting out of hand.

So, by the time their last night at RS-4 rolled around, Kilgor had surrounded himself with a cadre of hard-core followers. When they hit the brig at High Bluff he'd use them to build something bigger.

In the meantime there was the warm night air, a little bit of last minute slack from the guards, and Doc. Bit by bit, she was coming back from wherever she'd been, sharing confidences with Kilgor, and even laughing once in awhile.

Taking advantage of the unfenced compound they'd walked a little ways into the desert and stretched full length on the warm sand. Fingers intertwined they lay on the backs and looked up at the stars. Out here, away from city lights, they were visible in untold thousands.

"Beautiful aren't they," Doc said softly. "So pure and white . . . like diamonds on black velvet."

Kilgor smiled. "Yes, and a long ways off. I wish we could go there. Some place without uniforms and sand."

Doc sat up. "Ras, look!"

Kilgor looked in the direction of her pointing finger. A fireball blossomed on the distant horizon. Suddenly streaks of fire cut back and forth across the sky, sonic booms rolled across the land, and the sound of excited voices floated out from camp.

Kilgor looked at Doc, and she at him. Neither needed an explanation. The battle for Arista had begun.

Though called the "First Battle of Arista," it was actually little more than a Hothri feint. The bugs were a cautious lot and wished to test the planet's defenses prior to launching a major assault. The attack by a squadron of Hothri raiders lasted only twenty-seven minutes and was quickly repulsed.

Nonetheless it was shocking to see so much visible damage and realize it had occurred in such a short period of time. Early that morning the prisoners had been loaded onto four military transports and flown out of RS-4.

They were little more than lightly armored metal boxes kept aloft by an anti-grav field and propelled by jets. Due to their low operational ceiling and the considerable military activity at higher altitudes, the transports flew relatively low. This made the pilots nervous but gave Kilgor a great view. He didn't like what he saw.

Brief though it was, the Hothri attack had done a great deal of damage. Kilgor got a hollow feeling in his gut when he saw a burned out fusion plant, cratered expressways, the charred ruins of a small city, and long lines of olive drab vehicles twisting and turning through once peaceful countryside.

Doc touched his arm. "If they did this in half an hour, what could they do in a week?"

Kilgor shook his head but didn't speak. They both knew the answer. Somewhere Major Dieter, Colonel Dieter by now, was preparing the Guards for battle. A battle Kilgor couldn't fight.

At a distance, the High Bluff Military Correctional Facility, as it was officially known, looked like a high-tech castle. It was built in layers, like the tiers on an old fashioned birthday cake.

Although equipped with every security device known to man and designed to meet every conceivable emergency, the prison's architects had still placed the prison at the end of a small peninsula high above the sea. Though only twenty-five years old, the towering structure had the look of an ancient keep, making it even more forbidding.

Kilgor took one last look at freedom as his transport settled down behind the prison's high walls.

"Ras?"

Kilgor turned to look into Doc's eyes. *Damn, damn, damn. Why here? Why now? Instead of years ago when there were still choices to be made?*

He forced a smile. "Yes?"

"They'll separate us, Ras. . . . I'll miss you."

He didn't know they were coming until the words popped out. "I love you, Susan."

Doc smiled at the use of her real name. "I know you do, Ras. I've known for a long time. I love you, too. Don't forget that."

And then the two of them were pulled apart as guards pushed, pulled, and prodded prisoners out of the transports and into a large compound. Sergeant Major Giller would've been proud to see them form up and count off without being told.

In fact, they did it so well that High Bluff's Commandant,

Major Nancy Nithra was pleased. Although sitting in her office far underground, Nithra had watched the prisoners arrive via her wall sized vid screen and nodded her approval.

Sergeant Major Giller had done his job extremely well as usual. Nithra smiled. How surprised the slime balls would be to know Giller's actual rank! Giller was actually a Lt. Colonel, with a doctorate in sociology and a masters in psychology.

Turning away from the vid screen Nithra touched the alpha-numeric keyboard projected onto the surface of her spotless desk. A menu appeared, listing each one of the new prisoners, and ending with the words "Additional Comments."

Nithra speared this last selection with a bony finger. Text, along with supporting video flooded the surface of Nithra's desk, and she began to read Giller's report.

As usual the RS-4 staff had succeeded in splitting the prisoners into small groups and turning them against each other. It was a typical intake with the usual collection of sociopaths, psychopaths, and other scum. But wait . . . what was this? An unusual entry written in Giller's clipped style.

". . . It should be noted however, that this group of prisoners includes an extremely intelligent ex-officer with unusually good leadership skills. Ras Kilgor is aware of our attempts to divide the prisoner population into hostile subgroups and is taking steps to counter that strategy. At present he is building a cadre of followers drawn from the pool of non-accepted individuals. Some of these prisoners are extremely violent, but in spite of their severe mental and emotional problems, have latent leadership potential.

"Kilgor seems to recognize this potential and concentrates his efforts on those individuals.

"This leads me to conclude that Kilgor is not only building a group, he's building a rather special group, capable of extending his influence to a much broader population. He may even be laying the ground work for an invisible government within High Bluff.

"On one occasion I tried to isolate Kilgor through the use of group social pressure but failed. Not only did one prisoner rise to Kilgor's defense, but my revelations about his crimes backfired, and actually raised his social standing.

"In light of Kilgor's leadership ability, and negative potential, I recommend that he be placed in a maximum security cell and denied all contact with other prisoners.''

Nithra touched the surface of her desk and watched the report disappear. So the man they called the ''Monster of Maldura'' had arrived. Ever since his court martial she'd known that he'd turn up eventually but hadn't given the matter much thought.

The truth was that Nithra sympathized with Kilgor, and figured that given similar circumstances, she'd have done the same thing. Still, it was her duty to keep him inside High Bluff for the rest of his life, so that's what she'd do.

As for solitary confinement, well, that seemed a bit extreme. Maybe Giller had been in the desert too long. So Kilgor had some loons to watch his back? So what? The brig was full of similar groups and they'd keep him in check.

Satisfied with her decision, Major Nithra turned her attention to other things.

More than a month passed. The Second Battle of Arista was fought and won. This time the battle lasted a day and half. One of Arista's three fortified moons was neutralized, two orbital defense platforms were destroyed, fourteen cities were turned into radioactive slag, and 4,563,000 men, women and children were killed.

Now, the surviving population of Arista was preparing for the Third and, quite possibly, the Last Battle Of Arista. The one they might very well lose.

But not Kilgor, and not the other men and women of the High Bluff Military Correctional Facility. They spent their days turning rocks into gravel, dumping the gravel into chutes, and wondering where it went.

The truth was nowhere, since every truck on the planet had been confiscated by the military, and none were available for hauling gravel.

Kilgor rolled out of his rack to a morning like every other. His cell was a white cube, with only the utilitarian bunks, wash basin, and commode to break the hard straight lines. The floor was cold under his feet.

Three steps to the dispenser slot, grab two pairs of disposable overalls, and throw one at Murph. Ignore the other man's protest, empty his bladder, and brush his teeth. Another day had begun.

Kilgor was putting his boots on when the intercom went

off. "Prisoner Kilgor. Report to your door. A guard will escort you to the administration section. That is all."

Murph was worried. Although he had the smooth, untroubled features of a philosopher, he was a dyed-in-the-wool pessimist at heart.

"What's happening boss? The admin section? What if they brain-probe you?"

Kilgor forced a smile. Though worried, he couldn't let it show. "Brain probe? Nonsense. Major Nithra wants my body, that's all."

Murph laughed. "That'll be the day. I know her type. Firm but fully packed. That's how she likes 'em. Substantial, like me." Murph patted a small paunch.

"Full of it, like you," Kilgor answered, stepping up to the cell door.

The door recognized him, approved the thumb print provided by the guard outside, and swished open. Kilgor stepped out.

The guard's face was hidden behind a flesh colored mask. The guards all wore them and the masks all looked alike. They were an international barrier to communications. The masks made it more difficult to know the guards as people, to see their expressions, to probe their weaknesses.

"You know the rules," the guard said gruffly. "Walk five paces ahead, do exactly as I say, and keep your mouth shut."

Like most of the guards this one was sloppy. One by one, the more competent guards were leaving, headed for combat units, while second and third rate troops came in to replace them. This one was a joke, standing way too close, and damned near asking to have his butt kicked.

For the millionth time Kilgor considered taking the guard's blaster and shooting his way out. And for the millionth time he rejected a plan which would kill a lot of guards, end his life, and accomplish nothing.

He still wanted to live, still cared, still hoped. Would he feel the same way in five years? Ten? Twenty?

He thought of Susan and the glimpse he'd caught of her two days before. Her presence gave him hope somehow. Hope that he'd see her, talk to her, touch her hand.

News travels fast inside a prison and High Bluff was no exception. As Kilgor walked down a long series of sterile halls word of his journey rippled outwards like waves from the center of a pond.

Hand-talk jerked and fluttered as Kilgor passed groups of prisoners.

"Where ya headed? What's the deal? Anything I can do?" These questions and many more were asked and answered without the guard seeing a thing.

Kilgor was already a "somebody" inside the brig, leader of the prisoner council, and someone to be reckoned with.

Within weeks of their arrival Kilgor's Brig Rats had identified all of the social outcasts at High Bluff, recruited most of them, and quadrupled the group's size.

Then, using people like Freese, Bugs and Red as enforcers, Kilgor had taken control of the other groups. Things were touch-and-go for awhile as Kilgor's Rats went one-on-one with the heaviest muscle the other groups could bring to bear.

Battles were fought in the chow line, wars were waged in the showers, and scores were settled in the halls. But because most of Kilgor's troops were more than a little crazy, and willing to take unbelievable casualties, they won.

It proved his theory. Loners are tougher than joiners. They have to be in order to survive.

Once he had control, Kilgor took steps to end the wars. Alliances were forged, agreements struck, and many of the old abuses eliminated.

Kilgor's platform was simple: "This place is bad enough without making it worse." It was simple, straight forward, and quite sensible. It was also very popular.

So Kilgor's trip to the admin section constituted big news and the prison grapevine was full of it.

Kilgor had never been taken to the admin section before so he didn't know what to expect. The elevator was huge, large enough to hold an entire company of troops all at once, which was exactly what it was designed to do. In the case of a riot, the elevator could deliver lots of guards to every level of the prison in a short period of time. Outside of a motionless maintenance bot, the elevator was completely empty.

It dropped like a rock and came to a smooth stop. Kilgor stepped out into a hall full of troops. *Real* troops.

With help from a variety of utility bots they were moving furniture, unloading boxes from power pallets, and generally getting in each other's way.

Kilgor was surprised and knew his guard was, too. It

showed in the way he moved. Taking Kilgor by the elbow, a stupid move if there ever was one, the guard guided him towards a door marked "Commandant."

It hissed open and they stepped inside. It was a large well-lit room with a big desk and a wall-sized vid screen. Kilgor had expected to see a woman behind the desk, but not General Kelly.

He barely recognized her. The big, almost burly, woman present at his court martial had been replaced by a hollow-eyed scarecrow. The general's uniform hung around her in empty folds, and with a sudden shock, Kilgor realized that her left arm was missing.

She stood, winced with pain, and held our her right hand. "Hello, Kilgor. You look a helluva lot better than I feel."

She turned to the guard. "Haul ass, son. This prisoner's safe with me."

The guard took two steps backwards, delivered a half-hearted salute, performed a sloppy about-face, and left the room.

Kelly shook her head as the door closed behind him. "Barracks scrapings. What's this army coming to? No wonder Nithra volunteered for combat. Ah well, we would've taken her, anyway."

General Kelly sat on a corner of her desk and gestured towards a guest chair. "Sit down Kilgor . . . and stop looking at me like that."

Kilgor sat down. "Sorry general, I'm surprised to see you, that's all."

Kelly chuckled. "Bullshit. I'm one arm short, thirty pounds light, and look like hell warmed over."

She pointed at her empty sleeve. " 'Bout three weeks ago the bugs made a commando raid on HQ. Don't know why. Just to show they could, I guess. Zigged when I should've zagged. You'll like this though . . . the ugly bastards caught Hurd sitting on the can. Fried his ass!"

Kilgor smiled, not at Hurd's death, but at Kelly's irrepressible style. The woman was amazing. Then he thought about what she'd said, and the smile disappeared. "Arista HQ? They hit that?"

Kelly nodded soberly. "Scary ain't it? No big deal since we got the real important stuff stashed elsewhere . . . but frightening just the same."

"Things aren't going well?"

Kelly was silent for a moment before she spoke. Her eyes were deadly serious. "No, they aren't. We're arming children over the age of twelve. The navy's so short on equipment that they're wiring old men and women into missile guidance systems. Every home, office, and factory is a fortress. There's going to be one more battle, a big one, winner take all."

Kilgor jerked a thumb towards the hall. "That's what's going on here . . . you're fortifying High Bluff?"

Kelly nodded. "Right. This dump is being remodeled as a back-up command post and a surface-to-space missile battery." She gestured to the room. "A lot of it is underground."

Kilgor felt his heart thump a little faster. "What about the prisoners? What happens to us?"

Kelly smiled a crooked smile. "Well, that depends."

She touched the surface of her desk. A side door slid open and Struck stepped into the room. Kilgor hadn't seen him since RS-4. For reasons never explained Struck had been shipped somewhere else. Wait a minute, what was that uniform Struck was wearing? It was army instead of a marine, and bore the flashes of a captain, along with the crossed daggers of military intelligence.

Struck smiled and stuck out a huge right hand. "Hello Colonel. Long time no see."

Kilgor stood and shook the other man's hand. "Why do I have the feeling that I've been snookered?"

"Because you were," Struck said cheerfully. "General Kelly put me inside to track your progress."

Kelly nodded her agreement. "In spite of appearances to the contrary, Arista values good officers."

Kelly turned to Struck. "Captain, define 'good officers.' "

Struck smiled. "Yes mam. A 'good officer' is any officer that kills a lot of bugs."

Kelly nodded her satisfaction and turned back to Kilgor. "Damned right. And, since you killed a lot of bugs, I put Struck in there to keep an eye on you."

Kilgor remembered the evening when Struck had stood up to defend him. "I owe you one, Captain."

Struck shrugged. "I meant everything I said. The problem was that the General here forgot to pull me out until the last moment."

"He needed to lose a few pounds," Kelly responded loftily. "By the way, Struck monitored your behavior in here as well, so he's something of an expert on Ras Kilgor."

"You've got agents in here?" Kilgor asked. He'd expected a stoolie or two, but MI agents?

Kelly raised an eyebrow. "Of course. It's my job to know what's going on in this woman's army. That's how we weed out the really sadistic guards and incompetent commandants."

"Some of them, anyway," Struck put in sarcastically.

Kelly ignored him. "The point is, we thought you might come in handy someday. Now we need an answer to the following question: Has prison turned you bitter? If so, then you aren't worth a damn to me or anyone else."

Kelly, turned to Struck. "Well, Captain . . . what's the verdict? Is Kilgor worth a damn or not?"

Struck frowned. "That depends, General. I wouldn't describe Kilgor as bitter, but there's little doubt that he considered himself innocent, and bears the system a grudge."

Kelly laughed. "Not too surprising all things considered. The question is, can he command?"

Struck chuckled. "Can and does. He *runs* this prison. Kilgor could turn it upside down and inside out if he wanted to."

Kelly rubbed her stump. "Then why doesn't he?"

Struck shrugged. "This is only a guess mind you, but I suspect Kilgor has morals, a rather heavy burden for someone in his position."

Kelly smiled. "Is that right Kilgor? Have you got morals?"

Kilgor shifted his weight from one foot to the other. "There's some things I won't do . . . yes."

Kelly turned to Struck. "Would you follow Kilgor into battle?"

Struck looked at Kilgor and back to Kelly. "Any time, any place."

Kelly nodded, and reached into the side pocket of her camo jacket. She pulled out a small black box and tossed it Kilgor's way. "Welcome back, Colonel . . . we need your help."

Kilgor caught the box and lifted the lid. The comets glittered gold.

"They're yours," Kelly said, "the same ones Wanto ripped off your uniform. I kept them for you."

Kilgor's throat felt tight. He tried to speak but found he couldn't. Kelly understood and continued to speak.

"That's the good news. The bad news is that I can't give you a line unit. I pulled some G's at what's left of HQ, but not enough to restore your rank *and* your old unit. Nope, the truth is that if we weren't standing up to our belt buckles in bug poop, you'd be here for good."

Kilgor smiled. "That's okay General, I understand. So what's available?"

Kelly looked at Struck and they both laughed. It was Struck who answered. "Why, the Brig Rats, what else?"

Kilgor learned some interesting things during the next few days. The first time was that Kelly had been planning to "reactivate" military prisoners for some time. She'd seen the pattern of bug victories, understood what was coming, and made contingency plans. Military prisoners were only one aspect of those plans. It was through Kelly's foresight and long range planning that Arista had sufficient weapons to arm the civilian population.

The second thing Kilgor learned was his mission. The Brig Rats, formally designated as the First Battalion, Third Marines, would occupy and hold a partially completed orbital weapons platform known as Defender Seven. In Kelly's words, "Defender Seven was part of the friction, the resistance designed to slow the Hothri down, and give us a chance on the ground."

Defender Seven, along with three similar platforms and the two surviving moons, was to absorb the initial shock of the bug assault and hold as long as it possibly could. In the meantime, Kelly's ground forces, including the entire civilian population of Arista, would prepare a warm reception.

It was the perfect assignment for military prisoners. It would keep them away from Arista's regular troops, limit their chances of escape, and foreclose the possibility of retreat. If they won, so much the better, if they lost, so what?

It was a tough mission, but one Kilgor's marine and naval personnel were reasonably well trained for. It was also preferable to rotting in prison. Or so Kilgor assumed.

The third thing Kilgor learned was that taking control

from within, and taking command from without, were two different things.

As a prisoner, he'd been one of them, suffered the same indignities, opposed the same rules.

But the moment Kilgor reverted to officer status, he lost the credibility that went with being a Brig Rat and became an authority figure again.

Kilgor got his first glimpse of the problem when he summoned his original group of Brig Rats to give them the news.

Although word was out that something was going on, the prisoners didn't know what, and Kilgor wanted to keep it that way as long as he could.

Before destroying one social structure, he'd have to create another, and that's where his cronies came in. Given the fact that Kilgor had days rather than months to organize a full fledged battalion, there wasn't enough time to promote on merit. By turning his original cadre of Brig Rats into company commanders, Kilgor hoped to get a head start on pulling the outfit together. That was the theory anyway. The reality was something else.

Having gotten his hands on some camos to go with the comets, and commandeered a conference room just down the corridor from Kelly's office, Kilgor waited for the Brig Rats to file in. It was silly, but he looked forward to watching their faces as they took in his uniform, and the comets on his shoulders.

And then there was Susan. Would it still be there? The feeling that had existed between them? Or had it vanished, a victim of prison life?

Wires entered first, followed by Freese, Red, Bugs, and finally, Susan.

Kilgor drank her in, searched her face for clues that she was okay, signs that she felt the same joy he did. And the signs were there, in the warmth of her eyes, and the smile on her face.

Then the feelings were gone, stashed away like civilian clothes to be used when the time was right, submerged under a thousand years of military tradition.

Wires was the first to react. "Holy Sol! The bird of paradise took a shit on the boss's shoulders!"

Then came a confused babble of voices as everyone tried to speak at once. Kilgor held up a hand for silence. "Whoa! Hold on! Let me explain."

So they did, and by the time Kilgor was finished, most were scowling. Red was first to speak.

"You gotta be kidding boss . . . it sounds like a suicide mission to me. What's in it for us?"

Kilgor knew better than to talk about concepts like "freedom," and "independence," so he kept to the basics.

"The answer's simple, Red. Volunteer and you're back in the crotch, full pay, clean record."

"Big deal," Freese put in disgustedly. "I thought you were different Kilgor, a regular guy, but now I see you're like all the rest. Pure brass through and through. They screw you, throw you some comets, and you come running. It makes me sick."

Kilgor saw Susan start to say something but gave a tiny shake of his head. Anything she could say wouldn't be enough and might come back to haunt her. He was losing them pure and simple. Well, there were others, men and women less cynical or more eager to escape the brig.

Kilgor took a deep breath and got ready to send them away, when help came from an unexpected source . . . Bugs.

Bugs shook his head in disgust. "Freese . . . you ain't got the brains God gave corporals. Why not listen for a change? This ain't about us and them, it's about the friggin bugs killin' every damn thing on this planet, and using your momma's backyard to hatch their eggs.

"Now I don't know about you poop for brains, but I'd rather meet the bugs with a gun in my hands, than sittin' here in the brig waitin' to fry. I say we sign on and grease the bugs before they grease us."

No one seemed to have a ready reply, or if they did, the guts to deliver it in the face of Bugs' truculence. Although aware of Bugs's history, and the fact that he enjoyed killing Hothri, Kilgor was not about to question this unexpected support. He looked around the room.

"I think Bugs summed it up rather well. So, unless someone wants to wait for the bugs locked inside a cell, welcome to the First Battalion, Third Marines. From now on, each one of you holds the rank of Captain."

"Captain?" Red said enthusiastically. "No kidding? Hey this ain't so bad after all!"

"Oh really?" Wires asked sarcastically. "And what if someone puts an A-6 demo-pack under *your* bunk?"

Red made a rude gesture in her direction and Wires laughed.

Suddenly Kilgor had the support he needed. Susan smiled and he smiled back. Both were thinking the same thing. No matter what happened they'd deal with it together.

Defender Seven was shaped like a pie from which a single piece had been eaten. The platform was big, about a mile across, and its reflectorized surface rippled with light. During the initial stages of a battle, the platform's shiny hull would reflect laser based energy weapons.

Knowing that, the bugs would use missiles instead, which explained why Defender Seven's architects had specified so many anti-missile batteries. Unfortunately, thirty-two percent of them were nothing more than gaping black holes. Everything was in short supply.

Kilgor grimaced as the navy shuttle skimmed low and slow over the platform's hull. Army officers didn't get much training on the fine points of orbital warfare, but he was learning fast.

"You want another run, Colonel?"

The navy pilot was young, right out of advanced combat school, and cocky as hell. Defender Seven had only twelve of the thirty-six aero-space fighters it was entitled to, plus a couple of beat-up shuttles.

"Yeah," Kilgor responded. "Give me another run."

"Yes, sir."

The pilot put the shuttle into a tight turn and headed back across the upper surface of Defender Seven's hull.

Kilgor looked down into the black wedge where ten percent of the platform's hull was missing and saw pinpoints of light wink on and off as construction crews continued their work.

They'd never make it in time. According to Kelly, the Hothri fleet was already on its way.

That meant a ten percent hole in the platform's defensive weaponry, and if you drew straight lines out from the missing wedge, a regular highway for incoming bugs.

Once the battle began, their computers would take all of five or ten seconds to identify the dead spot and re-direct their forces to that approach. Kilgor made a mental note to do something about that.

On the plus side, Defender Seven was brand new, and

relatively undamaged from previous Hothri raids. Since the platform had been unarmed and offered no resistance, the Hothri left it pretty much alone.

According to the portacomp strapped to Kilgor's thigh, the platform had taken two missiles, one of which caused damage to six percent of Defender Seven's hull, while the other failed to go off at all. The damage had been repaired more than a week before.

That was the good news. Most of the rest was bad. Due to wartime shortages, the fortress was fifty-one percent short on long range energy weapons, eighty-seven percent short on missiles for what launchers it had, and well, the list went on and on.

The shuttle banked, turned, and skimmed "under" the platform's hull. Of course "up" and "down" don't mean much in space, but because Arista filled the viewscreens with her blue-white beauty, Kilgor thought of that direction as "down."

Up ahead, Kilgor saw hundreds of reflectorized balls hanging down from Defender Seven's hull, each connected by a temporary tether. He grinned. Here at least was something he had too many of.

Through some gigantic screw-up, the idiots in supply had sent him 423 remote energy projectors instead of the 125 he actually rated.

Once freed from their tethers, the REP's could propel themselves up to twenty miles out, where they would keep station on Defender Seven and provide defensive fire. Needless to say, Kilgor had no intention of giving the REP's away. He turned to the pilot.

"Home, James. I've seen enough."

The pilot, whose name really was "James," grinned. He goosed the shuttle's drives and scooted for the main lock. He'd be glad to dump the brass and grab some rack time.

Kilgor watched main entry port grow larger and felt a rock grow in his gut. As of yesterday there were 1467 convicted murderers, thieves, arsonists, and worse aboard Defender Seven.

Al of them, including the swabbies, were armed with full marine kit, including Zitter blast rifles, Smith 10mm slug guns, combat knives, and battle axes.

In addition there were crew-served weapons, rocket

launchers, a wide array of explosives, and just about every other weapon you could think of.

On the recommendation of his staff, Wires, Red, Freese, Bugs, and Susan, Kilgor had neglected to issue his troops any ammunition until now. As a matter of fact, live ammo was being issued right about now, and there was the possibility that he might step out of the main entry lock and into a full blown mutiny.

Would the Brig Rats stand by Arista? Would they follow his orders? Would they fight? His company commanders thought so . . . but nobody knew for sure.

The way things stood, Kilgor had 520 navy personnel to operate the platform's life support systems, heavy weapons, and twelve aerospace fighters. In fact, the pilots were the only people aboard *not* convicted of some crime.

Wires was in charge of communications, a one time CPO named Dolby was in charge of the platform's heavy weapons, and a cashiered Commander by the name of Stein was head of engineering.

They also had a manic-depressive medical officer named Potter, who, along with Susan, headed up the medical department.

There were 947 marines which Kilgor had divided up into three companies, each comprised of three one-hundred person platoons, plus a headquarters group consisting of forty-five technicians.

Red, Freese, and Bugs commanded a company each. Kilgor had noticed that their choices of lieutenants, sergeants, and corporals were not always the same ones he'd make, but there was no time to second guess them. They were either right or wrong. Time, and contact with the Hothri would tell.

The pilot came in too fast, fired his retros a hair too late, and hit hard. Kilgor gave him a dirty look and James blushed.

Damn it. The story would make the rounds and he'd catch hell from the other pilots.

The lock irised open, Kilgor stepped through, and heard the unfamiliar twittering of bosun's pipes. There was Wires, standing at attention, along with a side party of spotless marines. He knew many of them from prison.

Though no expert on naval tradition, Kilgor recognized this as the traditional ceremony welcoming a commanding officer aboard his or her vessel, and something more as well. His staff was letting him know that they had things under control.

Not only that, but the bulkhead just opposite the entry port bore a colorful, and completely unauthorized emblem. It was a large gray rat. The rat had ruby red eyes, a long pointy tail, and a lightning bolt clutched between long sharp teeth. Above the rat were the words, "First Battalion, Third Marines," and below it was the motto, "Touch Me If You Dare."

Kilgor made a production of inspecting the emblem. He could feel the tension build. What would the old man do? Would he freak out? Put the whole outfit on report? Most, if not all of the side party had served under officers who would do just that.

Kilgor turned to Captain Wires. He returned her salute. By common agreement the original Brig Rats still used their nicknames. They claimed it helped morale, and Kilgor had bowed to their judgement.

"An outstanding emblem Captain. Quite fitting, and well executed. My compliments to the artist. Please complete the forms required to make it official. Carry on." And with that Kilgor strode down the corridor.

Behind him Wires dismissed the side party, and they hurried off to tell all their friends. "The old man liked the emblem! He told Wires to file papers on it! I told you the sonovabitch was okay!"

And with that action, approved or not, the battalion forever known as the "Brig Rats" came into being.

The Hothri arrived thirty-seven hours later. There was nothing clever or subtle about their approach. Somewhere in their complicated social structure a decision had been made to take Arista, and take it they would, or die trying.

This time there would be no feints, no tricky maneuvers, just an all-out assault. Hundreds of ships would throw themselves at the less numerous human navy until the planet lay bare and ready for invasion.

Then wave after wave of troop ships would drop into orbit. Quickly their bellies would open to scatter thousands of egg-shaped landers across Arista's surface, each a durasteel seed, packed with alien life.

After that, the cleansing would begin. Where the Hothri

lay their eggs no threat could be allowed. Each and every human must die. So it had been, and so it must always be.

Kilgor forced himself to sip a cup of coffee. Outwardly he was calm and relaxed, but inside he churned with doubt. The bugs were coming, the detectors' screens were filled with them, but Defender Seven was far from ready. List after list of things undone crowded Kilgor's mind and fought for his attention.

The com tech's voice was calm. "Initial contact, five and counting."

Right. Deal with things as they are. Five and counting. Kilgor looked around. He would fight the first part of the battle from here, Command Center One, buried deep in Defender Seven's armored core.

Later, unless things went very well indeed, he would fight in the corridors themselves. Like every other man and woman aboard, Kilgor wore full space armor, and a full complement of personal weapons.

Command Center One was a circular room with six major exits. Each exit corresponded to one of the six major corridors which radiated out to the platform's perimeter.

Kilgor's command chair was equipped with four small repeater screens, powered so he could rotate a full 360 degrees, and capable of self-sustained operation for a full eight hours after fusion reaction shut-down.

From his position on a raised dais at the center of the room, Kilgor could see each of Defender Seven's forty-eight positions, and call up their screens at the touch of a button.

"Initial contact, four and counting."

Kilgor touched a button. A graphic representation of the bug attack force appeared on screen one. There were hundreds of red Hothri squares and only a scattering of green dots.

Kilgor winced as an entire clutch of green dots disappeared along with hundreds of human lives. The navy was suffering horribly. But they'd bought some time, a few priceless hours during which those on the ground could prepare and thousands of lives might be saved. And that was his mission as well, to buy Arista some time, and make the bugs pay.

"Initial contact, three and counting."

Kilgor put the coffee down and hoped no one saw his hand shake. He touched a button and sick bay appeared on screen four. Susan was there, working shoulder to shoulder with the other medical personnel, barely recognizable in her bulky armor.

Unaware of Kilgor's scrutiny she said something to the woman next to her and turned away. Kilgor bit his lip and wondered if they'd see each other again.

"Initial contact, two and counting."

Kilgor touched another button. Lieutenant James appeared on screen two. He was strapped into his aerospace fighter and awaiting launch. He looked very young. Aware of Kilgor's presence he gave a thumbs up.

"Take care of this tub Colonel. We'll need something to land on."

Kilgor smiled. "We'll be here Lieutenant. Burn some bugs for me."

"Initial contact, one and counting."

Kilgor switched away knowing James would launch thirty seconds later. The fighters were cutting it close but doing what they could to conserve on fuel.

A voice came over his headset. It belonged to Stein. "Engineering, sir. Screens at max. All systems green."

The next voice was unfamiliar. It belonged to Dr. Potter. He'd only heard it once or twice before. "Medical. We're here."

Then came Wires. "Communications, sir. All systems go."

Bugs followed. "Companies one, two, and three, in position and ready, sir."

Dolby was close behind. "Weapons, sir. Permission to fire."

Kilgor swallowed. "Thank you guns. Permission granted. Good luck everyone."

"We have enemy contact," the com tech droned, and the battle for Defender Seven began.

Lieutenant James fought heavy G's as his fighter flashed out and away from Defender Seven. The other fighters were behind him, eleven delta-shaped dealers of death, outnumbered and out-gunned.

Long thin fingers of blue light reached out to kill James, but he rolled right and slid in between them.

Missiles slithered from alien launch tubes, accelerated away, and sought the heat of his drives.

James laughed hysterically, launched missiles of his own, and watched them blossom left and right.

There, up ahead, a Hothri battleship, light stuttering from a hundred projectors, blotting out the stars beyond.

James centered his cross hairs in the middle of the Hothri hull, sent the picture to both of his torpedos, and fired.

Both hit the ship's defensive screen at the same time and went off in perfect unison. The energy released by the explosion drove the force field inward until it touched the alien hull. The battleship disappeared a fraction of a second later, quickly followed by James and his tiny fighter.

Kilgor saw but had no time to grieve. Dozens of Hothri fighters were swarming in towards the platform. Knowing their energy cannon wouldn't even scratch the platform's reflectorized hull, the bugs used torpedos instead, firing them in waves.

The force field held, but grew brighter and brighter, as it neared overload.

In the meantime Defender Seven fought back. Energy projectors reached out to destroy Hothri fighters with computerized efficiency. Missile after missile reached out, some intercepted, some intercepting.

Then, just as Kilgor had feared, the bugs located the wedge-shaped dead spot in the platform's defensive armament and vectored in.

Kilgor eyed his screens and touched a button. "Guns . . . Kilgor here. It's time to give the bugs our little surprise."

A hundred yards away in the fire control center, Dolby's ferret like face broke into a big grin, and his fist slammed down on a square of plastic. Dolby liked to kill things, aliens included.

Miles away, spread out along imaginary lines extending outwards from the unfinished section of hull, hundreds of remote energy projectors came to sudden life. Thanks to Wires and the jury rigged computer network she'd designed, each one of the REP's was slaved to Defender Seven's main battle computer.

Operating in synchronization, the projectors burped coherent light. Suddenly, the previously safe approach vector was transformed into a trap and the Hothri fighters exploded one after the other until none were left.

As soon as the last one was destroyed the REP's were repositioned to defend the platform's entire perimeter.

Kilgor took a quick electronic look around. The other defense platforms along with Arista's two surviving moon bases, were still in the fight. Much to his surprise twelve hours had elapsed since initial contact, twelve hours of preparation on the ground, twelve hours of additional life.

Kilgor took a tour of Defender Seven. He walked the corridors, inspected damage, and sympathized with his troops. He made sure a meal was served, sorted out logistical problems, and sent a report to Arista HQ. Kilgor doubted anyone would have time to read it, but what the hell, maybe a computer would absorb and make use of it.

Finally Kilgor returned to his quarters, took a quick shower, and collapsed on his bed. Two seconds later he was asleep.

It seemed like moments later when the intercom bonged over Kilgor's head. "Good morning, boss," Wires said cheerfully. "Time to rise and shine. The heavy stuff is on the way."

Kilgor rolled out of bed, slid into a fresh uniform, and donned his space armor. A few minutes later he entered the command center, accepted a cup of coffee from one of the technicians, and scanned the screens.

Wires was right. A wave of Hothri cruisers was in-bound for Arista. Their huge energy cannons reached out to pop the remote energy projectors like toy balloons. Minutes later they were through the cordon of REP's and coming in. The bugs were hosers, relying more on brute strength than finesse, and it was an unequal battle. Little by little Defender Seven began to die.

Explosions blossomed, artificial lightning flashed, and Kilgor floated on a sea of numbers, vectors and ratios. The entire hull shook under the massed impact of cruiser launched torpedos. A Klaxon started to bleat. A voice over-rode all the rest.

"Stein here. We lost the force field, sir. We're taking missile hits. Sorry, sir."

"Understood," Kilgor replied. "Shift all available power to our defensive armament. Guns . . . evacuate the projector emplacements. Dump the limiters. Give the bugs everything we've got."

Ensconced in the fire control center, Dolby grabbed his paunch and shifted it to a more comfortable position. He waved a lit and completely unauthorized cigar at a nearby gunner's mate. "Well, you heard the man, son. As soon as the crews are clear, dump the limiters, and red-line the projectors."

Coherent light rippled out from Defender Seven and a Hothri cruiser died. Then another, and another. With almost all of the platform's power to draw on, and operating way over spec, the projectors were punching holes through the Hothri fields.

Minutes stretched into hours before the inevitable happened. Defender Seven shook and rumbled as an overheated projector blew up.

Kilgor waited as long as he dared then pushed a button. "Nice shooting, guns . . . shut 'em down."

A quick check of Kilgor's screens showed that they'd earned another respite. Surprised by the destruction of their cruisers, and heavily engaged elsewhere, the bugs had given them a momentary break.

Kilgor took a video tour of his command. The flight deck was empty. By now all of the fighters would be low on fuel, but not one had returned. A quick check with fire control confirmed his suspicions. All of his fighters had been destroyed. Nevertheless the twelve pilots had taken eighteen Hothri ships with them.

Sick bay was organized chaos. Dr. Potter, Susan, and their team of medics were sorting the wounded according to the severity of their injuries and treating them in that order.

Zooming in, Kilgor saw Susan rip armor away from a woman's chest, and grab a dressing. Blood spurted upwards with each breath she took. Rolling the woman onto her wounded side, Susan applied a self-sealing dressing and taped it down.

Susan looked beautiful even with blood spattered across her armor and, he wanted to touch her. And then, just as Kilgor prepared to switch away she looked up, saw Kilgor's image on a monitor and waved.

Kilgor waved in return and forced himself to touch another button. Everywhere Kilgor looked he saw damage. Fires raged here and there, compartments were filled with smoke, burned out missile launchers hung useless in their bays, bodies lay in hallways, and some of the corridors were open to space.

But to his surprise, and immense pride, Kilgor saw other

things as well. Marines waiting for their turn in the fray, navy personnel struggling to keep damaged systems up and running, faces grinning through darkened visors, thumbs turned upwards, and individual acts of unbelievable heroism.

Kilgor took another tour of his command. This time it took longer. Entire sections were depressurized, the dead and wounded were everywhere, and there were endless problems to solve. He was down in life-support listening to their problems when Wires came over his ear plug.

"Here come the heavies boss . . . we're gonna take another pounding."

Ten minutes later Kilgor was in his command chair. He looked at Wires on the far side of the control room. She looked unconcerned, every hair of her black pageboy precisely in place, more officer than most he'd graduated with. Wires waved, and Kilgor raised his just-filled coffee cup in mock salute.

He checked the time. More than two days gained, each day packed with twenty-one wonderful hours, each hour red with blood.

"Thank you, Captain Wires. Prepare phase two."

Kilgor closed his visor, checked the seal, and activated his suit. He knew that elsewhere, every single person on Defender Seven, wounded included, was doing likewise. Verbal orders were avoided in case the bugs could hear.

It wasn't likely, but the aliens were damned close, and no one really knew what their equipment could and couldn't do.

Kilgor bit his lip as the Hothri battleships approached. There weren't that many of them, but each was big and extremely powerful. Behind them were thousands of transports each one packed with Hothri warriors. The Brig Rats might not stop them, but if things worked as planned, they'd thin 'em out and slow 'em down.

Wires was back. "Phase two's ready, sir. Standing by."

Kilgor crossed his fingers. "Thank you, Captain. Implement phase two."

It was the order that Dolby and Stein had been waiting for. Dolby flicked a switch and a series of explosions marched across the upper surface of Defender Seven's hull, culminating in a flash of brilliant light.

In the meantime Stein's blunt fingers danced over a keyboard and caused the platform to vent a tremendous amount of heat. Enough heat to simulate a sizeable explosion.

Elsewhere across the ship weapons fell silent, radars went dead, radios clicked off, sensors powered down, and locks cycled open to space.

It was a trick, a rather old trick at that, but one which the Hothri might fall for. The hull explosions had been real enough, all arranged by Red, but were directed outwards to cause as little damage as possible.

Kilgor hoped that the explosions, along with the heat loss, and the cessation of electronic activity would fool the bugs into believing that Defender Seven was dead. If the trick worked, the Hothri would get a nasty surprise. If it didn't, the Brig Rats wouldn't be around to worry about it, and bugs would roll on by.

Kilgor had nothing to go on except for a few low powered detectors. What he saw made him squirm and grit his teeth. The Hothri battle wagons were well within range now. Were they falling for it? Or simply waiting 'til they couldn't miss?

Light flared as the lead ship punched a hole through the platform's hull. The energy beam came so close to Freese's grunts that it momentarily warmed the deck under their feet.

Kilgor held his breath waiting for the waves of missiles, the jagged spears of alien light, but nothing happened. Then he understood. The bugs had prodded Defender Seven the same way a human might poke the body of a rabid dog.

Was it dead or just pretending? Well, there was no reaction, so most if not all the humans were dead. Now to make absolutely sure. Kilgor imagined a Hothri admiral detailing a transport to check things out.

And sure enough, as the battlewagons began to exchange blows with the heavily fortified missile batteries on Arista's surface, two transports peeled off from the Hothri fleet and approached Defender Seven.

Kilgor swallowed hard. Two! Holy Sol, one would've been challenge enough, two was damned near impossible. How many bugs did those things hold anyway? At least a thousand. That meant something like two-thousand bugs altogether, or odds of two to one, which was more than anything Kilgor had anticipated. Of course the swabbies would fight, too. That would even things a little.

Kilgor decided to take a chance. He chinned a button and spoke into his throat mic. "All right, Rats. You know the plan. Avoid contact until I give the word. Then grease 'em. Good hunting and good luck.''

Then came a long wait. The bugs were cautious. Hours passed. They sent out scouts, big things which moved with slow deliberation and wore body armor which echoed the insectoid lines of their bodies.

Kilgor could see the tanks on their backs and knew the aliens were breathing oxygen mixed with a trace of methane. If the Hothri managed to conquer Arista, everyone assumed that they'd introduce methane into the planet's atmosphere, both to make themselves comfortable and kill off the human engineered ecosystem. Relentless, implacable, ruthless. All were words that described the bugs.

The Hothri scouts signalled the ''all clear'' and more bugs came on board. Hundreds of them. Kilgor watched via the tiny low powered surveillance cameras which Wires had installed in all the main corridors. The bugs filled the main entry locks and pushed out from there.

Timing was everything now. If Kilgor moved too soon a substantial number of Hothri would be left outside, and if he acted too late, they'd run right into his troops.

Finally, when Kilgor estimated that the Hothri were no more than fifty yards from Red's troops, he opened the command channel and yelled ''now!''

A lot of things happened at once. Every lock aboard Defender Seven irised closed and welded itself shut.

Stein turned on the lights, and more importantly the heat, making it harder for the Hothri to use their infrared vision.

Wires flipped a switch and filled the corridors with random radar and sonar signals designed to jam, or at least hinder, the bugs built-in motion detectors.

And, with those things accomplished, Dolby fed power to the remaining energy cannon, and blew both of the Hothri transports into their component atoms.

The bugs could still attack them of course, but it would cost two-thousand of their own troops, and Kilgor hoped even the bugs would bulk at that. Apparently they did balk because no attack was immediately forthcoming. He chinned the command channel as he released his harness.

''Red, Freese, Bugs, it's party time, and our guests have arrived. Let's show 'em a good time.''

Marines opened fire all over the ship. The bugs died in droves at first. Surprised, confused by sensory jamming, and locked inside a durasteel combat zone, the Hothri took incredible casualties.

But the bugs were tough, and it wasn't long before they managed to regroup and launch a spirited counterattack.

What ensued was some of the worst fighting in the Hothri-human war. The battle for Defender Seven lasted for two full rotations, a bloody cat and mouse game played inside a metal cage, in which no quarter was given or asked.

The bugs were determined fighters and outnumbered the Brig Rats nearly two to one. They knew they were locked inside Defender Seven and gloried in it. They would win, and a thousand annums from now the poets would still praise their valor.

But humans had some advantages too. For one thing they were, as Wires put it, "rats in a trap," with nowhere else to go. But they were something else as well, they were proud, and determined to hold what no one thought they could.

But there was something else too, an advantage no one thought of until later, something which eventually turned the tide. The Brig Rats weren't normal. Most were psychopaths, homicidal maniacs, sociopaths, thieves, perverts, and worse.

The Brig Rats killed without compunction, without hesitation, and without mercy. Like Bugs, many of the humans enjoyed the violence and revelled in the opportunity to express their twisted psyches.

This give the Brig Rats something close to berserker status, and generated powerful emotions as well, emotions which rolled over the Hothri like waves of darkness.

Locked in a durasteel trap and besieged by human emotions the like of which they'd never encountered before, the Hothri gave in to despair.

Eventually the Hothri broke. By ones, twos and threes they ran, blasting their way through welded locks, spilling out through holes in the platform's hull, shooting each other in their haste to get away.

Finally, after the last Hothri had been killed, Kilgor stumbled down a hall. Stein was dead, as were Red, and Freese, but thanks to the second engineer, the corridor had been pressurized.

Elsewhere, Dolby was still taking potshots at Hothri

ships, Bugs had started a new finger collection, and Wires was in contact with Arista HQ.

Together with the other defense platforms and the moon bases, Defender Seven had delayed the Hothri for more than five days. It would be two more before the aliens landed in force. As Kilgor continued down the passageway he hoped it was enough.

Bodies lay everywhere, human and Hothri alike. The bulkheads were scorched, pocked, and smeared with blood. The butcher's bill was high, at least four hundred Brig Rats killed or wounded, but it could've been worse. Much worse.

Up ahead Kilgor saw a pile of bodies where the Hothri had attempted to take the sick bay and been repulsed by medics and walking wounded.

Was Susan somewhere in that pile? Her eyes empty of all life? Another name for his list of casualties?

Kilgor groaned as he tripped and fell against the bulkhead. There were two fingers missing from his right hand. His suit had pumped him full of drugs and blood volume expanders, but the effects were wearing off.

Then Kilgor was there, stepping over the bodies, praying he wouldn't see Susan's among them. Wait a minute, no, the face belonged to someone else.

Suddenly Susan was there, holding him up, pulling the visor up and away. She saw the stumps and called for help.

Hands grabbed Kilgor and lifted. Machinery hummed, needles slid through skin, and voices droned medical terminology.

Kilgor felt strangely light, as if he might float up and away but knew he couldn't. That would be deserting his post, running, fleeing in the face of the enemy.

Outside the battle for Arista still raged, but Kilgor looked up into calm gray eyes and smiled. His world was won.

# Hothri Tactics
## by Bill Fawcett

It should always be remembered that the Hothri are individuals with a high sense of group consciousness. This results in a strange combination of self-sacrifice and reluctant attack. The group awareness of the Hothri, when engaged, makes it difficult for them to accept casualties. Still, when fighting as individuals, the Hothri warriors are nearly fearless. They know they are part of a greater whole as they often can literally sense it. The result is a much lower regard for individuality as displayed by their near suicide courage. From the Hothri perspective the Aristan defenders are poorly organized and easily dispersed.

Another major factor that determines Hothri tactics is the instinctive need to protect their nesting areas, a result of the defenseless nature exhibited by the lover and mother sexes. The defense of the members of these sexes is mandated and pervades all Hothri behavior. The practical result of this instinctive pattern is that the Hothri are unable to leave any enemy contained behind their lines. All threats must be completely eliminated before continuing forward. This necessity takes priority over even primary space and land combat objectives.

Generally, the Hothri prefer sweeps and often assume formations more reminiscent of the Napoleonic Wars than modern combat. Their linear formations would do any 19th century Prussian general proud. In close combat they tend to attack or retreat in groups, carrying away their wounded whenever possible. When outnumbered the Hothri invariably seek out the most easily defended position and concentrate all of their forces there. Even more numerous human forces can find cornered Hothri units difficult opponents.

The Hothri rarely surrender. If they do it is almost invariably because they are defending mothers. In space, a small number of mothers and lovers accompany the fleet, but they stay far away from battle and remain under heavy escort. Feints that threaten their formation, even by light units, are always met with massive force, even if these forces have to be withdrawn from combat elsewhere.

Many of the early space battles followed a similar pattern: The Hothri appeared in large numbers and accepted casualties to neutralize any ships defending the base; then dropped large numbers in areas too distant for the enemies main defenses to affect the landings. These forces would scour the countryside, killing all humans encountered, until they could form a ring around the remaining defenders. Bombardment from space softened the final positions which were finally and methodically overrun.

Ships fleeing these battles are rarely pursued once they have definitely left the contested system. Some speculate that these tactics reflect the Hothri mandate to accumulate secure breeding grounds. Often the Hothri contaminate (by human standards) the atmosphere of any captured planet with quantities of methane. The most important result of the Hothri tactics is that it allows them to use their superior numbers to ensure any captured world is totally secure. This then allows the insectoids to concentrate most of their forces on the forward area, as was quickly becoming the situation over Arista itself.

# SUSPECT TERRAIN
## by Elizabeth Moon

MORNING LIGHT poured between the peaks, pummeling the mist hanging over the creek until it gave up and floated away in tatters. The air smelled of spicewood and hawberry, deep leaf-mold under the trees, fresh-broken rock where a slide had come down almost to the pasture level. Armitage lay back against cool wet grass, careless of the chill, and let his eyes rove the brightening sky. Maybe he'd see a reiver a-wing, even this early, hunting the slopes. The ground beneath him trembled . . . hoofbeats? He raised his head, looking for the horses and saw a line of them coming at a gallop, all tossing heads and hooves, manes flying wildly, great round bodies red and brown and bright gold. . . .

It was dark, and cold, and the air in his helmet stank of death. What shook the ground were brilliant flashes of violent light, too bright for vision, and then too dark afterward. His head ached savagely, he could not tell whether from the bad air or a blow. Had he slept or been knocked lopsided?

He reached out to either side and felt only the slimy sides of the hole. It must have been raining again. Armitage did not let himself remember rain falling on the green pastures where his father's draft horses had grazed. That was gone, wiped out, never to return, and if in some other place clean rain fell on green grass, it was for someone else, not for him. His world was here, wherever this was . . . he would remember, in just a bit, if he lived that long.

He did remember the war. He remembered the Hothri, who had violated someone's biological rule (he had never had the chance to learn what it was, only that it existed) about the maximum size of insectoids, and had also violated, in the process, some considerable number of rules and laws and planets and systems. They didn't like bright light, cool rain falling on green grass, big gentle drafters who ate lumps of beetroot and carrot out of your hand . . . but he wouldn't think about that.

Automatically, his hands found his weapons, and felt their way around the controls. As his fingers caught on the knobs and twirls that gave him control even with gloves, his mind cleared a bit more. The troopship, on its way . . . but he couldn't remember where from or to, if they'd even been told . . . the attack that broke up their convoy, which they'd known only by being slammed from side to side in the webs . . . the forced landing that left them somewhere . . .

It had to be Arista, because the gravity felt right, and he remembered that they'd been in suborbital transports, not deepspace. Yet the barren expanse of potholed mud and shattered rock had none of the amenities of a habitable planet. Except mud, which somehow the universe seemed to supply whenever and wherever a war was going on. The bit of his mind that remembered his father's library managed a wry chuckle at that, but the chuckle didn't make it to his mouth.

Another brilliant flash of violet-white threw his shadow onto the mud before him. The cold ground shook around his suited legs; he was massaged by the dying rumble of the explosion. He couldn't see anything useful before the light was gone, and the broad-scan sensors that should have been in his helmet, with replay facility for just such times, had gone out days ago. So had the suit radios. So had half the fancy junk that was supposed to make him able to go one-on-three with Hothri in their own ships.

With the next flash of light, he remembered that he was supposed to be anchoring the end of a defensive line. The Hothri had tried an assault landing—that's why they'd been hopped around the planet's curve. They were to counterattack, wherever it was—somewhere he'd never seen. Now, with the troopship blown, the colonel had said they'd try to set up somewhere, with the light artillery they'd taken off the ship, blow the Hothri that came after them. "Stupid idea," his sergeant had muttered. "But there aren't any smart ideas left. Gonna die, men, no use fretting about it. Nobody's coming out here to rescue us, not with the war going on where it matters."

Armitage had wanted to say, "We matter, too." But knew

that was nonsense. His D.I. had always said they were born to die, and so far his D.I. had been right all the way.

Armitage managed to tongue the right control in his helmet and got a warm mouthful of obviously recycled water. It tasted like the air smelled, and the ration chunk he got next wasn't much better. These combat suits weren't supposed to be good for much more than 48 hours, although they'd tanked up with enough air for lots longer. How much longer he wasn't sure, but the glowing control—one of the few telltales still working—was green. he checked his weapons controls again. He had ammunition, if only he could see a target. But he saw nothing move in the flashes of light that seared his eyes, nothing that looked like a Hothri ship or Hothri themselves.

The slap on his back brought a scream to his mouth before he could choke it off. He tried to whirl, staggered in the mud, and nearly fell. In the next flash he knew the shape of the suit was human. A helmet clanked against his, and a distorted voice said "Pull back—come on!" The heavy powered gauntlet of the other's suit grasped his arm and tugged. It was—it had better be—Garamond, the corporal. He felt someone else bump into him and slide into the hole he'd just vacated.

With the voice, with an order to follow, his mind abruptly recovered itself. They had, in fact, kept the Hothri busy; he remembered now that the bugs had a reputation for being unwilling to leave live enemies behind. While the Aristans couldn't quite surround the Hothri ground forces, the Hothri had chosen to stand and fight when they had every chance to disengage and do more damage elsewhere. For eight days, now, they had fought, and for eight days the Hothri transports had dared their meager but accurate artillery to land more troops. They had destroyed one transport before it landed, and cheered when it crashed and exploded. Two others had been disabled after landing with casualties. Many Hothri—how many Armitage had no idea, for they seemed to come in endless streams or waves when they attacked, and when they fell, their angular bodies collapsed in irregular heaps, like ants swept before a broom—many Hothri had died, shattered by rifle fire, the few remaining plasma guns, or the various explosive rounds lofted into their formations by mortar and antitank guns.

And every Hothri who landed there, who fell to their

weapons, was a Hothri not landing in some more vulnerable
area. It had cost the Aristans dearly; they had lost more than
half their men. But it had cost the Hothri more.

Now they were falling back to another set of holes dug
by those on the off rotation. And the colonel had had something in mind, he was sure, in the pattern of their withdrawal. The transport had gone down in the foothills of the
Greater Alps, a vast mountain range on Arista's less popu-
lated hemisphere. Each withdrawal had moved them toward
the escarpment that blocked the horizon toward the equator.
Armitage knew little about this hemisphere, and nothing of
the mountains besides their name. He had grown up with
the Lesser Alps rising over the sweet green pastures of his
father's farm. Walking or driving a team up the winding
road to Elise's farm (Entremont's farm, he corrected himself; she was only the third daughter) he had often looked
up to those majestic slopes, thinking them the perfect frame
for the fields and vineyards that lay around him. So they had
been, but the fields and vineyards were gone, blasted into
ash along with Elise and the rest of the Entremonts, and his
own parents and younger sister.

Armitage tore his mind away, once more, from the memory of those times, when Elise had reached up a basket of
berries, and he had given her his first man's kiss in reply.
He focused desperately on the mountains. These were
higher, wilder than those of home, the treeline barely up to
their knees, from whence long slopes of gray rock rose to
the ice-capped summits. Glaciers lurked there, the peculiar
green-blue color obvious against the snowfields.

Armitage grunted as he climbed along behind the man
who'd summoned him. He had always loved mountains, or
thought he had, but this everlasting uphill slogging, always
uphill with each shift, got to him. It would have been bad
enough if he'd been able to breathe the chill mountain air
instead of the ripe brew the tanks fed him, and if he hadn't
had to lug his weapons with him. He had no breath for
grumbling this way, and it seemed most unfair of all to be
deprived of a soldier's favorite recreation.

Colonel Casagar, a tough little man with bright gray eyes
and a deceptively soft voice, glanced from his topo maps to
the mountains, their shapes just returning with daylight from
the massive dark block they'd appeared at dawn.

"If the surveyors were honest, this is our best bet." His finger tapped precisely, and Major Perralt nodded. Perralt was a big man, whose strength and willingness to work hard had made him invaluable to a series of commanders. Now Perralt was hoping that the colonel didn't realize that, to him, all those mountain valleys looked the same—narrow and steep. He realized that Casagar was waiting for a comment of some sort.

"If you pull this off, you'll be a general."

"If I pull this off, I'll be dead." It was said without drama, the plain truth of a plain man, but a man utterly determined. Perralt glanced at him.

"Surely you can get high enough . . ."

"Someone may. But it's going to be chancy, at best. I will be with the lowest; it's only fair." At Perralt's continued look, he gave a quick lift of the shoulders. "Come now, you knew the situation when we came here. Even if they hadn't blasted our troopships, even if everything had gone perfectly, we'd have been in the same fix, only days or weeks later. No reinforcements, and orders to hold them as long as possible. Headquarters hoped they'd react just as they have, sending more of their troops here, relieving pressure back home—"

"I still don't see why the Hothri are wasting time on us."

Casagar shrugged again. "Nor I. You know the theory, that it's a biological imperative for them to follow up any resistance. Why they're doing it is immaterial. The point is, the more of them land here, and the more of them we keep busy, the fewer can be attacking the heartlands. But we can't keep them busy and escape safely at the same time." He sighed, looking out toward the distant plains where the Hothri ships slid out of the sky each night, and where by day the shattered hulls of their own troopships glittered in the sunlight that broke through every morning between the squall lines.

"We'll need to move faster," Perralt commented. "Once we pull back out of range—and that won't be far—we'll be unable to damage their landers. Unless you're going to use the last of the Esprit rockets—"

Casagar shook his head. "No. We'll need those later. And we can't move too fast—we want them to follow, to think they're pushing us back. I know it means more casu-alties, but it's the only way. If they give up on us and go away, we've failed.'' He grinned. ''But we won't. For whatever reason, they've decided to go this far. They'll want to finish, and we'll give them reasons to go on.''

Perralt wondered, not for the first time, just where Casagar had come from. His name was not Aristan, nor his accent, yet he knew all the current Aristan slang, and seemed to know all the right people. And he had a certain edge—more than military discipline, more than being used to authority. Perralt had known men of courage before and had been under fire more than once himself . . . it was not courage, in Casagar, but something else. A brightness, a brisk cheerfulness, a settled refusal to be dour or grim when dourness and grimness could be expected. Not flippancy, just . . . certainty? If anyone can somehow entrap a small army of Hothri in a mountain valley with our few remaining troops, thought Perralt, this one can. He wanted to be skeptical—it was in his family's traditional way to be skeptical—but Casagar elicted trust. Not feverish fanaticism, not that kind of blind loyalty, but trust.

Part of it was Casagar's broad knowledge of things Perralt had never thought to learn. When the Hothri attack on the troopships destroyed the holomap projectors, Casagar had old-fashioned topo maps, the kind Perralt hadn't seen since his first year in the Academy, rolled into an equally old-fashioned mapcase. He also had geological maps of the region, and while Perralt could read topo maps, he was at a loss to follow the meaning of the dashed and solid lines, the tiny arrows, the curious hatchings and colors, of the geological maps. Casagar had shrugged off Perralt's surprise with the quiet comment that no knowledge was useless to the military.

So now they were committed to leaving the more open country, in which they could maneuver, and would climb into a steep, narrowing valley. An obvious trap. The Hothri, Perralt understood, were supposed to think it was a trap for humans. He thought that himself, as he looked at the topo maps and mentally pictured the impassible walls of rock those stacked contour lines represented. Never go to ground without a back door to your burrow, his father had often said, when they were out hunting and he could see for himself what happened to animals that didn't have one. Once in that valley, there were no back doors, only the uncaring rock. Would they really be able to surround the Hothri pursuers, and do them any significant damage? He shrugged, silently, realizing that he had, after all, known he was going to die on this mission. He had not admitted it to himself, but the knowledge had been there, a subtle tension in his mind. Now it was out in the open, the tension eased, and he found himself very alert, very aware of the shapes of clouds, the color of light, the dirt ground into the skin of his own fingers.

"All right?" Casagar was watching him, and he wondered how much of his thoughts had shown on his face.

"I'm fine." Perralt found himself smiling more easily than he would have expected. Odd how many worries vanished, once he admitted the knowledge of death's certainty. Odd that he'd never achieved this calm before, in any of his other combat experiences. Surely he'd always known he could die—why was this different?

"We'll start moving back today, in whatever sunlight we get. I'd like to be *here*"—Casagar's finger tapped the map— "in three days."

Armitage had six hours in the dugout, six hours of what passed for real sleep, in which he knew he was not responsible for anything. The medics had looked him over after Garamond noticed the dint in his helmet. He had the mud to thank for his life, he was told. And the suit; he should have had a broken neck at the least, but the suit had protected his neck at the cost of throwing him violently on the ground—and the ground had been mud. He might have nightmares, the medics said, shaking their heads. He did not dream at all. When he woke, he could see daylight at the entrance, a pale colorless light that offered neither hope nor beauty. He felt as stiff as his suit, but he could move, and even think. He sniffed, finding no taint of halogens in the air, and wondered if he'd have to put the heavy stinking helmet back on. Probably. In the meantime, he dipped a cup of unrecycled water (or at least, not recycled in *his* suit), and took a chunk of the tinned meat laid out on an ammunition box. He had once thought it was bland and leathery; now it tasted better than any meal he could remember.

Garamond met him at the entrance. "Sarge bought it," he said. He didn't have to say more; he had moved up. Armitage nodded. Garamond led him to the others who would go back to the front. Armitage hoped he looked more alert than the others but knew he didn't. Everyone seemed to be staring at some infinite distance; a few twitched or shivered enough to make their suits hitch nervously. Garamond himself looked nothing like the suave ladies' man who had taken his squad through the bars outside the base and parted half of them (Armitage included) from their money playing his own demonic brand of baccarat. His bright black eyes were red-rimmed and looked bruised; he moved as stiffly as any of them. "The bugs have overrun the flanking positions, and they've landed another transport. Had to withdraw, or they'd have gotten in behind the lines. We can't reach the landing site now with anything we've got, so we're beginning a slow withdrawal on a narrower front."

"Helmets?" asked Armitage.

"Yeah. Captain thinks they're using some gas weapons—just their own breathing canisters and a little explosive's bad enough." Most of them groaned or spat eloquently into the mud. Garmond looked at Armitage. "You're in the middle this time, and be ready to pull back on the signal." He handed Armitage a narrow gray box. "*This* radio works—whoever's center gets it, and then you have to tap the two on either side. We're going to withdraw up there." He pointed, and Armitage looked up . . . and up . . . into mountains much nearer than he remembered.

For once it was not raining, and the clouds had lifted enough to show the valleys cut into the mountain wall.

"We're going into one of those?"

"Mmm. So I hear. The colonel has a plan, though what it is, I don't know. Maybe the bugs can't stand high altitude."

"And we can?" The thought of more uphill slogging appalled him; he had been this high before, but up there was the very home of mountain-sickness.

Garamond scowled at him but answered. "We've got the suits. Freibourne has the apparatus set up to recharge the tanks—as you'll find when you get your hoses hooked up again."

"I can hardly wait," muttered someone behind Armitage. "Freibourne—!" Freibourne was not the senior suit technician, who'd been killed in the landing, nor yet the second senior, but merely a teenage apprentice welder who'd been drafted and given six weeks instruction in suit repair.

"It means we'll have the high ground," Garamond said sharply. Armitage could sense his uncertainty. Looking around, he saw that they all did.

"They've got flyers," said someone tentatively. "They could strafe . . ."

Garamond shrugged. "If they could, they haven't. We'll have the rains another week or so; they don't like to fly in daylight anyway, and night flying in this weather, in the mountains . . . it's the best we can do. If they start using the flyers, well . . . then they do, that's all."

Armitage snapped his helmet closed and checked the hose connections before he stood. Garamond had been right about one thing; the air smelled better. Then he headed for his post, the others trailing. It was only a short hike downslope this time. Behind him the sleepsite emptied, the two remaining crawlers loaded with the heavier gear. Already the head of the retreating column was several klicks closer to one of the valley entrances.

The dull background crump of Hothri indirect fire sharpened as he got closer. At midday, the bugs rarely stirred, but they had their long-range guns on automatic to keep the Aristans at a safe distance. No one seemed to know how the things aimed—if they used temperature sensors, or what—and on the days with the heaviest rainfall the barrage was far from accurate. Today, though it wasn't raining, most of the fire seemed to be concentrating on the far right. Armitage spared little sympathy for the recipients; he'd been there only twelve hours before, and he'd earned his respite in the center. If they just wouldn't shift to pound the center for a few hours. . . .

He made it to his post without much trouble and slid into the comfortable excavation Delacrosse and Virain had occupied for two nights. Comfortable being a relative term, but muddy rock to stand on rather than mud alone was a definite improvement. He banged helmets with the former owners of this prime real estate, and sent them back up the slope. Dubarry slid into the hole behind him, and Meroux; they would operate the antitank gun. Half the hole was taken up with them, their weapon, and the stacked rounds for it. He had time, then, to arrange his own weapons, his ammunition, and even think, before the silvery draperies of the afternoon rains swept up from the distant coast and shut him into a little room walled with falling water and furnished with tedium and fear.

About midafternoon, as the rain fell more heavily, and he could feel the rocks beneath his boots sinking into the mire, the Hothri moved up. First he saw the bright muzzle flashes from their weapons through the rain, and then the mud splashing up, steaming, where their rounds fell. He looked sideways, where he could just make out a dimple on either side—Porouly to the left and Schnasser to the right. He waved, and they waved back, and so the signal passed. He remembered his working radio, clicked it on, and reported the renewed assault.

"Hold the line." Those orders hadn't changed. A thousand men had died following those orders, and the rest of them would die in time . . . but that didn't bear thinking of. Armitage looked at the antitank crew, busy with their weapon, and then ahead again. More muzzle flashes, brighter now. Mud gouted up not a meter in front of him, splattering his faceplate. Rain sluiced it away instantly. A thin fog crept along the ground, almost invisible in the spray the hard rain threw up about its feet. But the fog wasn't rain-colored. Armitage swallowed hard, very glad that Freibourne had recharged the tanks, for as sure as horses ate oats, that was gas. His throat felt tight; he told himself it could not be the gas, for he was safely inside his suit. He hoped.

Next he felt a vibration in his boots, carried through the rain-soaked soil. At first the bugs had attacked on foot (or claw, as some of the wits insisted on calling it), but in the past two days they'd begun to use tracked assault vehicles to lead an advance. These were smaller and flatter than the Aristan tanks, mounted with a single laser atop and two machine guns on the forward deck. Each one trailed one or two armored troop carriers, "so the bugs don't get their feet wet," someone had explained. As the Aristans didn't have enough antitank guns for the entire line, it had become a guessing game. Where would the Hothri send the main column today, and could the Aristans position the antitank crews so they wouldn't have far to travel?

Today they were fortunate, for out of the rain's shadow came another, low and dark. Meroux touched his helmet to Armitage's.

"Straight into the lion's mouth—couldn't be better." Then he turned away, and despite his ear protectors Armitage flinched as the antitank gun fired. He had barely seen the target, and the shell's passage through the rain distorted those smooth brushstrokes into a wild flurry. Then a colorful flare brightened the distance, and the ugly brownish stain of ruptured Hothri breathing tanks colored the clean blues and grays. Meroux held up one finger before turning back to his weapon.

That was but the first of many; the stack of antitank shells in the hole dwindled steadily. Apparently the Hothri had decided to throw the main force into the center this time, rather than trying to turn a flank. Twice a Hothri assault vehicle got within fifty meters of the line, and Hothri troops, their four jointed walking legs carrying them lightly over the mud, made it closer than that. Armitage fired mechanically, without thought, picking out of the falling rain the staccato movements imposed by Hothri structure, aiming, firing, finding another target. Beside him the antitank gun bucked and lurched in the mud as Meroux and Dubarry struggled to keep the braces even.

Armitage called back to HQ for more ammunition before dark, and it came as the last of the light faded from the sullen clouds. With it came orders—written orders, signed by the colonel—to withdraw "as soon as possible and maintain radio silence" which made Armitage furious. In the dark, in the mud, with the Hothri hot on their tails, they were supposed to slog uphill into unfamiliar country? And why send down more heavy ammunition if they were supposed to carry it back up? As if to emphasize the ridiculousness of the orders, the rain lifted as a gust of wind rolled along the ground and then swatted down again with renewed intensity, but this time angled by the wind.

The ammunition bearers were already straggling away, upslope to the old camp; Armitage managed to grab one arm and hold a brief, intense, and unsatisfactory conversation with a sulky private he knew only by name. His orders were to return at once; he had no orders to return carrying ammunition, and he wasn't about to involve himself in any affair between Armitage and the colonel. Before Armitage could marshal the words he wanted to use, the man was gone into the darkness, and he realized that he was being

left to make a decision no one in his position should have
to make.

"Generals make decisions," he muttered to himself in
the privacy of his helmet. "Colonels make decisions, even
captains . . . even sergeants. But privates make no decisions, that's what they always told me, and now—" Now,
he would decide when the line moved back . . . and if he
made that decision wrongly, it could not move back. The
orders said "as soon as possible" which meant if he didn't
think it was possible to carry back all that newly delivered
ammunition in the blowing rain (for the wind had risen),
then they wouldn't, yet. How long should he wait? What
had the colonel meant?

A gust of wind slapped his suit hard enough that he felt
it, even down in the hole. The bugs had trouble in high
wind; they could cling with their clawed feet, but when they
tried to move rapidly they sometimes overbalanced and tumbled along the ground. He peered into the dark, seeing the
random spots and blotches visible to anyone who strains to
see on a dark night. No muzzle flashes, no flares. Of course
the bugs didn't need as much light, preferring it in the red
range. They could be creeping close even now. He found
one of the flare rounds (he had eight of them) and fitted it
in his rifle, then aimed high and upwind. It functioned perfectly for once (some of them acted like tracer rounds which
the bugs were particularly good at tracking. They'd learned
early not to use tracers with bugs.) But all he could see, in
the few seconds of light, was falling rain and the usual messy
wet jumble of mud and rocks and broken machinery. Nothing that looked like a Hothri moved. He fired a few quick
rounds. Nothing in response, but the wind buffeted harder
as he tried to see.

It was two hours before Armitage managed to pass the
word to everyone, and get the withdrawal underway. The
Hothri artillery had begun to lay down patterns all along
the line, but nothing seemed to be moving forward under it.
This was small comfort when the ground leaped and jiggled
from a near miss, when the suit's override dampers suddenly held Armitage rigid. But for whatever reason—rain,
wind, or incompetence—the shells reached little beyond the
line itself, and once the men could overcome their reluctance to leave perfectly good holes and venture into the

open, they had only a short distance to go before they were beyond the shell patterns.

Not that it went without losses. On the far right, Marchant—who had been Armitage's bunkmate in boot camp—had lost suit integrity and half an arm to the same shell fragment. His partner Jeffries had a field clamp on the arm, but neither of them would leave. "We'll confuse them," Jeffries had explained. "They will follow, and then we'll fire into their flank—" Near them, two positions had been wiped out completely, although the bugs, concentrating on the center, hadn't taken advantage of the gap.

All along the line there were perhaps thirty wounded, and all but two chose to stay behind. So did their partners. They did not bother to explain. The realities were obvious without discussion. Anyone who had lost suit integrity, or power, could not make it where they were going. A partner's knife gave quick ease to those unable to fight or walk, but those who could still fight preferred a chance. Armitage argued with no one, and when the Aristans moved back, cloaked in night and blowing rain, he felt less guilt than he expected. The way things had gone so far, those who died tonight or tomorrow were the lucky ones.

For hours they struggled uphill, first to the old sleepsite, where they found a guide who led them on. Behind them, only the rain and wind moved; they heard the shells exploding, but that sound faded. It seemed forever that they had slogged through wet and wind and chill, their suits humming and clanking, the air in their helmets hissing. Finally they rested, still in their suits, huddled together with only the barest watch . . . the guide insisted that this was all that was needed, and they were all too tired to argue. When dawnlight seeped into the blowing rain, they could see nothing but tumbled rock and mud, none of it familiar, and no sign of the rest of the defenders. That day they continued, coming at last into forested country where they went in single file beside a brawling stream brown with runoff. Often enough they had to walk in it, with its eager current tugging at their ankles or knees; the route the guide took was choked with huge boulders and slippery, steep bluffs of mud. Around noon the rain stopped as usual, but the wind continued, moaning in the trees. They had taken their helmets off, since no one had seen any sign of Hothri on their track. The fresh air smelled wonderful, full of growing plants, flowers, and the rich earthy smell of the mud and rotting leafmold.

"Too bad there's a war," said Dubarry, plucking a delicate red flower that hung from a niche in the boulder. "This would be a good place for a picnic . . ."

"In sunshine," said Meroux firmly. Like the others, he was looking around warily. Armitage was as puzzled as the rest; surely they'd have seen some sign that the rest of the column had passed this way? Even heavy rains couldn't destroy all sign. He watched their guide, a heavy-browed man he couldn't remember seeing more than once or twice. The man looked at no one, munching his ration bar steadily. Could the guide be a deserter? A traitor of some kind? Armitage had just made up his mind to ask him some hard questions when the man stood, refastened his helmet, and gestured for them to follow.

Perralt had no idea how to go about it, but it had to be done. Too many others were wondering the same thing, and rumors had begun to spread where even he could hear them. He could see trouble coming, beyond the Hothri, when a few more became convinced. He straightened his shoulders, wished desperately for a clean uniform, and ducked into the command dugout.

Casagar was, as usual, bent over the maps, this time with dividers and a pen in his hands. He glanced up as Perralt came in, and went back to the map.

"Sir . . ."

"Yes, Major?" Whatever it was on the map, Casagar seemed fascinated.

"Sir, I need to talk with the colonel."

At that, Casagar looked up, nodded, and laid the dividers precisely on the map. He capped his pen, folded his arms, and said "Go on, Major."

"Sir, I hope the colonel will realize that my questions have nothing to do with his honor. . . ." That was ridiculous; you could not ask a man if he were an enemy agent without insulting his honor. But Perralt made himself plunge on. "It's only that the colonel isn't well known . . . I mean none of us know you. . . ."

The bright gray eyes met his. Whatever a traitor looked like, surely this wasn't it—a trim, fit, little man with honest eyes. "And you're wondering where I came from, is that it?"

"Well . . . yes, sir." That was part of it.

"You've recognized that I'm not Aristan by birth—my accent's pretty strong, I suppose. I was born on Davout, one of the out-colonies. Came here for my degrees—Dessalles never did have a university—and went home to join the Home Guard. When the war broke out, I transferred to offplanet duty with the fleet."

Perralt remembered Davout, one of the first planets lost to the Hothri, but knew nothing else about it or any of the other out-colonies. If Casagar's name and accent were Davout he would not know.

"It's just that we knew the other senior officers . . . General Duarte, Colonel Marish, Colonel Pachek, and then when they were all killed—"

"There was this stranger, not even Aristan, in command. And it bothered you. What did you think, that the Hothri had planted a turncoat among you?"

This was so exactly what he'd suspected that he could not keep from flushing; he felt the heat on his face. "Not only me, sir."

Casagar's eyebrows went up. "Oh? And is it a common topic of discussion, your turncoat colonel?"

"Sir, I never mentioned it. Whatever I thought myself . . . one does not speculate on such possibilities in such a dangerous situation. But some of the men and junior officers . . . they wonder, sir . . . all the familiar commanders dead, and your choice of tactics . . ."

Casagar cocked his head on one side. "Tell me, Major, do you have an armed squad waiting to arrest me if you decide I'm a traitor?"

Perralt felt a wave of anger; it was nothing to joke about. "With all due respect, sir, I thought this could be handled between officers and gentlemen."

"Major Perralt, I am not making fun of you. It would have been an intelligent thing to do, if you seriously believed I was a traitor, and I would not have been insulted, whether I was guilty or innocent. I suppose it would do no good to show you the original orders? No, of course not. If the Hothri could supply a traitorous colonel, they could supply me with fake orders, and personnel lists, and anything else to make me seem legitimate. And if you're so convinced, then the loss of our communications equipment and computers, and the equipment failures, all of that is part of the same scheme." Casagar squeezed his eyes closed, and when he opened them he looked around as if he saw a new world. Perhaps, Perralt thought, he did, having found suspicion where he was accustomed to trust.

"I have made bad mistakes," Casagar said, almost to himself. "I thought it was so clear, the only thing to do under the circumstances, and even you—" He looked straight at Perralt again, and his voice strengthened. "Even you, Major, have not really understood, have you?"

"No, sir," said Perralt, not giving in.

Casagar sighed, and hitched one hip up onto the table. "Very well. Let's try to clear this up. I'm not native Aristan, and I'm from a planet you know was taken by the Hothri. You can't get at the fleet records to see my date of transfer, and you might not believe the records if you saw them. I've been on Arista only eight months, came in with the Seventh . . . you'll know Admiral Koch by name, and if you've met him you'd remember the scar on the back of his left hand—but I could have got that from a photograph. I had met Colonel Marish and General Duarte; when the landing response teams were being formed, they asked if I'd care to serve there. General Duarte checked my background with Admiral Koch. Of course, he's not alive to explain that, and you could choose to believe I made it up." For the first time, anger leaked into his usually level voice. "I'm helpless to clear myself, for exactly those reasons you'd expect a guilty person to have devised."

"It is not only the opportunity," said Perralt, stiffly.

"No. I see that. If I had chosen to throw all my forces at the Hothri landing site, however foolishly, or if I'd chosen to retreat into the forest and try to escape, I suppose you'd have fewer doubts."

The tone was crisp, once more devoid of anger, and Perralt couldn't help smiling. "Sir, in the first case I'd be dead and have no worries. In the second . . . well . . . it would be less wasteful."

"Would it?" Casagar beckoned. "Come here and look at this, and this time *listen* to what I'm telling you. And no, I won't take this opportunity to knock you on the head."

Perralt flushed again but moved up to look at Casagar's

hand holding the dividers on the stacked lines that meant the mountain escarpment.

"Major, we had orders to prevent the Hothri landing, if we could, or engage and occupy them if we couldn't stop them. As you know, our transports were attacked even as we landed, and we lost men and vital equipment immediately—with more to come in the first hours. We did not have enough left to prevent a Hothri landing. But we could—and did—harry them. Smart human commanders who found a remote landing site infested with troublesome defenders would just pull out and go land somewhere else, but the Hothri are—luckily for Arista—different. They kept coming, and we kept killing them. That worked as long as we had enough men and material to keep them boxed near their landing site."

"I understand *that*," said Perralt grumpily.

"If you do, then you understand that we had to pull back, or be wiped out with decreasing Hothri losses. The question facing me then was how to pull back, and where, and how we could do the most damage to the Hothri in the process."

"I still don't see why we could not operate as a mobile strike force. There's plenty of rough country at hand."

"Because the rains will stop any day now, and once the Hothri have control of the air—which they will, because we don't have adequate anti-aircraft weapons—our so-called mobile strike force is dead meat."

"How do you know the rains will stop?" asked Perralt.

"First, it was in the briefing given to the senior officers, and second, I make it a practice to know something about all the environmental components of a field of battle. Third, the end of the rains is signalled by increasing winds—as we've had the past day or so. The more you know, the less chance there is to be caught in someone else's trap. Besides, the Hothri aren't going to be moving from here on the ground—they wanted this as a secure landing site for their spacecraft. They'd use suborbital and aircraft to transport their troops from here to the cities. So a mobile strike force would have nothing to do but snipe at the landing site, and we have dropped below a size that could do that effectively."

Put that way, it made sense, but Perralt still had questions. "But why this retreat into a blind trap?"

"It's either that, Major, or wander around in the brush

and trees waiting to be picked off by the Hothri flyers. Or even a stray column that just wants to go human-hunting. We'd do no good in the sense of keeping them busy or doing them harm, and in six months—actually much less—we'd all be just as dead. This way . . . this way we make them pay for our deaths, at ratios that may do them enough harm to help Arista. Can't you see that?''

Perralt could, but he could also see how hard it was going to be to convince the others. His face must have shown that, because Casagar sighed again.

"If they're all about to plot a mutiny, I suppose I'd better take the time to convince them otherwise. What do you think it will take?'' Perralt noticed that this assumed he himself no longer thought Casagar a traitor. He didn't want to ask himself, because he could see no clear alternative to Casagar's plan. No better ideas rose up to suggest themselves, no brilliant tactical coups popped out of his memory of military history lectures.

"Well,'' he said at last, "You're going to have to talk to them. The officers, at least.''

"And you?'' Casagar put the question Perralt had hoped to escape. He spread his hands.

"Sir, I can't think of anything else. You've answered my objections. Actually—if you *were* a Hothri plant, you've been doing them a lot of damage, and aside from retreating as soon as we landed, trying to save ourselves by hiding in the hills—'' He shook his head. "No, I can see that wouldn't have done Arista any good, while what we did may have helped. It's not like anything I ever read about, but it's the best choice out of bad ones, I suppose. I don't like it, but then . . . war's full of things I don't like. If you'll excuse me—'' Casagar nodded, and Perralt went back out, his mind in a whirl. Would it seem so sensible the next day or the next, when they had their backs to a stone wall and the Hothri moving in on them?

Casagar had gathered all the remaining officers. Perralt watched their faces as they listened to the colonel's final explanation of his plan. Fatigue, despair, sullenness, confusion, and on two or three, growing comprehension that turned to horror.

Casagar paused, reading the same signals as Perralt. "You don't think it will work, I gather?''

Girond, lately a captain and now a major, clambered up. "Begging the colonel's pardon, but it seems too simple to work—like trying a rabbit snare on a cow."

Casagar smiled in a way that Perralt had learned meant he was pleased. Why now? Perralt wondered. "It's a matter of scale, Major Girond," Casagar said. "This is really nothing more than the classic battle of Marathon, only we haven't the human reserves in the wings. We have the planet itself, the mountains."

"But, sir . . . rockslides? I've seen rockslides, and yes, they'll kill a few, perhaps block pursuit behind us for awhile, until the bugs climb over. But the colonel seems to think they'll act like a couple of thousand reinforcements—"

"Five thousand fresh men couldn't do what those slopes will do," said Casagar briskly. "Come—none of you are geologists, nor have any of you done fieldwork in these mountains." He nodded at Captain Solomon, who had once boasted of his mountaineering skills. "Tell them, Eugene— what velocity will an avalanche reach down slopes like these?"

"It depends," began Solomon cautiously, but at Casagar's nod he went on to speak of snow avalanches and mud-slides, rockfalls and rockslides, describing how they moved downslope at more than 100 kilometers per hour, splashing high on opposite slopes, veering wildly down narrow mountain valleys to destroy everything in their path.

"And that's the smaller ones," Casagar said. "There are records—all the way back to Old Earth—of slides so huge, so destructive, that they reshape not only the valley and valley walls, but extend beyond that valley to its outwash. It requires very large, very steep mountains, with very unstable rock strata. The steeper the slope, the faster the slide travels, the more rock it can move, and the farther it goes."

"Wait—you're not thinking of making a slide that could reach to the Hothri landing site—?"

"No—probably not. But it may spill out a kilometer or more—the outwash fan from this valley is steep; it's one reason I chose it. No, what I intend is to destabilize both valley walls, in sequence from the head of the valley to its outlet. Right now, at the end of the rains, those steep-pitched shales and slates are full of water. Water reduces friction between rock strata just as it does between your boot and the rock. I once saw a shaped charge shake loose a ten-meter thick layer and send it sliding on a month's worth of heavy rains. Not here, but the principle's the same. The Hothri can't fight gravity any more than we can. Even a ship's shields would have trouble with that much mass moving that fast.''

"So all that rock—whole or broken, is supposed to come crashing down on the Hothri and their equipment, and send them tumbling down the valley under it?'' asked Barthe, whose family had been rich, and who could not let any discussion go on long without his contribution. Casagar nodded. "And where will we be? If it can splash as high as Solomon said, can we climb above it?''

"Most of us, no. The rocket crews maybe, although being above the splash puts you in the zone where separation occurs. The thing is, gentlemen, the concussion of the explosions and other slides may—and probably will—induce sympathetic slides everywhere in the valley. There will be no safe place.''

"But sir—'' Girond stopped abruptly, and reddened.

"It's all right, Major; all the rest are thinking the same thing. Why would I choose a plan that is almost sure to kill all of us?'' Casagar smiled again, a slightly challenging smile. "I'm sure you've all read your military history, and I assume you remember the Iron Duke of Wellington.'' No one answered; he nodded as if in answer to a question of his own and went on. "At Waterloo, when hard-pressed by Napoleon's forces, his comment was 'Hard pounding, gentlemen; we shall see who pounds longest.' You would understand calling in artillery or airstrikes on our position, if it were necessary.'' Heads nodded. "We have had hard pounding, and I am calling in the hardest pounding, the best and only reinforcements, we can get. We have eroded their forces considerably—amazingly, I think—but from here on, the Hothri can kill more of us with less risk to themselves . . . unless we stake all of this trap and let the mountains of Arista join the defense. If with loss of our last hundreds we can destroy their thousands, it is worth that loss. I myself will be on the valley floor.''

He paused for that to sink in, and when the faces were thoughtful but calm, he went on. "There is one thing. Our rear-guard was directed not to this valley, but to another nearby. I believe, in the storm that night, the Hothri will be unable to trace them. If they do, they'll be no worse off than we are. But if the Hothri do not trace them, they're in a smaller, shallower, valley with more cover and more stable rock. They may survive. I have sent with them a written report of this entire expedition, and my plans. It may be that if the Hothri are defeated, these men will be found alive, and our work known. At least the report may be found, even if they do not survive.''

Up the valley the Hothri came, the tracked assault vehicles lurching over the smaller boulders, between the larger ones. Skirmish teams afoot flanked them. There had been no rain since the previous morning, and the Hothri had probably moved all day and night. Through his scopes, Perralt could see the shiny carapaces bob over the uneven ground, even though sunlight barely touched the highest peaks he could see. He had gone up one of the terraces with a functioning radio to keep track of the Hothri advance. From here, forty meters above the valley floor, he had an excellent view of the colonel's plan. At the head of the valley, as if hopelessly trapped but determined to fight to the death, the Aristans had clumped their forces beneath a three hundred meter cliff. If a Hothri had been where he was, it could have seen how few they were—and with a scope could have seen how ragged, how many suits were holed, how many wounded, how few heavy weapons remained to them. Given that view, a Hothri might decide to drop a few shells on them and let be.

But the Hothri were down in the valley. A *lot* of Hothri were in the valley; a column that ran all the way back to the entrance, and perhaps beyond. A trail of ants on a line of honey, he thought bitterly, looking for the honeypot at the end. They could never have defeated this many Hothri, could not have held them even another day in straight fighting. The colonel was right about one thing, and Perralt had the grace to admit he might be right about many others. *I was never the officer I thought I was,* he admitted to himself, *despite my rank in the Academy, despite my combat experience. I am not bad—I am brave enough, and I care for my men, but—but Casagar is right. If we had all known all we could know, if we humans would ever realize that all knowledge really is connected, and useful, and that recognizing a trap before you're in it is better than having the courage to chew off your leg, or even lie in wait for the trapper* . . . His thoughts cut off abruptly as he caught a light signal from one of the rocket teams on the opposite slope.

The Hothri were still entering the valley, apparently determined to overmatch the humans enough to need no second battle. An observer even nearer the valley entrance reported that a ring of tanks had made it to the top of the outwash slope and come to a stop. More infantry were coming in. Perralt looked back to the valley floor and saw that the Hothri were almost in close-firing range. He had worried that they might try an artillery barrage before the rocket teams could set off the slides, but the colonel said that would do almost as well.

"As long as they are in the valley—whoever makes the first loud noise will set it off. The rockets are probably not necessary, but I want to be certain."

Perralt thumbed the radio's control. "Colonel?"

"Here. How close?"

"Their advance lines are perhaps 200 meters; the main body is a few hundred meters behind that, and it's solid from there back. They've brought up heavier vehicles—tanks, the observer says—to the outwash slope. My estimate is well over two thousand, maybe as many as four . . ."

"Artillery?"

"Nothing that I can see but the guns on their assault vehicles. None reported."

"Very good, then—"

"Colonel Casagar," Perralt interrupted hastily. "Before you give the order, sir, there's something I must say. I'm sorry I suspected you of being an enemy agent; I'm honored to have served under you."

There was a pause, then Casagar replied. "Perralt, you have nothing to apologize for. You've been supportive, you've followed what must have seemed cockeyed orders, you are brave and you care for your troops. Times like these breed suspicions. Besides . . . you ought to know . . . the Hothri think I *am* their agent."

"What!"

"We have only moments, but you deserve the truth, Perralt, before we die. In one way only your suspicions were correct: I was a reserve officer on Thormelde, captured in a Hothri attack. They wanted a prisoner, and despite all I could do . . . Anyway, they 'converted' me, and to make

my long story short, planted me on Arista to do just what
they think I've done—bottle up a regiment and deliver at
least 500 prisoners."

"But—"

"Let me finish, Perralt. They think this valley is safe;
they expect to launch gas canisters and knock us out, because they think our suits are no longer operational. They
think they can convert the others as easily as they converted
me." A brief pause, in which Perralt stared fixedly at the
sunlight touching the top of the slope across from him, his
mind blind with panic. "They're angry that I cost them so
many casualties in the past few days, just to convince you
that I was really what I claimed; they would probably have
followed us here for that only." Another pause, and then
Casagar's voice regained its wonted brisk cheerfulness.
"They don't know I was a geologist before I was drafted
into the reserves; they don't know one damn thing about the
geology of terrestrial planets. They had to believe I was
truly their turncoat to fall for this rather obvious trap, and
I hope you'll forgive what I had to do for that. But I am
human, though not Aristan; my death will prove what loyalty I have."

"You . . . you *lied,*" breathed Perralt.

"Yes. And you, with your blunt honesty, felt it. But under that lie, Perralt, was the truth you wanted. As you saw
on down below; we hurt them badly. As you will see, in
the few minutes left to us. God bless you, Perralt, and
Arista."

Perralt could neither bless nor curse in reply; fury and
sorrow and amazement struggled for dominance in his mind,
trapping his tongue.

"And now it's time, Perralt, and I must know if you trust
me enough to follow this last command."

"I . . . if I don't, you'll signal from down there, won't
you?"

"Yes."

Perralt drew himself up, wondering if Casagar peered upward with his scope, or if this was an empty gesture, and
saluted briskly. "Sir, I'm waiting. . . ."

"Go ahead, then."

"On your order."

The shadow of the ridge behind him was fleeing down the
opposite slope as Perralt picked up his own rifle and sighted

at the leading Hothri team. "Fire," came the word from
the radio, and he squeezed the trigger. His aim did not
matter; it was the sound, the flat crack of the rifle, that
signalled the rocket teams. From above and to his left he
heard the pop and roar as the first team on his side launched
their Esprit. A few seconds later, when the crack of his rifle
had crossed the valley floor, he saw the plume of vapor from
the first team opposite. Immediately behind him, a brisk
rattle of loose scree began, triggered by his shot and the
Esprit launching.

He could see the white vapor trail of both Esprits crossing
the valley, making an X against the dark rocks. He followed
the one from his side to its impact just below the ridge-top;
a massive roiling ball of flame and vapor obliterated his
view of its target before the wind blew it away. Then the
thunder of it came to him, just as the roar of an impact on
his side of the valley made him grab for his ear protectors.

Across the valley he saw dust still rising and then realized
that the explosion had triggered a rockslide. It looked piti-
fully small and much slower than he expected, no more than
the slithering of sand down the side of a sandpile when
children are playing. Sorrow clenched his heart, as much
for Casagar's lie as for the failure of their plans. He had
wanted so to believe in one last truth before he died. But
the ground rumbled beneath him, so heavily that his ear
protectors couldn't handle it. He glanced left, and saw boulders the size of tables jouncing down the slope beyond the
terrace; when he looked up, he saw an immense bulge of
broken rock and soil hanging in midair, hardly seeming to
fall except that individual pebbles grew into house-sized
blocks as they approached.

He tore his gaze away from this to the opposite side, just
in time to see the vapor trails of two more Esprits crossing
farther down the valley. He looked down; the Hothri advance had stopped, and the neat column seemed to be
breaking up. Across . . . across was a gray-brown wave that
fell endlessly, slowly and then faster, so fast it was no longer visible as a mass of rock or soil, but a smooth blurred
surface that rippled like muddy water pouring down a gully.

Dust rose from its leading edge now, clouding his vision,
but he felt in his bootsoles the rising rumble, like twenty
thousand organs all playing their longest pipes. When he
glanced upvalley to see what was happening to the pitiful

clump of human fighters, he was just in time to watch the
slow fall of part of the cliff behind them, a great chunk of
rock that crumbled as it fell . . . he could not see its final
fall because now the froth of those immense avalanches,
great spurts and clouds of rockdust, rose higher than his
terrace. The noise was vast, beyond comprehension; his
mind seemed to turn into itself and hide. He had retreated
to the middle of the terrace, half-hoping that the approaching chaos would miss him, though he had no idea what he
would do if he survived. See how much damage had been
done, he supposed, though it was clear that Casagar's plan
was working.

And then a tongue of wet rock and mud slopped up across
the terrace and gathered him in, one more bit of organic
debris on its way to scour the valley and its outwash slope.

Morning light blazed upon the peaks, swept down the
western slope of their valley, and swallowed the mist hanging over the noisy little river. The air smelled of spicewood
and hawberry, leafmold under the needled mountain trees,
unknown flowers starring the lush grass. Armitage lay back
against the grass with the others, free of the encumbering,
smelly combat suit. They had all bathed in the river, braving
its chill and the uneven rolling rocks of its bed. Now, damp
and chilly, but welcoming the sunlight and its promise of a
warmer day, they sprawled in forgotten luxury, scratching
and stretching at will. No Hothri had found them yet, and
the rear-guard said none had followed them—they had seen
the hordes going by in the distance, all headed for another
valley entrance. So for this day, they counted themselves
safe—and if they died later, they'd have had one last day of
pleasure.

Armitage lay his head on his arms and let the grass tickle
his ears and forehead. He wondered if the pink starry flower
in front of his nose was related to the white starry flower
that had grown in their upper fields. He wondered what the
others thought about the letter the colonel had written them,
the one he'd opened yesterday and shared around. No one
had said anything about it at all. It was safer to wonder
about botany.

The ground beneath him trembled, a faint quiver that grew
stronger for several minutes, then died away. All the men
were looking at each other. Armitage looked west to the

valley's sheltering ridge. A roiling cloud rose at some distance beyond, and blew away on a wind from the mountains. Reivers rose from the high ground, lifting easily on air currents to circle gradually in that direction. Armitage watched their dark wings silently.

"Was that it?" asked Meroux after awhile, as they all watched the cloud disperse.

Armitage shrugged. "What else? It is not a cavalry charge."

"Do you suppose it worked, what he said? Trapped the bugs in there, too?"

"Probably. We have to hope so, or they'll be hunting us."

None of them said what Armitage was thinking, what they were probably all thinking. They were the witnesses, but the glory belonged to those in the other valley, buried under rocks where no reiver could find them.

Armitage lay back down, squinting against the sunlight that now warmed his cold skin. As he closed his eyes, he thought again of his father's farm, and their horses, this time without as much pain. It was gone; it would never come again; but he was alive in another mountain valley, and if Arista survived he would farm again. He would find another woman to love as he had once loved Elise, and they would have children. He owed the others that.

# Irregulars
## by Bill Fawcett

Throughout history, hard-pressed nations such as ancient Egypt and Persia have improvised armaments on their merchant vessels. English freebooters of the fifteenth century contributed more toward British naval domination than the island's weak formal navy. Fighting under Letters of Marque, civilian owned vessels once terrorized the Carribean. Later, the British East India and Hudson Bay Companies armed and sailed their own ships.

The incentive for arming civilian vessels is always necessity. This changes little in space as became apparent in the desperate situation Arista faced in their war with the Hothri. It was simply cheaper and quicker to place weapons on an existing hull than to scrap build a naval vessel. In Arista's case, with all of their docks filled, any civilian ship that could be armed was added to their defense ranks as a supplement to those few they could manufacture.

Once the Hothri were able to penetrate the Aristan system, they quickly destroyed the orbital dockyards. Soon these merchant vessels were the only additions the Aristans could make to their diminishing navy. Designated as "militia," these irregular naval ships were manned almost entirely by local asteroid miners and refugees from overrun Aristan colonies.

# RAGE OF AN ANGEL
## by S. N. Lewitt

MORE THAN ANYTHING about the Hothri, Claude
Dessales hated their cruisers. The fighters were dangerous,
angry hornets stirred up and on patrol. The dreadnoughts
carried more in their bellies like mother bugs, but it was
the cruisers that had cut Arista off from aid and had pum-
meled her cities and fields and defenders. And Claude Dessales was determined to get one. Not because she needed
to show the regulars at Chapelle St. Anne Base, or even
because she wanted revenge. It was simply a matter of eras-
ing a mistake. A lot of mistakes, unfortunately.

The girls were flying well. They emerged from behind
the second moon in perfect step formation, bursting into
speed suddenly as they left black out. Ranged ahead were
the Hothri hordes, just like the briefing man had said, looking like a garbage heap around a fat shiny globe.

"Talley-ho," Dessales muttered but didn't bother flick-
ing on the transmitter. Even Goneaux couldn't miss this
target dead ahead and bigger than all of Arista behind them.

Hothri fighters detached themselves from the edge of the
mass and flew straight for the group. Dessales smiled. They
knew this was coming, and their orders reinforced their
preference. Don't bother with the small fry.

Claude threw the Balgin hard to starboard and above at
the same time, twisted around inverted and then threw on
the speed. The Balgin was a sweet bird, alright, and even
pulling heavy G's she stayed stable and built speed.

The Hothri fighters followed, trying to mimic the tricky
turn and shoot. Claude saw the flickers in her peripheral
vision and pushed the Balgin even faster, jinking hard but
not cutting the speed.

Behind, one of the Hothri had gone into a flat spin that
deteriorated quickly. Another shot off on the wrong trajectory, and the one that had originally been the leader was

lying dead in the vacuum. Too much pressure for the bug to take, Claude thought. That carapace could take a lot of punishment, but once the pressure got too high it went like an eggshell under a brick. At least the briefing boys thought so. No one had ever seen the results.

The last one though, that one could fly. Claude could feel it on her, riding her sixes, maybe losing a little in the speed department, but a good plasma blast would plug up the difference in no time. She could feel the alien behind her, targeting, loading, making her body itch with the strangely prescient knowledge.

*Come on, Elizabeth,* she prayed. If pure will had form, it would have become a laser, slashing through the pursuer and striking her wingman as well. Elizabeth Goneaux had better get her aim together for this one or . . .

The blast lit her canopy from behind. *Good shooting, kid,* she thought back to Goneaux, a silent apology for having doubted the girl. But Elizabeth was too young to be out here, had too little experience back home running revenuers and shooting out rival supply vans. Dessales couldn't help but doubt the child's skill. She was only sixteen and even the regulars didn't take them that green.

No time to think of that now. They were free of the threat only for a moment. Ahead lay the cluster, denser than any star field Claude had seen in her forty-seven years. She couldn't find the other element, Suzanne Hoffman with Leonie Benoit on her wing. She only hoped they were still on her after that little maneuver, although Benoit would be mortified at losing the leader. They all knew better—had convinced the briefing boys of it, too, and that hadn't been easy.

So they could come out and do—this. Take the little Balgins against the main Hothri force and keep them occupied. That was the mission, Dessales reminded herself. Keep them occupied as long as possible. Tie up ships here, make the bugs concentrate on the constant, miserable infiltration of Balgins. And above all, keep them away from the main Force, massing behind moon three and ready to break through Hothri lines. Just enough time to let them get away, to get to light, that was all they needed.

And then, dead ahead, she saw an assortment of Hothri four-seaters that looked for all the world like the assortment at the pastry counter on Saturday morning. Gleeful, Des-

sales laughed and targeted her first plasma bomb. She came
in close, seeking visible contact so she could make out the
lines of the alien markings on her target.

As she released, the fireships came to and began their
usual "towering inferno" effect. Dessales broke the Balgin
hard and fast to the right, cutting back from the blazing
laser-yard at a near one-eighty. At least they couldn't fire
and pile on velocity at the same time or the Balgin would
be a decently crisp fried shrimp by now. But as she completed the break she found herself nearly face-on with Goneaux's craft, close enough that she could see pale horror
on the girl's face.

*Damn you, Elizabeth, I always break right.* She slammed
the small vehicle into a hard dive. *Hard enough to stay alive
with the bugs. Don't need to avoid you too.* Braced for impact, Dessales expected any second to hear the ragged shear
as her nose shredded Goneaux's fuselage.

But for once Elizabeth had done something right. She'd
managed to pull the opposite direction and flew directly
away from Dessales. Claude sighed, partly with impatience
at her inexperienced wingman. In the normal course of
things Goneaux would learn sooner or later, but this time
there was no later. There was only now.

Elizabeth came around and formed up again, and this
time Claude could see Suzanne and Leonie take their places.
She smiled. They must have been herding the four-seaters
over to where she had been ready to bomb them. Naturally,
Leonie would have fired as well, catching the escape vehicles in the crossfire.

For the first time since they had come from behind the
radio shadow of the second moon Claude opened communications. "Let's get to the Force," was all she said.

They rolled around and arced back through the radio-
dead ring to the second moon. As they came through the
glittering particles of ring-ice they met up the main contingent of their Force. Sixteen Balgin in this group alone harassing the bugs today, and four other groups had been
scheduled to go.

As they passed the radio margin Claude watched another
Force bursting through the ring to harry the Hothri in her
stead. Leave them no sleep, at least what it is that passes
for sleep among them. Let them know that they are never
safe, that there is never time to rest. Wear them down until

exhaustion makes their judgement fail and their reflexes jagged. Most of all, keep them occupied so they never even notice when the main fleet breaks through. Claude Dessales ran through the global mission objectives in her head. She didn't realize that she had uttered them as a prayer.

Sixteen Balgin went out in their Force. Fourteen came back. According to the statistics that was very good. According to Claude Dessales it was bad enough, but at least it wasn't any of her girls. Not yet. And they had accounted for at least six confirmed kills of the thirty credited to the Force. That made Claude very proud indeed. After all, the regulars had said it was time they ate their words.

"You're looking for volunteers. I've got more hours than any three of you put together," she had said in the auditorium of the regional gymnasium, the only room big enough to hold section meetings. It wasn't really the auditorium anymore, either, now that the Civil Defense had taken it over as an armory and training facility. But that was where regional meetings had always been held, and habit was hard to overcome.

"Maybe if we went over to the Base at Chapelle St. Anne they would settle it?" the programmer said hesitantly. He was home guard, over-age for service in even the Civil Defense, but in spite of his years he still didn't command respect. Always deferring to the authorities, the regulars, somebody, Coordinator Mittner never wanted to take responsibility for anything. It had been the same with the sewage treatment plant, the generating facility, even the building of Chapelle St. Anne itself.

"Besides," Mittner went on, stalling for time, "your group is all girls. We can't be risking our ladies in this kind of mission. For pure defense, maybe . . ."

"If this isn't defense I don't know what is," Suzanne had cut him off. Dear Suzanne. She didn't take attitude from anyone. "After all, if the main fleet doesn't break out now then there's a real good chance we're all going to die. And, Coordinator, I don't think the Hothri have your outdated sense of chivalry."

Mittner turned red and his full cheeks made him look like a balloon under far too much internal pressure. Claude Dessales had been tempted to giggle for the first time in at least ten years. He positively sputtered . . . which was to be ex-

pected, naturally. If he had trouble with Claude and Elizabeth and Leonie, then Suzanne would be completely beyond
his comprehension. And she had even worn her old flight
suit to the meeting to put Mittner in his place. No matter
how much the coordinator wanted to convey the impression
that he had been vital to the spreading of Aristan colonial
efforts to the southernmost continent, everyone knew that
he had rarely left the city limits of Nouvelle Strassbourg.
Suzanne, however, had been a bush pilot down south in the
early days and no one intimidated her. She was perfectly
ready to go head-on with the commander of the base himself, if need be.

That was just the thing Claude needed. Mittner wasn't
afraid of her. No, he just hated her guts, for which she
couldn't blame him, since she had fended him off her second moon mining claim after Henri had died. And Mittner
had lusted after those mining rights as he had after nothing
else in his life. Too bad. Little did he know there wasn't
much on the backside of Faker's Ball except a lot of nickel
and a pretty full fuel cache.

Which was a fact no one knew about. She should have
reported it to the base, or the Civil Defense unit, but it
wasn't easy to get to and, while fuel was critical, her Balgin
was more important. To be honest, she had simply forgotten, and it would look worse now.

The Balgins were what the military wanted, anyway. They
were originally built as bush runners, perfectly adapted to
Arista's growing military needs and for commuting to mining claims on her three moons. The fact that some bush
runners had supplemented their income with the sale of various beverages and luxury items not reported to the Nouvelle Strassbourg tax authorities had gone unmentioned . . .
until it was noted by the military that the aforementioned
runners had adapted the Balgins for exceptional speed and
maneuverability.

They were only lightly armed. Aristans didn't shoot other
Aristans, even runners and tax collectors, so armaments
were for protection against local fauna. But the military
could correct that easily enough. A laser mount on the nose
and wingtips and a plasma cannon rack tacked on to the
belly corrected that. The Balgin did not become fighters or
bombers in any traditional sense, but they were wonderful

evasive craft and perfectly built to harass the bugs and get away clean.

Which was one of the jobs of the Civil Defense. Originally they had been organized merely in case of land invasion, but their mandate had grown enormously as the regulars took high losses and even larger numbers were recruited to the main fleet now off-planet. Claude had been involved in that first organization. Only a third generation Aristan, this planet was more than just her home. She loved it fiercely, protectively, the way she loved her two sons who were with the main fleet. And she would defend it with the same dedication.

She had tried to volunteer for the regulars with her children. After all, she had nearly a thousand hours logged in Balgins alone, shuttling to Faker's Ball and running overpriced supplies down to the southern continent. But the regulars weren't interested in taking, as they put it so politely, women of a certain age. *Old enough to be your mother,* she had thought, looking at the recruiter.

But age had taught Claude that it was easier to avoid authority than openly defy it. So she had immediately become active in organizing the Civil Defense. They had run classes for children on how to take cover in case of attack, had dug tunnels and shelters, and supplied them with food, blankets, and auxiliary generators. They flew low patterns with the Balgins, honing techniques learned against the tax police and adapting them to Hothri capabilities. Eventually, even the former taxmen joined the group and taught tactics with Claude.

Now the regulars needed a diversion. Excellent. The Balgins had been designed for this, as if someone had seen into the future and knew that they would be needed for more than simple colonial runs. The only problem was that the base had asked Mittner to find volunteers. And there were no volunteers to Mittner's liking.

Claude was about to say something more when a young woman walked up and whispered something in the coordinator's ear. It seemed like he listened, thought for a moment, and then couldn't make up his mind.

"Look, Coordinator," Suzanne was saying. "No one cut me any slack as a bush pilot. I'm not about to sit on my can while a bunch of bugs turn my home into carbon. You got that? Either you let us do something now, inside this military strategy, or we're just going to take matters into our own hands. After all, our grandparents didn't come here because it was easy and they didn't leave when their hands got a little dirty.''

The entire auditorium erupted in cheers. The coordinator stood and waved both arms at the crowd to sit down and come to order. No one did anything of the kind. Claude jumped up and grabbed Suzanne's hand and held it high in the air.

Later that night Suzanne came to dinner. Claude's house was still, with only the two of them sitting on the floor in the living room sipping wine. ''You know,'' Suzanne said softly. ''There's a good chance we won't survive.''

Claude nodded. ''I know.'' She took in the room, the walls her grandparents had built with their own hands from rough-hewn planks of the trees that had once stood on this land. Time and work had smoothed the boards and filled the chinks with white plaster. Her mother had made the rug they sat on, hooked together from bits of rag that Claude could still identify. That blue piece had been her father's militia uniform, and the fine white muslin had been her own christening dress. Holocubes stood on the table, her sons, her and Henri on their wedding day.

Now Henri was gone, killed in the first Hothri attack. She might never know if the boys made it, but she would rather be dead than know for a fact they were. Beyond that there was this precious land, hers, as close as her own flesh. She could not imagine anyone else owning it.

*What the hell did the Hothri want, anyway?* Claude wondered. They could hardly stand the smell of the air, the gravity was a touch high for them, they didn't eat anything the Aristans grew, wanted nothing the Aristans had so far as she could see.

Perhaps that was the worst part, the part that made it worth dying. It was one thing for someone else who might love the land to take it, but for bugs who couldn't even appreciate what they would gain, that was unthinkable.

And at forty-seven, Claude Dessales still felt young. Still felt almost immortal, although she knew in her mind that was a delusion. The fire that had made her take the claim on Faker's Ball and never give it up, never give up her personal Balgin or her fuel cache as well, that sheer obstinacy was enough to goad her on. Taken together, all her reasons formed a single and overwhelming equation.

"Time."

Claude came awake instantly, surprised to see Elizabeth standing over her with a cup of coffee. "For the mission briefing," Elizabeth explained.

Claude zipped into her suit and noticed a new patch on the shoulder. She didn't know what it meant or where it had come from, or even who had steamed it on while she had slept. There was no time to worry about it now. She took the coffee from Elizabeth and drained it in three gulps, burning her mouth in the process. Then she followed the girl into the briefing room.

They were the last pilots from the Force to arrive. There were fourteen in the room. So the two who hadn't come back had already been replaced. Or maybe it had been longer than Dessales thought. She had no idea how long she had been asleep, only that it hadn't been long enough. A week would hardly be long enough. She blinked. Sleep was a luxury she didn't have time for. They were badly overextended with only six groups from the Civil Defense, but that didn't alter their objective. Harry the enemy constantly. Don't give them a moment of silence, maintain constant attack, and above all, keep their attention.

Dessales didn't even know why they bothered with the briefings. The mission outline seemed plain enough to her, although there were some minor points such as how the Force should coordinate their harassment.

"We're getting to them," the briefing officer told them. He was a regular and wore all the little attachments that went with his official status. "They have more fighters on patrol all the time now, and intelligence figures they're stretched very thin. At least on double shifts. Skills are deteriorating and fighters are easier to lure from their base ships and even their groups. They don't fly elements the way we do; they stick to their groups of four. This gives them more firepower but makes them less flexible. Mass over finesse."

There was a general snort from the assembled Force. That fit the Hothri profile dead on, and they had the experience to know it.

"We want you to lure them out near the edge of our moon

shadow. While you were all resting, a team of jacques, the very best regulars, you know, planted a few surprises. The point is, take the fighters in through. We want the lighters and maybe the larger ships to follow.''

Claude smiled broadly when she saw the plan. It was even worth listening to this stick in a uniform. Good enough that she would have been proud of it herself. As it was, she couldn't wait to fly.

The Balgins were ready, prepped by the crew chiefs while the flyers had been on down time. The crew chiefs were mixed, regular and Civil Defense, but Claude's was Willie Hunt who had been the best Balgin mechanic within a thousand klicks of Chapelle St. Anne. She didn't do much preflight, that would be an insult to Willie's special talents and his pride. Instead she merely strapped on the bird and told Willie to release the locks. She saw him smile through the transparent canopy and was rewarded. Willie Hunt had never been seen to smile unless he approved. Obviously he approved of Claude.

They took off as in regular formation at twenty second intervals, and the shaking of powering up had hardly settled before Claude could see Faker's Ball below her. Only a touch of glitter in the rough terrain, she had spotted those craters so many times before when landing with supplies and hope. Hope for a major find this time, and hope for a little peace and quiet away from what was becoming too bustling a center at Chapelle St. Anne. The claim twinkled under the Balgin's burners and then she was far into the dark and starless night.

But there was an array of light ahead of them, the energy complex of the Hothri fleet. From this distance they seemed massed, more numerous than she had seen them before. And more menacing. Taking the briefing boy's data that they were shaky and overwrought was pure faith, and faith was something Claude had never had. Around her was the sullen dark of the minefield, the matte clusters dead even against the brilliance of the oncoming Force.

Willie had been better than usual. He had programmed the minefield map into the navigational software so she didn't even have to make corrections herself. *Bless you, Willie Hunt.* She couldn't see the mines at all, and that was both frightening and reassuring. Maybe they weren't there.

And then the computer buzzed her all clear and in the open, nothing but vacuum black between her and the enemy.

She found her target immediately, a group of four already coming forward from the protection of the cruiser's large guns to engage. Bad judgement. A lime green pilot would know better. Maybe the intel geeks were right and the Hothri were as vulnerable to stress and exhaustion as humans.

She touched her transmitter and said, "Eye in the needle." They were merely Civil Defense. They didn't have to use the approved regular code for a configuration. Suzanne and Leonie and Elizabeth knew what she meant.

They formed up around her, Elizabeth and Leonie "up" and to each side, Suzanne dead below. They held position only long enough for the Hothri to note and begin their weapons sequence. Before the bugs ever fired, Leonie and Elizabeth broke to the sides and down, circling outward as Suzanne and Claude broke opposite up and down and poured on the speed. They quite literally "wove" the Hothri into a pattern, herding them together as a group. Then, in a move so perfectly timed that it had to be pure artistry, all four doubled back on their trails and recrossed. Each of them hit the center point at exact twenty second intervals and then looped further back toward the minefield. It looked like they were beating a retreat before the overwhelming firepower of the enemy, dodging and splitting to keep from getting caught in the energy onslaught directed at them.

It only looked like a retreat. Oh, Willie had done better than beautifully this time. The entire group entered the minefield at the same time. Their spacing looked random and panicked. In fact, they were placed to pull the Hothri fighters exactly to the dark mine clusters that lay silently between them.

*Let them come all the way,* Claude thought. She held that wish hard as she dodged through the booby-trapped sector of space. *Let them collect.* The mines were attracted to burner energy and attached themselves to anything that manifested that. Aristan ships sent out a signal that kept the mines away. Any ship not broadcasting, theoretically, would be covered with tiny black boils that would erupt with as much power as a good close shot with the plasma cannon.

The group continued to weave. Claude didn't bother to tune into Hothri frequencies; she couldn't make any sense of their chittering in any case. But she still kept radio dis-

cipline among her group. They knew what to do. They'd
practiced this weave movement a hundred times before.

She and Suzanne had perfected the maneuver with Henri
and Suzanne's friend Paul, running unlicensed tabac seed-
lings down to farmers in the south. The profits on tabac
were enormous, big enough to take the risk, and they had
worked the route and the method before they ever tried with
contraband. And for about seven Aristan years they had had
a very good business, until Paul got caught and sentenced
to L'isle Jamais.

The final pass turned all four Balgin around and back
toward enemy space. But this time they went around the
minefield, not through it. Better to leave some of the munitions for someone else. One or two of those matte black
bubbles was deadly enough. And if the jacques had put a
time-delay on them then there was even hope of getting one
of the cruisers or more. Claude liked the idea very much.

"Let's go home," she said into the transmitter.

The group formed on her again. Now the Hothri who had
been pursuing them were angry, and their firepower increased. But the Balgin had been built for speed, stripped
for speed, and Willie Hunt had been a racing champion for
ten seasons before his son started taking the titles.

They ran back in step pattern, Suzanne and Leonie in the
lead this time, Claude and Elizabeth in the rear. Claude
heard her receiver buzz twice before she responded. She
was more angry at the prospect of losing radio discipline
than worried about anything being wrong.

"Fuel going red," Elizabeth said.

Claude went cold. Fuel critical was worse than enemy
fire. Pilot error, it had to be. Elizabeth didn't have enough
experience for a mission like this, Dessales had known that
from the begining. She had tried to dissuade the child, but
Elizabeth was at that age that combined a simple belief in
perfect justice and a sense of immortality, which between
the two produced extreme heroism and hardheaded stupid-
ity. This was the latter. Elizabeth should have turned back
as soon as she noted her fuel was low.

"Can you make it back?" Claude demanded.

There was a choke at the other end. Or maybe it was
merely flack getting in the way of the transmission. Claude
held her breath and flew, keeping her speed up. On her
scope she could see Elizabeth lagging behind. And on her

sixes were a group of very mad Hothri throwing megatons of plasma bombs.

"See you later," Elizabeth said, and Claude heard the hysteria under her control. Or maybe it was only her imagination, her own hysteria. She was the group leader, she was responsible, and it was no surprise that Elizabeth was the first to go.

The scope showed it flat in orange on black. At least Dessales didn't have to watch the girl eject in the pilot's capsule, see her Balgin and then the tiny capsule consumed by enemy fire.

Her hand shook ever so slightly, rocking her controls and causing the Balgin to shudder even so delicately. The one kill must have slaked the Hothri rage—they were no longer being pursued so singlemindedly. Her own fuel was well in the black. That was the first and most important lesson, fuel is life. No skill, no shooting, no justice, and no speed can save you from fuel shortage. Elizabeth had been too young to understand the vital importance, the elegance even, of that simple lesson. Goneaux, at sixteen, had been far too sophisticated to worry about something as basic as fuel. And now she would never be more than sixteen, would never worry about age or energy or children or adulthood. She had had all of those in her last few seconds before the enemy had turned her to cinder.

And then the screen blazed, everything completely absorbed in the orange haze. The Hothri she had led through the minefield had blown. The mines, on time destruct, had waited until they were back in the pack. Claude wondered woodenly how many they had taken out with that explosion. Surely they hadn't had time to come aboard one of the great dreadnoughts and blow it from the inside out. Or maybe one of the others from another group in the Force had done it. She prayed. Only a dreadnought blowing its drive would blank the screen like that.

*Elizabeth, they are for you,* Claude said silently. *And you will find them all in Hell, and they will serve you, like the slaves killed with the Pharoahs.* Dessales didn't know where she'd picked up that bit of trivia, but somehow it seemed right.

Elizabeth Goneaux had been born without fear. That was the only way Claude and Henri Dessales could explain her attitude. Of all the refugee children she was the one who didn't cringe, didn't cry, didn't jump and dive at every loud noise. Instead she had turned and made faces at the cowards who surrounded her.

Undersized for her age and anger, Claude assumed that she must have been from Angelique. What a name for a mudball, but the one-percenters from Arista had thought it beautiful. Angelique had not been the first colony world to fall to the Hothri, only the most furious.

They had been way out on the fringe, as far as they could get and still be called part of the Aristan Wave. The settlers were the kind who found the new cities of Arista too closed-in for their taste, and the wilderness becoming too tame. Too many bush pilots, too much contact with humanity, they were the edge who wanted to push on to more open spaces. If it had been practical, Henri had once said, they were the types who would probably prefer an asteroid each. When the Hothri came the settlers were all killed because not one of them surrendered.

What did the Hothri want with those worlds? Nothing had been done at all on Angelique, so far as Claude had heard. The mudball was empty, tilled fields filling up once again with wild grasses. In fifty years the trees will have grown back and there will be no evidence of human settlement there at all.

The very idea was appalling to Claude, whose whole life had been a process of taming and civilizing the land, bringing it under cultivation to serve man as men served it. She thought about the great tracts of forest that had become rich farmland, how the first wave of settlers had practiced slash-and-burn. Quick and dirty, it cleared acres and fertilized them with ash. No matter to those first few that the ash would be leeched out in a few years and the soil depleted. There was plenty of land for the taking on Arista.

Claude's generation had done things very differently. The land isn't ours, she had been taught from her first days at school. The land belongs to the future. We are its caretakers, and it is up to us to leave it richer for our being there. So the forests became lush green fields. Cows grazed the grassland and chickens ran free range in the yard. Geese announced visitors, ducks took over the ponds, and the gentle hills started to produce wheat and cabbage and haricot beans.

On Angelique the tamed acres were falling back to wild as the Hothri ignored the rich potential of the small planet and pressed on their attack.

The children had been sent on to Arista. The colonists of Angelique had thought of Arista as being the bastion of humanity, impervious to attack. Compared to Angelique, perhaps it was. Three adults made the trip with the children—a pilot so old that his license would have been revoked on Arista for slow reflexes, a teacher whose limbs were twisted from a disease that could have been treated easily on a more civilized world, and a young woman who had been born without eyes. These would be useless fighting against the aliens but could chaperone the children to safety.

Elizabeth Goneaux had been the first off the battered transport, the first to explore her new world. She hadn't been cautious then, either, running head-first into Henri, who was on duty at the port. He had brought her home. Her, and six other children.

Three of those six were later adopted by other couples in the Chapelle St. Anne area. Two were within a year of their majority and went off and joined the regulars as soon as they had come of age. One of the children had died, supposedly of cancer caused by radiation exposure while still on Angelique. Claude privately held the opinion that it had been sorrow and not radiation, but there was no use telling that to the hospital techs.

Elizabeth had stayed. She had never been like a daughter, exactly. There were still things about Angelique that she never told any of the Dessales clan. Like who her parents were, what their farm had been like, or what had happened when they heard the Hothri had come. She had known that they had welcomed the aliens at first, wary as they would be of any stranger but not ready to fight. That ended when the supply shuttle from Vink was vaporized in friendly space.

To Elizabeth, fighting Hothri was what adults did when they weren't farming or mining. She learned to fly before she left Angelique, and once on the Dessales farm she began to show her skill. When the Civil Defense was formed she begged Claude to join.

"But I can fly the Balgin better than any of them," she had said, curling her lip contemptuously at the thought of the Schrantz gang getting in on the action.

Claude had to agree. If the Schrantz youngsters, already older than Elizabeth but without nearly her skill, were accepted, then she could hardly keep Elizabeth back. And it was only Civil Defense, she reminded herself, their job to do the things the regulars couldn't do while fighting the Hothri. Patrolling the sector, making sure that none of the little alien vehicles slipped through, watching for Balgins in distress, running shuttle missions to the moons and out to the big ships. Bringing them fresh produce, cheese, meat, butter, the things that made Arista so very desirable. So worthy of all their lives.

Claude did not cry when they returned to the base this time, even with Elizabeth dead. The girl had done all she knew how to do. And Elizabeth had been a child of war. Claude could hardly imagine her in peacetime, calculating crop rotation and fertilization techniques, trying to keep the cache on Faker's Ball secure just to raise Mittner's blood pressure. Those things didn't suit Elizabeth at all.

And they no longer suited Claude, either. She had been at war too long, had lost too much. Only the fleet was left, if they were able to break the cordon.

Suzanne and Leonie left her alone during the rest period. No one even pressed her to come and eat, reminded her that she needed her strength. There was enough delicacy left among them that they were left to their losses alone.

Claude slept and sat in silence. At first there was nothing at all in the silence. Then whisps of memory came together, bound to something far colder than hate. There was simply necessity . . . revenge. She could get a cruiser. And if she was lucky she could do it. She had a plan and it was a good one.

The more she thought the more she knew that she was right. A lopsided smile crossed her face. Pleasure cut through the nothingness of loss.

No one questioned her when she checked over the Balgin. Even Willie gave her a guided tour instead of his usual huff that his work was perfect, and that if she didn't trust him she could get another mechanic.

She strapped in and asked for clearance to lift. Maybe they were surprised, but no one was going to stop her. This was the Civil Defense, after all. They were not regulars, not subject to the checks and counter-checks the regulars insisted on. Perhaps that was why the military didn't trust the Civil Defense. Not because they were civilians per se, or cowards, but because they weren't predictable.

She took the Balgin out but didn't arc high over the horizon through the radio shadow and out. No, this time she stayed low, skimming the dust, headed to the crater field. Headed to Faker's Ball.

It was still sparkling the way she remembered it. The dome was deflated, the hut and tool shed of the mining camp sat quietly under the plastic drape like some summer cottage waiting for the owners to open up. Claude spared one sorry look in that direction, and released a wry snort as she realized that Mittner would probably be the next person to air-up the dome. But that wasn't her destination.

On the other side of the crater, in a deep niche of their own, were two torpedo tanks full of fuel. She rolled the Balgin down on the hard-packed strip and slapped her faceplate down. There was only a moment of nostalgia as she got out and inspected the tanks. For all the years they had been sitting there, they were in perfect condition. No problem. In the lower lunar gravity it wasn't difficult for her to haul them, one at a time, over to the Balgin. They fit perfectly where the plasma cannon had been attached, even down to the same gauge locking pins. She wouldn't be needing the cannon on this run, and Suzanne would know where to come looking when the ordnance were needed.

Full fuel tanks did mass more than the plasma cannon set-up. The Balgin lifted like a pregnant cow. It didn't like the extra mass and the off-balance of the sloshing under its carriage, but it had no choice.

Alone on this side of the moon there was nothing at all in the sky. Even Arista was out of view. Only a faint sprinkle of ring dust shimmered across the sky, two distant stars twinkling through. Claude Dessales thought it was the most beautiful sight she had ever seen. With a sigh she turned the little craft away and back to the far too crowded Hothri main fleet.

One single little Balgin not coming in on any flight schedule without any Force was a surprise. The Hothri didn't mass out at her the way they had in the past, when she had been flying formation with the rest of the group. Now they hesitated, not sure what to make of this straggler. Perhaps

they thought it was one of their own who had captured a
human vessel.

*To hell with what they're thinking,* Claude said to herself,
clearing her mind. They were aliens. Who knew how they
thought or if they did at all. She didn't care. They were
enemy, that was the only important thing.

She put on the speed. The Balgin, even with the additional mass, pulled forward hard against the vacuum. She
could feel the sluggishness under the start, the strain in the
lines, and she fought it for every scrap of power the tiny
craft had. Pushed it farther, harder, willing it to a higher
and higher speed.

She felt like she was flying on will alone, her own abso-
lute concentration against the massed might of the enemy.
*Don't see me. Come on, faster.* She knew the thing could
only put on so much. Every nanosecond more she squeezed
out of it was that much closer to the red line.

Not that it mattered. For the very first time she could
ignore that binding limit. Harder, harder, she coaxed the
engine against the night. And it responded. Willie Hunt
must have known. In his heart he had tuned the Balgin to
racing standards, to an edge Claude had never approached
before.

Her blood was on fire, her skin stung as if it was whipped
with the racial memory of atmosphere. Speed burned in her
veins, it dried her mouth, it was wrested from the very core
of her being. Speed. Pure, brilliant, beyond anything she
could have imagined. She was drunk with it, crazy.

And she was beyond the enemy now. There was no way
they could respond to her in time, no way the merely mortal
reflexes of any species could catch her. She raced to the
heart of the Hothri fleet just as they realized they were at
risk.

Claude smiled. There were two cruisers dead ahead, close
together—so close that if she got one, the neutrino shower
from the dying drive should catch the other. Around them
glowed the nimbus of their shields, shields created by technology for the tools of technology. Created to keep blasting
energy out. Never created to deflect a ballistic fighter at
close range. Never meant to keep craziness from piercing
reality in a space so insane that it superseded whatever reality persisted.

No triggering device was needed for the fuel cells on the

undercarriage. Impact alone was enough to set them off as her own ignition flared and caught. The shields would even spread the blaze faster, energy from them feeding the raging explosion that would blossom across the blackness like a time-lapse flower, like a star going nova.

The power had fused with her essence. Claude Dessales no longer existed, even though, for the moment, she still lived. Instead there was only flame and rage, power and intent. She became something far more than human, and far more alien than even the enemy. For a moment, she became a god.

And as a god, the eternal goddess of war, she was immortal as the little Balgin shredded through the shields and skin of the alien cruiser, turning it into the brightest star in Arista's sky.

Back on Arista there was a ceremony where the name of the base was changed. It wasn't the largest base by any means, but it was appropriate . . . from Chapelle St. Anne to Chapelle St. Claude.

"Only there wasn't any St. Claude, was there?" Leonie asked Suzanne.

The older woman smiled and watched the new cornerstone laid, the plaque set in the ground. How had Claude known the exact moment the main fleet had approached the Hothri cordon? She had been radio dark, completely cut off and on her own. Still, her action had surely diverted enemy attention at the critical moment.

"I don't know about saints," Suzanne said. "But there had to have been an angel."

# Total War

## by Bill Fawcett

In a series of space battles, the Aristan Navy was driven from space. At first the mine fields, mobile missiles, and platforms were able to discourage Hothri landings. But they were almost entirely ineffective in preventing high speed bombing runs, and even less effective in dealing with the swarms of missiles launched from the Hothri's superior position at the top of Arista's gravity well.

Many of the vital industries and military positions were protected in hardened sites. The 3.5 million (of an initial five million) surviving, non-combatant population was less fortunate. When it became apparent that there would soon be Hothri landings on an unprecedented scale, it was admitted that there weren't enough defenders to protect even a small portion of the planet.

During the Napoleonic wars Prussia and Russia faced a similar problem. Confronted with superior numbers of French veterans and a shortage of trained troops, they armed large numbers of Landwehr and interspersed them with their own highly trained soldiers. On Arista an effort was made to arm virtually everyone old enough to fire a weapon. Advanced training techniques would instruct these otherwise untrained civilians on how to fire the weapons, but could not prepare them for the realities of combat.

Historically, the Landwehr often fought valiantly, but suffered massive casualties. Un-named and commanded by teachers, retired soldiers, and local police officers, the Aristan Landwehr often fought with a tenacity and courage that surprised even themselves.

The first Hothri landings were greeted with ferocity, though at great cost to the planet's adult population. With the Hothri maintaining complete control of the air and space over the battlefield, the casualty toll rose quickly. Any show of Aristan resistance was often met with air strikes and strafing from slowed orbiting space ships.

After several days the Hothri made a final, massive attempt to overwhelm the remaining defenses. No one knew how many humans were alive and capable of fighting. Field communications were non-existent or jammed. In almost total disarray, the diminished Aristan military united with the skeletal civilian reserves to face this final challenge. The average age of the these last remaining Landwehr was fifteen years.

# UNREALITY

## by Jody Lynn Nye

JUST LAST WEEK, they were standing in the lavatory, smoking illegal herb sticks, comparing hair styles and boyfriends. Today, they huddled together under the musty floors of the school building, hiding from warriors of an alien invasion that the news services had screamed was coming for weeks. By the smell, Thari could tell that a whole bunch of the kids huddled around her had wet their pants in fear, and not all of them were the baby-graders. Some of them were her own age, thirteen Standard. It wasn't fair that the children of Arista should have to suffer for the attack that their elders, military bosses, had made on the Hothri.

The Hothri could read each other's minds, so all of them instantly knew about anything that happened to one of them. They were seven-foot tall bugs that looked a lot like ants and breathed through their chests. Some human soldiers or something had killed some of the Hothri, and the rest of the Hothri went berserk. That was how Thari heard it. Now they were going to kill all the humans in the galaxy, and especially those on Arista. For months afterward, Thari had nightmares about giant bugs.

She was calmer now than she was at the beginning. There were only three things that you could do with the invasion imminent: leave the planet—which only the rich people could afford to do—fleeing toward the end of the galaxy that the bugs hadn't yet reached; kill yourself, as some of the kids in her block had done; or cope. It was the cheapest way to go.

Thari was a little surprised to find the inner strength in herself not to follow those of her friends who had hanged, monoxided, or lasered themselves to escape. Her father, Marcel, was a communications tech. He had offered to send Thari, her mother, and six-year-old brother, Patrice, away once they knew the attack was coming, but he told them he would have to stay. In the event of an emergency, he needed to remain on duty at his transmission post so their fellow Aristans would know they weren't alone. No matter where they were, they could tune in to Station Duxieme and hear another human voice, which might spell the difference for them between sanity and fearful madness. To him, his duty was obvious. His quiet heroism had steeled her, and she went through the school drills with his voice in her ears.

The school hadn't even dismissed the children during the first Aristan War. No one in their province knew it had taken place until it was over. In about thirty-four minutes flat, over a hundred thousand people in Arista's principal town were dead, blasted from space. The Hothri hadn't bothered to land. They sprayed bombs across the globe, picking off prime targets in population centers, and then flew away.

The Second War was longer, but it killed most of the army and the space navy. There was no one much left to defend the planet except the men and women judged unfit for service, the elderly, and the children. It wasn't fair, Thari thought, clutching her newly issued laser rifle. *Children shouldn't have to fight wars. There should be grownups to defend us.*

The landscape outside the building was unrecognizable. Shelling and firebombing from the Hothri ships had wrecked and burned every building from the town center out to a radius of over fifty miles. Thari didn't like to think of the fates of the people unlucky enough not to be near Civil Defense shelters. Her family had a storm cellar underneath their house, where her mother and brother were hiding. Of course, her father wasn't in it. The communications tower was lying in shattered fragments from a blast it sustained during the Second War. The soldiers who had sorted through the wreckage looking for bodies wouldn't let her near when they found her father. He was dead, of course. Her mother, who had to claim the body, was devastated. When the surviving officers came to ask Thari to join the Youth Brigade and defend Arista, Thari's mother had said only one thing, "No." Maman had guns and explosives which were for blasting stumps and rocks out of their field, but which she planned to use on the Hothri if they came. But Thari had

gone anyway. She didn't want the other kids in the flitterbus
to think she was a coward. Besides, her father would surely
have wanted her to do it. She still couldn't believe he was
dead.

Some of the volunteers were as young as eleven and
twelve years of age. Thari and the gang with whom she used
to hang out struck a clique immediately, volunteering to
work together in a team.

Thari wasn't panicking because it wasn't real to her yet.
She was holding an assault gun, but it had never been fired,
most particularly not by her. The sleep tapes she had listened to taught her how to fire and maintain it perfectly,
educated her mind and nerves—her hands knew where to
hold it and what to push—but she had never actually pulled
the trigger. She could tell which of her gang were afraid—
it showed in their eyes even while they were acting tough.
Thari understood. If she felt the same way, she too would
have concealed her feelings for fear of being teased as a
weakling. The appearance of strength was vital. Otherwise,
the army of schoolchildren would deteriorate into helpless,
useless rabble as one after another broke down, and they all
knew it.

The underground chamber where they were sheltered
beneath the school was built for food storage in the first
days of Arista's colonization. It was a big, chilly, ceramic-
lined box with only ceiling grilles and the open doors for
ventilation. Since they didn't dare to run the noisy fans for
long, the air was heavy except for five minutes on the hour
when the danger of suffocation outweighed the fear of the
invaders. Light was provided by cool-lanterns, placed in
the middle of each company's section like tribal bonfires
around which the student soldiers huddled. Thari knew she
had been there two days, but without the sun, there was
no way to tell when one day ended and the next began.

Guilbert, one of her gang, sat next to the lantern with
his head down. He was plugged into his portable computer
game, one of the few amusements allowed in the shelter
because the commander said that it didn't give off enough
electrical impulses to be noticed by the Hothri. Thari knew
Guilbert's toy well. It was a family heirloom, passed down
from his many-times great grandfather, who had lived on
Earth. It was good that the games were permitted. Otherwise there was too much time for imagination.

The tiny backlit screen reflected off Guilbert's set teeth, and sweat beaded on his forehead as he destroyed imaginary enemies over and over again. He followed orders given to him, and smiled to show he acknowledged them, but no more. The captain of Thari's team, a marine wounded in space combat, explained that Guilbert was suffering from a kind of shock. Guilbert had seen his house blown up with everyone inside it after he had gone out to collect milk from the delivery flitter. The flitter driver brought the hysterical boy to army hospital. After three days he had calmed down, but he never spoke again. Captain Gavrielle said she expected Guilbert would function perfectly well in combat, but she was concerned if he would ever adjust again to a normal life after the war was over.

Thari liked Gavrielle, who was the only one in the company who spoke of what would happen afterwards. Most of the other seasoned soldiers were cautious or cagey, not willing to engender hope in their young charges. Only the deranged didn't understand how slim their chances of survival were, but Thari wanted to hear someone talk about peace and hope again, even if it was all lies. Gavrielle had a prostethic left arm and shoulder joint, the result of a firefight with the ant-people. The wound had been cauterized by the flamethrower-like weapons the Hothri carried. They left her carcass for dead. Only six of her shipmates out of a thousand had survived, all in a similar condition, and yet she still believed in hope, which heartened her young charges. Gavrielle had probably been assigned to handle the children's army because she knew how to keep them from falling into utter despair.

Her talent for psychology was actively needed by Guilbert's buddy, Mimione. Mimi, the tallest girl in Thari's class, had shown unusual talent for empathy, which was great since she planned to become a doctor, but a positive detriment near the Hothri. The ant-people broadcast their feelings on a wide band which even ordinary humans could sense sometimes. When the Hothri were agitated, Mimi was agitated. She wasn't the only one of her kind; other creches reported the problem, and not only among children. Some felt it all the time; others, like Mimi, seemed to be affected in proportion to the distance between them and the enemy.

"That's good," Gavrielle had said encouragingly. "We can use you as an early warning system to tell if the Hothri are nearby."

Thari could tell that Captain Gavrielle had earned Mimi's lifelong gratitude for that. The others were starting to consider Mimione a danger. What if the Hothri could receive Mimi's feelings, too? There were twice as many who didn't believe that she was receiving any sensations at all, didn't believe in empathy, and thought the girl was insane. As far as Thari was concerned, it didn't matter if you believed or not; you couldn't disregard her accuracy. As a result, everyone had their eye on Mimione, wondering when she would have her next attack.

After a while she couldn't stand the silence any longer. She nudged Friedrich, one of her best friends in the clique, who had been appointed her 'buddy' by the captain. The two of them were unofficial corporals for the team, and did special errands for Gavrielle whenever she had something to do.

"Fray?" she said.

The stocky boy was drowsing, elbow and head resting on one knee. "Wha'?"

"When do you suppose something will happen? I'll go crazy sitting in here too long, staring at the walls."

"Maybe never," Friedrich replied, coming awake all at once as he always did. His irises were a curious red-brown, like the light behind a cat's eyes. Fray was something of an all-around athlete. He could shoot and throw with accuracy, run and jump well, and he was very strong. He needed fewer hours with the teaching tapes than the others did. Thari envied him. Her only claim to excellence was that she could run fast, a useless talent in the face of Hothri flamethrowers. Fray shook his straight red-brown hair out of his face. "You could listen to the tapes again."

"No, I want to do something. I'm bored!"

Fray's eyes glittered mockingly. "Do you want to go with me? There's a quiet corner near the cooling room we could use. I promise not to be boring."

Thari gaped at him. *"Mais non!* Be serious, for once. What would they say?" She glanced warily at the colonel, who was conferring with three of the six captains, seated between two cool-lanterns in the middle of the gigantic chamber.

The youth lifted one shoulder disdainfully. "They think we're going to die soon. I don't think they would care what we do. Are you afraid they'll tell your mother?"

"Yes! She would be horrified that I lost it to a lowly pig like you."

"If you change your mind . . ." he offered temptingly. "This could be your last chance."

"I refuse to think this is my last anything," Thari announced firmly.

"If you are bored," Gavrielle's gentle voice interrupted them, "you can help Captain Dauvime's assistant distribute food from stores. It's time for supper."

The group ate their canned rations in the dimness, chatting in low voices over the meal. There was some speculation, overheard from other groups and passed from youth to youth, as to when the brigade might be called out to fight. There was no armor for such small warriors, so only the adults would face the Hothri directly. The children were to fight guerrilla style, firing from cover. They knew from radio-to-radio transmissions that other groups had been destroyed by the marching troops of Hothri. Thari shrugged. None of it felt real since the news came over electronic media. There was no immediacy. Bang, bang, like on Guilbert's screen. Game over, start a new one.

The air was getting so heavy Thari had trouble keeping her eyes open. Must be close to ventilation time, she thought sleepily, chewing the same tasteless mouthful again and again. As if in response to her thought, the heavy fans clashed once and began their ponderous humming. The air began to stir, and fresh breezes gently brushed Thari's grateful face. She swallowed and reached for another bite. There was a sudden, stifled whimper from the far side of the lantern. Mimi was beginning to twitch.

Gavrielle went to her, imposing in her battle armor, and put a gentle hand on the girl's shoulder.

"What's wrong, petite?"

"The hate. It's stronger than before," the girl said, looking up at the captain with worried eyes. "They're close by."

"Give her a sedative," Fray growled impatiently, lowering one knee and raising the other to brace his plate. The food was uninteresting, but no one threw away a bite. It was too precious.

"Could the Hothri have heard the fans go on?" Gavrielle asked, shushing Fray with one hand while watching Mimi.

Alarmed, Thari snatched the laser rifle off the floor and looked to her captain for guidance.

"There's been no report of Hothri near here," Gavrielle began, soothingly. "We'll wait until there's verification from outside."

A huge crash shook the building, and a little piece of the ceiling cracked away and fell toward the floor. Everyone watched it fall, dull-eyed until the section hit the ground and splintered with an explosive bang. The six Youth Brigade commanders rushed to confer in the middle of the floor with their colonel as everyone began to talk at once.

"Silence!" the colonel bellowed, raking an eye across the astonished faces of the students. The six commanders bent to hear the muffled voices coming suddenly over the colonel's command receiver unit. He gestured sharply, and the captains scattered to their companies.

Gavrielle strode back to the lantern. With her prosthetic hand, she jerked the earplugs out of Guilbert's ears, and signaled for attention.

"We move out now," she ordered the group crisply, whipping her long tail of brown hair around her head and pinning it in place. "This position is no longer safe. We've been ordered to relocate as quickly as we can. Gather your gear. Follow me." She put on her helmet, and the power lights of her suit sprang to life, red and yellow in the darkness.

The gang stumbled to its feet. Two of the teens were kicked awake in haste by their fellows. They rose, glaring, and were given their orders by Gavrielle. Each of them was issued a backpack containing a small medikit, a blanket, a knife, and two weeks worth of iron rations. On her command they shouldered their rifles and lined up in rows of two, facing the exit. In order, the companies filed outside.

"Be prepared to run for cover if we are attacked," Gavrielle reminded them.

They could come and drop a bomb on her head the next minute, for all Thari cared. She was enjoying the fresh air and the feel of the sun on her hair and face. It was welcome after sitting in the school ice box for two days. She took a deep breath and let it out in a happy little sigh. Fray, walk-

ing beside her, peered at her out of the corner of his eye
and gave her a lopsided grin.

At the top of the long concrete staircase, Gavrielle peeled
off from the line of students in front of her and veered to
the left, into the angle of shadow cast by the noon sun. Her
company, surprised, hastily corrected its direction and
marched after her. Marching in formation had evidently
been one of the lessons on the soma tapes, Thari decided,
snickering. Everyone was putting the same foot forward at
the same time. During school pep rallies the students
couldn't walk in step if you tied their left feet together in a
line. The gun bumped on her back with the rhythm of the
march.

Mimi was behind her. Thari could hear the sensitive's
breath coming in short, pained gasps, and Victor, her boy-
friend, whispering encouragement to her in an undertone.
The school grounds were a disaster, even worse than they
had been when the brigade went into hiding. The most recent bombing had shaken down what little remained of the
school building, leaving it in heaps of ruined brick, glass,
and wooden beams. The grass was fried brown and crisp
where it stood. Only the scorched tips moved in the breeze.
The blades of grass broke off under their feet as the students
marched across it.

"Aren't we getting transportation?" asked a girl named
Hildie from several ranks behind Thari.

The gang sneered, shooting scornful glances over their
shoulders at the girl, who blanched. Not that every one of
them wasn't wondering the same thing, Thari thought, remembering the flitterbus that had gathered them from their
homes.

"We are not going that far," Gavrielle announced patiently, and sped up to a brisk walk. "Stay on the rough
path. You will be more invisible to enemy optics that way."

It felt funny to be sneaking furtively across the fields in
broad daylight, but that was when it was safest to move.
The Hothri were nearly blind in bright lights. It was common knowledge that they saw heat instead of light. Thari
felt they were fortunate that it was a hot, sunny day, when
the very ground was baking with heat. The parched grass
seemed to be shimmering around them.

The pairs of students moved slowly and far apart on the
broadest, rockiest path. In another two hundred paces, they

were in the village. Nothing much was recognizable. Everything was in worse shape than before the last bombing. Blackened, shard-sharp pieces of tree boles pointing angrily to the sky were the only evidence that what they were walking in had been a very beautiful city park.

"Where are we going?" one of the small kids asked.

"To Arista Gardens," Gavrielle said shortly. "Please remain silent."

Her warning was ignored. "Arista Gardens!" The whisper flew along the attenuated rank of teenagers. That was the premiere party ground on the continent. The amusement park! The dance hall! The rose promenade! Thari's heart lifted, and she picked up her feet instead of shuffling them on the hot stones.

"We are not going there to play," Gavrielle cautioned them, observing the change in morale somewhat sadly. "It isn't what you remember. We are to be stationed there. The bombing of the school building was the Hothri's way of telling us they are landing a force in this area."

"Do you see?" Thari hissed at Fray. "Mimione was right."

Within two hours, they were on the grounds of the Arista Gardens. To say that it had changed was more than understatement—it was a falsehood. Thari felt very old, walking through the ruins of what had been a beautiful parkland.

Arista Gardens was designed to be an entertainment complex for anyone and everyone. No visit to Arista was complete without a trip to the Gardens. There were broad green lawns and gardens in which one could picnic. A lake was kept stocked with game fish, and there were canoes and pedal boats available for rent if one wanted to enjoy the lake. The beach along one edge was lined with white sand trucked in from the ocean shore. A music complex boasted a band shell where famous pop and classical groups played for the customers who relaxed on the lawns, and a dance hall for those who felt like being more active. There was a full sized, permanent carnival, complete with rides and try-your-skills games and an arcade.

Where the green lawn had been was bare, pitted ground. Scraps of colored paper and torn pennants blowing between tree stumps were all that remained of the gay decor of the Gardens. Everything else was burned black. The walls of the arcade had fallen outward like a horrible flower, reveal-ing the exploded shells of the computer game consoles hunched amid the debris on the interior floor. Some of the babies in the files began to cry. Thari couldn't connect the ruin before her with the famous amusement park, and de-cided she wouldn't try. It was a new place, and it had always looked like this.

Gavrielle permitted them to stroll slowly during day-light, but cautioned that as soon as it began to grow dark, they had to return to the shelters. "The ants are abroad at night, and they can see you by the heat in your body. Noth-ing is important enough to go out during the night. To-morrow a marine force will rendezvous with us here."

Left with free time, Thari and the gang promptly made for the fun house, one of the few amusement buildings left standing. None of the gaudy paint which had covered it remained. The outside was scorched and pitted with flame, but it was intact. Fray was the first to enter the steel-framed building. He disappeared into the darkness while his friends waited impatiently for him to give the all clear.

Suddenly, from the blackness, there came a horrible shriek, which died away into an agonized moan.

"The ants! The ants have got him!" Mimi cried.

Guns in hand, the teenagers rushed into the dark build-ing. "Fray! Friedrich!" they shouted.

Thari stumbled on an uneven step, and realized the floor was moving. "The funhouse is turned on," she called to the others, and flailed to keep her balance.

Victor switched on a miniature lamp he kept at his belt and guided them up the steps and through a crooked door into a hallway. "This was always my favorite amusement," he explained, waving them after him. "We can find him quickly!"

"Ha ha ha!" Fray's voice sounded like it was coming from all around them. "That's the oldest trick in the data-file! And you fell for it!"

The teens stopped, shocked, as the boy's laugh reverber-ated off the metal walls. "I'm going to kill you, Fray," Thari fumed, casting around for her friend. "We thought you'd been eaten by ants. Where are you?"

"Over here!" Fray waved to them from the end of the corridor. They ran to him, and found they were looking at their own reflections, and he was gone.

"It's the house of mirrors," Victor announced.

"Sorry! I'm over here!" Fray called, beckoning from another turn in the path. "And over here!" a third image caroled happily behind them.

The other teens turned around and around.

"Now I'm disoriented," Mimione complained. "Which way did we come in?"

"Look, I'm really here," said Fray's voice. In the shadows behind them, a figure stood with arm raised. They ran to it. Thari threw her arms around its waist, and recoiled with a shriek.

"He's dead!"

Victor inspected the form. "It's a dummy. There are many set up in here to confuse people walking through the maze. The operators move them in and out."

Guilbert and two of the others, Valerie and Claus, vanished into the darkness, but soon came back to the center of the maze.

"We can't figure how to get out," said Valerie. "Every turn we took came to a dead end."

Suddenly, Fray was among them, his eyes glinting. "You give up too easily, my friends. It's simple if you know the secret."

"How did you get here from the other mirror so fast?" Thari demanded, grabbing Fray's arm to make certain he was real.

"There's sliding doors every fifth panel," the youth explained, pushing one open. "Also makes it easy to get around to the exit. It's confusing with all these mirrors."

"We noticed," said Mimi, sarcastically, looming over the unrepentant boy with all her extra inches of height.

"I declare this fun house our private province," Fray said, pulling out a package of herb sticks and passing them around. "Shall we smoke on it?"

It was the morning of the second day since they had left the school building, five days since Thari had seen her mother. It felt like it had been much longer.

The stored food began to run out after two days. Their group was better off than some they spoke to by radio, because Fray was raised a vegetarian, and he showed them what leaves and plants growing near their hiding place would make a healthy meal. Thari missed meat and peanut butter, but she had to admit she had never felt so healthy in her life.

Still, she felt that they were only playing a game of hide-and-seek. Outside, a physical education teacher would clap her hands and cry *"Allons, mes enfants!"* She and her friends would go running into the classroom like they did in the baby-grades, laughing, smug that they'd been able to elude the seeker. There was even an air of camping out when they bedded down in an underground, hollow, metal control room underneath the burned shell of the round-about, and watched the sun through a highframed slot in the wall that let in air but was nearly invisible from street level. Gavrielle made them sleep most of the day so they would be alert during the night when the ant-people were abroad. Thari liked to stay up long enough to see the sunrise.

The marines bivouacked in Arista Gardens had been dec-imated by the Hothri in a minutes-long ship-to-ship engage-ment. Their armor was clean and polished, but it looked timeworn, as did the faces of the men and women wearing it. The marines treated the children tenderly, even rever-ently, as the future of Arista. This drove Thari's gang wild with irritation. They felt their forced adulthood and wanted to converse with the marines as equals.

"Forget it," Victor dismissed them after another frus-trating attempt to gain information from the tired soldiers. "They simply don't know how to talk to us. All they want to do is rest until the ants get here."

Thari felt sorry for them. They trained all their lives to do something that would be over in five minutes. She was surprised they didn't go crazy in training. "I suppose it's because of the discipline training."

"Who cares?" Claus wanted to know. "Let's go into the labyrinth and change the walls around."

One evening, Thari was awakened by Gavrielle, who clapped a hand over the girl's mouth to keep her from crying out. As Thari stared, the captain snapped out her orders in a hush. "Wake the others. Tell them to arm, and BE QUIET."

She nodded her comprehension and Gavrielle turned away. Thari rolled over and touched Fray's arm.

Mimi was thrashing in her sleep. She came awake in a panic, nearly biting off Thari's silencing hand.

"Get your gun," Thari said. "They're here."

"I dreamed them," Mimi whispered. "They're horrible!"

Outside the children's shelter, the marines were hurrying about in the dying light. Under shouted orders, they blasted up rows of concrete barriers out of the midway pavements. As the stonework cooled under white, steamy blasts from a hoselike contraption, the soldiers ranged themselves.

"We have just enough time to hide ourselves," Gavrielle explained to her force. The children were wideyed and nervous. "The marines will do most of the fighting. You are defending them so they can accomplish their task. Teamwork!"

They divided into two groups, one on either side of the midway, with Fray in charge of one and Victor leading the other. Thari's tiny band pressed itself into the angle of a standing wall. It was cold, but Gavrielle assured them it would help conceal them and confuse the Hothri, who saw infrared heat, not light.

Gradually, the more sensitive among them grew agitated. Mimione was so hysterical that Thari was afraid she'd run screaming from their hiding place.

"Shut up," one of the girls hissed from the back ranks.

"Not her again! Smother her! Shoot her!" Fray growled, turning around and shoving his face into Mimi's. "You're going to give our position away to the ants, being hysterical like that. We ought to kill you and stop your misery."

"You've always been a psychopath," Thari ordered in a strong whisper, pushing him away from Mimi. "Leave her alone. It isn't her fault. You've always been against Mimi, even back in school. You didn't want her to join the gang. I didn't understand why. What's the matter, did she refuse to go with you one night?"

"What would you know about it? You've never refused to go with anyone in your life, I bet," Fray snapped hurtfully.

"Moron!" Stung, Thari kicked at him, and he grabbed her ankle and raised it so she had to hop.

"Does the truth hurt?" Fray gloated, red eyes glittering.

"That's enough!" Gavrielle shot over her shoulder. "Silence in the ranks!"

"Stop it," Thari said to Fray, wrenching her leg out of his hand. "Mimione might sound crazy now, but one day, we're going to go back to being in school. She'll just be one of us again."

Fray looked at her darkly, and she saw sadness in his face. "We're never going back to being the same. Even if this ends and we're still alive."

Thari knew what he meant and felt her heart sink, because it was true. He was right. "I don't want this to be my whole life, Fray," she said quietly. "I'll remember it, but I won't let it rule me."

The hot gaze dropped. "Still friends?" he murmured.

"Forever," Thari promised firmly. "Come on. Help me."

Together, they hustled Mimi into a storage shed nestled in a corner of the garden walls. Thari gave her a tranquiltab from her own medikit pouch and stayed with the girl, talking to her until she calmed down. Fray stood guard at the door, and signaled with his gun barrel when it was safe to move out.

The three of them crept around the ruined wall until Gavrielle could see them. She motioned forward with one hand, and Thari stared. The Hothri ships, silent as moths, were landing on the midway and disgorging hordes of troops. They marched out in perfect formation until the marines' white-hot spotlights hit them.

They didn't exactly look like ants, Thari decided, although she could see where the name came from. They just looked more like ants than anything else, except for the locustish back end sticking out behind like a full diaper. They moved with a terrifying grace, even in their haste, stooped figures with bonelessly fluid limbs. As one, the Hothri reached around to their backs and dragged forward blunt metal nozzles attached to hoses. Flame sprang from each nozzle searing the night. Thari pressed herself into the cold wall, making herself as small as possible. When the roaring ceased, she risked a peek around the wall's edge.

The flames didn't reach far enough to take out the spotlights, which were at the distant end of the midway. Yell-

ing, a number of Arista's marines charged forward, hitting
the ground and rolling after firing off explosive charges.

The charges detonated with a howl which temporarily
deafened the children. When the noise ceased, Gavrielle,
who had been watching the marine's commander, gestured
frantically. "Now, petites! Spread out and fire on the
Hothri!"

Thari elbow-wriggled down the backmost row of concrete barriers to her assigned position and poked the nose
of her rifle between two shards of fused stone. Within seconds, a Hothri appeared in her sights, a towering, ugly
menace. She squeezed the trigger as the sleep tapes had
taught her, and a big section of the ant-person's thorax
exploded. Thari lowered her gun sights to stare at the
Hothri whose arms were twitching with uncontrollable reaction. It never let go of its gun, though. In its pain, it
fired madly at the sky, the walls, anything. Thari ducked,
and flames washed over her head and swirled away. The
heat lasted only a few seconds and died away, so she risked
another look at the Hothri.

Thick, ugly-colored fluid poured from its wound. It continued to fire wildly, hitting marines or its own nestmates,
or nothing at all, until it spun slowly to the ground and
stopped moving.

"That was easy," she thought, dismayed, still staring at
the corpse. Steam rose in a thin stream from the extin-
guished flamethrower's nozzle, as if the monster's spirit
was floating away. Otherwise, dead it meant as little to
Thari as it had alive. Mechanically, she picked another
target, and shot at it. This time, she didn't watch the Hothri
die.

The marines numbered as many as the enemy, but they
couldn't seem to match the perfect response of the Hothri
troop. Thari remembered that the ant-people could read
each others' minds. You couldn't assail their organization,
so you had to attack the whole group mind, confuse them.
For her life, she couldn't figure out how you could do it.

The battle seemed like a cross between a computer game
and a video show. In the foreground, Hothri charged past
the barriers and were shot down by the students' fire. They
would rake the barriers with flame, and start to crawl over
the banks of concrete, but died before they reached the children. In the background, marines and Hothri skirmished.

At first, it looked as though the marines couldn't lose. It was their battlefield. Their troop had been divided into small parties for the maximum capability of movement and flexibility, and the minimum for mass casualties. It was not enough. As a row of Hothri came under attack by a party of Aristans, the other ant-people rushed over to join in the kill, sacrificing individuals of their group to protect a greater number. That there were fewer human's dead on the field led Thari to believe that more of them were alive, until she noticed a cluster of the Hothri carrying away the still-twitching body of a human woman.

Mimi jabbed her urgently with the edge of her gun butt. "What are they doing? Where are they taking her?"

"They eat human flesh," Fray said grimly.

"We've got to save her! We can't let the monsters have her!" Mimi began to stand up.

"Down, petites!" Gavrielle called from the end of the row, kneeling so they could see her. "Down!"

A Hothri soldier observed her breaking from cover and scurried forward, raking the captain with the wrist-thick flame of its weapon. Shrieking her agony, Gavrielle fired back on it, but her gun was only a sniper's weapon. In horror, the children watched her armor turn black and melt. The faceplate became opaque, and crackled with black lines. Thari screamed at the Hothri to stop. Fray was the quickest to recover, and shot at the ant soldier, swearing. It was well armored, and the boy's hands were shaking too much to hit it cleanly. The woman's body dropped to the ground, and the Hothri swarmed over the barriers to claim it. Thari cried out and then stifled it with both hands pressed to her mouth, hoping the Hothri couldn't hear her and take them all, too.

"Save her," Guilbert begged, desperately, crawling into Fray's bunker. "She mustn't die."

"Save yourself," Fray snarled, elbowing the boy away. "She's already dead. She wouldn't want us to sacrifice ourselves for her corpse."

"Go back to your post, Guilbert," Thari ordered, trying to keep her voice steady. "Protect the marines. That's what she'd want us to do." Weeping, Guilbert crawled back, and grimly set his gun barrel on the wall. Fray seemed unaffected, but Thari knew him well enough to understand how shaken he was by Gavrielle's death.

Through her tears, Thari huddled over her rifle butt and
fired at any Hothri she saw. Furiously, she blasted round
after round at enemy bodies, cutting one nearly in half until
Fray shouted at her to stop wasting ammunition. Helplessly
they watched the marines being backed gradually toward the
top of the midway, a position from which the children knew
there was only one narrow escape, easily blocked. The
Hothri were deliberately forcing separate parties together,
herding them like well-trained dogs managing a flock of
sheep. The humans fought desperately, leaving burned and
bleeding Hothri carcasses strewn on the fairway, but they
still edged inexorably toward the trap.

"They're all going to get killed back there," Fray
growled. "They need to regroup, but they can't get around
the ants."

"I know, but we can't help them," Thari hissed.

"I will! Protect the marines, isn't that what you said Gavrielle would want?"

"What are you going to do?" Thari grabbed out at his
arm, but he evaded her.

With a wild yell, Fray burst out of his hiding place and
blasted the nearest Hothri apart. The ant exploded in yellow
goo, its corpse dropping backward across the bodies of a
knot of Aristan marines.

"Catch me if you can, bugs!" he cried. "Come on!"

It was like watching him on the playing field in one of
his finest games, Thari thought as she and the gang ran
behind him. As if charmed, he dodged and hopped, evad-
ing the Hothri's efforts to grab or shoot him. Nothing
touched him as he headed toward the fun house.

They piled in through the door after him and squeezed
in behind the nearest sliding mirror just as the Hothri bar-
reled in the door. Slinging his rifle over his shoulder, he
felt for the switches to turn on all of the fun house's mech-
anisms, and heard squeals and scrabbling as the tilting
room's wobbling floor caught the ant-people by surprise.

Thari dashed to a peephole and gazed through it.
"They're falling down. What are we doing with them in
here?"

"Confusing them," Fray said. "A distraction, long
enough for the marines to reorganize. It can't last long before they find us."

Concealed behind the shifting panels, the students fired

at the Hothri, who were casting about in chittering confusion, trying to find their assailants. The walls were thin,
but they were steel, and that was cold enough to make the
Hothri's infrared vision all but useless.

In the hall of mirrors, Fray and Claus pushed one after
another of the dummies out into the maze. Only a split
second before the panel slid shut, the Hothri appeared at
the maze's mouth. Thari gawked and pointed. Fray shoved
her roughly into the bowels of the fun house, but not before the Hothri saw them. A brief tendril of flame brushed
Fray's shoulder and back, and he howled. Thari and Mimione beat out his burning clothing and sprayed anesthetic
on his skin.

"Radiation, that hurts!" Fray growled. One-handed, he
hoisted the rifle to a peephole and waited for the Hothri to
find their dummy substitutes and start the fireworks.

The effect was greater than any of them could have
wished. The dummies blazed up satisfactorily, but the repeated blasts from the ants' flamethrowers heated the metal
corridors to the boiling point. Their chitinous feet started
melting to the floor, making it impossible for them to get
out of each other's way. The ones whose feet weren't stuck
beat on the walls as they turned around and around, trying
to find a way through the narrow paths of the maze.

Moving from peephole to peephole in the narrower passageway behind the scenes, the teenagers shot at the Hothri,
reveling savagely in the squeals of anger and agony. They
felt as if they were getting revenge for Gavrielle's horrible
death.

The temperature of the whole maze was beginning to rise
too high for the children to remain.

"Come on," Fray ordered. "It's been long enough. Try
to get out. Anyone left behind is meat!"

Through the darkened, hot tunnel, they felt their way back
to the entrance. Claus stumbled out first and staggered down
the ramp wiping sweat out of his eyes. "Run!" Fray ordered him from behind. "Don't walk! Hurry!"

Fray threw himself out of the door of the fun house, with
Thari and the others in hot pursuit. "Blast it!" he shouted
at the marines, waving his rifle over his head. "Blast it!
They're inside!"

The Hothri remaining outside clearly understood what
the boy's wild gesticulations meant, but it was too late to

do anything but telegraph the details of their doom to their comrades trapped inside. The marine commander ordered a strike on the building, and the whistling of ordnance fire pierced their eardrums. Even before Thari and the others had fairly hit the ground a hundred yards away, the building exploded with a rumbling roar. Flames washed out of the hulk, followed by a shower of debris which rained on them for several minutes. Dozens of hot little pebbles landed on Thari, burning through her clothes and leaving itchy red blisters on her skin, but she ignored them, meeting Fray's triumphant grin with her own.

Few ants were left alive after Fray's cunning maneuver. With a hasty pat of congratulations, the marine commander ordered the children to shelter while his soldiers pursued the last of them. The teenagers hastened back to the roundabout chamber and huddled together.

There were wounds to bind, and everyone was hungry. Thari moved in a daze, carrying bandages and comforting friends who had lost friends. It wasn't for hours that she noticed with deep shock that Guilbert hadn't come back.

"He's dead," one of the other girls told her gently, putting an arm around her neck and sitting next to her as she had done to console their grief. "He sat shooting at the Hothri, and never moved when they came over the barriers right at him. He was brave."

"It was just a computer game to him," Thari said. "It wasn't real."

They didn't dare to emerge from their hiding place all the next day, even in the daytime. On the radio, they heard reports that Hothri troops were using their infrared vision to ferret out concealed humans and kill them. Now leaderless, the children felt too vulnerable to expose themselves, in case the scrabbling of the ants came again. The marines hadn't come back, but Fray saw that as a good sign, that they didn't need to come back.

Days passed. Food was beginning to run genuinely short in the shelter, but the children were afraid to venture out for forage. Thari looked at Fray expectantly, hoping that he would have an idea before they started eating each other. Then she cursed herself for such a thought, remembering poor Gavrielle.

"One more day," the boy ordered them. "We'll wait. The war is still going on. Listen to the communications unit."

Tension grew during that day, the longest they had ever experienced in their lives. The place was beginning to stink because they couldn't go outside to relieve themselves, and the chemical toilets were giving up the ghost.

"The ants will come back during the night," Claus said, challengingly. In their hearts, they knew Fray was right to make them keep hidden, but with nothing to do but worry— not even eat—tempers were flaring. "Why can't we go out now? The locust-bottoms don't want to stress themselves in the sunlight."

"The ants can't be trusted. They're smart, and they're angry. They will wait until we think we're safe, and then WHOOSH!" Fray pantomimed a flamethrower. The other boy recoiled.

Night came slowly. Thari couldn't remember when she had been so tired, but between anxiety and hunger, she couldn't relax enough to sleep. The children watched each other, worrying if another attack was imminent. Thari counted backward. It had been nine days since the war started. She and Fray had been fighting constantly. Everyone was at each other's throats; everyone except for Mimione.

The tall girl sat propped in a corner, staring into the open space between the ceiling and the walls which acted as their window and door into the eight-foot-deep shelter. There was a curious expression on her face, as if she was watching something. Thari glanced over her shoulder. There was nothing there except for the few stars one could see in Arista's skies and the first lights of false dawn.

"What's wrong?" Thari asked, crawling over to her friend.

"They're gone," Mimi said, wonderingly. "The ants are gone."

"Bullshit," stated Fray. "Why would they just leave? They're winning."

Mimi held out her hands to him. "No, the feelings are all gone. I feel wonderful. It's like the static has cleared. The ants are gone."

"Are you sure?" Thari asked, cautiously.

There were jeers of disbelief. Ignoring them, Mimi made

for the edge of the wall and hoisted herself up and through in an effortless movement that made Thari sigh with admiration. She remembered that Mimione was a growing favorite among the gym teachers to go to the World Olympics. Slinging her rifle across her back and scrambling up with less grace, Thari followed her, ignoring Fray's shouts. He pulled at her leg, and she kicked at him.

Emerging onto the scorched grass, Thari and Mimi looked around. It was dead quiet except for tiny rustling noises. Thari hit the spotlight on her rifle at once and pinpointed a human head. It was another hideout, only yards from theirs, and she never knew it was there. The face gasped, and Thari turned off the beam.

"It's okay," she called, so surprised at herself that her voice died from an initial shout to a murmur. She looked at Mimione, who nodded approval. The head popped down out of sight.

"Oops, I scared him off," Thari said sadly. "Well, he'll come out again soon. I wonder if they have any food?"

"Sparks, I'm tired," Mimi said, throwing herself full length on the ground and staring at the growing pinkness at the far end of the sky. Thari lay down next to her with her rifle at the ready, in case of a last minute attack by the ants, but there hadn't been even a report of one for twenty-four hours. She was ready to believe Mimi, that there weren't going to be any more Hothri.

One by one, humans, alerted by whatever means they had that the threat had ended, crept out into the sunlight from the other bunker. Most of them were half-starved, wounded, so exhausted that they had only enough strength to emerge from their burrows to crawl out and lie in the light, gaining strength. Encouraged by Mimi, the children came out, too. Last to emerge, Fray stood and stretched, and cast himself down next to Thari. Gently, he took her hand.

"It's over," Thari said sadly, staring at the sunrise. "It's funny, but I can't feel anything. I'm only tired, and I'm dying to get something to eat. I know my friends are dead, and everything is ruined, but all I feel is numbness."

"One day you'll just cry and cry," Fray told her, but his voice lacked its usual sardonic edge.

"I think someday, you'll cry, too." Thari said defensively.

"Maybe it will be the same day," he said, smiling at her and squeezing her fingers.

"Now, that's pushing reality too far," Thari grinned.

# Desperate Gambles
## by Bill Fawcett

There is a great tradition of desperate, last-hope military gambles. In 1299 B.C. Ramses II gambled and won when he led his bodyguard in a suicide charge against the entire Hittite army. Later in 48 B.C. Caesar led his legions against Pompeii's larger force and drove them from the field by sheer elan. For Caesar, bucking the odds worked, and he became the first Emperor of Rome. Marc Antony took a chance at sinking Augustus's ship before assistance could arrive. He failed and died by his own hand.

Later, Napoleon took the calculated risk that Davout would march his French Corps farther and faster than ever before and arrive in time to reinforce his weak right flank. Davout arrived and Austerlitz became Napoleon's greatest victory. Gallipoli should have ended the First World War years early. Instead Churchill lost a gamble and hundreds of soldiers paid the cost. During World War II the American Navy, outnumbered three to one in carriers and over six to one in surface ships, risked destruction on the chance that they correctly understood a partially decoded message. They were right, but even so, the Battle of Midway nearly ended in disaster.

In the same war another desperate gamble didn't work. Hitler had hoped his attack across the Ardennes would convince the western allies to make a separate peace with him. During the Vietnam War the French bet that the Viet Minh couldn't take the losses or emplace the cumbersome artillery of the period on the slopes near Dien Bien Phu. They were wrong at the cost, ultimately, of tens of thousands of French and American lives.

If military victory is imminent there is no need to take a desperate gamble. In the preceding situations the generals, many the greatest in history, had to risk all at long odds. Most were calculated risks based on their best judgement.

Picket's Charge at Gettysburg was similar to battle-winning attacks Lee had ordered earlier in the American Civil War. Lee had been forced to charge, to take the offensive against all advice, even against his stated preference, because the South had to have a victory. A draw forced them back to Virginia, just as his gamble's failure did. This is another example of an ancient captain taking a huge risk in the face of almost certain defeat.

So too was the Hothri-Human war, where it became obvious that nothing was going to stop the alien invaders. They massively outnumbered the human defenders in both warships and soldiers. The Hothri were too methodical to make any mistakes that might endanger their now inevitable victory. They didn't need to do anything except land and overwhelm the remaining defenders. The Aristan Navy had no choice but to take a desperate gamble. They had nothing to lose.

# BREAKOUT

## by Robert Sheckley

THE Command and Computation room of the battlecruiser *Eindhoven* was the size of a ballroom, but not nearly as gaudy. The color plan was subdued pastels; fighting fleets don't go in for bright colors, even indoors. The vast room was open-plan, extending the entire width of the ship. It was divided into levels, for the Aristan Navy had long ago given up the closed office arrangements of the past. In the C & C room, if the intercoms failed, you could shout orders from command (on its own raised section) to the computation section, four rows at the center. These rows were filled with computers, most of them manned by technicians, working with data that concerned the ongoing battle for Arista. The technicians were dressed in battle gray with scarlet collars. Most of them wore the rose trefoil that had been awarded their squadron for heroism in the attack on Double Star Pass.

One of these men was Corporal Adams. He was working alone in a small plastic-walled cubbyhole in the back. Small, insignificant-looking, with a tiny moustache, Adams's official rating was ordinary computerman. But he had turned out to be adept at number manipulation.

He had been more than willing to try his hand at the problem De Vries had set him—a problem no one had been able to solve yet. Granted that no ship could be traced once it had entered FTL mode, since no radio waves were propagated in that medium, De Vries suggested another approach. What if you plotted the vectors of the alien ships coming out of FTL space, extended those lines backwards, applied the standard correction, and averaged them? Might that not reveal their point of origin? Could the alien home world be discovered that way?

The problem wasn't quite so simple as that. There were additional corrections to be made concerning the courses.

But Adams had been able to find the standard math formulas in the ship's computer library.

Ten minutes ago he had signalled Commander De Vries that he had a result.

De Vries entered the cubbyhole. Adams was so engrossed in going over his data that he didn't hear the commander enter, and jumped when De Vries said, "What did you come up with, Corporal?"

"Here's what I've got," Adams said, handing De Vries a piece of paper with coordinates scrawled on it.

De Vries was tall and thin. At twenty-seven, he wasn't much older than Adams. With his dark ruddy skin and shock of black hair, many people thought he was part American Indian. But De Vries was Afghani on his mother's side, Flemish on his father's.

De Vries tapped the coordinates with a finger. "You think the Hothri home world is there?"

"Hey!" Adams said. "I've got no idea at all about that. You told me to work with the data in this way and I did. We know that a lot of Hothri ships seem to come out into normal space along similar vectors. Maybe that shows the direction to the home world. Or maybe they're all coming from a tavern out in space where they go to drink up their methane boilermakers before coming here to shoot us up. I warn you, skipper, neither the assumption nor the data can be classed as reliable."

"It'll have to do," De Vries said. "It's all we got."

Adams shrugged. "Sometimes all you've got isn't good enough."

"But you can never know that until you try to use it," De Vries said. He left the computation room and made his way back to the bridge.

The *Eindhoven*, like the rest of his small fleet, had dug itself in to the soil of Arista. Covered by reinforced earth and concrete, the ships were almost impregnable to Hothri bombing. Although they couldn't be hurt themselves, they also couldn't do much good. They kept on firing away at the Hothri ships when they came screaming in for their bombing and beaming runs, but didn't score a lot of hits. That was natural enough—they were designed to operate in the vacuum of space, not as buried fortresses. But there was no sense keeping them in space when they were outnumbered almost ten to one by the Hothri fleet that had been attacking Arista for the last five years.

If these coordinates were true, there was something De Vries could do, a way he could break out of the stagnant and losing defensive situation he'd been in since taking station at this far-flung planet. But it was a hell of a gamble, he thought. And with the planet of Arista under increasingly heavy attack, he couldn't even be sure of getting his fleet off-planet safely. He would have to think about this. Perhaps if Guthrie's Free Corps were to stage a diversion . . . But they would never agree.

De Vries was on his way to the meeting he had set up with Mira Falken, the Aristan council representative to the fleet, when a breathless crewman hurried up to him. "Urgent message, sir." It was a pneumo from Martin Havilland, the political officer aboard the *Eindhoven*. "Need to see you urgently." De Vries cursed under his breath. It was a new practice on the part of the government, sending along a political officer with a fleet. In theory, De Vries was in command; but only of military decisions. Havilland, the political officer, was supposed to advise on political consequences. Since a firm line had never been drawn between what was military and what was political, this was a sure recipe for confusion, expecially when there was little sympathy between the two men to begin with.

De Vries decided to see Havilland in his own territory. The political officer was in his own little stateroom, reading up on "Human Dimensions," the most recent effort by the Ministry of Information, also known as Propaganda Central. He put down his book when De Vries entered. He was a few years older than De Vries, a broad-faced man with a tendency toward corpulence and a firm belief in his own omnipotence.

"What's up, Commander? I know something is going on but no one has advised me as to what it is."

"I've called a meeting with the Arista representative," De Vries said.

"Without informing me?"

"It didn't involve the political side. Only military."

"You might not be the best judge of that, Commander De Vries. I wish you had consulted me. Why have you called this meeting?"

"To review the situation with Mira Falken. This planet is becoming undefendable."

Havilland nodded grudgingly. He couldn't have failed to notice that the Hothri fleet was now carrying out its bombing missions almost unopposed. "What are you going to propose?"

De Vries thought before answering. He hadn't wanted to involve Havilland in this. The man was sure to disapprove.

"There's only one thing we can do. Stage a breakout."

"You mean going off-planet with the League forces under your command?"

"Yes, plus any ships the corporations will give me."

"The intention being, I suppose, a sudden attack upon the enemy?"

"Something like that," De Vries said.

"What did you have in mind, specifically?"

"I can't discuss it with you, yet."

"And why not, may I ask?"

"It is a military matter. You are a political officer. Your opinions on my course of action would not be useful."

Havilland scowled at this. "May I remind you, Commander, that military decisions flow from political situations, not the other way around?"

"I'm well aware of that theory. But politics must give way to military necessity. We can't defend this place much longer. The Hothri have greatly increased their bombing efficiency over the past year. We are increasingly outgunned, and some of the ships have been taking serious hits, despite being dug in. It won't be much longer before the Hothri mount an all-out assault. When that happens, we all go down in flames.

"That's gloomy thinking, Commander."

"It's realistic."

"Realism is not the only factor we have to consider."

"None of the others make any sense without it," De Vries said. "I must go now. We'll talk later."

"Just a minute!" Havilland said. "I have more questions to ask!" But De Vries had already gone.

He took the elevator from his ship to ground level. The armored car was waiting to take him to the deep cavern where the government of Arista was trying to carry on the defence of the planet. The vehicle bounced along the cratered road, while overhead, in Arista's dark skies, another battle was shaping up. All would be quiet for a while. Then suddenly, abruptly, one side or the other would open up. This time the skies were suddenly filled with a shower of small green flares from space. They were a new species of high-explosive bomb, traveling downward in eccentric orbits to fool the defence gunners. Lights flashed and flared, then De Vries saw the sudden rush of net-webs, a hastily improvised but effective defense flung up to gather in the flare explosions. Meanwhile, other weapons had entered the fight. Heavy plasma cannons, boxcar bombs, Simple Simons. The ground shook as bombs penetrated the city shields, causing further wreckage. The air was humid and dark, and smelled of explosives and damp smoke. Arista had been a lovely planet. But now De Vries felt the sense of hellishness that comes to a place under continual attack. The sense of doom was closing in; an inexorable enemy was tightening its grip.

The command car moved quickly over the road and descended into the cavern of Mmult. De Vries knew that this was one of the biggest cavern systems on the planet. It had been selected as the Command Bunker, a place relatively secure from the Hothri bombs and torpedoes. It was just starting to come under attack as the planet's outer defences were stripped away day after day. De Vries followed the cavern until he came to a branching of the extensive tunneling system that characterized this level. Here were the big bronze doors that sealed off the Aristan living section. He went through them, and through a separate set of pressure locks, and then he was in the final retreat of the Aristan people. War had reduced them to an underground bunker on their own planet.

De Vries was hurrying to his meeting with Mira Falken when a man ran out of a side corridor and seized his hand. "De Vries? I need to see you urgently." It was Charles Guthrie, Commander of the Guthrie Free Corps.

"A word with you, Commander?"

"Please make it brief, Mr. Guthrie."

Charles Guthrie had been second in command of the Security Corps of the planet Thistle. When the planet was overwhelmed by the Hothri, the men of Guthrie's ships who managed to escape the ensuing debacle elected Guthrie their commander. Like so many Free Corps people before them, Guthrie and his men were interested mainly in profits. Any patriotism they might have had burned out with the loss of their home world.

Since the beginning of the war, various Free Corps had sprung up—collections of men and armed vessels who flew the flags of obscure human-occupied planets which were not engaged in the war, or recently, the remnants of space fleets from planets which had fallen to the Hothri. These men, who owned allegiance to no one, signed with various planetary fleets as auxiliaries. Since they were under independent command, they didn't always obey the orders of the senior commanders. Sometimes they attacked the enemy with great courage, but often without orders. More often, they deemed caution the better part of valor and waited to see how a particular engagement would go before committing themselves. They were an annoyance to the regular commanders. But there was little choice. At this desperate time in the war, any armed vessels were welcomed. The Free Corps were not reliable, but they were better than nothing at all.

Guthrie was a large man just going to flab. He had curly red hair, a big nose, beetling eyebrows.

"What can I do for you?" De Vries asked.

"Well," Guthrie said, "I could beat around the bush, but I might as well get down to it. Commander, the position here is untenable. The handwriting is on the wall. This planet has had it."

"I don't share your pessimism," De Vries said, putting on an air of confidence he didn't feel. "We're just about holding our own. As the lines are driven in, our defense becomes stiffer. And help is sure to come soon."

Guthrie shook his head. "Save that talk for the Aristan nobles, Commander. The Hothri are getting closer and closer to breaking down the last shields defending our military installations. Another couple of weeks and they'll have us at their mercy. And you know as well as I do what the mercy of a Hothri is like."

Secretly, De Vries agreed with him. But he couldn't let it show. "Nonsense, Guthrie. We still have a few tricks up our sleeves."

"Like what?" Guthrie said. "Never mind, I don't want to embarrass you. The situation is clear. We have no reinforcements from the League and none are due. We've had it. It's time to pack it in, Commander.''

"I don't agree with your assessment," De Vries said. "But why are you telling me all this?"

"I've had a meeting with my senior commanders. They all agree that the risks here have become unacceptable.''

"So what do you think we should do?" De Vries asked. "Surrender? You know what the Hothri do to humans they capture.''

"I don't know what *you* should do, Commander," Guthrie said. "But I do know what *I* have to do. Me and my men are getting out of here.''

"You have a contract with us!"

"Our wages haven't been paid for over six months!"

"They will be! You have the council's guarantee!"

"Just now," Guthrie said, "that guarantee isn't worth diddly squat. I'm sorry, Commander, we're leaving. I thought it only right to tell you. Some of the men just wanted to leave a note and blast off.''

De Vries was furious, but he managed to choke down his rage. Guthrie's departure would leave the northern sector dangerously undermanned.

"How in hell," De Vries asked, "do you expect to get your ships out past the Hothri guns?"

"Once we're out there, we'll signal them that we're going over to non-combatant status. They'll let us through. They did it for the garrison of Kaneel.''

Kaneel was a small planet that had capitulated to the aliens after its Free Corps defenders had gotten away. The Hothri hadn't attacked the Free Corps ships.

"They might not let you go this time," De Vries said.

Guthrie chuckled. "These accounts of the Hothri killing all humans are greatly exaggerated. They only kill the ones who oppose them. We'll be all right, Commander. If you like, we can try to negotiate a favorable capitulation for you Aristans.''

"Don't do me any favors," Guthrie said. "No fleet under my command is going to surrender.''

"Suit yourself," Guthrie said. "My corps is ready for immediate departure. We'll leave within the hour.'' He took a piece of paper out of his pocket and handed it to De Vries. "Here's our flight plan. Tell your people not to fire on us.''

"Do what you have to do," De Vries said. "And I'll do what I have to do."

On his way to the main meeting room, De Vries's mind was working furiously. Guthrie's departure was a disaster. Was there some way he could turn it into a triumph? He had the feeling that he could, if only he could think of something. . . .

He pushed Guthrie's flight plan into his pocket. His fingers closed over another scrap of paper. The coordinates for the Hothri planet!

And then it came to him. Suddenly, a plan formed in his head. A risky plan. But they had no alternative. Doing nothing was even riskier. The question was, would the Aristans go for it?

Before the disastrous war, the Aristans had prided themselves on their good management and careful ways. They had done wonders with their dark little planet—turning it into a garden world that produced food for populations much greater than its own modest five million. But all of that had been before the war, before the determined siege by the Hothri.

The distant League had promised them assistance after the Hothri attacks became too much for the local militia. But all they received were a few dozen worn out ships. More reinforcements were promised later. The reinforcements never came. The humans on other worlds were badly pressed as Hothri victories mounted. Alone, Arista was doing the best it could, but at this point the war was going badly for humanity. Weak spots in the defenses had to be shored up. But try to explain that to a proud and independent people who had to stand by and watch their planet be bombed into rubble!

Mira Falken was waiting for him in the council meeting room. She was a member of the old nobility that made a home on Arista and did so much to bring civilization to the planet during its first hectic decade. Nobility was not a prerequisite of high office on this planet, and Mira had given away any claims she had to noble status long ago. She was fiercely republican, utterly devoted to her planet's cause. Highly intelligent, slender and arrow-straight despite her eighty-seven years, she was the unanimous choice among the Aristan leaders as their liaison with the League Navy.

This was an office of some importance. Due to the demands of modern warfare, decisions affecting millions of people often had to be made rapidly, without any time for a plebiscite or council vote. The Aristans entrusted Mira with the power to make those decisions.

She was of medium height, slender, gray-eyed. Her hair was brown, well speckled with gray. Longevity treatments made her appear no older than her late forties. She wore a belted one-piece silver-gray jumpsuit. Her only badge of office was a square silver plaque worn around her neck. It displayed the entwined lily and dagger emblem of high office on Arista.

"I'd better give you the latest news," De Vries said. "Charles Guthrie and his Free Corps won't be with us any longer. They have decided our cause is hopeless, and they are departing within the hour."

Mira betrayed no emotion. "Indeed?"

"This is a blow to us," De Vries went on. "But it also presents us with a very great opportunity."

"An opportunity to do what, Commander?"

De Vries said, "What I had in mind was a breakout of the fleet."

"You mean leave your dug-in positions?"

"Exactly."

"But whatever for?"

"The way things are going," De Vries said, "and without outside help—which I do not expect—we can't hold out more than a month, six weeks at the outside."

"I am aware of that, too, Commander. I think of very little else these days."

"We have to do something about it."

"Yes, of course. But what?"

"I have recently received information," De Vries said, "that will allow me to take my fleet through FTL space to the vicinity of the Hothri home world."

"There's no way you could do that," Falken said. "No human has ever been to the Hothri home world. Its destination is unknown. And it has been proven that you can't trace a ship's course when it's in FTL mode."

"All of that is well known," De Vries said. "But one of the scientists aboard my ship has come up with an ingenious solution. By notating and averaging the vectors of Hothri ships coming out of FTL space, he believes a course can be traced back to their home world.'' He thought Corp. Adams would forgive him for passing him off as a scientist.

"So you would abandon Arista, just as Guthrie did? Without your fleet, the Hothri would be here in a week.''

"I'm not abandoning you," De Vries said. "I'm trying to save your lives."

"How, Commander?''

"You know it yourself. Even with my ships dug in on the ground, we can't keep the Hothri out. You've seen for yourselves how our defenses are being staved in. There's no relief force from the League. I'm sorry, but that's how it is. We have only one possibility. If I can bring my fleet to their home world, they'll have to pull out of here in order to save their planet."

"You think they'd leave the home world unguarded?'' Mira asked.

"Yes, that's precisely what I think. The size of the attacks they're mounting against us and other League planets convinces me they're throwing in everything they've got in hopes of a quick victory. Why should they guard their home world? No human has ever seen it. FTL can't be traced. These are their safeguards. I think we'll find no more than a light screen force at the home world."

"Commander, is your fleet large enough to reduce an entire world?''

"It will be," De Vries said, "when you give me permission to take about half of the Aristan militia."

Mira said, "that would give Arista about a week before they overwhelmed us."

"Yes.''

"I understand the necessity of doing this. You're asking us to give away our own forces in favor of your one last roll of the dice—all or nothing, win or lose."

"Those are the terms of the war we are engaged in.''

"Well," said Mira, "you make a good case. I will confer with my colleagues. Tomorrow I'll tell you our decision."

"No," De Vries said.

"I beg your pardon, Commander?''

"It must be made here and now.''

"And why?''

"In order to get my ships off this planet," De Vries said, "I need a diversion."

"A diversion? But none is possible, unless you throw the militia at them."

"We'll do that, but I need the militia to help me attack the Hothri world."

"What, then?"

"Guthrie and his Free Corps are leaving about half an hour from now. We have their proposed route on file. I propose that within minutes after Guthrie lifts, when the attention of the Hothri will be riveted on him and the militia diversion, my fleet and the rest of the militia get away by a polar direction."

"You want to take off immediately?"

"It is the only possible way."

Mira said, "It shall be as you say. But I shall go with you."

"Noble Falken," De Vries began, "much as I would welcome you aboard in ordinary circumstances, our precedented situation . . ."

He stopped when she raised one slender hand. "Don't bother arguing," she said. "You are only wasting the time you claimed was so valuable. If you will lead the way? . . ."

De Vries knew when he was overmatched. Mira Falken was coming aboard.

Everything had to be done with great haste. All ships on Arista had been at full alert battle stations around the clock as the battle for Arista came toward its climax. De Vries led Mira Falken aboard the *Eindhoven* and swung into action. The crew was well-drilled and used to leaping to full alert after months of relative inactivity. De Vries, at his console in the command section, swiftly flipped switches and touched light-sensitive panels, opening the communications system. He issued orders to the fleet and waited, drumming his fingers impatiently on the textured gray plastic of the console until the last of them had reported their readiness for immediate departure.

"Noble Falken," De Vries said, "Please take the acceleration couch over there and strap yourself in. We're going to be piling on the G's on this exit."

"Very well, Commander," Mira said. "But one thought has been bothering me. What if the Hothri are alert to this possibility of your breaking out? What if Guthrie made an arrangement with them beforehand? It's not impossible, is it?"

"Not at all," De Vries said. "That sort of thing has happened before. We just have to take our chances."

"I know that. But to lead the breakout in your own flagship . . . isn't that inviting disaster? Shouldn't one of the smaller ships clear the way?"

"That's not the optimum computation," De Vries said. "I've worked this out before. If they have a full-sized battle group waiting for us, this fleet has had it anyway. If it's only a light screen, my dreadnought is better equipped to break through than any other in my command."

"I hope you're right. It's a desperate plan, but I agree, there's no other."

"We'll know pretty soon," De Vries said.

"I'm scared, Commander. Oh, not for myself. I've already led a full life. It's the others I'm thinking about, all of those millions of Arista, waiting, hoping we come up with something."

"I'm thinking of them, too," De Vries said. "If I could think of any other way to save them, believe me, I'd take it. But we have no choice, and that makes it simpler. Either this plan works or we're all dogmeat."

A crewman reported. "All ready, sir!"

De Vries looked at Falken. She said, "Good luck," and went to the acceleration couch. De Vries went to his own, looked around, saw everything in readiness. The Free Corps was lifting on schedule.

"Standard power!"

The ship seemed to grunt, shook itself like a sleepy bull, and lifted itself out of its earth pit. De Vries ordered full power. The ship seemed to strain for a moment, as though reluctant to leave its safe shelter on Arista, so fortress-like, then made up its mind and leaped upward. Faster, faster. Through monitors they could watch the planet fall away and dwindle, first to a dark, cloud-covered ball, then to a dot. Other views showed the remaining ships of the fleet coming out behind them. Further back still, red and green winks of light showed the ships of the Arista militia following. On the far side of the planet lights flared as the smaller militia ships threw themselves at the Hothri.

"OK," De Vries said. "We're out of the atmosphere." He signaled the astrogation officer. "Take down these coordinates.'' He rattled off a string of numbers. ''Broadcast them to all ships. Tell me when they have all acknowledged.''

''Now,'' Mira said, ''you're going to see if you can find their home world?''

De Vries nodded.

''What is that orange light flashing on your display?''

De Vries looked at it and smiled. ''That's a signal from the political officer. No doubt he wants to put in a word or two of advice.'' He made no effort to answer.

''Aren't you going to talk to him?''

''Not now. Whatever he has to say wouldn't be useful. Finding the Hothri is a military matter, not a political one.''

Moments later the communications officer was back on line. ''All ships acknowledge, sir. Controls are set to your coordinates.''

De Vries turned to Mira. ''Ready for the jump into FTL mode?''

''Yes, but I don't know what it entails. Do we strap down again?''

''No. But it gives some people a peculiar feeling in the pit of the stomach. Nothing serious, but its better to be warned.''

De Vries turned to their annunciator. ''All ships. Execute the move into FTL mode!''

According to Corp. Adams's calculations, the journey in FTL mode would take just under twenty-eight hours ship's time. At the end of this time *Eindhoven* and the other ships came out into normal space again. De Vries turned on the vision ports and began a visual search of the space they were in. Mira and the crew waited, scarcely daring to breathe.

At last Mira asked, ''What do you see? Is there a planet out there?''

''Look for yourself,'' De Vries said, his voice flat, expressionless.

Mira looked around. It was apparent that they were in deep space. She could see nothing that looked like the fiery disk of a nearby sun. Just the distant pinpoints of the stars. And something else. She shifted to the lower right-hand quadrant. De Vries turned up the magnification.

''What's that?'' she asked.

"It seems to be a space fleet," De Vries said. At maximum magnification he could see, spread in a wide band across the darkness of space, a line of ten ships, lights blazing from their port holes, shifting and changing position as they closed on the fleet and then came to a halt.

De Vries called to the intelligence officer, "What do you make of them, Alex?"

"I wish we could get a little closer," Alex said. "Near as I can make out, no ship like these was ever fabricated on any human world. Let's try a simulation for a better look."

Alex punched keys. An intercam recorded the image of the nearest ship and, using simulation techniques, produced a close-up view. The ship was monstrous-looking, a solid, misshapen bulge of metal and glass that resembled the grotesque head of a creature, half dwarf and half dragon.

"Weird-looking craft," De Vries commented. "Do the Hothri ever use a configuration like that?"

"That ship has none of the Hothri characteristics. Commander, I don't think you've found the Hothri home world. But you have gotten a whole new space fleet of unknown origin and disposition. It looks somewhat larger than ours."

"Are they armed?" De Vries asked.

Alex studied the images, then turned back to De Vries. "Oh yes, sir, they're armed."

"Then the next question," Mira said, "is are they friendly or unfriendly?"

De Vries sent a signal to the communications officer. "Contact them, Mr. Manfred."

But that was easier said than done.

The communications room of the superdreadnought *Eindhoven* was a small room crowded with equipment. Green cat's eyes expanded and shrank from various visual displays. A graphic equalizer showed jagged lines. There was the constant hum of machinery, the stifling warmth that comes on these ships. There were low rumbling noises from time to time; signs that the ship was working. The lights in this room were low, indirect. The dials of the instruments gave light enough.

De Vries and Mira were in the room, gathered behind Manfred. He was young, barely twenty. His blonde hair was shaved close to the skull. His features were delicate, boyish. There was another man in the room, too. This was Carson, a hulk of a man. He hardly looked the type to be the alien linguistics officer. But so he was. Since a new alien language is not often encountered, especially in these war years of diminished spatial exploration, Carson doubled as assistant gunnery officer.

De Vries and the others entered. Manfred started to get to his feet to salute.

De Vries said, "At ease, Manfred. Do you have anything new?"

"Just the same old stuff, sir."

"Any visuals yet?"

"No. Their screens are up. They're broadcasting only on a narrow voice-only channel."

"Let Carson hear it."

Before Manfred could act, Havilland entered the room.

"Commander De Vries! I should have been notified of this! The first contact with a hitherto unknown alien race—that is a political matter!"

"Given the situation," De Vries said, "I consider it at present a purely military concern. Their fleet is armed and larger than ours. We're standing toe to toe and all hell could break out any moment. Communication is imperative if we are to preserve our lives long enough to be useful to Arista."

Mira said, "I'm glad to hear you mention Arista, Commander. I believe the idea was to find the Hothri home planet. There's no evidence of it around here, is there?"

"None whatsoever," De Vries said.

"Then your guess has failed and you have doomed our planet."

Havilland said, "I can assure you, noble lady, he did it without the approval of the merchants, whose representative I am."

"And what would you have suggested?" Mira Falken asked him.

"That we return to Arista and fight!"

"But you know the situation was hopeless."

"Duty indicated that we stand by your people and die with them, if necessary. If we ever get out of this, which I very much doubt, I'll see to it that Commander De Vries gets the punishment he so richly deserves."

"That's wonderful!" Mira said, her voice heavy with sarcasm. "The Commander's plan may have misfired, but at least he is actively trying to save our people."

"Noble Falken, I don't understand your attitude."

"I'm sure you don't. Commander, do you have any ideas now?"

"I'm playing it as it comes up," De Vries said. "Extemporizing. The first thing we need to know is something about that fleet. Manfred, play the tape of the alien's announcement."

Manfred punched a button. A tape recorder whirred into action. A sound came out of a nearby loudspeaker. It was difficult to characterize. It combined qualities of hiss and chatter. When Carson slowed it down, you could make out several voices, or separate components of voice. The sound was high-pitched, jagged, filled with nervous energy. There were no discernible words.

"Well, Carson?" De Vries asked.

"I'd like to hear it again," Carson said. "Through headphones. And I'll need to be able to vary the speed." Carson played it several times, then took off the headphones.

"I'll give you a preliminary diagnosis, sir. I can't even identify the group that it belongs to. There are sounds in there that no race we've encountered, human or alien, has ever made. I know the main characteristics of the three human groups and the twenty-seven alien groups so far identified. This stuff belongs to none of them."

"I don't suppose they've shown any comprehension of our messages?" De Vries said.

"I tried ten major language groups when I transmitted your message to them," Manfred said.

Havilland said, "Well, isn't that just great? You bring us here in a great rush to bomb the Hothri home planet, and now we're face to face with an armed alien fleet that we can't even communicate with. What do we do, go on trading gibberish until someone starts shooting?"

De Vries ignored the political officer's feeble attempt at satire. He turned to his aide. "Jamieson, prepare the launch for my immediate departure."

The Political Officer said, "What are you thinking about now? You aren't thinking of going to the aliens, are you?"

"What else?"

"But you can't talk with them!"

"That doesn't mean," De Vries said, "that I can't communicate with them."

\* \* \*

De Vries's fleet was on full alert, ready to start firing, standing toe to toe with the alien fleet. The launch, a dot of light, detached itself from the underbelly of the dreadnought *Eindhoven*. Starlight flashed on its steel-gray side as it drifted away from the mother ship. Its jets came on, silent in the vacuum of space. It began moving toward the alien fleet—a grouping that consisted of just ten large ships. Their shapes were monstrous, with bulbs and fins and metallic members of all sorts. They looked more like a strange head or gigantic octopi than a human's conception of a space-craft. Each ship would be a match for the *Eindhoven*.

"What makes you believe they won't blast us as we approach them?"

"They're probably too civilized for that," De Vries said. "At least I hope so. But we won't get anywhere waiting until we understand their language."

The launch approached. On the nearest alien ship, three blue lights flickered frantically. De Vries saw them and ordered the launch to hold its present position. "What do you think, Carson?"

Carson shrugged. He had no referents to go by, no base-line to figure from. He had brought along a computerized Translator.

"What's this?" Myra asked.

A big hatch had opened in the foremost alien ship. From within, blue and green lights glowed weirdly.

"Take the ship into it," De Vries told the helmsman.

They entered the alien ship, moving slowly. Once they were within, the doors closed. Air flowed into the vacuum. Their dials indicated that it was a breathable atmosphere. They filed out one by one.

At the far end of the hold, a door dilated. A figure came through. Although it wore a space suit, its insectile appearance was apparent.

"My God!" Carson said. "It even has an ovipositer!"

"Steady," De Vries said.

"Sugar," Carson babbled, "that's what insects like, sugar. But I forgot to bring any. Oh, my God, Commander, what do we do now?"

"Get hold of yourself," De Vries snapped. "Let's see if we can make any sense out of it now that we're face to face."

Carson didn't seem up to approaching the alien by himself. De Vries made a mental note of it. Carson would be recommended for planetside duty if they ever got out of this. He approached the alien by himself.

When he was three feet from it, the alien let out a staccato sound that combined a hiss and a high-speed chirp.

"That's probably a warning signal," De Vries said. "Did you get it, Carson?"

"Yes, sir," Carson said. "I'm recording all of this."

"Now," De Vries said, "let's see if we can make any sense out of his bag of gibberish."

De Vries, with the computerized Translator in his hand, was trying to decipher the creature's utterances. The Translator was able to break down sounds and relate them to a universal phonetic alphabet. Mira watched, alarmed, and worried for the commander. The alien was so big! One misunderstanding and it could crush De Vries to death before they could do anything about it. Although she was sick with anxiety for her besieged planet, something in her heart went out to this quiet but intrepid man. Dr. Vries was just doing what a commander in the navy ought to do; it was business as usual. Yet she couldn't help thinking that it was something special that he was doing now, something beyond the call of duty.

And yet, even with all his courage, what could De Vries do? If the computerized Translator couldn't help, how could he be expected to achieve any communication? And what if he did succeed and these creatures turned out to be enemies? A fine spot they'd be in then!

There was a hiatus. Time seemed to stand still as the commander and the alien stood face to face. The alien, large, long, with a complexity of body form that showed in the detailing of his spacesuit, seemed to be coming to the end of his patience. His antennae were beginning to twitch with an emotion Mira could only ascribe to nervousness. And the hell of it was, the alien seemed to have something to say to De Vries. Something urgent. You could infer that by his general twitchiness, the increasingly rapid clicking of his mandibles. What was he trying to tell De Vries?

There was a flurry of antennae movements on the part of the alien. De Vries watched as the alien repeated its gestures several more times. Then he turned to the other humans.

"I think he wants me to stay aboard his ship. I will do so

immediately. The rest of you will take the launch back to
the *Eindhoven* and wait for me. If I'm not back in four
hours, set coordinates for Arista, go back, and see what you
can do.''

"We don't want to leave you!" Mira said.

"I don't particularly want to stay, either," De Vries said.
"But it seems like the best way. Probably the only way.
And there's no sense in risking more lives than is strictly
necessary. Go back, Mira. With a little luck, I'll join you
soon.''

"And if you don't have even a little luck?"

De Vries smiled very faintly but did not answer. He
turned to his communication officer.

"Carson!"

"Sir!"

"Get these people back to the *Eindhoven*. On the double,
Mister! Stand by for four hours. If I'm not back in that time,
control reverts to Havilland. It's a pity, but he'll be senior
officer aboard.''

Aboard the *Eindhoven*, time passed with agonizing slow-
ness. Everyone was watching, either at the vision ports or
the magnifying telescopes that were used for close-in course-
spotting. The two fleets seemed to hang in space, two globes
of colored dots, facing each other, waiting for a signal to
tell them what to do next.

"How long is it now?" Mira asked.

"It's getting close to four hours," Carson said.

"He didn't give himself long enough," Mira said. "We
have to give him more time.''

"It's not up to me," Carson said. "You'd better talk to
Havilland.''

When she approached him, Havilland was not sympathetic. "I have no choice in the matter. Captain De Vries
is in command here. Despite our differences, I am subor-
dinate to him. He left me clear orders. He asked for four
hours, no longer." He looked at his watch. "In exactly
seven minutes I propose to lift ship.''

"For God's sake!" Myra cried. "Can't you try being human for a change?''

Havilland gave her a small smile. "Human is what I am
and what I do is what humans do. I follow orders." He
turned from her. "Power room. Are the engines up?''

"Yes sir, ready to go."

"Then stand by for orders."

"There's still almost six minutes," Mira said.

"I'm just getting ready."

"You don't think De Vries will come back, do you?"

"Don't be so accusing. It's not my fault. No, I don't think he will."

A minute, two minutes passed. Time had gone by so slowly at first. The four hours De Vries had given himself had stretched in Mira's mind like an eternity. But now the time was almost up. Havilland was calling for a checkout of all takeoff procedures. Mira knew that at the end of it, he would power up and go. And that would be the end of De Vries.

"Something approaching, sir!" a lookout reported.

"What is it?"

"Can't make it out yet, sir . . . Wait a minute. Yes, it's an alien ship, a small one, about the size of our launch."

"He's returning!" Mira cried, weak-kneed with relief.

"That is an unwarranted assumption," Havilland said. "This could be a ruse. That launch could be mined, ready to blow us up when it's near enough."

The gunnery control came on the line. "Orders, sir?"

"All of you, hear this," Havilland said. "I want every gun and missile trained on that launch. But don't fire until I give the word."

The launch crept slowly toward the *Eindhoven*. Externally, it looked like a cylinder, without windows or distinguishing features. The armament of the fleet tracked it as it moved.

"Stand ready," Havilland said. "Be prepared to fire on my signal. I'll count to three. One, two—"

"Wait!" cried Mira.

Immediately after her Carson said, "The launch has stopped, sir! They're ejecting something!"

"Take aim on it," Havilland said. "Steady, now—"

"It's a man in a spacesuit," Carson cried.

"It's De Vries!" Mira said.

"That is an unwarranted assumption," Havilland said. "For all we know it could be nothing more than De Vries's spacesuit packed with plasma and set to go off."

"I think it's De Vries inside," Carson said, checking his instruments. "The heat-signature—"

"I can't take any chances," Havilland said. "Stand ready. . . ."

Mira said, choosing her words with care, "If you destroy that spacesuit, Mr. Havilland, I will make it my life's work to bring you to court-martial and have you cashiered from the service . . . unless I can arrange to have you hanged, which would be much better."

"There's no reason for you to take that tone with me," Havilland said. "This is extreme war conditions. I'm just taking normal precautions."

"Contact!" Carson cried as the spacesuit came up against the hull of the *Eindhoven*.

"Nothing has happened," Mira pointed out.

"They could be waiting to explode it inside, by remote," Havilland said. He was greeted by stony silence. "Very well, bring it aboard."

Commander De Vries was cramped from his long hours in space armor, but he was brisk and businesslike as always. Once out of the armor he got onto his control panel at once. "Navigation? Take these coordinates. Relay them to the fleet. Tell everyone to be prepared to execute on my order."

He turned to Mira and Havilland. "They're on our side. They are a race known as the d'Tarth. That's the closest I can come to pronouncing it."

"And they are friendly?" Havilland said.

"Let's say they're not unfriendly. They share at least one thing with us. They too want to destroy the Hothri."

"How did you learn all this?" Havilland asked. "We obviously don't share any language with them, and I somehow doubt you learned theirs in the few hours you spent with them."

"I think we'll be a long time learning their language," De Vries said. "They don't have anything like our sentence structure. I don't even know if they have separate words. They hiss and chirp and we can't even form most of their sounds."

"How did you learn about their hatred of the Hothri?"

Just then a signal was received telling that the fleet had acknowledged setting the new coordinates and were now standing by for further orders.

"Get ready," De Vries said. He turned to Havilland and Mira Falken. "One picture, they say, is worth a thousand words. The reason the alien wanted so badly for me to go into his ship was because he had drawing materials there.''

"He drew his situation for you?"

"Not exactly," De Vries said. "I did most of the drawing."

He took from the pouch of his spaceship launch a handful of crumpled sheets of heavy paper. It looked like some kind of papyrus. There were drawings on them.

"Here's the most important one," De Vries said. He showed them the sheet. There was no mistaking the characteristic outline of a Hothri warrior.

"Good work, Commander. But how did you discover they were enemies of the Hothri?"

"See that tear in the middle of the page? I got the idea when the d'Tarth pulled out a sort of dagger and drove it through the center of the paper."

De Vries displayed the rest of the sheets. They showed a d'Tarth fleet approaching a planet; intercepted by a Hothri fleet; getting badly mauled; retreating with ten ships remaining.

"You consider that evidence?" Havilland asked.

"Evidence enough for me," De Vries said. "These people fought a battle with the Hothri and lost. This is the area of the battle. We traced the vectors of Hothri ships. But they weren't going to their home world. They were coming here."

"Well, it's good to have allies," Havilland said. "Now what?"

"As planned, we are going to the Hothri world to finish what we began."

"But your coordinates were wrong! They brought us here!"

"Correct. But the new coordinates—the ones the d'Tarth gave me—are correct. They'll take us to the Hothri planet."

"And what about the d'Tarth?"

"They're coming, too. They accepted my proposal that we make a combined attack."

"I'd like to suggest," Havilland said, "that making a joint attack with a new and untried ally definitely falls into the political arena. I strongly advise that we report this to the League, and get a firm directive before we commit ourselves to unknown complications and possible treachery."

"There's no time for that," De Vries said. Into the annunciator he said, "All ships! Stand by for orders!"

"But what if it's a trap?"

"Then we've had it. Execute the course order!"

The *Eindhoven* winked out of sight. A moment later, the rest of the ships at his command also disappeared into FTL space.

The d'Tarth fleet hung there for a moment. Then, close to simultaneously, they, too winked out.

The reappearance of the combined fleets in the vicinity of the long-sought-for Hothri world is a matter of universal history. On Arista, the day is celebrated as the important occasion when De Vries's counter-tactics resulted in the Hothri fleet being hastily recalled to the home world, and Arista was saved.

Of course, it wasn't quite so easy as that. But that was the beginning of the end of the war against the Hothri.

# BEYOND THE IMAGINATION